The
AMERICAN
WIFE

BOOKS BY CHRYSTYNA LUCYK-BERGER

Chrystyna Lucyk-Berger

The

AMERICAN
WIFE

bookouture

Published by Bookouture in 2023

An imprint of Storyfire Ltd.
Carmelite House
50 Victoria Embankment
London EC4Y 0DZ

www.bookouture.com

ISBN: 978-1-80314-736-9
eBook ISBN: 978-1-80314-735-2

Dedicated to all members of the Austrian resistance in WW2

FOREWORD

After the Nazi party took control of Germany in 1933, the U.S. ambassador in Berlin expressed his concern about the atrocities conducted by Adolf Hitler's regime on Jews and on dissenters, as well as rising violence against American tourists. President Roosevelt's Department of State issued some guidelines but did not strongarm Germany so as not to ruffle feathers.

In November 1933, U.S. Secretary of State Cordell Hull received a telegram from an Austrian minister. The telegram contained a warning from a German diplomat predicting that the Austrian government could not, and would not, last. He further stated that if the Nazi party were to take control in Austria, it would spark a brutal anti-Semitic pogrom throughout the country.

U.S. officials dismissed these warnings.

The following summer, the Austrian chancellor was assassinated by Nazi followers. The preceding Austrian leader illegalized the Nazi party, but it was too late.

The U.S. was additionally warned that the number of clandestine Nazi party members was exponentially growing in

Austria. The news was treated as an opinion with no evidence and much to Europe's eventual detriment. Because, like a powerful undercurrent, the Austrian Nazis were indeed steering the course of their country's fate.

They were just waiting for the right time to surface...

PART ONE

MAY–DECEMBER 1937

1

SPRING 1937

A Minnesota winter is like a warrior who falls, gets back up, and keeps on fighting regardless how wounded.

The day before her flight to Tokyo, Kitty Larsson had been certain that spring had arrived for good. But overnight, snowfall had ridden in on the coattails of a late-night storm. As she looked through the long beveled glass at the front entrance of the mansion, the budding trees along Summit Avenue were covered with white powder again. The yard of the Larsson mansion had turned into a surreal world of iridescent green beneath a protective layer of soft snow. In the spring bed that Kitty had planted, white powder balanced on unopened tulip bulbs, had put a mantle on the heads of daisies, and clung like cotton candy to the lilac branches.

A Ford Cabriolet pulled up outside. Kitty considered the woolen ostrich-trim hat on the rack and the leather gloves she'd set aside. They would only take up space in her luggage because where she was going the last signs of winter were long gone. She decided against the hat and spun around to pick up the two travel cases off the marble floor.

"Sam, my taxi's here! Are you coming?"

Facing the gleaming wooden staircase, she eyed her mother's favorite Oriental tapestry hanging on the wall at the top of the landing. It depicted the *hanami*, the viewing of the cherry blossoms in Japan. Where Kitty would soon be.

A door shut softly above and footsteps sounded on the thick rug in the hallway. Kitty swung the cases at her side until Sam finally appeared. Her little brother was dressed in a suit and tie, grinning at her, a big fat book under his arm. Probably anatomy or organic chemistry, or whatever other tome a medical student had to read.

"You're not planning on stealing out before saying goodbye," he said, jogging down the stairs.

Kitty set her luggage down again and hugged him tightly. "My plane leaves in two hours. Taxi's here already. And with this snow..."

Sam pulled away, his blue eyes alight. "Nils has a subtle way of extracting you from Maman's claws, doesn't he?"

She laughed because there was nothing subtle about their older brother. Not even his name, which he consistently had to correct people's pronunciation of—"It's a long e, like *kneels*."

Kitty lightly punched Sam's arm. "Who says no to Nils, especially if he sends an all-expenses-paid offer?"

"Nobody says no to the big brother," Sam agreed. "Don't get too sauced, Kit. And give Nils a hug when you see him." He peered down the corridor. "Am I the last one to see you off? Where's the Senator?"

"Dad got a personal invitation from Roosevelt and Hull. Top secret stuff, apparently. He caught the last flight to D.C. while you slept at the campus library." Kitty winked. "Or wherever it was you say you slept."

"It was the library," Sam stressed. "What about Maman?"

"She was gone even before I got up. You know how Claudette gets when she has to sit over finals."

"Right... Which reminds me. I've got to get to campus." Sam

hugged her once more. "Enjoy yourself, Kit. Enjoy the reprieve from the..." He jerked his head at the portrait above the fireplace where their parents, forever preserved in oils, watched over them.

In the painting, Claudette was standing next to the high-backed chair, chin lifted, her high cheekbones a deep blush. Her green almond-shaped eyes gazed critically beneath her dark arched eyebrows. Kitty could imagine how nervous her mother had made the artist, and likely commented on everything in her native French although she'd moved to Boston when she was seven.

The Senator—as Kitty and her brothers fondly referred to their father—was sitting. Had to be, for if Arne Larsson had been the one standing, the painter would have had to cut him off at the torso. His white-blond hair—nowadays just white—was smoothed back, his mouth stern, but his blue eyes gave away that soft interior Kitty depended on when she needed buffering from her mother.

"I'll enjoy my time in Tokyo," she quipped to Sam, "if you promise to at least have some friends over. Have a party. Break out the gin and the shaker. Go on a little bender. Just a little one, Sam."

"I've got finals," Sam said with his easy grin. "But I will be happy when the steam releases from this pressure cooker you've turned this house into."

Kitty snorted. "It's always my fault, right?"

"Yes, it is. But I love you anyway. Now, get going."

He gave her an affectionate kiss on the cheek, reached for the heavier bag and swung open the door for her. She gazed at him for a long while, suddenly sad to be leaving him again so soon. To Kitty—and the rest of the family—her baby brother was perfect, and nobody resented him for it. Whereas Nils had both the Senator's looks and disposition, the youngest in the family had inherited the family's ambition and Claudette's elegant and southern French features. As for Kitty, if it weren't for the obvious Scandinavian bone structure and blond hair, she would have accepted that she'd been adopted.

Sam turned on his gangster voice. "Go on, chum. Get outta here."

As she stepped into the chill air, the taxi driver jumped out and collected the luggage from her. Kitty crawled into the Ford, the back window fogged over with cold. She drew a heart into it with her index finger before waving goodbye to Sam. The automobile pulled away from the curb and drove along Summit Avenue, the vehicle passing beneath the arc of snow-laden oaks and maples.

"St. Paul airport, Miss Larsson?" the driver asked. "Which flight?"

"Pan Am. San Francisco."

"Is that your final destination?"

Kitty shook her head. "Tokyo. In three days."

He whistled. "All the way to Japan?"

"Yeah," Kitty glanced at the passing winter landscape. "Where it's a heck of a lot warmer."

And where she had a full week before she had to face her angry and disappointed mother again.

It was turbulence that bounced Kitty awake. Her neighbor was a man in an expensive suit and Fedora. He held the morning edition of the *San Francisco Chronicle*, which he had folded back. He had barely muttered a greeting back to her when she boarded her connecting flight, and had kept to himself. The headline screamed attention.

JAPAN'S STARTLING MOVE...

The rest was hidden by the fold. To hell with protocol. She wanted to read the article.

"Good morning," Kitty said brightly.

The Fedora bobbed once, a flash of a thin-lipped smile, before her seatmate made a point of hiding behind his paper. She wrinkled her nose and looked around. Bored, she reached for her pocketbook and withdrew the telegram Nils had sent her late last week. It had come on the heels of Kitty's last fight with her mother.

> I could arrange an escape from your latest fiasco. If you're serious about becoming a Foreign Service officer, it wouldn't hurt to come out and network. Say the word and I'll arrange it.

Kitty had said the word. Immediately. The ticket and the itinerary were delivered to the Larsson mansion the very next morning.

Then Claudette found out about it.

"I'll join you in Japan," her mother said in a decisive tone. "We could go right after I correct my students' exams."

To Kitty's relief, the Senator came to the rescue, suggesting Claudette wait until he'd returned from a policy meeting in D.C. They could visit her art historian colleagues in Kyoto before joining Kitty in Tokyo for the cherry blossom festival. Her mother acquiesced, adding, "I'm just so glad that Nils is no longer in Berlin socializing with Nazis..."

When the pilot announced that they could now see Tokyo city, Kitty lifted her shade and peeked out. Hundreds of sunrise-pink trees lined the city's parks and boulevards.

"Like clouds of cotton candy," Kitty said to the window. She laughed softly. Sam would point out the alliteration and her love affair with flowers, then try to make a haiku out of it.

The view disappeared as the airplane descended toward the airport, and the man next to her muttered something.

"Pardon?" Kitty asked brightly.

He indicated his copy of the newspaper. "All that pink cotton candy can't cushion the sound of sabers rattling."

She beamed, not quite sure what he meant, but appreciating his alliteration right back at her. This was her chance. "Would you mind lending me the—"

But he was already packing the newspaper into his briefcase. As the plane bumped and rolled onto the tarmac, he rubbed the side of his mouth with his index finger. "You might want to wipe that off."

Kitty dropped her head and snatched the compact mirror from her pocketbook. There was a dried white crust alongside her mouth. Her makeup was also a mess. She could hear Claudette exclaiming: *Tu finiras par me tuer, Kitty!*

Cheeks flaring, she found a tissue and tidied up, the man already at the exit before she finally gathered her things to disembark. It was a muggy spring day, and she was about to descend the passenger staircase when Kitty pulled up. There was something electric in the air, as if there were thousands of taut strings humming above her. Everything appeared to be familiar: the smiling stewardess at the bottom of the stairway, the streaming passengers bumping luggage and chatting excitedly on their way into the airport, the pilot lounging against the cockpit door. Kitty was blocking the way for the rest of the passengers.

"Did you forget something?" the stewardess behind her asked. She was holding a parasol. "Is this yours?"

It wasn't hers, and Kitty wasn't forgetting anything. She had the sensation that she'd reached a life-changing portal and if she moved on, there would be no way back. But there were passengers squirming behind her, waiting to get off. So she took the steps and joined the current of tourists.

· · ·

On the other side of Customs, Kitty spotted a quaint brown and red limousine parked alongside the curb, its headlights the size and shape of half watermelons. A Japanese man was holding a sign with *Larsson* written on it. He was dressed in burgundy livery with *Imperial Hotel* embroidered above the pocket in gold thread. The closely shorn hair beneath the cap gleamed white against his brown skin.

"Miss Larsson?" He peered up at her when she approached. "I take you to Imperial Hotel."

"Thank you very much."

The Imperial Hotel, Kitty had learned from her parents, was where many dignitaries stayed. Meanwhile, as a new embassy was being allocated in the city, the American diplomats were operating and living from the hotel.

"You're going to find a pretty international atmosphere," her dad had promised. "With recent political developments, Japan's attracting a host of junkets. Everyone is playing the country like a chessboard."

Exactly the kind of thing Kitty was attracted to: intrigue and politics. And there seemed to be plenty of both, judging by the number of military trucks peppering the wide boulevards, with policemen standing guard outside every important-looking building.

"Is there trouble?" Kitty asked the driver, but he squinted at her through the rearview mirror and just flashed her a wide smile.

"Almost there, Miss Larsson."

Just then, he turned into the drive of the Imperial Hotel and parked beneath the portico. To her left, a long, rectangular fountain rippled where water lilies floated, cracked open like eggshells. The driver removed her bags from the trunk and she followed him inside. Broad burgundy-and-gold carpeted steps led them to the sunken lobby.

After he'd lugged her bags to the front desk, Kitty gave him a few American dollars before smiling at the young man behind the desk as he politely welcomed her to Tokyo in impeccable English. "You have a couple of messages, Miss Larsson."

He handed her two envelopes. The first contained a thick card and Kitty recognized Nils's handwriting. Her brother would meet her at breakfast the next morning and urged her to "sleep it off." She smirked. The second message was a telegram from her parents. They would be landing in Kyoto that day and would see her in Tokyo before the end of the following week.

Still looking for a newspaper—English, French, German, or Russian, any of them would do—Kitty found only a stack of brochures with illustrations of smiling tourists strolling beneath cherry trees, Mount Fuji in the background and the program for the 1937 festival.

She turned around. Opposite the lobby was a long area. Lounge chairs were set between towering pillars below a temple-like roof. Glass clinked from somewhere among them, which had to be the bar. Someone would likely have left an issue lying behind, and she would finally understand what the heck had happened in Japan since she had left Minnesota.

The clerk called to her, the room key in his hand. Just before she turned to go, another military truck sped past the hotel entrance. The clerk had also seen it. His gaze scraped over her before he ducked his head.

"There appears to be trouble in the city," Kitty said.

His expression dissolved into a patronizing smile. "Everything is quite well, Miss Larsson. Many tourists. It's the *sakura* season. Extra precautions to keep our visitors safe."

Again, he bent over the pile of receipts. When the phone rang, his eyes betrayed relief.

Kitty instructed the porter to take her bags to her room, told him she would follow later and headed towards the lounge.

Safe? she thought. *Safe from what?*

2

SPRING 1937

Next morning, Nils was already in the lobby when Kitty came down. She paused, a grin spreading across her face. He was Viking-sized and even when Nils spoke softly, like he was doing now, everyone within a hundred feet could hear him.

She tiptoed behind him. When she was close enough, she reached up and cupped her hands over his eyes.

"Guess who!"

Her brother wrenched himself free and snatched her up into a bear hug. He was nearly a half foot taller than she was, and broad-shouldered. His dark blond hair was pomaded back, revealing his high forehead.

"Kitty," he boomed. She had to laugh. Compared to the small, demure, and soft-spoken hotel personnel, her brother had crash-landed in this lobby like a great Easter Island sculpture.

"It's good to see you," she said. "Thank you for the escape."

"Rose is a little jealous," Nils said. "She says that sending her back to Boston from Berlin to have the baby alone is grounds for divorce."

"I spoke to Rose the day before I left. She'll be fine."

"You mean *I'll* be fine."

"Happy wife, happy life!" Kitty laughed.

"She's glad to be out of Berlin, anyway. It's only a couple months, and then she can start packing for Tokyo." He held Kitty at arm's length and scoured her with his eyes. "I know you prefer your breakfasts late. Are you hungry already, or do you want to go for a walk and spill the beans first?"

"Walk," Kitty said. "I'm still jet-lagged."

Nils steered her towards the exit.

"So are you going to tell me why you really invited me to Japan?" Kitty asked.

"You mean besides getting you out of the way of Maman's fury?"

She hooked her arm into his elbow to keep up with his great stride. They passed the long rectangular fountain and waited at the curb. "Darling, since when have you ever been interested in my fights with Claudette?"

Nils feigned insult as he raised his hat to halt the persistent traffic. They crossed the road and headed towards the Imperial Palace Gardens. "You know I always went to bat for you."

"You left the house when I was twelve," Kitty teased. "I hadn't even gotten started with her yet."

"You two were at it from the day you were born. Maman wanted a perfect little French dolly and what she got was her husband's sporting spirit in the shape of a veritable tomboy. You can out-smoke, outdrink, and outshoot most of our father's cronies."

"Stop it now. I am perfectly feminine."

Nils assessed her with some amusement, but Kitty also saw his approval. "You are now. Snagging two fiancés and breaking it off with them within hours of having to walk down the aisle. A vicious feline indeed!"

"Don't exaggerate or you're going to be just like Claudette. It was two weeks before the wedding with Todd Hall. And four months with Hank. Hardly *hours*."

Chuckling, Nils led her through the garden gates. Tourists and locals strolled relatively unhindered beneath the blossoming plum and cherry trees. Kitty looked around, taking in the parading parasols, the bright lanterns dangling from trees, and the colorful rowboats gliding along the moats. Music played somewhere in the garden and she could smell frying fish and perfumed rice. The sun broke through the intermittent clouds creating shadow plays along the walkway.

She veered off to the merchant booths lined up along one pathway. They displayed everything from postcards to smoked fish, trinkets with Japanese calligraphy, sugared red beans, and pickled blossoms.

Nils was still on about Claudette. "Our mother's not so bad, Kitty. She fought hard to win that tenure at the university. She's a woman. She's French. She's tiny on top of that and specializes in Japanese tapestries. You've got to be really, really passionate about something like that to convince a university board to take you on. And you're very unforgiving to still be calling her Claudette all these years."

Kitty blew him a kiss. "You know I love her. It's a mother–daughter thing. And I only call her that behind her back."

Nils nudged her appreciatively and put an arm around her shoulder. They stopped at the next booth, and she ordered a bowl of noodles and broth, the savory smells too rich to resist. She turned to ask Nils if he wanted to order too, but he had drifted off to the nearest arched bridge and was leaning against the railing, distracted. She paid for her bowl and went to him. He pushed away and smiled when she dangled some noodles on her chopstick and fed them to him.

"Everything all right with you? With you and Rose?" Kitty asked.

He took the bowl from her and began rapidly downing two more servings of noodles before she could recover her breakfast.

"You mean with the baby? Rose is Boston Irish and tough as

nails. With six sisters watching over her, heck knows they don't want me around."

"Is she happy about coming to Tokyo afterwards?"

"She married a diplomat. She knows what to expect."

"That's the trouble, isn't it?" Kitty said softly. "You get married and..." She drank the broth.

"Sounds like you have no regrets about breaking it off with Congressman Hall."

Kitty rolled her eyes. "As soon as he was finished with his house, I was supposed to be another furnishing he wanted to install."

Nils winced and looked back out on the moat. "He wouldn't have known what to do with that bubbling genius beneath your shallow facade."

Kitty flinched, but Nils's smile was gentle. "The parents are frustrated because they don't understand what it is you want, Kit. So, what is it that you want?"

"I want to do what you're doing," she said, pointing the chopsticks. She remembered that was bad luck, and dipped them back in the bowl before becoming a spectacle.

"Be careful what you wish for," Nils cautioned.

"I don't want to be careful," she argued. "I want to do something that makes a difference. After what I've seen and experienced these last years, I want to see the United States adopt more humane immigration policies. I want to be a foreign service officer."

Nils nodded and affectionately ruffled her hair before she could duck away. "My sister, all of twenty-four and she wants to leave her mark on the world."

Kitty faced him, a little miserable.

He picked up the empty bowl and returned it to the stand, then led her over the moat. "I suspected all this. That's one of the reasons I sent for you."

"You sent for me?" Kitty laughed. "At your service, sir!"

But Nils was very sober now. "The escalations between Manchuria and Imperial Japan have got our office on full alert. Everyone at the Department of State has their attention on developments in Europe. Germany in particular, and Italy. Spain. But Japan really should be on our radar, mostly because I think Hitler is taking cues from them."

"I've been wondering what's going on. I went to the hotel bar to find a paper last night, but a group of gossiping diplomatic attachés from three different countries absorbed me." After the second gin rickey, she had forgotten she'd been hunting for information.

Nils gave her a knowing look but he was still serious. "We believe Japan is going to invade China. We don't know when, nobody does. But likely very soon."

"Intriguing..." Kitty remembered what her seat partner on the Pan Am flight had said about sabers rattling.

Nils studied her. "You're almost done with your diplomatic service training. I could get you a job with us here, if you like Tokyo. Have a look around. It might do you some good to have a few bodies of water between, you know, the parents and yourself."

The idea excited her. "Would I be an officer?"

"Easy, Kit. Secretarial first. Besides, it's Japan. But there are reassignments in—"

Nils suddenly looked over her shoulder, startled. Kitty turned to see what it was. But it wasn't a what. It was a who. A man—*debonair* was the word that popped into her head—with a mop of light brown curls, and dimples, deep ones, was heading straight for them. He wore a light wool blazer, and a white shirt, both definitely European. He stretched out his hand, his smile brilliant as if his mind was spinning with happy memories.

"Nils Larsson? Nobody could mistake you, could they?" The stranger pumped Nils's hand. "I think I heard you before I saw you."

Her brother stammered. "Edgar Ragatz. By God, man. It's been years, old chap."

Kitty burst out laughing. "Old chap? Let me guess, you two met at Oxford. I can always tell as soon as Nils adopts that British accent. Top o' the morning to you, guv'nor! But yours?" She peered at the handsome stranger. "It's not British."

The man's gaze landed on Kitty. Blue-green eyes, more blue. Now green. Kitty had to straighten. She felt as if she'd been running and suddenly slammed straight into a wall. His smile wavered, and she sensed how his brain switched from Nils to zeroing in on her. Then his hand was in hers, and he bent over it.

"Dr. Edgar Ragatz. From Vienna. I'm sorry I never made it to your wedding. I was in—"

"Ha!" Nils boomed. "This isn't Rose. This is my sister, Gertrude."

Mortified, Kitty shot Nils a look that should have slayed her Viking hulk of a brother, but Nils scrunched his face.

"What?" he said. "It is your name, right?"

"*Kitty*," she said acidly in Nils's direction. "Just Kitty."

He never introduced her by her Christian name but Dr. Ragatz had recovered from his faux pas, and now he took her hand to his lips.

"It is my pleasure, Kitty." His eyes were on her knuckles before he looked up with that delightful smile.

This time, Kitty was certain she would never be able to breathe again. His gaze was direct, intent, and, to her delight, she recognized mischief. Wit, layered amid deep intelligence. Layers and layers of it.

"What are you doing here, Edgar?" Nils asked him. "In Tokyo, I mean. Besides openly charming my sister, that is."

Edgar's look lightly danced over Kitty again. She felt heat creeping into her face, looked down and wrung the fabric strap of her trench coat around her finger.

"I'm with the Department of Foreign Economics in Vienna. That's where I landed after Oxford."

Nils guffawed. "I knew you would make it big." He turned to Kitty. "This man here, he was in every club, every society, taking the lead."

"Only when you weren't," Dr. Ragatz said. "I'm here on business for two or three days before my uncle has to fly back." Again, the look towards Kitty before he showed Nils his full attention again. "And you? Are you still carrying diplomatic pouches across borders?"

Nils shook his head. "Promoted. Secretary to the consul general here."

"Congratulations!" Edgar exclaimed. He clapped Nils on the back before smiling at Kitty again. "Then you're likely at the ball tonight. At the Imperial? Both of you?"

Nils nodded. "We're there. Aren't we, Kitty?"

Kitty tore her gaze away from that long, graceful neck, the perfect dimples, those eyes. His voice was satin-smooth and that accent was even more delicious than a Parisian's. "Yes, I'm going. I packed a dress and everything."

"Wonderful," Edgar said, opening his arms a little. "I look forward to seeing you there."

He may as well have been in that garden with her alone. Kitty had never heard anything more intimate. She felt physically ripped when they parted.

Trying to keep her demeanor casual as she and Nils walked on, Kitty asked, "How do you know him?"

"You guessed right. Oxford. He studied international and economic law in Vienna, and decided he'd try something else for a change. He studied in France, too."

"In Paris? Like me?"

"No, in the Alps somewhere. I can't remember exactly. French literature, though. That's something you two have in common."

"Law and literature," Kitty mused. "Intriguing combination."

"You're going to turn around now," Nils teased. "Don't do it, Kitty. Don't—"

"Too late," she shot back. She caught Edgar watching them from the bridge. Was it possible to see that smile from so far away? He raised his hand. She raised hers back.

Nils groaned. "Kitty's struck again."

"I beg your pardon?" she said. "I did no such thing."

But struck she was. And she wondered if it was too late to check the seating arrangements for the dinner. She had to make sure Dr. Edgar Ragatz would be at their table tonight.

3

SPRING 1937

Edgar was sweeping Kitty off her feet, quite literally. Acutely aware of his hand on the small of her back, she followed his lead over the ballroom dance floor. He was such a good dancer, she felt as if she was floating.

The moment she and Nils had arrived, she spotted Dr. Ragatz lingering near the entrance to the ballroom. Smiling broadly, he announced that Kitty and Nils were assigned to the same dinner table as he was. Kitty had feigned surprise, but Nils had harrumphed and pinched her arm.

During dinner, she'd hardly touched her meal. She didn't have to. Listening to Edgar talk was like dining on crisp apple strudel with warm vanilla sauce poured over it every time he laughed, and she wanted to drown in it. As Edgar and Nils exchanged stories, they kept Kitty laughing and she even forgot to drink her wine. Then Edgar asked her to dance.

Kitty held back a sudden urge to laugh now, giddy about the fact that she was in Tokyo, waltzing with a dashing Austrian.

"I've been wondering about something since the park," he suddenly said. He didn't miss a step as he spoke.

"Let me guess," Kitty said. "You want to know how Gertrude became Kitty?"

He brightened. "How did you know that?"

"The Senator—my father, that is—always called me Gertie." Kitty pressed in closer as another couple swung near them. The danger was gone, but Edgar did not release her.

"I'm listening," he said. She'd rather he spoke—that accent of his was divine.

"Dad called me Gertie but when my brother, Sam, was still a baby, he pronounced it Kitty. And it—"

"Sticked?"

"Stuck," she corrected.

Edgar's chuckle vibrated against her. "You enjoy telling that story, don't you?"

She smiled to herself. That punchline was the one thing that Kitty was certain about; the one sure thing about who she was, wherever she was in the world. The rest of it—her life, especially as of tonight—that was all up in the air. And she was hoping for a good landing spot, and not only when the music stopped.

He ushered her off the floor when it did. "Drink?"

"Yes, please."

She could still feel the heat of his palm on her lower back although he was no longer touching her, and she moved slowly ahead of him so as not to lose the sensation. They stopped at a pair of lounge chairs and Edgar whisked two glasses of champagne from a passing waiter's tray. Then he moved his seat directly next to hers. They watched the theater of a party before them, the lap of Kitty's dark blue satin gown glowing like sapphire beneath the light of the chandeliers.

"Do you know all these people?" Kitty asked, balancing her glass on the armrest.

Edgar scanned the crowd. "Some. Most."

Kitty smiled slowly. "Anyone I should know?"

He mocked scrutiny. "Some," he said. "Most. Over there, the people talking to Nils now. That's the former ambassador to Manchuria, Sempo Sugihara and his wife, Yukiko."

"It is just one big jolly boys' club, isn't it?"

"And their wives," he mused. "Or lovers..."

Kitty observed the Japanese couple and decided on the spot that she liked them, so she was surprised when Edgar leaned in close enough to whisper into her ear.

"That is his second wife, there. Sugihara-san's first wife was Russian. His time in Russia changed him."

Kitty delighted in the shivers he was sending down her neck and was disappointed when he moved away. "Are you saying he's a communist now?"

Edgar shrugged slyly. "Nobody knows. But he was transferred to Manchuria and there was a bloody incident soon after." Edgar continued, his voice low so she had to bend in his direction: "People got killed. Tokyo sent for him, questioned him. Soon after, he divorced his wife and resigned. Word is that Sugihara-san disagrees with Japan's policies in China, and believes the fascism of the West is infecting Imperial Japan."

Fascinated, Kitty glanced up at him, his aqua-green eyes steady on her. She leaned in close but whispered anyway. "Tell me, Dr. Ragatz, are you a spy?"

Edgar laughed. "Only a lawyer, and a bit of a gossip maybe. I do, however, believe that we should be watching developments here. It's little things, little nudges, but..." He studied her, "America is not aware, or refuses to acknowledge, that they are one of the dominoes in the chain, together with Europe. If Japan pushes the first domino over..." He flicked his finger and drew a line over the people in the room.

Kitty mulled this over. "Italy severed its relationship with China, right?"

Edgar's smile was slow, his eyes flashed interest. "Indeed."

"Mussolini's son-in-law was here to negotiate the sale of weapons and military equipment to Japan."

He sat back and studied her. "How do you know so much? Perhaps you are the one who works in espionage?"

"I read," Kitty said.

Edgar laughed and jerked his chin towards where Nils was now drifting to another group of diplomats and guests. "I'd say you have an awful lot of curiosity. If I were your brother, I'd be very careful."

"Ha," Kitty said. "I come from a family of politicians and diplomats. Discretion is in my blood, Dr. Ragatz."

"That's my uncle he is speaking to now." Edgar pointed to Nils standing with a smallish, mustached man wearing gold wire-framed glasses. Nils put a hand on the man's shoulder and maneuvered in front of him so that he seemed to swallow the Austrian whole.

Kitty turned her attention to Edgar again. "You're involved in foreign economic policies. Where do you think the dominoes are going to fall hardest now?"

Edgar looked thoughtful for a moment. "Japan wants to expand influence politically and militarily. Hitler is keeping his eye on Japan. For him, their occupation of Manchuria justifies the Nazi party's own doctrines of racial superiority."

"So what you're saying," Kitty said, "is Hitler is looking to Japan for inspiration."

His mouth twitched and there was a flash of admiration.

Turning her chair to face him, she propped her elbows on her lap, making the space between them intimate again, as they'd been in the park earlier that morning. "Do you think Austria will rejoin Germany?" Kitty asked.

"You come right to the point, don't you?" he teased.

Kitty smiled deliciously. "Subtlety is not my strength."

Edgar's eyes suddenly glided behind her, and Kitty also

scanned the dynamics unfolding in the ballroom. "We'll see where—"

"The dominoes fall," Kitty finished.

By the flash in his eye and that dimpled smile, she was certain that he was as aroused by their discussion as she was. She leaned back and crossed her leg, her foot very close to his shin. He glanced down but did not move away. Instead, he rested his arm on the chair, his wrist dangling over the edge, his fingers hovering just above the point of her high-heeled pump.

"What is it that you studied, Kitty Larsson?"

"Life sciences. All of it: politics, diplomacy, social studies, psychology, languages, literature—you name it. My university is right here, in places like this. I hated studying but I have always wanted to know it all." She winked.

Edgar raised an index finger at her, chuckling. "I caught that. *Know it all*." He propped his chin in his hand, his finger strumming his smile, his eyes bright. "You are fascinating, Gertrude Larsson."

"Nobody calls me that."

"My mother would insist." He winked back.

Kitty laughed wickedly. "I'll let you in on a little secret that you can share with your mother. When Maman refused to refer to me as Kitty, I started calling her Claudette. She stopped calling me Gertrude. But Sam and Nils got a kick out of that little rebellion. I still call her Claudette behind her back. She hates it even more than 'Mom.'"

Edgar chuckled, that delicious smile revealed again as his hand tapped the armrest. "Sam is like the two of you, then?"

"Heavens no. Sam is much more adorable."

"I can't believe it."

"I have a question for you." Kitty reached over and put her hand on his. Edgar immediately lifted his fingers and rested them over hers.

"And I have a question for him, too," said a voice behind Kitty.

She twisted around and looked up at Nils.

"Sorry to sneak up on you like that. Kitty, would you mind if I speak with Dr. Ragatz for a few minutes?"

Of course she would mind, but it was her brother's earnest expression that made her bite back the retort. She looked at the spot where he'd been standing with Edgar's uncle, but the Austrian ambassador was nowhere to be seen.

"I suppose I could powder my nose." Regretfully, she withdrew her hand from beneath Edgar's. "Be careful, my brother just digested your uncle."

"Come back, will you?" Edgar's eyes followed her as she stood up.

She drifted away. The devil himself wouldn't be able to keep her away from him. She was charged by their conversation, drunk on it. Her head swam. Her insides fizzed with excitement.

The powder room was bustling with women in colorful ball gowns, the various fabrics rustling and whispering as Kitty walked in. Perfumes from a variety of lands—spices, flowers, herbs, and musk—competed for air. But the strongest scent of all was power. Pocketbooks snapped, lipstick tubes popped. Besides the various skin colors and distinctive facial features, the jewelry and fashion revealed hints of each woman's origin. Kitty thought the whole world was represented in this little room; the wives and lovers of diplomats, politicians, and policymakers.

She remembered something Rose had said to her when Kitty first noticed her sister-in-law refer to Nils's career as "our work."

"Yes, it's ours," Rose had explained. "Who do you think pulls all the strings behind the scenes?"

Kitty caught sight of her reflection behind three rows of

ladies primping in the light and wondered whether she could ever be satisfied with only that.

Pushing forward into the huddle, she reminded herself she'd had the chance already. She could have helped Todd Hall become a star in Washington, but not at the expense of playing second fiddle. Edgar was out there now, and he was something else. Todd Hall had never spoken with her the way Edgar had.

Kitty quickly put on a fresh layer of lipstick before venturing back out. Her heart skipped a beat when she saw that another couple was sitting in their chairs. Edgar and Nils were gone.

It took her a while before she found the men near the temple-like bar. She paused behind one of the pillars and watched them. Edgar was speaking, animated and serious. Nils, his head bent low, was listening intently.

There was something so expressly European about Edgar; so gentlemanly and terribly seductive. From his stature to the way his wrist flicked when he spoke. His entire aura spoke of class and education, of old-world values, and generations of blue blood. He had both feet firmly on the ground, and had paid attention to her like it mattered.

So why did she feel so shy? So uncertain? She had never wanted someone to like her this much, ever. She smirked to herself. Probably because the whole situation was hopeless, that was why.

She forced herself forward. Now Nils was talking, his voice a low growl. She was going to salvage what she could before he put Edgar to sleep with his talk of politics and problems nobody in this hotel was capable of solving at this time of night.

"Boys!" Kitty called. She slipped her arm into the crook of Edgar's elbow. "Is my brother trying to scare you off now?"

Nils looked annoyed but she raised her chin at him, daring him to ruin the rest of her night.

"Nils?" Edgar prompted.

"What you're telling me is very distressing, Dr. Ragatz." His look was hostile, and Kitty frowned.

"Maybe we should save it for tomorrow?" Edgar suggested gently, but the Austrian's smile was strained. He indicated the direction of the ballroom. "You said you like big band music, Miss Larsson."

"I have a better idea." She wanted to be alone with Edgar. Whatever it was that had dampened the boys' earlier Oxford-riddled chumminess was not as important right now.

Nils took a step towards her as if he were about to whisk her away. "I thought I'd introduce you to some people, like we'd discussed."

"Later, Nils." She clutched Edgar's arm tighter. "I'm here for a week, and all these people live here. Besides, they're all sopping drunk, and we're not." She pulled Edgar closer to the bar where champagne sat on ice. "See you at breakfast, Nils," she called over her shoulder.

"Room four-twelve," she said to the bartender. After plucking two bottles from the ice bucket, one in each hand, she beamed at Edgar. "Let's take these for a walk, shall we?"

4

SPRING 1937

The sun was rising over Tokyo Bay. When Kitty looked inland, the distant snowy peak of Mount Fuji reflected the orange-red of the early morning sky. Edgar sat next to her on the bench, his white tie undone, the top collar of his shirt open. She was wearing his coat over her shoulders, her shoeless feet pulled up beneath her, the gown's wrap spread over both their laps. Edgar's hand rested between them on the bench, and when he spoke, sometimes she felt his fingers brush the fabric of her dress so subtly that she was nearly convinced it was unintentional.

She draped her arm over the back of the bench, turning to face him and propping her head on her hand. "Back to your family. Nils told me that your father is the director of the War Archives. Your mother plans social events for Viennese high society, of which your younger sister is a part of. And—according to you—spoiled. A lot of people assume I'm a spoiled socialite, too."

Edgar grinned. "You're not. But Margit? She is very much."

"She'll grow out of it."

His eyebrows shot up. "Your faith in her is stunning."

Kitty laughed, conscious that she was tossing her hair and

willing herself to stop. "Goodness knows, I did. Grow out of it and escape, that is."

Edgar's eyes crinkled in laughter, and she was once again struck by how gorgeous this man was. He was nearly ten years her senior and very charming, as well as proving to be delightfully fun. And his attraction to her was like static electricity between them.

"And after Oxford?" she purred, her lids feeling heavy. She wanted to snuggle into him, lay her head in his lap, but it was too soon. "You came full circle and became a lawyer."

"Something like that. My uncle will be retiring soon. He's pushing me to become a full-fledged diplomat."

Kitty sat up straight. "I want to be a foreign service officer." She waved her hand in front of her body. "But not many women are, if at all."

Edgar's eyes turned dark aqua, almost like the water in the harbor. "I have no doubt you'd be the first."

She flushed at that.

They had begun their conversation as most couples would, a veritable interview in the search for common values, a connection beyond the obvious physical attraction they felt for one another. So they worked to impress. He told her of his education at an elitist *Gymnasium*, she told him of her first boarding school experience. Both of them had been pranksters. After they drank the first bottle of champagne, exchanging stories about how they pulled the wool over their victims' eyes, that feeling that she had to impress Edgar dissolved beneath heaps of laughter.

They spoke of their fathers' influences on their jobs and their mothers' influences on their upbringing. Very soon, they turned to comparing their cultures and their countries, which inevitably led back to politics, an interest they most certainly had in common.

"You should have been a lawyer," Edgar said.

"No offense, but no," Kitty laughed. "I like playing politics, but through the back door." She remembered suddenly how Nils had left Edgar's uncle and the change in mood it had brought. It was a risk, but she wanted to know what had happened. "So, what's really going on with Austria?"

Edgar shrugged, sobering a little, but his smile was still easy. "The political pot is boiling over. Getting rid of our monarchy after the Great War simply meant a whole slew of autocrats were waiting to take over."

"I have to be honest, I was a little relieved if not surprised that the Nazi party was made illegal in Austria."

Edgar looked down at his lap for a moment. "Don't think for a second that the Nazis are buried. Just look at Vienna. It is very anti-Semitic and it's very modern to think like this these days. But where do you think they are taking their cues?"

"From Germany, of course."

Edgar gave her a look as if to say she should think again.

"Certainly not from Austria?" She leaned in deliciously.

He tapped the side of his nose. "So thick, you can smell them. They're everywhere."

Kitty shifted a little, not sure how to interpret this bit but not wanting to be like her big brother and crushing all the fun with earnestness. A fisherman's boat puttered into the harbor and she heard crates being unloaded at the wharf across the water.

Edgar followed her gaze. "Even your President Roosevelt doesn't take his Jewish constituents seriously. When Nils was working for the previous ambassador in Berlin, his alarms about Hitler's hate for the Jews went unheeded."

Now it was Kitty who shrugged uncomfortably, the lining of Edgar's tuxedo rustling softly against her bare arms. "I'm not sure what all the fuss is about either way. Why does everyone pick on them?"

Edgar turned to face her, his arm resting over his crossed

leg. "If it's not the Jews, we'd find someone else to pick on, as you say. A few years ago, Vienna's communist party achieved great things for the common worker in the city. But an uprising crushed that, and now—ta-da! we have welcomed Austrofascism with Kurt Schuschnigg as our chancellor. In return, we lumped the Jews together with the communists and vice versa. Double the impact when striking fear into the hearts of men."

He was being ironic, but it still sent a chill down her spine. He was not wrong. She knew that. She looked out onto the water again. A goose splashed softly out of the reeds, and six little gray, downy goslings followed.

Edgar was smiling at her again, one eyebrow cocked. "Anything else I can clear up for you, Miss Larsson?"

"Uff," Kitty breathed. "I think I just sucked all the joy from our conversation with my question. I guess I am a bit like Nils."

"Not at all," Edgar murmured. "I find speaking with you terribly exhilarating."

She laughed, head tipped back.

He stretched his index finger over to her wrist and stroked it, sending a shiver of pleasure through her. "I have a feeling, Kitty Larsson, that I would have to spend a lifetime discovering everything about you."

Her stomach flipped. "You're not so boring yourself."

They gazed at one another and then a yawn caught her unawares. She apologized and he rose, offering his hand.

"Let me take you back to the Imperial. You're exhausted."

Kitty glanced down at the empty champagne bottles and her discarded heels. The sun was growing warmer. With a sense of remorse, she took his hand and got to her feet, picking up the shoes by the slings.

"Actually, I'm rather starving. But look at me, like Cinderella, ousted from the ball."

Edgar's smile was slow as he gazed at her. "I don't want the night to end either."

It was one statement but everything shifted for her and she felt light. Eyes locked on his, Kitty knew she could say anything to this man, and it would be understood, accepted. There were no games. No silly need to flirt and skirt around their desire for one another any longer.

"I could freshen up," she said, "and meet you for breakfast?"

"I think that is a wonderful idea. But not at the hotel. I have a place I would love to take you. There's a little seaside resort, about half an hour away from here. I have a car. You're American. You'll love it. It has no top."

Kitty laughed. "I'll be sure to wear my scarf, then. It's a fabulous idea."

He offered his hand and she took it, following him along the wharf. "I'm not prepared to return to that—"

"Gladiator's arena?" Kitty shaded her face from the sun.

"Fascinating," Edgar murmured. Something changed in his expression and Kitty's heart somersaulted. Gently, he tugged her back to him. He lifted his hand and caressed her cheek. She dropped her head into his palm, relishing his hold.

"You have a strong face," he murmured. "It's beautiful. You are beautiful."

When he drew her face to him, she let him.

"You inflame my romantic imaginations, Miss Larsson."

"Let's hope I live up to your expectations, Dr. Ragatz. I would hate to see your fantasies go up in smoke."

Edgar's lips were soft against hers, brushing gently, pulling back. "Not in the least."

But Kitty could never have enough of that mouth. She grasped his upper arms and drew him closer, and this time, Edgar kissed her in a way that Kitty just knew.

She knew she had landed.

. . .

To avoid the crowd at the breakfast room and hotel lounge, Kitty and Edgar snuck in through the back, surprising the Imperial kitchen staff and dashing for the service elevator in their disheveled outfits. Edgar was staying two floors above hers and he kissed her just before the elevator closed again and whisked him away.

Back in her room, Kitty had no sooner finished freshening up than she heard the knock. She didn't have to ask who it was. She could feel it was him.

"Gertrude Larsson," he called softly from behind the door.

"It's Kitty. Just Kitty," she said with mock exasperation.

There was a pause and she could hear him chuckling. Then, "Kitty?"

She liked the way he said her name—regardless which one —with that voice and that Austrian accent wrapped around each letter. "Yes?"

"I missed you when I was upstairs."

Kitty bit down on her knuckles and pressed her ear up against the door. The anticipation was crackling in the hallway. She took in a deep, quiet breath and held it. Her face hurt from the permanent smile she'd worn since they'd met.

"You're here, right?" His voice was low but she could hear him as if he were in the room with her. His cheek had to be resting right next to hers on the other side. She only nodded. "I need to tell you, Kitty, I think I could fall in love with you."

"When you know for certain, Edgar, tell me."

"If you have breakfast with me, I'll tell you."

"If you tell me," she said, "I'll have breakfast with you."

Again that chuckle, rolling down his chest. "I know I could love you."

She slid her hand down to the doorknob, her reply ready the moment she saw Edgar's face, but then she heard Nils's voice booming down the hallway.

"Is my sister in there?"

Kitty flung open the door and stepped out. "Reporting for duty, sir!"

Her brother looked her up and down. She looked herself up and down. She was wearing a pair of white leisure trousers, a navy-blue blouse and patterned scarf, and sensible pumps. Absolutely presentable. She had even brushed out her curls and put up her hair in anticipation of the ride in Edgar's convertible.

"Maman and Dad are here," Nils said, his eyes skittering between her and Edgar. "They arrived from Kyoto late last night."

"What?" Kitty cried. "Where?"

"In the breakfast room. They sent me on a one-man search party when you didn't answer your door."

Kitty groaned but didn't even have an opportunity to pull her brother into a conspiracy that would entail excusing her for a day of sightseeing, shopping, anything so that she could just have a few more precious hours with Edgar, because Nils then turned to Edgar. "And you and I need to finish our conversation from last night. Is there a place where we can talk?"

"Must we?" Edgar pulled a tortured face, his tone laced with sarcasm.

"Absolutely. If what your uncle tells me—"

Edgar held up a hand. "We can go to my suite. I'm upstairs."

Nils shot Kitty a warning look. "I'd get downstairs if I were you, young lady."

Kitty clicked her heels and saluted him. "Yes, sir. Right away, sir." She turned to Edgar and said sweetly, "Will you write to me? I'll likely have to do jail time."

He winked. "Then I'll write. Better yet, I'll come break you out."

Nils groaned and Kitty bit her lip to stop laughing.

"Ta-ta." She reached up and brushed a kiss across her brother's cheek, then Edgar's. "I'll see you as soon as you two have done your important conniving and I've placated my parents."

. . .

Her parents were finished with breakfast. Not a spot on Claudette's plate. A peeled eggshell lay on the Senator's. He was reading the paper, folded in half at the side of his dish. Claudette was lounging in the chair, her coffee cup resting in her palm.

She brightened when Kitty walked up to the table.

"There you are. We've been looking all over."

"Maman. Dad. What are you two already doing here?"

Kitty's mother pouted and pointed at the Senator. "He's been called back to Washington. Everything is cut to three days, and I was not going to leave without seeing something of the festival in Tokyo."

Her dad finished his article and rose, removing a chair for Kitty.

She sat down and fingered the perfect white and pink orchid in the vase to feel whether it was real or fake. It was real. "You want to pick up the conversation from before I left for Tokyo. Let's get it over with."

"You think we're nagging, Kitty. We're not nagging," Claudette said. "We're worried about you. Aren't we, Arne?"

Kitty's father shrugged and tipped his head. "Should we be?"

Claudette placed her cup on the table and patted her mouth with her napkin. "Kitty, I just—I worry that if you keep losing yourself to distraction, you'll never find the best version of yourself. That's all."

Kitty clenched her hands beneath the table.

"Look," her dad said, and this time his placating tone made Kitty turn to her old habit of picking her nails. Claudette was quick to tap Kitty's hand down. Her father winced and tried again.

"Nils put your name in for a position in Tokyo. He said he'd see to it that you get an important department. Who knows, Kitty. Maybe oversee the typist pool or..." He must have seen her expression because he swallowed.

"Would she just *stay* here?" Claudette's eyes went accusingly wide. "She has only enough things to wear for a week. Don't be ridiculous."

"So that Nils can babysit me?" Kitty muttered. "No thank you. I appreciate it and everything, but Japan is not progressive enough. A woman here... Nope. I want to be a foreign service officer."

"Kitty," her dad started, "I don't know any place that would take you abroad as an FSO officer."

"But it doesn't mean that I can't work my way up." She leaned into the table and grinned at her dad. "I'm good at this. I know how to drink—"

Claudette clicked her tongue. Kitty drove her point homeward.

"I function well at parties. I know how to talk. But best of all, Dad, and you know this, I'm a great listener."

"Really, Kitty?" Claudette scolded. "Then listen to your father and take a position in D.C., or even in St. Paul."

"Now, honey." The Senator's mouth twitched, and Kitty beamed when he turned to her mother. "She does have a point."

Claudette sighed heavily. "We should talk to Nils. Where is he, by the way?"

"Probably scaring Edgar off." Kitty immediately regretted mentioning his name.

"Edgar?" Her mother wiggled like a worm on a hook. She looked to the Senator for help. "Who in God's name is Edgar now?"

Kitty sighed. "Dad, I'm being tested for the diplomatic license in just under two months. I want to work abroad. I'm going to ask them to place me somewhere in Europe. I speak

French, German and some Russian. I can certainly be useful. I want to be in Europe."

"Is this Edgar in Europe?" Claudette asked, still looking to the Senator for answers.

Kitty ignored her, watching her dad lean back and cross his arms.

"I can help you get to Paris. I've got some people I know, and they know some people."

"Yes, Paris. Paris would be good," Claudette said. "I can ask your aunt Julia to arrange everything. Is Edgar French, too?"

"No, Maman. And he's not an American."

Paris, Kitty calculated, was not that far from Vienna. That was, if she and Edgar were heading where she thought they were heading. And the way her heart hurt just at the thought of all that distance—even not being on the same floor in the same hotel—then maybe Paris would also not be close enough.

"Berlin," she said, avoiding the obvious. "What about Berlin?"

Claudette smacked her lips and made a disgusted noise. "Nils just got out and you want to go in—"

"Or Paris," Kitty said, just to keep the peace. "Dad?"

Her father nodded. "I'll look into it."

"So how was Kyoto, Maman?" Kitty asked brightly.

Diverted by the question, Claudette was updating Kitty on all that she had seen and done with her art history colleagues when suddenly Nils entered the hotel lobby. When had he left? He was heading straight for the elevators at lightning speed. Kitty dashed out of the breakfast room, Claudette calling after her in that exasperated tone. *Kitty, not again!*

She managed to get to Nils just before the elevator doors opened.

"Hey, where's Edgar?"

Nils looked sheepish.

"What?" Kitty huffed a laugh. "Did you murder him and leave him in the park, or what?"

"He had to leave. He has to catch a flight back to Europe."

Her voice revealed her disbelief. "Did you do the big brother thing and scare him off?"

Nils peered at her. "Come on, Kitty. You're the one who keeps getting cold feet. Maybe I'm protecting him from you."

It was an automatic response, Kitty had no idea she was even capable of it, but she balled a fist and punched Nils hard in the upper arm.

"Gertrude!" Claudette cried. She and the Senator had hurried after her.

It was then that Kitty saw a convertible pull up to the hotel portico. Edgar appeared and got into a car with his uncle. She rushed to the window and rapped on the glass, but it was much too thick.

"Kitty." Nils stepped up to her and put his big hands on her shoulders. "There's no time for goodbye now."

There was always time for goodbye.

Nils fished a small envelope out of his breast pocket—the hotel's stationery. "He gave me this."

Kitty took it and went back to the tall windows. She opened the card and glanced over the words, keeping her eye on Edgar. But he wasn't even looking.

It seems I really must write to you. I know you were joking. I was not. I meant what I said. I really could love you. This is not a passing fancy, believe what my heart has been saying to you since I first saw you. This is not the end. It is only the beginning. I will write and beg your forgiveness for this rushed departure until you give it to me. And God willing, we will see each other sooner rather than later. When we do, I will beg your forgiveness, again and again in futile hope that you believe how very sincere I am.

Your devoted Edgar

She folded the card closed and pressed it to her. The car was gone. But those sparks—no, not sparks—this was something solid. Edgar felt like a calling. A destiny, even. Meeting him was propelling her on a journey. With or without him, she knew what she had to do next.

The Senator was speaking with Nils, and Claudette had her hands on her hips. Kitty marched up to her dad and tossed Nils a defiant, scathing look.

"There is something you can do, Dad," she said.

The Senator tipped his head. "All right, Kit. What is it?"

"You know people everywhere. Drum up someone who can get me into the consulate in Vienna."

"Vienna is only a legation, Kit. A branch of Berlin. It's not Paris. It's a small staff. You might get on the typing pool but nothing more than that. Certainly not in a position where you could work your way up to a foreign service officer."

"Vienna," she said firmly, and looked out the window. "I know what I want."

5

SUMMER 1937

From the moment Kitty stepped off the train in Vienna, she was looking for signs of Edgar. A few times, her heart would jump at the sight of a tall, slender man, brown hair, or a suit, or a similar gait. But it would be an absolute coincidence if she ran into him in the first moments of her arrival, and she did not really believe in such things, mainly because Edgar did not know that she had moved to Austria.

At first glance, Vienna was much as Kitty had remembered it from her whirlwind tour through Europe years earlier. The Baroque and Neo-classical buildings along the *Ringstrassen* were still impressive. The lush gardens were blooming in the July heat. The palaces, the horse-drawn Fiakers, the city hall and parliament, were all familiar and lavish sights.

But on that previous visit she'd been a tourist. As a newly arrived resident, she was also aware of the nuances playing beneath the facades. She stepped over dark liquid streaks that sloped from the base of the buildings towards the curbs; pools not only made by dogs but by men relieving themselves. She saw workers wearing signs around their necks, complaining about the lack of work, the price of food, or shortage of justice.

Beer bottles lay smashed along the streets. Right outside the main train station Kitty saw a gang of children with ruined shoes, moth-eaten tunics and dirty faces. And if the billboards and placards were any indication, Vienna was embroiled in an identity crisis.

On the fringes of the Great Depression, Kitty had experienced something similar, witnessing the stark contrast between her lifestyle and the circumstances of those who had not fared well after the economy crashed. She had never felt comfortable with it, and she was very glad she'd rejected her father's offer of an apartment and chosen instead to room with one of the women from the U.S. legation.

The address she'd been given was somewhere between the Belvedere Palace and the Danube River—a lot of land to get lost in. She had taken a tram to what she'd thought was the right stop, but now she wandered through curved streets and hit dead ends, or narrow alleys that led nowhere. The streets changed names depending which side of the road she was on. She was hot, tired and anxious. Worst of all, she was beginning to regret not informing Edgar that she was coming to Vienna, but he had made her uncertain.

It started when the tone in Edgar's first letter on returning home was decidedly less ardent. She had written back, telling him she had forgiven him, and that she had wished they could have continued that day in Tokyo. His next letter arrived weeks later. He was funny, informative, but neutral. He never said he loved her again, and he never again signed off as her *devoted Edgar*.

It did not make sense to her until she flew to Boston to visit her new niece, Molly. Nils was helping Rose to pack up for Japan, and Kitty cornered him and laid herself bare.

"I'm suffering," she said. "What happened in Tokyo? You and Edgar stopped being chummy during the ball. What are you not telling me?"

Nils barely looked at her. "Not everything is as it appears on the surface, Kitty."

"I thought you two were friends."

"We were. People change. We have our differences. Listen to me, Kit, go to Paris. Forget Vienna. Forget Edgar."

"Come now, Nils," she'd scoffed. "You of all people should understand how I like being in the middle of the excitement."

Nils had lost his temper. "You know that people are not who you think they are. You of all people. I mean, look at you. You jilted two guys in under two years."

Squaring up to her brother, Kitty had demanded, "What are you not telling me?"

He'd shaken his head, thrown his wife a pleading look and then put his hands on Kitty's shoulders. "Maybe it's my fault. He's a very earnest man. He comes from a very traditional family. Catholic, loyal to the former monarchy. Maybe I let it slip that you left two men hanging at the—"

"Oh, you are a pistol," Kitty sneered. "Just ace, Nils."

Her brother looked away. "That probably wasn't the right thing to do."

"Probably?" Kitty cried. She blinked the sting at the back of her eyes away. "If you were trying to make me miserable, you've succeeded."

"I wasn't, Kitty."

"Could've fooled me."

It was then that she had decided not to tell Edgar she was coming. If she was going to salvage anything, it would have to be face to face, but first she needed to find her feet.

A woman in a bright yellow sari with frizzy blond hair and a red dot in the middle of her forehead stopped in front of Kitty. "You are lost?"

"I'm looking for the Rabenhofsiedlung," Kitty said. Before

her, a huge network of apartment buildings stretched as far as she could see. They were brown-brick and concrete with double-paned windows. The complex was more modern than most buildings in the city center.

"This is it," the woman said, and waved in all four directions. "Which part do you need?"

Kitty showed her the address and the woman led her past tastefully appointed gardens, a kindergarten where she heard children singing, and a theater with an extensive program on the billboard. The contrast to what Kitty had seen immediately around the train station was stunning. The woman soon stopped at one of the entrances. Kitty thanked her and looked for the bell with Millicent Hoffmann's name on it.

Having envisioned a secretarial spinster type, she was not prepared for the curvy and vivacious woman who waited on the fifth floor. Millicent Hoffmann was about Kitty's age, dark hair, bright pink lipstick and dark green eyes.

She stuck out her hand and Kitty took it.

"Millie," her new roommate said. "Welcome to Vienna. It's so exciting to have someone new here. Sarah left for the Paris embassy two months ago, and the place has just been so empty. Come in."

Millie ushered Kitty in, telling her she was from upstate New York, which explained the East Coast accent. She swayed as she walked in a well-cut suit, unconsciously twisting a pearl necklace with one finger.

The apartment consisted of a whole lot of eclectic furniture and decorations. Nothing really matched. There were a variety of kilims scattered on the floor. A window seat was decorated with several pillows, one hand-embroidered with an Alpine scene. Kitty stroked the potted fern to discover it was fake, as was the palm tree in the corner.

Millie looked apologetic. "Someone decided it wasn't worth

keeping real plants, in case the apartment stayed empty for a while."

"Of course. It's all so... cheerful." Kitty was charmed.

"Everyone kind of leaves something behind when they get reassigned," Millie said. "These paperbacks? All romance. Not mine, though. I prefer non-fiction."

She pointed to a stack of back issues of *The American Foreign Service Journal*. "I'm going to be a career diplomat," Millie announced, and hustled out into the corridor.

Kitty raised her eyebrows. "I see." She liked her very much already.

She followed Millie and looked into the next room, a bedroom. It was a small space and high-ceilinged with a single bed and a simple oak dresser and matching wardrobe.

"That's my room," Millie said. "Yours is down the hall."

The next room was furnished similarly. On the dresser were Viennese and Austrian knick-knacks. A wine glass with the Prater Ferris Wheel. There was also a snow globe containing a horse-drawn Fiaker with two dappled gray horses in front of the Vienna opera house. Kitty shook it and replaced it.

"I'm keeping them," Kitty said.

"Home sweet home," Millie called. "Come on, I'll show you the rest of the apartment."

Her new roommate chattered away as she showed the tiny kitchen and bathroom, then grinned again. "That's it. This is home. So which one is it? Love or money?"

Kitty frowned, not understanding the question.

"We only leave our countries voluntarily for love or for money. You don't look like you need the money."

Kitty flushed.

Millie wagged a finger. "OK, who is he? Tell me all about him."

"An Austrian diplomat."

Millie blew a soft whistle. "Holy moly. And is it serious?"

"I guess I'll find out," Kitty said. To get off the subject, she claimed she was exhausted, which she was. Millie bustled into the kitchen and left her to it.

Just the thought of Edgar not being thrilled about seeing her was enough to make her feel nauseated, but she wasn't going to tell that to a perfect stranger.

Back in her room, she viewed the landscape outside her window. A wall of apartments that looked just like hers on the outside. Five stories below, a man sat on a bench dwarfed by the surrounding white and pink hydrangea bushes. She decided that tomorrow she would go down there, cut a few blooms and spread them around the apartment.

She wondered what Edgar would be doing right now. What he saw outside his windows. And if he spotted her below one, would he be happy to see her or treat her as a colleague's little sister? Kitty drew the muslin curtains and threw herself on the bed.

The trip had been long, but she rolled over and opened the small case containing Edgar's letters. She should call him. She would hear it in his voice whether he was happy that she was in Vienna. But the apartment had no telephone. A post office probably would. Or the consulate.

"Tomorrow," she said, and pressed the cards to her chest before falling instantly asleep.

A hearty breakfast was waiting for her the next morning and Millie, who felt it necessary to divulge all the office gossip, got to the point only after Kitty had eaten.

"You're the new personal assistant to the chargé d'affaires, Mr. John Cooper Wiley. He's pretty new himself."

"What's he like?"

Millie smiled. "I think you two are going to get on like a house on fire."

The office was located twenty minutes on foot from the apartment, just a couple of streets away from the Belvedere Palace. There was a wrought-iron gate around the complex, and a garden that served as a *Hof* for not just the U.S. legation but several other embassies and a large legal office. Millie took Kitty on the rounds of the building. The employees could come through the garden off the side street in the back. They were checked in by a guard. The foyer floor was of swirled gray and green marble tile. A grand staircase led to the next floor with a long corridor going to the left and right wings of the building. Millie led Kitty to a big airy room with windows looking out onto the courtyard.

All the assistants who served the foreign service officers and the legation officials were located in this one large room. Their bosses' offices were adjacent. Millie stopped before a pretty dark blonde in a floral dress. She was tall with bird-bone wrists, wore very little makeup, but her most distinctive feature were her dark, sharply etched eyebrows.

"This is Miss Mary Rosen. She is one of our best."

"So, I've heard," Kitty beamed.

But Mary Rosen, her brown eyes shifting over the lines on her document, nodded curtly at the typewriter. "Yes, and I've heard that your father got you this job."

Kitty bit her lip and glanced at Millie.

"Anyway," Millie stressed loudly, "I was hoping you could bring Kitty up to speed regarding Mr. Cooper Wiley's expectations?"

Mary's gaze darted to Kitty as she continued typing. "Soon as I'm done here."

Millie patted Kitty's arm and moved on to an empty desk with only a phone and a typewriter on it. She pointed to a door behind it where a plaque reading *John Cooper Wiley, Chargé d'Affaires* hung.

"Cooper usually comes in at nine. He'll call you on this line here when he needs you."

"Thanks," Kitty said, eyeing the telephone. She could ring Edgar right from here and the very thought of hearing his voice —that rich accent, that gorgeous, silken laugh—set her heart racing.

"Is there anything I should do right now?" Kitty asked.

Millie glanced over at Mary. "She'll take over from here."

Mary rose at the same time as she yanked out the final sheet, added it to the papers she'd already typed, aligned the pile and handed it to Millie.

"Please take these downstairs," Mary said, then turned to Kitty. "Follow me."

Kitty looked regretfully at the telephone, wishing she could call Edgar, then followed Mary across the office.

"You took my job," Mary called over her shoulder. "I've been waiting for this position, I was next in line, and doing excellent work, according to Cooper. So let's see what you're made of."

Kitty bit her lip again. "I'm so—"

But Mary was already striding out the door. "We have four Foreign Service Officers here. Mr. Morris—"

"Yes, that's Millie's boss." Kitty caught up to her, then named the remaining three officers.

Mary stopped and tipped her head. "How impertinent."

"I'm sorry. Millie got me up to speed this morning."

"Is that so," Mary said drily. "What do you need me for then?" She strode on down the corridor, but continued talking while Kitty hurried after her. Essentially it was a repeat of Millie's tour, but Kitty did not say another word.

They returned to the main room and Mary led Kitty back to her desk. "Anyway, when Cooper—don't call him that to his face—gets in, he'll say hello, and you just wait until he rings for you. You'll be busy all day. Lunch is at half past twelve—you'll have to get used to the slang around here; we've all been living in Vienna for quite some time and have adapted to the locals' version of British English—and you get two ten-minute breaks, one at ten thirty and one at three thirty. We usually take lunch at the little tavern on the corner. You can join us today if you'd like."

Kitty smiled, surprised. "Thank you. About the phone—there's someone I need to reach in Vienna. How do I place a call outside?"

Mary's smile was a grimace, as if she had found something in her teeth. "We finish at six, but only if the work is done. Cooper tends to work late. No personal calls."

Sharp disappointment stabbed right through her. "I see."

Kitty went to her desk and Mary returned to her seat, pulled a folder out of a box and rolled in a fresh sheet of paper into the typewriter.

Millie tiptoed over. "Hey, Kitty. I'm pretty sure Cooper won't keep you late tonight. There's a great jazz club called Achmed Beh and on Thursdays it's a real gas. So, I'm taking you down there tonight. There are some people I'd love you to meet."

Just then a man in wire-rimmed glasses, a hat, and a suit coat flung over his shoulder walked into the room. The pool of secretaries kept typing, banging, filing, but all of them straightened and greeted him, and he returned their greetings.

"Mr. Cooper Wiley?" Kitty said, sticking her hand out. "I'm—"

"Arne's daughter. Gertrude Larsson?"

"Please, it's Kitty."

He nodded. He had the kind of eyes that drooped downwards, but his smile lifted them. "All right, Kitty. Come on into my office, and bring that pile of newspapers."

There was a stack on top of the filing cabinet next to his door. She scooped them up and hurried after him. She fanned them out on his desk and in one glance saw that they were in German, French and English. He whisked off the first English language one and pointed to the headline.

"I reckon now that Japan has invaded China, we're headed for a whole new phase in geopolitics." He looked up, openly assessing her before indicating that she should take a seat. "We're both new here. Let's get acquainted. I was looking for a new assistant when your father called me."

"I'm afraid someone believes she got overlooked."

"You ladies will sort that out between yourselves. Buy Mary lunch or something. She likes expensive things."

Kitty was not convinced Mary would be so easily appeased.

Cooper reached into his drawer, pulled out a packet of Chesterfields, and offered her one. She declined. He tapped the end on the desk before lighting it. "I need someone like you, Kitty. Someone who understands and can navigate the game, you understand? I've heard about you from a number of people already. I think you're perfect for the job here."

She flushed. What exactly had he heard then?

"I'll be counting on you a lot. I communicate with Berlin often, and I want you on those calls, taking notes. I protocol all communications. We document everything. I've got diplomatic briefs, reports, cables and pouches you'll need to prepare. Miss Rosen and Miss Hoffmann will help you with the procedures. I'll tell you when it's time to go home. You have a family you need to get to?"

"No, sir..."

"I do. My wife is Irena. You'll meet her soon. And the other thing you're responsible for are all the functions we put on. The events, the lectures, the parties. Everything that requires my good suits and appearances. You've signed a document that says you'll be criminally charged for spilling any secrets?"

Kitty cocked her head. "Yes, sir."

Cooper grinned. "Good. That's good. I'll be reading the

papers and my stack of cables here. Take the French and German papers, if you will. I want a summary of anything that you think is important for our office to know. Everything."

"Yes, sir." She turned to go.

"Miss Larsson?" She decided he had kind eyes. "You prefer to go by Kitty? When I introduce you to others, I mean."

"If you would, sir."

He seemed to mull something over as he scanned the next page on his desk. "I can tell you grew up with a father who's served in the military."

"Yes, sir."

He assessed her anew. Kitty tried not to fidget.

"They call me Cooper out there. I know that. We'll keep that between us, though, shall we?"

She nodded.

"Brace yourself for a run of work. I do a lot of reporting. The Department of State likes that kind of thing."

Her stomach in her throat, Kitty drummed her fingers on the desk as the phone on the other end buzzed. The office was empty, but everyone would be returning from lunch in a matter of minutes. She'd ducked out of the tavern on the excuse that she needed to retrieve something and had hurried back in hopes that the room would be empty. It was.

Edgar answered on the tenth ring, slightly breathless. *"Hier spricht Doktor Ragatz."*

"Hello, Edgar. It's Kitty."

A split second of silence during which she held her breath and then Edgar's voice, jubilant. "Kitty? Is that really you?"

Her heart did a flip and she exhaled with relief. "It certainly is. I'm in Europe."

"Im Ernst? Seriously? Where are you calling from?"

"From the third district."

"You're here? In Vienna? When?"

She laughed. "When what?"

"When can I see you?"

She looked out the window and put a hand beneath her ribs to still her breathing. "I'm working. Until six, I think."

"Let me guess, you got a position at the consulate."

"Yes."

"I'll be there at six. On the dot. Darling, I can't wait to see you. I can't believe it. You're here. You're really here!"

She could not stop smiling for the rest of the day and the hours flew. Cooper had a hundred things for her to do and a lecture to send invitations to, and she loved the work, but she was on tenterhooks.

"Kitty." Millie was hovering over her desk.

She looked up from the report she was typing up.

"I just came up from the foyer, where there's a charming prince asking for you. He's pacing the hall as if you're about to give birth. And he's brought flowers."

"Good Lord!" Kitty looked up at the clock: 6:10 p.m.

"What a dish," Millie said, bending low. "I understand why you insisted on coming here."

Kitty grinned at the typewriter, her hands shaking. "I'm almost done. Would you mind telling him? Ten more minutes." She glanced back at Cooper's door. "You think he's done with me?"

Suddenly Cooper stepped out, his briefcase and coat in his hand. He looked taken aback at Millie's silly grin. Her eyes darted to the clock. Cooper stuck his hat on his head. "Miss Larsson, you can finish the report tomorrow morning. Just lock it up in the cabinet before you go, will you?"

"I guess Achmed Beh and the gang will have to wait," Millie said as he left.

"Thursday comes again next week."

With Millie ahead of her, Kitty hurried to gather up her

things and popped into the restroom to check herself in the mirror. She shook off the nerves and went to the top of the stairs.

Edgar turned the moment she reached the landing, a bundle of purple larkspur and white lysantheum under his arm. A broad grin broke across his entire face. He was like a light bulb, and she was caught in his glow.

He opened his arms and his embrace was warm, and safe, and intimate. Like a promise between future lovers.

"There was something I wanted to say," she whispered into his ear.

"I could really love you," he whispered back.

"Yes."

6

SUMMER 1937

An infatuation it was not. For the next weeks, as late summer's green began taking on a tinge of gold, Kitty never made it to a Thursday-night drink with Millie. Instead, she was off with Edgar exploring Vienna, attending the opera, sitting in cafes, meeting Viennese society at ritzy dinners everywhere from the Hotel Metropole to the Belvedere. She met royalty and businessmen, as well as artists, politicians and plenty of side characters that—based on the delicious gossip Edgar and she shared after the parties—Kitty suspected made a living from racketeering.

With a finger stuck in every veritable society and club, Kitty had a hard time keeping all of Edgar's friends and business acquaintances straight. But his eyes shone with pride as he watched them receive her warmly. He positively glowed when she made his acquaintances and friends laugh.

"I don't know what it is about you," Edgar confessed one day. "But you have a knack of charming people into telling you some of their most scandalous secrets."

Kitty's knowledge of German helped her to quickly adapt to the local dialect, too. With its affected, bored inflection, and over-enunciation, she compared Viennese to the Southern dialects in the United States.

One Friday, Edgar came around with a car and they motored out to the Vienna Woods. Seamlessly, Kitty glided between her world at the consulate, her life as Millie's roommate, and the established European society in Edgar's world.

And in that world, that he should have access to a country estate was almost expected. When he asked her to motor out with him for the weekend to the Vienna Woods, Kitty anticipated finally having some time alone with him. Because up to that point, their social events never allowed them much time for intimacy.

"So, tell me about the place we're going to," she said.

"It's our family cottage." He grinned at her. "A little time away from the bustle of the city, away from the perpetual complaints."

What Kitty had not expected was that their "quiet getaway" involved hosting three other couples. To her absolute frustration, Edgar was all too happy to play house with her, but they were still sleeping in separate rooms.

"Why?" she pouted as he escorted her to her room. She dodged his kiss. She was prepared to rip his clothing off as he prepared to turn in for the night, to his own room.

He caressed her tenderly and kissed her forehead, which increased her disappointment. "I don't ever want you to leave me high and dry at the altar, Kitty Larsson. I'm sure about you. But you are in a foreign country. In a foreign culture. It's not just me you have to consider." He lifted his hands in surrender and slowly turned all the way around.

"This is it. This is me. All of it. But I cannot separate myself from the things that have shaped me. So, I want you to be certain about me. Certain, darling, the way I am certain about you."

"I am certain about you," she said.

"Are you? All of it?"

She opened her arms and nodded. "I am ready to embrace it all, Dr. Ragatz. Absolutely."

He cocked his head, those green-blue eyes flashing with emotion and tenderness. "Good. But not with everyone here."

She could have screamed. Later, she relished the anticipation of making love to him. His words heightened her awareness, too. Yes, Vienna was different to Minnesota, to Washington, D.C. even, but not so drastically. It was Europe. Charming. Layered with history and a good dollop of intrigue. And save for the splashes of social conflict she witnessed on the streets between the classes, what wasn't there to love?

If she was not at a function or event with Edgar, Kitty was planning and attending one for and with Cooper and his wife, Irena. The social circles often grazed one another, because one thing Vienna most certainly had to offer was the variety of cultures and a rich expat community. She was in her element and Edgar was part of that.

Under Kitty's attention to detail, the consulate's events and diplomatic junkets were a roaring success. Kitty dressed the part, looked the part and spoke the part. She was at every lecture with Cooper, every local function. She liked both him and Irena very much. Cooper praised Kitty openly, repeatedly assured her that her presence was appreciated, and lauded her ability to speak to anyone from the service providers to royalty.

Dignitaries laughed with Kitty when she was around, were impressed by her language skills or the time she took to understand their culture and their issues. Only on occasion did Edgar's attendances cross with Kitty's functions, and that was when Kitty really noticed that Edgar had either changed or sometimes had a different persona.

The Viennese Edgar was not as relaxed and spontaneous as he had been in Tokyo. The phrases "as is appropriate" and "how things are done here" were his favorites, and Kitty yearned for him to lighten up a little more, like he'd been in Japan. He had actually once told her to "stop being like all the loud Americans." Where was the man who'd dashed for the service elevator of the hotel to avoid the diplomatic society at breakfast?

Even in the whirlwind of their budding romance, Kitty recognized other signs around the districts that might have attributed to Edgar's tension. The poor were out begging for work. There were protests about the lack of bread or other basic needs. The high prices for rent. She sometimes skirted by leftover marks of violence on the streets, reading about the arrests of demonstrators in that day's paper afterwards. Other alarming signals cropped up, mostly about the economy. Companies paused their projects, such as construction, because of uncertainties, which led to layoffs and further unemployment, and more riots by Vienna's aggravated working class. Vienna was shuddering beneath Kitty's feet, like the warning signs of an earthquake.

Shortly after the visit to the country cottage, Edgar picked her up and took her to one of the many gardens in the city. They lay on a blanket beneath a willow, the litter of their picnic on the grass as they stretched out. Their wine glasses were propped up against the picnic basket within reach. The days were growing shorter, and it was late dusk already. After work, their trysts were simply too short before night fell.

As she rested her head on his belly, Edgar stroked her hair. They were both very quiet but she was aware of everything about him, and she felt he was in tune with her. When two boys passed by, playing with a ball, and their mother scolded them to hurry along, they simultaneously turned their heads to watch.

Edgar sighed against her. "You have no idea how I ache for you, Kitty. No idea."

"I do, though. Because I am in great pain myself."

"I love you," he said.

"No, I love you." She lifted her head to look him in the eye.

He smiled and drew a stalk of grass over her forehead, her nose, her lips. "I love you *more*."

"Not possible." She snapped at the stalk before he danced it lightly on her chin. "It's me who loves you more."

"War is brewing Kitty."

She rolled onto her stomach and propped her head, mildly alarmed at the switch. Was this what was holding him back?

"America will likely face away," he said.

"Roosevelt's administration thinks it's Europe's problem," she said. "And it is."

Edgar raised himself on his elbow and nodded up at the hanging branches.

Kitty caught her bottom lip. "That's the administration's stance not mine..."

He turned his head to her, his features sharper now. "You'd be hard pressed to convince the Germans they have chosen the Nazi party incorrectly. The Reich is making a real recovery under Herr Hitler."

Kitty's eyebrows shot up. "Do they willingly ignore the brutality and violence? That Hitler even had his own people murdered just three years ago? I'm astounded that none of the other countries have the guts to take the man down."

"Why must they? He's doing his job, isn't he? Considering where Germany was after the Great War..." His questions were rhetorical. Kitty answered anyway.

"Only when Germany, Austria, and Italy threaten to become more powerful than Britain, France and the United States, will anyone act," she said.

Edgar reached over and handed her wine glass to her before raising his.

"To peace," he said.

"And if that's not possible, then here's to being on the good team."

"Who else are you rooting for then?" Edgar asked.

She raised her glass and inched closer to him. "I'm rooting for you right now."

He leaned in and kissed her. "Where will we go from here?"

He was alluding. She was not.

"Who knows? Eventually, however, to bed."

His grin was slow. "Then let me get you home."

It was twilight by the time they left the park and they clung to one another as if breaking up for the night would mean wrenching their own limbs off.

"I don't want to go home," Kitty said as he led her to the streetcar stop.

"I live over there." He pointed to a building on the other side of Rennweg—one of many that looked the same. "I'm on the top floor."

They were already crossing the street and she waited as he unlocked the entrance before leading her to the elevator and slamming the gate shut. Again, she shivered with anticipation. He inserted a key and pressed the top button. When they reached the last floor, Kitty realized they were in the foyer of one very large penthouse. Edgar stepped aside and she was taken aback when a man appeared. He was in his forties and had a bald head, slightly sagging jowls, and bright blue eyes. He looked very grave and very formal.

"This is Jerzy," Edgar said, handing him the picnic basket and his suit coat. "Jerzy, this is Miss Larsson. Would you mind seeing to a couple of gin rickeys, please? With ice, if you would be so kind."

"Yes, Dr. Ragatz." Jerzy's look darted over Kitty quickly before he turned and left them in the foyer.

"And that will be all, Jerzy," Edgar called. "You may leave for the night."

"Thank you, sir."

"You have a butler," Kitty said. "Polish?"

Edgar nodded. "He came with the apartment, an uncle's inheritance."

The furnishings were stately and conservative and very much befitting a bachelor's apartment. Edgar showed her to the study, the walls bulging with trophies of boiled deer skulls and stuffed marmots and badgers as decoration.

"These aren't mine. Uncle Andreas used to be a hunter," Edgar said by way of explanation. "I'm still trying to figure out when to redecorate." He gazed at her, his arm around her waist. "The whole place could use a woman's touch…"

Another hint. She knew where this could be leading but Kitty did not bite.

He took her by the hand and led her through the rest of the apartment. It was stylish, but darkened by the wood paneling everywhere. Two gin rickeys were waiting for them in the sitting room. The Jugendstil chandelier high above them cast only a dim glow. Kitty wondered how often Edgar had brought women here and given Jerzy the "and that will be all after you make the room romantic" instructions. But then Edgar had her in his arms, was kissing her throat, swaying against her, and murmuring her name.

She wrapped her arms around his neck, the ice in her glass tinkling softly.

Pulling away, he gently took it from her hand, placed it on the sideboard next to his, turned around and swept her into his arms.

Making love to him was like nothing she'd experienced before. They were passionate, confident, gentle and holding back their hunger with tender patience. They had all the time in the world. She fell asleep in his arms and awoke to the flickering of candlelight. Edgar was awake, naked, tiptoeing from one candle to the next until the room was bright. He slipped back under the dark green sheets, and pulled her close.

"I have been hoping for this, Kitty. I've been dreaming about you and I was in such agony after I left you in Japan. Marry me, darling. I don't ever want to be without you again."

"When?" Kitty rolled over and propped herself on her arm. She bit her bottom lip.

He mirrored her and brushed back a hair from her face. "Tomorrow. All right, Christmas. New Year's. Soon."

"My parents are going to kill me."

Those dimples deepened. "It will be over and done with before you can change your mind."

Kitty laughed. "You're serious, aren't you?"

"Dead serious. When it's right, it's right. I think we make a good team."

"A team," she said.

"A team," Edgar said. "Will you be my *Frau*, Miss Larsson? *Mein Gott*, that sounded awful."

Kitty searched his face and laughed softly.

"What is it?"

"Gertrude Ragatz," she said. "Very authentic Germanic name."

"You'll always be my Kitty, though." He draped an arm over her hip and pulled her closer, not just his words like soft vanilla, but his touch as well. "You strong, beautiful woman. You are the only one for me. The only one."

"I have to make a call." She scooted to the edge of the mattress.

"Now? You're naked. You want to go like that?"

Kitty whisked the sheet off and scurried to the door before Edgar could reach and grab it back.

"You're the one who's naked," she laughed. She turned back to him and leaned against the doorframe, one arm raised over her head. She loved his body. She loved the sight of him in that bed. She belonged here. Right next to him. And still, she had to make a joke about it.

"Yes," she purred teasingly. "I have to call now. Before I change my mind."

Edgar grinned and fell onto his back, groaning.

"A Christmas wedding?" shrieked Claudette. "You *are* just like her, Kitty Larsson!"

"Like who, Mother?" Kitty yawned. Not even her mother could ruin the moment.

Edgar was grinning at her against the wall, a towel wrapped around his waist.

"That ambassador's daughter," Claudette cried. "She married Alfred Stern just this past summer. Came back from Berlin, after all that news of a Commie boyfriend and married one of the richest men in New York."

"I'm nothing like her..."

Claudette huffed when Kitty's father chuckled on the other receiver.

"You are going to be in Europe for Christmas anyway," Kitty said. "What about Sam?"

"I'm here," her brother chimed in. "And I'm not missing this for the world. Good thing you're doing this before I begin my residency."

"Only for you, little brother, only for you."

She answered all their questions, the conviction so strong that her parents finally acquiesced. She hung up and turned to wrap her arms around Edgar.

"We're getting married," she said.

"We're getting married," Edgar said. "Now, to meet my parents."

"Are they anything like mine?" Kitty laughed.

"Worse," Edgar said with a shrug. The way he stroked her hair and looked at her, Kitty almost believed he was serious.

The minute Kitty walked into the Ragatz home in the Cottage District, she was on edge, and by the time they actually sat down to dinner, Kitty realized that—although Edgar had not yet sprung the news on them—his family was anxious about her presence, as if bad news—not good—was coming their way. Winning their approval was going to be a tough job.

The Ragatzes' enormous villa in the affluent eighteenth district was relatively new, built just fifteen years before. Both of Edgar's parents came from money and wanted everyone to know it. Josef, Edgar's father, was the quintessential patriarch, and peered at Kitty from afar as if he were examining a new species. He greeted her by saying, "You're quite tall."

Edgar's mother, Dorothea, on the other hand, greeted her with a look that went from head to toe, and a smack of her dark red lips. "*Nah*," she said, which in Viennese was a "Well" but may as well have meant, "No." She was a carefully coiffed blond, blue-eyed Upper-Austrian with skin treated by loads of creams and cosmetics, a haute couture dress, and extravagant jewelry. She eyed Kitty critically, which did not bother her. She recognized the type. Her mother was very similar but her arrogance was nowhere this high. Dorothea was authentically mean. Yet, Kitty wanted Edgar's mother to at least approve of her, as she did not know any son whose mother's opinion did not count.

The spitting image of her mother but thirty years younger, Edgar's sister, Margit, had the same tilt of her mother's chin, the haughty mien, and careful distance, as if Kitty were hot coal and if touched, would leave black marks.

Naturally, as Edgar had warned, Dorothea Ragatz completely ignored Kitty's request to call her anything but

Gertrude, rolling the rs and adding the *eh* at the end as if Kitty hailed directly from Sweden and not Minnesota.

Josef Ragatz led the tour of the house, drawing attention to the architectural detail while Dorothea pointed out the artifacts.

"This we got on safari, *Gerrtrroohdeh*." She rubbed one of a pair of ivory tusks that stood nearly as tall as Edgar. She then indicated a gigantic blue-and-white vase filled with gold and ruby gladiolas. "And this, *Gerrtrroohdeh*, we received as a gift from my brother, the ambassador. It's from China."

There was war regalia as well, no doubt from Josef Ragatz's work at the war archives or from his own experiences in the Great War. Medals, and commemorative plates, a saber, a dagger and a rifle hanging above the tiled oven in the dining room. Kitty admired everything politely, the air thin and cold, as if the Ragatzes lived at a much higher altitude.

At dinner, served on gold-rimmed porcelain plates, Josef led the conversation talking about politics and unsubtly criticizing Americans.

"The United States has no reason to fear an Austrian union with Germany. For us, it would simply mean strengthening our conservative, anti-socialist and anti-democratic forces."

"Anti-democratic?" Kitty started. "But—"

"I understand," Herr Ragatz interrupted. "As an American, you are confused by the term. But Austria was ruled by a monarchy until recently. And when we look to the United States, we see chaos. Not order. Austrians like order. As for the social democrats, the communists infiltrated them very quickly."

"Surely, that can't be right," Kitty said. "I see places they built up, like the Rabenhof where I live, and I'd say their one crime is that they tried to bridge the gap between the classes."

Josef Ragatz held up his hand as if he were swearing on the Bible. "Come now, Miss Larsson. You and I can both agree that none of us want to be anything like the Soviet Union. Can we?"

"Of course," Edgar answered. He reached for her hand under the table and squeezed it. Kitty had not realized she was clenching her fist until then. She clutched his hand for a second before stabbing her broth with her spoon.

"You can ask Edgar," Herr Ragatz continued. "The civil servant is loyal to the governing institution, Miss Larsson. We swore allegiance to the Habsburgs. We swore allegiance to Dollfuss. We now have Schuschnigg."

Kitty swallowed and said very sweetly, "Then you did swear allegiance to the social democrats."

Frau Ragatz looked as if she'd been slapped. Margit looked up from her plate, startled, but her eyes lit up with amusement. Kitty recognized something of herself in Edgar's sister.

Herr Ragatz's earlobes turned bright pink. "We've always been suspicious of the idea of a democratic Austria. You Americans can't possibly understand what I mean. You have no culture."

Kitty gaped at him but Frau Ragatz picked up the small bell on the table, ringing it violently.

The second course came, followed by the third, and the rest of the meal was a very miserable affair. Edgar tried to get Kitty to talk about her family—impressing on his parents that the Larssons were also quite wealthy and renowned—to which his parents hardly reacted. But she had lost the drive to win the Ragatzes over. Maybe another day.

Which was why, when Edgar pushed back his chair and rose, Kitty yanked the hem of his coat.

"Let's just elope and send them a cable," she whispered.

"It will be all right." He chucked her under the chin. "I have some news," he announced to the rest of the diners around the table.

Herr Ragatz noisily lay his knife down on the plate. Frau

Ragatz shot her husband a knowing look, then tilted her chin upwards, one hand nervously fingering the ends of her Marcel waves. Margit folded her arms and her mouth twitched.

"*Mutter*," Edgar began, raising his glass. "*Vater*. I'm delighted that you have warmed to Kitty so quickly..."

Kitty coughed, covering her mouth with her napkin. "Sorry," she said. "I must have swallowed wrong."

Was that a shimmer of hope in Dorothea Ragatz's eyes? That Kitty would keel over dead before her son could make the surprise announcement, which was so obvious already?

Edgar was undeterred. "Kitty and I are getting married."

Kitty ducked her head to avoid the storm that was bound to blow over.

"So soon?" Dorothea said, her hand falling onto the table none too gracefully. Her astonishment screeched over Kitty. "But you have just met."

"But she's an American," Josef Ragatz said at the same time. "Are you planning on moving to America?"

Edgar was confounding. He was beaming, the awful reactions bouncing off him as if he were wearing a shield. Only Margit's simpering turned into an exuberant smile. She grabbed her mother's arm and shook it.

"I knew it! A wedding!" she cried. "We must book the Palais Liechtenstein. And the ceremony at the Gersthof, here. But the reception, at the Palais. Can you imagine, Mother?"

Kitty's eyes were wide and she was shaking her head, but Margit waved her hands like a football cheerleader.

"Mother and I will help take care of all the details, Kitty. You must let us, because we know everyone. Simply everyone. It will be spectacular. When, Edgar? When do you plan to get married?"

Grinning from ear to ear, Edgar sat back down, snapped his napkin with sheer satisfaction and nodded at his sister. "New Year's Eve."

This set off another alarm from Dorothea. How could he? He knew that the Ragatzes were always invited to some royal New Year's Eve party every year. Certainly they could choose a better date. Margit's jaw dropped. A spring wedding? Why not a spring wedding? They couldn't coordinate anything proper at least until the spring. But Josef Ragatz looked up from the table and said, "Enough! Our son is getting married."

He rose and shook Edgar's hand, then clapped him on the shoulder. He then offered Kitty his congratulations like a peace offering. To Kitty's surprise, her future sister-in-law rose, glided around the table, and threw her arms around Kitty's neck.

"Welcome to the family," she said, and kissed Kitty's cheeks on either side. "I'm going to do everything I can to make it the event of the year. I promise."

Kitty rose from her seat, still stunned, and embraced her carefully, catching Edgar's beaming expression. Dorothea may as well have raised her white napkin to wave in the air. She congratulated Kitty next, and by the end of the night, there was a softer atmosphere in the room.

"*Wiener Schmäh*," Edgar said to Kitty after they were back in the car. "The Viennese art of dry humor. I think you've just been baptized in it."

7

FALL 1937

Kitty was engrossed in an ominous report Cooper had asked her to analyze about Hitler's occupation in the Sudetenland.

It is our deepest concern that Hitler will not stop there, she wrote in the margins. *He likely has his eyes set on invading the whole of Czechoslovakia.*

With a feeling that someone was watching her, she looked up to find Millie standing a foot away from her desk, arms crossed.

"Before you get hitched and disappear altogether," she warned, "you must join me at Achmed Beh's. You've been promising me for months that you will come one Thursday."

Kitty groaned. "Edgar is picking me up at five sharp. We haven't even begun making arrangements. So, before my future mother and sister-in-law take over all the wedding preparations, we're going to the Vienna Woods, to the cottage—"

Millie leaned in close, her green eyes daring Kitty to disappoint. "You've been to that cottage. You must experience the jazz club and especially Judith and the gang."

"Is this a new band?"

Millie tittered, shaking her dark hair. "I'm not telling you.

Besides, you'll be thrilled to get away from stuffy Viennese high society."

That part was certainly tempting. The Ragatzes had raised the bar of expectations on Kitty, and it was getting rather oppressive. She glanced at the phone, then the clock. It was four. Edgar would have already left the office. "I promise you. Promise-promise-promise that I'll come next week. Promise."

Millie pursed her lips and raised an index finger. "I'm holding you to that, Kitty Larsson."

Kitty was done by quarter to five and began gathering her things, Millie already heading out the door when the phone rang. Mary Rosen looked from her typewriter and raised a penciled eyebrow. Her dyed blond hair was beginning to show dark roots, but otherwise, she was impeccable and pointed a carefully manicured finger towards the phone.

Kitty sighed and returned to her desk.

"Darling," Edgar said apologetically. "I won't make it."

"I'm so sorry to hear that," Kitty said into the phone, trying to make it sound like business. It was the third time he was canceling on her in a week but she could tell by Edgar's voice during his next set of excuses that he was pinching his nose and rubbing his eyes like he did when he was irritated.

"There is simply too much going on at the moment," Edgar finished. "I'm wondering whether we should postpone the wedding."

Kitty's heart tumbled. "*Im Ernst?* You mean that?"

"No," he said testily. "Of course not. It's just—"

"Don't tell me it's just another Viennese joke. I don't find it funny," she whispered. Kitty turned her chair around just as Mary shot her a dirty look.

"You sound like you're afraid of karma. I promise I won't leave you at the altar." Edgar laughed drily.

Aching for him, Kitty did not find it funny. But he'd said

they were a team and that meant mutual support. "Work is work. Do what you need to do."

"Listen, Herr Messner is here. You remember? The general director of the rubber manufacturer? I can't really talk. I'll call you tomorrow. We'll get away by Saturday for a night."

Saturday? Her request for a day off had been for naught. "Till then," Kitty sighed.

Millie suddenly hurried back in. "I forgot something. Hey? Why are you looking so glum?"

"I've been stiffed."

"You're coming, then?" Millie cried, and Mary shushed them both without pausing in her typing.

Kitty tried to muster up some enthusiasm about it. "It seems so. I'll walk home with you."

As Kitty followed Millie out to the street, she could not shake off the uneasy feeling that Edgar was avoiding her.

Swanky was certainly the order of the night. Entering Achmed Beh's, which sat like a ruby jewel in the midst of Petersplatz, Kitty shifted from occidental to Oriental. From the Moroccan lanterns to the gold-painted columns, the marble dance floor and Turkish carpets, the place was made to transport patrons south of the Mediterranean. A band of musicians accompanied a dark-haired woman in a glittering gold bikini, performing a contortionist's routine in a pair of high-heeled straps. Kitty watched for a moment, impressed not only by the woman's ability but by the costume, which appeared high quality.

Millie grabbed her by the hand and led her past the spectacle. The club's interior was separated into various areas by plaster walls shaped into pointed arches and onion domes, and splattered with geometric patterns and arabesques. Men in fezzes smoked from water pipes, and elegantly dressed women puffed from long cigarette holders. Kitty saw immediately that it was a tourist hotspot—the foreigners all took up the tables around the floor near the stage while expats and Vienna's celebrities hid away in the back.

Millie stopped at a round table where a petite woman was sitting with a Maltese in her lap, and a large glass of wine. The woman had short red hair and dark-framed glasses. When she stood to greet them, the little white dog wriggled in her arms. Kitty admired the woman's stylish black pantsuit and heavy gold jewelry.

"This is Judith Liebherr," Millie announced over the clash of cymbals from the stage. The contortionist was finished and the patrons applauded, but she continued shouting near Kitty's ear. "Judith is one of the most respected fashion designers in Vienna. She also helps with the costuming for the shows here and at Der Keller."

The woman took Kitty's hand and blew two air kisses. Behind the thick lenses were owlish, coffee-colored eyes. She wore lipstick and the candlelight revealed fine wrinkles around her mouth. Kitty guessed the woman was somewhere in her fifties.

"*Grüß Gott*, Frau Liebherr."

Frau Liebherr smiled warmly. The music, more swing than jazz, was very loud, so she had to nearly stand on tiptoe to be heard. "You're an American. We'll dispense with the formalities. I'm Judith. And Millie has told us all so much about you, already."

Millie took a seat opposite Judith, and Kitty sat between the two. When the music stopped, Judith turned in her chair and waved towards a dark corner. Kitty expected a waiter to appear. Instead, she had to keep herself from gawping at the sight of a huge man with a bullish face. He was oversized in both height and girth, solid as a rock beneath the row of straining shirt buttons. He bent over Judith, who pointed out Kitty.

"This is Big Charlie," Judith then said to her. "His name is

Karl Grossmann, but the Americans gave him the nickname and that's what we call him now."

"The Americans?" Kitty wondered.

"Big Charlie is an international champion wrestler. He was supposed to go to the Olympics in Berlin last summer but he's Jewish and so he boycotted." Judith said it so matter-of-factly that Kitty was still spluttering as Big Charlie reached for her hand.

He had a large, flat nose, dark eyes that were set too close, and short, tight curls on his head that reminded Kitty of a Greco-Roman centurion. And he was shy, as if wholly apologetic about how intimidating he was.

A short and curt introduction was all he managed before he offered to get them drinks. The musicians suddenly stood and announced the feature band and an all-Black group settled in before striking up with a light and upbeat jazz tune, a lot more soothing than the previous cacophony.

Millie leaned over. "Big Charlie is everyone's mentor in a way. He took Oskar—that's Judith's son—under his wing, as well as Khan, whom you'll meet soon enough. Before they were pursuing their own things, Big Charlie gave them jobs with the city."

Kitty smiled at Judith. "So you all know each other from way back? Millie calls you 'the gang.'"

The fashion designer nodded, a fond expression on her face as she glanced at Charlie. "We all live in the same neighborhood and look out for one another. What about you? Millie mentioned you have a sweetheart here."

"They're getting married on New Year's Eve," Millie called next to her. "Oh Kitty, Judith should design your dress!"

Judith clasped her hands. "You can come by the studio, Kitty. Have a look."

"I will," Kitty promised. Though she could imagine her mother would be devastated if she was not involved.

Big Charlie brought them a round of drinks and another guest. From the full-moon face, high cheekbones, and the slanted eyes, which were a startling gray-blue, Kitty guessed this was Khan. He looked Mongolian.

Khan handed a glass of champagne to Judith, and gin rickeys for Kitty and Millie and they introduced him to Kitty. She could not help but smile. Despite the fact that they were all so vastly different, each of them was endearing and it was easy to imagine how they all fit together. She wanted to as well.

Khan was graceful and elegant, in a nice suit, and silver cufflinks.

"The band's from America," he said. "They're the feature tonight. You want to dance?"

Kitty agreed and he led her to the marble dance floor at the front of the club. She was surprised at how gracefully he took her into his arms and led her to the music.

"So, your name is Khan," Kitty said. "Where—"

"Alikhan, actually. But Khan is what everyone calls me."

"Where are you from?"

"Sixth district," Khan said. "Now I live in the ninth. Big traveler." That *Wiener Schmäh* again.

Embarrassed, she apologized. "I meant, where does your family originate from?"

"I know what you meant," Khan said with a smile. "Kazakhstan. My father's a chef. My mother runs a little bookshop. They came here as teenagers. I'm as Viennese as they get."

Kitty laughed. "I can hear that! So what do you do?"

His smile was patient and Kitty sensed she had stuck her foot in her mouth again.

"I'm a businessman."

Businessman was as generic as one could get and it meant that she should stop prying. Edgar had once pointed out that the typical American question came across as judgmental.

After the song, Khan led her back to the group where Big

Charlie was propped up on his elbows, talking to Judith. He pulled away when Kitty reached the table and moved a chair for her to sit between Judith and himself. The dog rose and balanced himself on Judith's lap.

Kitty patted his head. "What's his name?"

"August Macke," Judith said. "Or just Macke."

"The painter," Kitty said.

Judith tilted her head, smiling. "Indeed. How did you know?"

"My mother used to drag us to all the art museums."

"How nice," Judith said.

"Not really," Kitty said. "I preferred to be out with my dad, riding, hunting, fishing. Most of all, I love to shoot on the range."

Judith looked stunned and Big Charlie crossed his arms and sat back. His shoulders bounced up and down, a sure sign that she had made him laugh, which delighted her.

"Any other talents we should know about?" Judith asked.

Kitty played along. "I am pretty darned good at card games."

Big Charlie rapped a knuckle on the table. "Hear that, Khan? She's a card player."

Millie whooped. "Me, too."

Kitty burst out laughing again, looking to Millie and Khan in turn. "Millicent Hoffmann, you sure are full of surprises. I should have come a long time ago."

Judith smiled and tapped Kitty's thigh. "We're heading to Der Keller next. I want you to meet Oskar. It's his club in Mariahilf. His partner, Agnes, is singing tonight."

Millie came around and linked her arm into Kitty's. "Be prepared to be scandalized."

Kitty wrapped an arm around Millie's waist and kissed her cheek. "I can't wait."

. . .

Judith took side streets to the main thoroughfare on Museumstrasse and the whole "gang," as Millie still referred to the group, jumped a streetcar heading to Mariahilf, a part of the city Kitty had not really explored before.

As they stood in the middle of the carriage, Khan told her about how he worked with Oskar and Big Charlie as a "sewage rat" beneath Vienna. "It's a fascinating underworld," Khan said and winked.

Just then, Macke started growling in Judith's arms. Kitty turned to see a square-faced man frowning at the group. He glared at Khan and Kitty moved between him and her new friends to block the stranger's view. The streetcar slowed to a stop.

"This is ours," Khan called. He helped Judith down, then caught Millie as she hopped off. They turned into a narrow alley and Judith stopped before a large steel door with a single bulb hanging above it. *Der Keller: Stage Door!* was written on a glued-on sign. Judith produced a key. Kitty followed the group into a dark corridor, and passed two rooms. The doors stood open and Kitty spotted two women in suits and hats admiring themselves, and each other, in a dressing room. The sound of music and laughter came from far ahead, and Kitty smelled cigarette smoke and the sweeter, earthier scent of marijuana.

Before she could inquire about the kind of club they were in, Judith bustled by and was already calling out in a sing-song voice at the door further down. "Agnes, darling? How's the dress? Let me look."

The rest of the group pushed into the small dressing room and Kitty saw a stunning blonde with heavy eyeshadow and thin, penciled eyebrows, rubbing rouge into her cheeks. She would have been more beautiful if it wasn't for the cigarette dangling from her lips.

"Agnes, *Liebling*..." Judith clucked and preened around the woman, making her stand up. "I could still make an adjustment here."

The woman was wearing a sequined ruby red gown with a scooped neckline. She could have been Marlene Dietrich, Kitty thought, but she was too thin in the hips. Too flat in the chest. And that was when she realized Agnes was not a woman at all.

Embarrassed, Kitty directed her gaze to a black-and-white photo stuck in the corner of the mirror. Two handsome men in very stylish suits and hats smiled into the camera. The Eiffel Tower was in the background.

She looked at Agnes again, and Judith plucked the photo out of the mirror.

"This is my son, Oskar," she said, pointing to the younger man. He was desperately handsome, with dark chiseled features and soft eyes that hinted at a tragic air. He wore a white-tie tuxedo with a rose in the buttonhole and curls that hung around his ears.

The second man was a bit older, wearing a top hat and white tie with a longer tux coat. Kitty peered at him then at the woman in the mirror.

"This is Agnes." Judith handed the photo back to the woman in the mirror.

"Delighted to meet you, darling. By day, I'm Artur Horváth," Agnes said, facing Kitty now. He had a deep, brittle voice. "But by night..." He rubbed his hands along his sides, and laughed, shaking the mane of his golden wig.

Kitty recovered quickly and introduced herself. She'd been to drag queen shows in San Francisco and in Paris, but in Vienna—now a very conservative Vienna—this was a surprise.

Millie and Judith helped Agnes finish up, and Kitty stood on the fringes, watching the warm dynamics unfolding. They reminded her of people she had met in the secreted clubs of major cities, and even at the college after lectures; people who were authentic, and had nothing to hide. Not here. Not with one another. It was a relief from the stuffiness of Edgar's family, of the Viennese circuit.

When Big Charlie drifted over to her, she playfully nudged him in the side. He'd taken off his suit coat and now had one thumb hooked through his suspender.

"And you taught Oskar how to box?" She was still trying to put the image of Judith's son together with someone who would take and give a beating in the ring.

Big Charlie bounced his head. "Nobody ever called him a sissy again."

Kitty grinned. "No, I guess not."

He pointed to Artur. "Him, too. And Khan. They can all take good care of themselves."

Kitty realized what he meant, and she looked at the group anew. Of course they were together. Nobody in her world would accept any of these people individually, and suddenly she felt a deep need to preserve them as they were.

Two little boys ran in, out of breath. They ducked around Big Charlie's legs and dropped a packet of cigarettes on Agnes' dressing table. The eldest had a satisfied grin.

"You little monkeys," Artur clucked. "What took so long?" He dropped coins into each outstretched palm. "Hannes, Max, say hello and skedaddle. Make sure you eat something in the kitchen."

Announcing that she was ready, Agnes headed for the door just as a man in tuxedo with a rose in a buttonhole swept gracefully in. The second man in the photo, Oskar. Judith's son. His hair was now carefully groomed back and his adoration for Artur was obvious.

"*Liebling*, you're on in two. What's the hold-up?" he scolded, then grinned at the rest of the group. "Of course, I should have known. They've pounced upon you..."

Judith cupped his face in her hands and kissed his cheeks.

Afterwards, his look landed on Kitty. Gracefully, he moved to her and took her hand.

"Millie has finally managed to lure you into these depths. You must have a glass of champagne with me."

"My pleasure," Kitty beamed.

Oskar led her out towards the stage.

"Scandalous, isn't it?" Millie chided behind her. "It's our little secret, this gang. Nobody else in the office would understand."

Kitty grasped Oskar's elbow and chuckled. "I've already determined not to share you."

"Not even with Edgar?" Millie whispered next to her.

"Maybe not."

And that thought surprised Kitty more than anything that evening.

The next afternoon, after sleeping off the booze, Kitty awoke to find a vase full of red roses on the coffee table with a small card.

I'm so sorry again, darling. Come to the cottage in the Vienna Woods on Saturday. I'll meet the 11:30 train. Have a good day at work. Your devoted Edgar

He'd even forgotten she had the day off today.

Kitty fingered the roses. Ruby red. Each one perfect. Each one looking exactly like the other.

Millie had also left a note; it said she'd found the evening wonderful, and she'd signed off with *Welcome to the gang*. It left Kitty feeling warm again, remembering Oskar. She'd chatted away the night over a shared bottle of champagne, and he practiced his French on her. Agnes had sung two sets and was as good as, if not better than, Marlene Dietrich. Kitty adored Khan, who had revealed that he had real street smarts and a very sharp wit. Big Charlie was a big overstuffed bear beneath that tough exterior, and everyone's guardian. And Judith, whom Kitty could hardly wait to see again, was warm and kind, and a most exceptionally talented designer, as Kitty had discovered while sifting through Agnes' gowns.

With a start, she realized that the gang offered a haven away from Vienna's conservative high society, and this time she really doubted that Edgar had ever experienced something like this. Or whether he would understand it.

Every woman had to have her secrets, Claudette had often said. This one would be Kitty's little indulgence.

8

DECEMBER 1937

Kitty's family arrived on the weekend of the second advent with just under four weeks to go to her New Year's Eve wedding.

The following Tuesday, on a bright and chilly morning, she led Claudette through alleys and parks to the Palais des Beaux Arts and Judith's studio. A golden globe was perched on top of the roof. At the corner entrance, Kitty pressed the button next to the sign that said *Studio JuLi - 3. Stock.* She glanced over her shoulder, towards the park kitty-corner from the building. A woman, dressed in ragged layers, was huddled on a blanket on the ground next to a handwritten sign.

Before Kitty could go over and give her some coins, the door buzzed and Claudette pushed through into the spacious marble-floored anteroom. There were Etruscan bronze reliefs on both sides, a baroque mirror, and perfectly round hedges in Roman pots next to the broad stairs leading to the elevator. Kitty pulled aside the accordion gate and stepped back to let her mother in first. Claudette shuffled the small box in her arms that she'd carried all the way from the hotel.

"I wish you had let me take care of this in Paris," Claudette complained.

Straining to remain gentle, Kitty told her she wanted to choose her own gown. "I promise you, Maman, Judith is a top designer here. Besides, I waited for you to get here so that we can make a decision together."

Judith appeared with a whining Macke in her arms. He wriggled and squirmed at the sight of Kitty. Kitty let him nuzzle her hand before Judith set him down.

Wearing a dark blue wool dress with a layered necklace of three gold chains, Judith shook hands with Claudette first, then kissed Kitty's cheeks. She had a sheer chiffon scarf pinned to her left shoulder with an emerald and gold brooch.

Eyeing the box in Claudette's hands, Judith spoke French. "Is this your gown?"

Claudette reluctantly held it out to her. "It's the lace. My gown would never have fit Kitty. I'm a petite size and she is—"

"A big-boned Swedish-American," Kitty finished with a strained smile.

Judith's charm never wavered. "Then she shall have a perfectly suitable gown designed only for her."

Inside the studio, Claudette marveled at the tastefully appointed décor in layers of white and ivory, gold and silver. A large crystal chandelier hung in the middle of the ceiling and two baroque-styled mirrors were propped up on either end of the room. Judith led them to a trio of velvet lounge chairs and a middle-aged woman with gray streaks in her dark hair appeared carrying two champagne glasses.

"Thank you, Bella," Judith said.

They talked over the aperitifs and Judith commented on the high quality of the lace, then wrote notes in a fancy leather-bound drawing book. By the way her hand flowed over the pages, Kitty guessed she was adjusting initial sketches. She was a little disappointed when Judith closed the book and held it against herself.

"I have a few samples I want you to try. I'll share my ideas then. Is that suitable?"

"Samples?" Claudette appeared astonished. "I thought you only did haute couture."

"It's quite a new idea these days," Judith said, lightly touching Claudette's arm. "But I promise you, most designers are working off the rack now. We work from a basis, and go from there."

"Who?" Claudette snapped. "Who is doing it?"

Judith rested her chin between forefinger and thumb. "Do you know Kurt Ehrenfreud in Amsterdam? Or Haus Gerson in Berlin? It's the counterpart to London's Harrods."

"*Pas possible*," Claudette murmured, her suspicion only slightly dissipated.

"But never at the cost of true haute couture," Judith assured. "Salt and pepper. We can do both."

Claudette looked thoughtful.

Kitty reached out and caressed her mother's arm. "Relax a little, won't you?"

Her mother nodded and Kitty pecked her cheek.

Judith was her usual ball of energy. As Claudette visibly held back from commenting much, Kitty tried on four of the JuLi gowns before Judith returned to her drawing table. She then motioned for Claudette to look first. Kitty peered over her mother's shoulder and took in a deep breath.

The dress was simple with few adornments and very elegant. Claudette's lace was now a cape that would replace the veil for the reception.

"I would suggest slipper satin," Judith confirmed, sketching more lines. "Slightly off the shoulder, here, and here..."

"I love the V-cut at the collar," Kitty said.

"*Très chic*," Claudette murmured.

"The sleeves have the same V at the wrists. They are three-quarters length, and I know it's winter, but I fear that if we take the sleeves all the way down, it will ruin the look." Judith traced the length of the sleeves lighter in pencil.

"I see," Claudette conceded. "Yes, quite."

Her mother was actually smiling. With renewed energy, Kitty admired the broad satin sash with her, which tied at the waist, and the modern straight train of the gown.

Judith flipped to the next page, and Kitty's eyes widened. The entire back of the gown and train was seeded with a row of pearl buttons. Claudette's approval was evident by the tears shining in her eyes. Kitty leaned against her, giddy with excitement. Judith had created a *chef-d'oeuvre* and, more importantly, harmony between mother and daughter.

"It is *exquis*," Claudette breathed.

Kitty agreed. "Truly perfect."

"Then let's get started," Judith said and called her assistant back.

Just as they finished taking down all the measurements, the bell buzzed.

Macke raised his head from his little basket where he'd been sleeping.

"That must be Margit," Kitty said. "Edgar's sister."

Judith waved Bella to the door and Margit was ushered in shortly after. Macke leaped out of his basket and barked at her. Margit pulled back, wrapping her fox-pelt stole tighter around her shoulders. When Bella scooped up the dog, Judith apologized and introduced herself, but Margit was dismissive and distracted.

"Were there problems with the flowers?" Kitty asked, hoping it wasn't the dog that was getting her hackles up.

"Not at all," Margit sniffed. She looked around the studio. "Can we go?"

Claudette began gathering her coat and bag, replacing the lid of her box over the lace but Bella came out with another glass of champagne. Without looking at her, Margit waved the woman off.

"I booked a table at Palais Kempinski."

Appalled by her rudeness, Kitty could only look to Judith, who politely assured Margit that they were finished.

Kitty agreed to return for the fitting in two weeks and kissed the woman's cheeks, thanking her profusely as a way to apologize for Margit.

Edgar's sister turned on her heel and was out the door before Kitty and her mother caught up to her at the elevator.

"What time did you book for?" Kitty asked, irritably.

Margit checked her wristwatch. "One o'clock."

"But then we have plenty of time," Kitty said.

"It's on the other side of the city and I want to be there when Mother arrives," Margit replied in German. "Or she'll wonder where we are."

Outside, Margit walked briskly ahead and Kitty caught sight of the beggar woman in the park. Again, she wanted to give her some money, but Claudette, at that very moment, nudged Kitty.

"What have we done?" she whispered.

"Heck if I know."

Thankfully, by the time the three women reached the restaurant, Margit was pleasant and polite again as the waiter led them to their table. While they waited, she shared the details about the flowers, then promised Claudette she would show her where the reception would take place. Kitty leaned back and let the two women get mired in the details.

Frau Ragatz showed up twenty minutes late in a show of agitation but with a gleam in her eye. "I talked the caterer down to a twelve percent discount," she said before she even took a seat. "These are hard times. Everyone is looking for work. How is the gown?"

Before Kitty could formulate an answer, Margit rose and excused herself.

"I just got here," Frau Ragatz protested.

Margit gave her a meaningful look and jerked her head in the direction of the ladies' room. Kitty watched them weave through the restaurant.

"Very intense, those two," Claudette said. "You thought I was bad..."

"I'm going to see what that's all about," Kitty whispered and pecked her mother's cheek.

She made a beeline to the back of the restaurant, stopping just before the powder room, and pulled the handle open just a little, but she could hear Frau Ragatz's raised voice.

"... her dress designed by a Jewess?"

"Yes, *Mutter*," Margit said.

Frau Ragatz huffed. "But that cannot be allowed! What will our friends say?"

Margit murmured something that Kitty could not make out.

"You're right," Frau Ragatz announced decidedly. "Madame Larsson is probably unaware or I'm certain she would interfere. I'll make sure to set *Gerrtrroohdeh* straight. However, we will get through the wedding, first."

Kitty backed away from the door and hurried back to the table.

"Everything all right?" Claudette frowned as she watched Kitty take her seat.

"Everything's fine," Kitty muttered. Margit was nothing but a spiteful, hateful, cold fish.

"You don't marry the family, Kitty," her mother told her. She may as well have said, *Don't you dare cancel the wedding on me this time.*

Kitty reached over the table and patted her mother's hand, attempting a bit more conviction. "Everything is perfectly fine."

But Claudette was wrong about one thing. Kitty was

marrying into the family. From across the room, she watched the two Ragatz women return, their conspiracy "to set Kitty straight" obvious in the smug and determined expressions.

Relieved when her parents announced they would stay in that evening, Kitty grabbed Sam from his hotel room and headed to the Rathausplatz, where Christmas lights were strung up between booths selling *Glühwein* and glass ornaments, pretzels and Alpine cowbells.

Holiday music piped through the megaphones attached to the tops of lampposts. Choirs sang at one end of the market, and a string quartet played on the other. Tourists arrived in horse-drawn carriages, and a massive Christmas tree stood in the middle of it all. It wasn't until they had their first mulled wine in hand that Sam asked her straight out.

"Is everything OK, Kit?"

"No. It's not."

Sam slowly tipped his head. "Are we going to go through this—"

But Kitty elbowed him in the ribs. They had reached a fire in a steel drum and a dejected-looking boy was trying to fish out a burned potato. Kitty took the boy's hand and pressed several coins into it. "Go buy yourself a pretzel or something," she said.

Sam watched the boy toss the potato between his hands and scamper off to the nearest food stall.

"We're here flashing our wealth," Kitty said. "Planning an extravagant wedding and these people... Do you remember when you dragged me to Iowa, to that camp? They assigned me to that kitchen."

"You were so disgusted," Sam said fondly.

"And you were so brave. You jumped right in and helped the nurses. You watched the doctors."

"That's when I knew I would follow through with medicine."

Kitty caught her bottom lip in her teeth. "And me? I've been behaving like a spoiled brat, just like Margit."

"No, you haven't, Kit. You learned to grow vegetables, remember? You started gardening at home. You've got a job in foreign service."

"Gardening, Sam? And being a secretary? Holy smokes. Look around. It's not enough."

"So do something more."

Kitty rolled her eyes. "Frau Ragatz is going to look down her nose at everything I try to do."

Sam blinked at her, warming his hands over a fire in yet another barrel. "*Gerrtrroohdeh* Larsson, are you scared of Edgar's mother?"

Kitty grinned, then shrugged. "I don't want to make Edgar unhappy."

"We can live like we do and still do good in the world, Kit. Don't let Dad's job disenchant you. One person at a time. That's how I got through that camp in Iowa."

"One person at a time. First ones I'm going to have to work on are my future-in-laws. I'm not so sure they're going to let me get away with anything."

"What's really going on, Kit?"

"You mean besides the fact that my wedding gown is being designed by a *Jewess*?"

"That's harsh," Sam scoffed.

"The family is ironclad in old monarchist ideals. At lunch, Frau Ragatz gave me a lecture about expected behaviors and practices among the Viennese elites. I think even Maman was perturbed."

"What kind of expectations and practices? You have to learn how to waltz?"

Kitty rolled her eyes.

Sam chuckled. He paid for a hot pretzel and tore half for her. "You talk like you're some kind of Cinderella who didn't grow up with a public and rich set of parents herself."

"This is different, Sam. It's like I've been sent to the past century and should be wearing corsets."

"And that's not what you want."

"I want Edgar," Kitty insisted. "I know I shouldn't care about the rest..."

"Don't underestimate the power of wanting to belong."

Kitty peered at him and he cocked his head, chewing. She pretended to pick off a crumb and sipped her mulled wine.

"Anyway," she finally said, "to answer your unasked question, no, I'm not canceling the wedding."

"Besides your scary, medieval in-laws, how do you like living in Vienna?" Sam asked.

"It's quite the project in social studies," Kitty said. She led him through the stalls and told him about Khan, and Big Charlie, then about Agnes and Oskar.

"I just adore the gang," Kitty said. "You would too."

Sam was examining her again, that grin wavering. "I can only imagine how Edgar must have reacted to Agnes."

"Why? He wasn't even there."

"He wasn't?"

"I was out with Millie."

"And what did he say when you told him?" When she did not answer right away, Sam's eyes went big. "You didn't tell your fiancée about your friends?"

"Not everything, I suppose."

"Kit... Are they your friends or your pet project? You collect people like some collect stray animals off the street."

She frowned. "Friends."

"Are they coming to the wedding?"

She prickled.

"Agnes? Is she singing at your wedding?"

"What are you going on about, Sam? Can you imagine someone like Agnes being forced in the same room as those overstuffed guests? I invited Judith, of course. And Millie is coming with Khan. I spared the others of Frau Ragatz."

"That's very gracious of you, Kit, to protect your friends like that."

Still stinging, Kitty said, "I'll admit you have the purest heart of gold, Sam. I suppose I am still learning not to be a beast."

"Nah, Kit. You're just constantly looking for approval. You make a big show of everything to see how people will react. Except with Edgar maybe. You're a girl... a woman, sorry... and sometimes you make noise to get noticed."

"I don't need to look for his approval. I know he loves me."

Sam grinned. "Well, then that's your answer, isn't it? He's the right one for you."

Kitty looked at the tower clock ahead of her as it chimed eight. Right on time, Edgar appeared and called out to them. Her future husband, that gait she now knew well, was heading straight for them.

Grinning, she looked at her brother. "You're right, Sam. I can have it both ways. And that guy, there, he's going to help me. I know he will."

Edgar reached them and took her into his arms, kissing her cheek, then took Sam's outstretched hand. "How are you doing future brother-in-law?"

"I'm ready for a warm tavern," Sam said.

"Then I know just the place," Kitty said, and beamed at Edgar. It was time Edgar got to know all of her. "Do you know Achmed Beh?"

"The one you go to with Millie?" Edgar asked.

A little bit surprised, Kitty winked at Sam.

"See?" she whispered. "He pays attention already."

9

NEW YEAR'S EVE 1937

The Palais Liechtenstein's stateroom was decadent with chandeliers, baroque ornamentations and oil paintings. Set up along the high arched windows, the family table contained the wedding party and the immediate Larsson and Ragatz members. As the guests applauded Herr Ragatz for his speech, Edgar strode over and clapped him on the shoulder. Kitty leaned back and watched the big band musicians setting up.

The guests began to break away from their seating places, some into a carefully choreographed dance of business associates brushing up against local power brokers. Even Edgar was already drifting to a group of these men and Kitty recognized some of his friends. Herr Ragatz was shamelessly shaking hands, patting shoulders and nudging favors from other notables.

Next to her, Margit cocked an eyebrow as if to start a conversation, but Kitty picked up her wine glass and rose to gaze out the windows. Outside, in the garden, strands of white Christmas lights glowed beneath the snow on a row of rounded boxwood hedges.

For a quiet moment, Kitty scanned the guests again. Some

of the people the Larssons had invited had said that, after Hitler's occupation in the Sudetenland, it was not safe to visit Austria. Utter nonsense, thought Kitty. Others, like Kitty's best friend in St. Paul, had very valid excuses for not being able to attend her last-minute wedding.

Sighing, Kitty looked for Rose and Nils only to find them talking to family friends. Since their arrival from Tokyo, Nils had been cool and Kitty had asked whether he disapproved of Edgar.

"No, Kitty."

"Do you mistrust him?"

Nils had hesitated. A split second was all it was, but he quickly sugarcoated it and started going out of his way to be warmer with her after that. But Kitty never saw that chumminess between the two men like that first day in the Imperial Gardens, and even now she wondered what had transpired. And it was not just coming from Nils. Because Edgar, who was returning to the table now, seemed to also be skirting around her brother—only a few feet away—as he suddenly veered off and shook hands with a man who had a mustache just like Hitler.

At the sight of Judith coming, Kitty beamed, relieved for the distraction. Millie and Khan were following the designer.

"Edgar," Kitty called to her husband and waved him over. "There's someone I want you to meet."

Edgar excused himself from the mustached man, and shook hands with each of her friends, and accepted their congratulations graciously.

Judith peered at him. "It was a beautiful ceremony, Dr. Ragatz. Your wife has most excellent taste. You are very lucky."

"Yes, thank you. Thank you very much."

His eyes were elsewhere, however, taking in everything else in the room. He then seemed to have found what he was looking for. "Darling, I wanted to introduce you to some people. Will you join me?"

Kitty bit back a sharp retort. "Give me a minute."

"Super," he said, and beamed at the group again. "Enjoy yourselves."

Kitty watched him go. "So many people to greet. Can you imagine if everyone had come?"

She kissed each of the women, and embraced Khan before raising her glass to toast with them. "I think my husband"—she relished calling Edgar that—"is also a little irritated that most everything had been Margit's and Frau Ragatz's doing."

Judith covered her mouth. "And there I go complimenting their work. What a *faux pas*."

"But the dress is all you," Kitty assured her. "Claudette loves what you did with the lace, by the way. Especially the veil for the ceremony."

Judith's smile widened. "Big Charlie, Artur and Oskar send their love."

As Kitty had suspected, after sending last-minute invitations to them, they had sent their excuses and she'd rubbed it into Sam's face, too.

She was soon laughing with her friends, until Kitty saw the man hired to coordinate the reception burst through the side doors. He hurried over to Frau Ragatz near the middle of the family table. He was likely receiving the next commands in the woman's orchestrated agenda.

"I think they're about to bring the cake," Kitty said. She searched for Edgar and found him talking to two men near the bar.

"Go fetch that dish of a husband," Millie commanded. "I don't need to eat another bite, but I'll always make room for cake."

Kitty headed across the dance floor to the bar but suddenly Sam appeared.

"You did it. I'm so proud of you, Kit." He threw his arms around her. Her brother was overly affectionate when he drank.

He then indicated the family table over her shoulder. "Since you'll likely skip smashing the cake into Edgar's face, why don't you call Margit up and do it to her. That woman is really bitter about something. A little fun would do her good."

Kitty put a finger to her lips and shushed him, laughing. "I don't think that's how I want to start my new life."

"She'd be so pretty," Sam said in a loud whisper, "if she would just get rid of that permanent simper."

Just then, the side doors of the reception hall opened and two waiters wheeled out a towering cake on a trolley. It was decorated with red marzipan roses and star lilies over five tiers. The guests applauded and marveled at the artistry. Kitty looked for Edgar, but the two men he'd been talking to were the only ones left at the bar. They looked as if they had just lost money on a bet.

People were calling for her husband. She saw Herr Ragatz surveying the crowd and Kitty theatrically shrugged her shoulders when his questioning gaze landed on her.

She gave the immediate guests an apologetic look and pointed to the door. "I'll just go find my knight in shining armor," she announced. "He's probably looking for his sword to slay that gigantic thing over there."

Outside the ballroom, she headed for the front of the palace. There were guests from another New Year's Eve party, music seeping through a second event room. People from both parties were mingling in the foyer and the staircase where a huge shrouded outline of 1938 hung between them.

There he was, her husband, with Nils. There was also another man dressed in a tuxedo. He was broad and tall, with brushed-back hair. Save for his thick upper lip, he reminded Kitty of Nils a little bit. She recognized him but could not place from where. The three men were huddled on low seats around a small table in the hall above. Nils was listening to the stranger and Edgar was twisting his new ring on his finger. As she came to the top of the stairs, she could hear that the stranger had a British accent.

Her husband rose and put an arm around her waist.

"I've been looking all over for you," she told Edgar.

Nils said, "We'll be right with you."

"It's the cake. The guests are all waiting." She turned to the stranger. "I'm terribly sorry. I know we've met but..."

"You are the new Mrs. Ragatz. My congratulations to you both." The man shook her hand. He had piercing blue eyes. He carried himself as if he'd grown up in the military. "I'm Thomas Kendrick."

Kitty recognized the name and the face now. "From the British legation."

Edgar's hold tightened around her waist and his expression was visibly strained.

"That's correct," Kendrick replied.

"He's the station chief," Nils said.

"But of course," Kitty said. "I'm John Cooper Wiley's secretary."

Kendrick nodded. "We met at the Wileys' home not long ago."

"That's it." She indicated Nils and Edgar. "So you all know each other."

The Brit cleared his throat and a sheepish look flicked between Nils and Edgar.

"You could say that," Kendrick said.

"I had no idea you were a guest at the wedding," Kitty started but Kendrick pointed to the other ballroom.

"I'm with the consulate's New Year's Eve party."

"But you must come for a drink," Kitty insisted.

Edgar chuckled. "Darling, I think we'd better hurry before our guests hop on that monstrosity of a cake themselves. Kendrick, do come by. We'll toast at midnight."

Kendrick squinted. "I'd like to be part of ushering in a new year with you, Dr. Ragatz." He shook Nils's hand vigorously. "Happy New Year."

Kitty watched him go before Nils accompanied her and Edgar back to the ballroom.

"Are you happy, darling?" Edgar asked her as a few immediate guests cheered at their arrival.

"Very," Kitty said, but she wondered what that had all been about with Kendrick. And with Nils? It had not been chummy; it had all been much too serious to appear so, but what she did sense was some sort of alignment again.

Suddenly, there was a bigger whoop and more applause as the majority now spotted them at the entrance. Edgar kissed her cheek and escorted her to the cake. They cut it together and fed one another the first bites just before the music started up.

Grinning, Edgar offered his arm and they danced their first dance as husband and wife to a traditional Viennese waltz. They held one another's look before laughing, and she was filled with happiness.

Afterwards, her father waited for her and Edgar swept over to his mother.

"Hey, Dad." She gave him her hand. "What song did you pick?"

"For my little girl?" he said. "I should have picked something a little more charlatan, but you might like this." He signaled the band. It took Kitty a moment but she recognized "Someone to Watch Over Me".

"Well," she let him pull her in. "I do love Ella."

But she noticed that some of the Ragatzes' guests had drifted off the floor with wrinkled noses.

When Edgar retrieved her again, she asked for a break. He must have sensed her mood. "Are you all right, darling?"

"I feel somewhat... adrift." She indicated a group of men who surrounded Herr Ragatz. "Who are they all, Edgar? And why here, at our wedding?"

They were seated at the front table again, and her husband held her hand as he crossed a leg. "You want me to introduce you or gossip?"

Kitty leaned into him. "Gossip."

"All right. The man with the funny mustache with my father—"

"Hitler mustache," Kitty whispered daringly, recognizing the man Edgar had been with earlier.

Edgar pursed his lips. "All the rage these days. That's August Eigruber. He's from Steyr in Upper Austria. He's a— what do you Americans call it? Big wig in iron and steel."

Kitty cocked her head. "A business acquaintance then?"

Edgar shrugged, and looked out at the crowd of people. "Business. Recreation. He's my father's friend, *Liebling*."

"Your father knows everyone, doesn't he? OK, let's do the next one. Those two men over there at the bar. They've hardly moved all night. You were talking with them earlier."

Edgar folded his arms over his chest and pursed his lips. "Business acquaintances of mine."

Kitty nudged him. "Come on. You were in deep discussions with them. Spill it. What was so important that you put frowns on their faces?"

"You're imagining things, Kitty Larsson."

She huffed. "Kitty Ragatz now."

He kissed her hand apologetically but was still distracted. He used her hand to point the two men out. "The one on the left, that's Baldur von Shirach. I know him from Berlin. And next to him, Rudolf Schloss. He's also from Berlin."

"Berlin? Then why are they at our wedding?"

Edgar did not respond at first, then he took in a deep breath. "I think we were drinking beers together not too long ago and I threw out the invitation. Why wouldn't I want to show off my beautiful wife?"

"It's the dress," Kitty said.

"It's you, darling," Edgar stressed.

She glanced at the clock on the wall above the stage and musicians. "And how do you know Kendrick, anyway?"

"Kendrick is Kendrick," Edgar said. "Everyone knows him. He's kind of a permanent installation in Vienna's expat community. My office has frequent dealings with him and he does throw some of the most famous parties in the city."

"Anyway," she continued lightly. "I'm glad to see you and Nils have made up."

"Made up?"

"I thought he was completely against us getting married, but he seems satisfied enough."

"Does his approval matter that much to you?"

Kitty flushed. "I suppose so. I had no idea that it had."

"Big brothers." Edgar kissed her hand once more. "*Komm.* Let's dance."

After Edgar, she was obliged to dance with some of the other men, including August Eigruber, whom she decided she did not like. She excused herself afterwards and sought out Khan.

"Will you dance with the bride?" she asked.

He was flattered and began to head to the floor with her but the band stopped playing. The leader announced that everyone should fetch another glass of champagne. It was twenty to midnight. He called the couple to the front of the stage and Edgar suddenly came from nowhere and snatched her hand. Kitty threw Khan an apologetic look.

Turning her focus on a search for her parents or her brothers, she did not find them immediately either. Instead, Edgar finished thanking everyone and cracked jokes onstage, then he was leading her into the middle of the crowd where Josef and Dorothea Ragatz, along with their family members, waited. Kitty looked for Claudette. For the Senator. For Nils and Rose, and Sam.

The band leader announced a few minutes to midnight. There was a scramble for glasses. Horns and whistles were so loud, Kitty covered her ears but laughed anyway. Corks popped and glasses clinked. A new group was pressing in on Kitty and Edgar. Well-wishes and slaps on the back for the groom, open assessments for the bride. She recognized the three men he'd pointed out to her earlier; Eigruber from Steyr, the two men from Berlin. Their wives or companions, one very, very young, were smiling at Kitty, preening around her. They were complimenting her in Berlin dialect, which Kitty struggled to understand especially with the increasing noise. Then the band director announced the countdown.

The men closed the circle around Edgar as they raised their glasses and shouted with the countdown.

"Ten!"

An explosion sent a shudder through the crowd. All heads turned to the high windows of the hall. Fireworks scattered across the sky outside.

"Nine!"

Kitty stood on tiptoe. Sam was coming through the crowd toward her, but two laughing girls, both very pretty, snatched him. Sam allowed them to drag him away.

"Eight!"

One of the women was asking Kitty something, her glass raised in Kitty's face. The fireworks reflected off it.

"Your gown," the woman repeated in English. "Who designed it? It's stunning!"

"Seven!"

"JuLi," Kitty shouted. "You might know the label?"

"Six!"

Another of the women twisted her red lips, and exclaimed in Viennese dialect, "Isn't it a Jewish house?"

The flashes of embarrassment and disapproval reflected in the next explosion.

"Five!"

The fireworks increased in frequency.

"Four!"

"Well, the Jews have added an element of chic to German clothing," the third woman, older than the other two, said loudly. "Even Magda Goebbels says that."

"Three!"

The other two women nodded, the shift of opinion evident on their faces. Kitty looked around.

"Two!"

Not even Edgar was near her. But he was reaching for her.

"One!"

Kitty broke away from the women.

"Happy New Year, darling," her husband shouted into her ear.

But she could not find her voice.

When Edgar swung Kitty into the New Year's waltz, she caught sight of Nils watching her. He was holding Rose against him, and kissed the top of his wife's head, but his eyes remained on Kitty. Edgar spun her around, and the next time Kitty spotted Nils, she craned her neck. Her big brother was mouthing something.

I love you? Or maybe it was, *Happy New Year.*

But what she read from his expression was that warning he'd given her at least twice before.

Be careful.

PART TWO

MARCH–AUGUST 1938

10

MARCH 1938

In a careful trot over muddy fields, Kitty steered the roan horse back over the knoll and along the woods. Two deer bounded across the field in the opposite direction, followed by the appearance of the Ragatzes' cottage roof above the treetops.

In need of some fresh air and exercise, and after Edgar had been on yet another trip away, they'd informed her in-laws that they were reserving the use of the Vienna Woods cottage for that weekend. That first morning, Kitty and Edgar had made love before racing one another to the stables for a ride, but not before warning the kitchen they'd return only for brunch.

She broke into a broad smile as Edgar rode up next to her. The cold March air on Kitty's cheeks, the winter melt and the snowdrops blooming alongside the needle-covered forest path, were promising that spring was just around the bend.

"I know it's only been three months, but I feel like we might be honeymooning for the rest of our lives," she teased.

Edgar gave her the kind of grin where his whole face scrunched up in near laughter.

"Or it's your dimples," she said. And his eyes, she thought.

Those blue-green eyes that reminded her of the Mediterranean they'd visited in Italy.

"That was the point of marrying you, Frau Ragatz. *Flitterwochen für die Ewigkeit.* A forever honeymoon. If only it weren't for all these business trips. I miss you before I am even gone."

She blew him a kiss. "You'll make it up to me, darling. Every time you return, I'm going to peel back another layer of you."

"Let's get that blood flowing again," he called and urged his mare forward. "I can't wait for you to peel something else off."

Laughing, Kitty shifted in the saddle and transitioned her horse into a canter.

They stayed on the drier forest floor on the return to the cottage. A row of birch trees lined the road up to the *Hof.* The Ragatzes referred to the country home as "the cottage," but the place had once been a working farm. There was an old barn and adjacent stable. Next door, stood a low building which had been used as a workshop in earlier days but now apparently held a whole lot of bric-a-brac. Kitty had seen the hints of clutter through the cobwebbed windows. Further on down the property, next to a pond, was a guesthouse that doubled as a study when Herr Ragatz—or Edgar—needed a quiet place to work.

Back in the stable yard, Kitty dismounted and Edgar yanked her to him and kissed her. The horses nickered.

"Do you think—"

"They'll serve us brunch in bed?" Kitty teased.

With matching wistful looks, they turned to the house, then to one another, and shook their heads. This was something she loved about the two of them. They were nearly always in harmony, whether something banal like this or in their lovemaking. They finished each other's sentences, were often thinking about the same things, and always looking for reasons to touch one another. In the evenings, when they'd finish making love, they read passages from their books aloud.

Kitty pulled Edgar to her now and gazed at him, her heart full.

Edgar nuzzled her neck. "May I then persuade you to skip brunch as well?"

"I'm positively starving," Kitty admonished and stepped away before he could kiss her again. "No more of that until I've had eggs, and pancakes and bacon, and maybe even half a loaf of toast."

Edgar laughed. "You and your American breakfasts."

"Hardly," Kitty retorted. "Although I will say that the *Kaiserschmarren* here do have a leg up on the American pancake."

Suddenly, the cottage door opened and Jerzy, Edgar's butler, stood on the stoop. He fidgeted, as if unsure whether he should interrupt their interlude.

"I think we're about to be scolded," Edgar muttered in her ear. "Good morning, Jerzy. What is it?"

In response, Jerzy came down the stoop, a slip of paper in his hand. His usual stone-faced demeanor was now a version of grave concern. "Your father's just called. He says it's very urgent."

Edgar looked at the note and winced. "I'll be right there. We'll just put the horses in."

"I can do that," Kitty offered.

She watched the men go into the house and eyed the pathway to the stoop. She could do something with that plain square of patched lawn. Perhaps plant some lilies and roses and spruce up the landscape. If Frau Ragatz would approve, which was doubtful.

She slid off the horse saddles and brushed the animals clean of mud before draping blankets over them. Next, she filled the trough and added water. Outside, wind swirled dust and debris over the threshold of the barn. Kitty heard a clanging sound and then a dull bang. At the end of the barn, a door had been pried open by the wind. She went to shut it when something on the floor caught her eye. The note from Jerzy. Edgar must have dropped it outside and it had blown in on the wind.

She picked it up.

S-I needs a meeting. Call right away.

Kitty frowned. It was a strange way to write a person's initials. Jerzy had written *S-I*. Not *S.I.*

The door creaked open again on the next gust and this time, Kitty removed the chain and looked inside. It was an empty barn. There were boards with chains attached to them, and troughs, maybe for cows or sheep. Old straw was scattered about on the floor. Her eyes adjusted to the darker room and she stepped inside. The weak sunlight seeped in through the window where dust motes danced. Otherwise, the air was still, the wind muffled by the stone wall, creating a sensation that she was underwater.

She explored the open stable but just before she turned to go, her foot scuffed against something. Kitty looked down. A pile of straw, but whatever she'd felt had been solid. She brushed the strands away with her boot and revealed an iron ring. Another few brushes with her foot and she realized she was standing over a trapdoor.

"Kitty?"

Edgar was outside. She turned around, glanced at the note again. *S-I*. Who was that? She tucked it into her blazer pocket.

"In here," she called.

Edgar appeared in the threshold just as she reached it.

"Hey. I didn't know this was here."

He looked around as if something were amiss. "Nobody uses it anymore. Are you ready?"

"Sure."

"Good. I have to return to the city after breakfast."

"Why?"

"Hitler has threatened to invade Austria."

Kitty straightened. "What? When?"

She followed him out, but he was all business.

"It's about Sunday's referendum—"

"About the union with Germany?" Kitty asked.

"Our chancellor has done it this time."

Kitty immediately thought of the banners she'd seen on a few of the department stores on Mariahilfstrasse earlier that week. *The same blood belongs in a united Reich! Your honor, pure! Your blood, loyal!*

She hurried to catch up to her husband as he marched up to the cottage.

"Changed the rules..." Edgar muttered.

"Who changed what rules?"

"You can't just do that," he said, still talking to himself. "Raising the legal voting age to twenty-six. Schuschnigg knows the younger people support the NSDAP."

Kitty followed on her husband's heels as he directed Jerzy to get them packed up. As he moved about the house, it was as if he were putting miles between them. It was not so much the situation that caused her concern. She was well aware of Germany's interest in uniting Austria with the Third Reich. What gripped her was Edgar's anger, the way her husband transformed before her very eyes, and she wondered exactly how close he was to the men in power. And why it appeared that they relied on him so much.

They motored back to the city, but Edgar was terse. This was not the same man she'd awoken to that morning.

"Do you think the Austrians will vote to unite with Germany?"

Edgar stared ahead, gripping the steering wheel. "The Nazis will make sure we do."

She considered this. "Your job will be at stake."

"Why do you say that?" he bit back.

"Certainly, if there is a regime change, you won't be able to stay on at the Department of Foreign Economics."

"Why not? I'm uninteresting to the NSDAP."

She frowned. "What does that mean? Uninteresting?"

"I do my job. I never caused anyone concern or said anything for or against one regime or the other. I've always been neutral. Like Switzerland."

That was not what she had meant about staying on. She recalled he had said something similar after the Austrian radio broadcasted a speech by Hitler. In it, the Führer had declared, *The German Reich is no longer willing to tolerate the suppression of ten million Germans across its borders.*

Kitty remembered it word for word because she'd had to type up the translation for D.C. That evening, as a fire crackled and Edgar and she had held snifters of cognac in their hands, she had asked her husband exactly which Germans were being suppressed, and was the number of Austrians who supported joining the Reich really growing or was it propaganda?

"Austria is a nation used to regime change," Edgar had told her. "If we unite with Germany, it will simply be viewed as yet another shift in power. Our citizens remain loyal to whoever is at the helm. All those years as a monarchy transformed us into servants to the state. I am just a loyal bureaucrat, fulfilling my duty. You heard my father when you first met him. We never learned any other way."

Whether it was the booze, the warmth, a full stomach, or simply her undying devotion to her new husband, Kitty had thought she understood.

Realizing the danger in his words now, she shifted in her seat to face him. "Would you join the party if they asked you?"

"I'm a diplomat, Kitty. A civil servant. And a very experienced and respected one at that. The likelihood is they will not get rid of me."

Again, he seemed to deliberately misunderstand her question. Kitty slumped back and her thoughts suddenly turned to Judith. She had not seen her friend or the gang since the wedding. First, she and Edgar had left for their honeymoon, a skiing tour of the Alps in Switzerland, a jaunt along the western coast of Italy and then a stopover at the lake districts in Upper Austria to ski. When Kitty had returned to work, there was a mountain of catching up to do.

Kitty looked over at Edgar. Austria joining the Third Reich would mean the Nazi party would take control. What would that mean for Judith? Or Oskar? She shuddered, remembering the stories of brutality and force Nils had reported to the family when he was stationed in Berlin.

The week before, Cooper had assigned Kitty to build up a new pool responsible for summarizing the intelligence they'd gathered from their sources. As a result, Kitty had become familiar with a certain Captain Wallace. Captain Wallace's intel focused on the Austrian political circles.

According to Wallace... Wallace reports...

How many times had she read and typed that? Followed by what he'd heard from key personalities:

The good of Austria lies in the hands of a greater Germany...

The crowd chanted, Heim ins Reich!—*home into the Reich!—several times before police broke them up...*

Pure blood. Nationhood of Aryans. A false-flag operation in Poland or France is not to be discounted such as the Germans have done with snatching the Sudetenland...

"I might put in a call to Cooper," Kitty said to Edgar's profile. "See if he needs me."

He barely acknowledged that he'd heard her except to slow down. But his jaw was still clenching and unclenching. At least she had upset him. At least he was thinking about her words.

"My parents suggested we meet for dinner," he said moments later.

"When?"

"Tonight."

"But you're working."

"Yes. At the villa, with my father."

She frowned at this. "On what, exactly?"

"He has questions. And his colleagues want to know the legal ground our chancellor is standing on. Anyway, why don't you meet me for dinner there?"

Kitty sighed. If Cooper had needed her, he would have already called. She wanted a reason to go see Judith. Urgently. The way Edgar was behaving and with his laissez-faire attitude, she knew her friend would at least soothe Kitty's anxieties with some laughter, a cocktail, maybe a visit to Achmed Beh's with the rest of the gang. Anything more joyful, because dinner with the Ragatzes was the most joyless activity Kitty could imagine.

They entered the city limits and Kitty sat forward, peering through the windshield. Edgar copied her. There were banners slung across the road. Those occasional signs declaring German nationalism had multiplied overnight. A crowd was gathered in one of the squares, someone screaming into a loudhailer.

"Look at what our chancellor is up against," Edgar muttered. "Certainly you can see he's trying to work against the popular will. There's a lot of support for unification."

As far as Kitty—and her eye—could see, there was. "That doesn't mean it's the right thing to do."

"That's rich, coming from the woman who grew up in a democracy..."

Kitty shot him a surprised look. He remained stone-faced. As they passed the street that would lead to Der Keller, her thoughts returned to the gang. After the jazz club tour she had taken Edgar on, she knew that he was not all that interested in her group of friends. He'd been genial, polite, but his laughter had been forced and he'd had an irritated look on his face. Later, when she'd asked him about it, he said it had been "amusing" and that, no, he did not need to repeat the experience. On instinct, she had not even taken him to Oskar's club.

"I'll drop you off at the apartment," Edgar said. "Then I have to go. You'll manage to my parents' with public transportation."

Edgar rounded the corner. They were right between Judith's studio and the park nearby. Judith worked on her sketches at the studio on Fridays.

"Drop me off here?" she said. "I'll walk."

Edgar looked around before pulling up to the curb. "You sure?"

"You bet." She reached over to give him a peck, but he grasped her hand, remorseful.

"I heard you, Kitty. I did. I just don't know the answers. I don't know what I'm going to do. Don't let it disturb you, all right? I'm sorry." He stroked her cheek, caught her look and held it.

"OK." She kissed him, got out and watched him drive away, that furrow of concentration creasing his brow again.

Instead of heading to the Rennweg penthouse, she crossed the road and started for Studio JuLi. She took the stairs to the third floor and was a bit out of breath when Judith opened the door to her.

"Kitty, what's wrong? You look unwell. Are you sick?"

"Not yet," she said. "Got any coffee?"

It was the first time she'd felt she could breathe since Jerzy delivered that note to Edgar and disrupted her entire weekend.

As Judith tinkered in the back, Macke pranced around Kitty's feet. She picked him up and carried him to one of the walls where Judith's illustrations hung. She recognized some of Agnes' gowns, and the costumes from Achmed Beh's. Others were very avant-garde designs that were exciting and imaginative. Judith was wasted here in Vienna. She really should be in Paris, Kitty thought. Or New York.

"Judith?" she called, placing Macke onto the sofa. She caught the whiff of coffee. "Are you all right?"

Judith reappeared in the threshold. "I'm all right. Why?"

Kitty gazed at her. "You mean a lot to me, you and the gang. I've missed you all. If there's anything, ever, that I can do, you know I will, right?"

"*Lieb*," Judith said. "That's really nice. The same goes for you. Now I know that something is really bothering you."

Kitty stroked Macke's little head. "*Und wie!*" And how! "I hope you've got time for me."

Judith came in with the coffee. "Always."

11

MARCH 1938

Judith and Kitty were in the lounge chairs in the studio, the untouched cups of coffee on the table between them. The muslin curtains were inhaling and exhaling the breeze from the cracked open windows.

"Pure blood," Judith scoffed. "Vienna surges with so many races, Kitty. Now imagine all those races relying on their own nationalism, and their political leaders exploiting that fervor for their own means."

"The United States really only has two parties, and they're hard enough to track. I'm not familiar with all the latest details of Austria's political landscape," Kitty admitted. She sat up, reached for the coffee. Judith had made fresh whipped cream. "All I understand is that democracy seemed to be taking flight here. What happened?"

Judith sniffed. "The nationalists got very uncomfortable when they saw that workers were fighting for, and earning, rights. They had rights, Kitty. We also had a two-class system. Poor and rich. When the socialists were in power, they installed new housing, gardens, civic centers, swimming pools, schools.

They gave voice to a class of people who'd never really had one before. But then the radical right ganged up on them."

Kitty sighed. "Edgar says the nationalists accuse the socialists of bringing Vienna to the brink of collapse."

"Yes, these are the same people who nostalgically yearn for *das schöne, alte Wien*."

"The beautiful old Vienna," Kitty translated into English. "Like his parents."

Judith tilted her head. "But not Edgar?"

"He and I are aligned on nearly everything." Kitty frowned. "At least, that's what I thought, until today."

"Don't take the influence of culture too lightly," Judith warned. "The fact is that both of you come from very different worlds."

Kitty did not like that. She stood and went to the window, looking at the little park just below. A man in a hat was lounging against the lamppost, reading a paper. It was an odd place to be reading a paper.

"I mean, would it ever work in America?" Judith asked.

"What?" Kitty turned away from the window.

"Socialism."

"Not for lack of trying." She plucked her cup of coffee from the table and leaned against the back of the chair. "Some of the things Vienna has done for its city would never even get off the ground in America."

"Why?"

"Because anything good for all the people is not profitable. That's not how America works; not how our politicians work for America."

"But it's in your constitution, Kitty. By the people, for the people."

"Yeah," Kitty said and lifted her cup at Judith. "But only for the *right* people."

Judith sighed heavily. "It started with Seyss-Inquart in parliament and—"

"Wait. Arthur Seyss-Inquart?" Kitty set her cup onto the windowsill. "Good Lord, how could I forget? I'm so stupid!" She reached into her pocket and retrieved the note she'd found in the barn. *S-I.* She looked up at Judith. "I think I know who my husband is meeting."

"The head of Austria's Nazi party?" Judith sat up. "The man Hitler will likely appoint chancellor if Austria unites with Germany?"

Wide-eyed, Kitty nodded. *I can't wait to peel back each layer of you...* That was what she had said to Edgar, but suddenly she was very frightened of what she might discover lying underneath.

Judith came to her side. "Give him a chance to explain," she urged, giving her arm a squeeze. "My late husband was also a career politician. You and I both know how complex these things are."

Kitty bit her lip. "You're right. Of course you're right. I believe in Edgar. I really do."

"You're a smart girl. You know what to do."

Kitty embraced Judith. "I'm going to tell you again. If this happens—if Austria joins Germany—I want you to know Millie and I will make sure you and Oskar are safe."

Judith looked surprised. "My husband was an Austrian colonel, decorated in the last war. What's there to worry about?"

Kitty hesitated a moment before she forced herself to smile. "Sure. What's there to worry about then?"

At the Ragatzes' villa, Kitty handed her coat to the butler at the door. In the dining room, she expected a room full of those faces she'd seen at her wedding. The people that Captain Wallace had been recently reporting on. Instead, she was disappointed to find that only Margit, Edgar, and her parents-in-law were lingering around the table, obviously waiting for her.

"I'm so sorry I'm late," Kitty said.

Josef Ragatz greeted her half-heartedly. Dorothea Ragatz did not hide her annoyance as she smacked her lips and pointed that sharp chin upwards. Margit smiled at Kitty, then quickly returned her attention to her mother.

"Americans are always late," Kitty's sister-in-law said as if to calm Dorothea.

Kitty pecked Edgar's cheek as he held a chair out for her. "Looks like I missed the party," she murmured.

"Not at all."

She greeted everyone properly and waited as one of the servants poured wine.

"And?" She fidgeted with her napkin. "Did you get all the questions answered? It must have been a very short meeting?"

Edgar fingered the rim of his empty plate. "I'm afraid we have bigger issues right now."

"Why's that?" Kitty asked.

Josef tugged at his mustache. "The German Wehrmacht has mobilized on the border."

"This is bad," she said to Edgar. "Will there even be a referendum?"

His parents tossed one another a knowing look.

"Not the sham of one the chancellor was planning," Josef huffed.

"But Austria can't really be serious about giving up her sovereignty?" Kitty said.

Dorothea threw up her hand. The servants carrying in their soup stopped in their tracks.

"My child," Josef began, and Kitty prickled under his condescending gaze. "It seems you do not understand the signific-icant gains that will fall to Austria by joining Germany, the additional territory and the additional population. Why, that would turn Germany into the largest state in Europe! We would increase the workforce, and not just with unskilled labor. Austria has an abundance of trained specialists, especially in iron, metallurgy, and the construction industries."

Kitty pictured that man Eigruber, with the Hitler-style mustache at her wedding; the one who was in the iron and steel industry. She eyed her father-in-law. *We would increase the work force...*

Startled, she put a hand on Edgar's arm. Was his father an NSDAP supporter? But Margit surprised her even more.

Quietly her sister-in-law said, "It's either here, or Hitler will invade Poland. Likely, he'll go after both."

For a brief moment, Kitty locked eyes with Edgar's sister. Frau Ragatz suddenly tutted and rapped her knuckle next to Margit's plate.

"He will go where he believes the Germans need him," Dorothea claimed.

Josef seemed to have ignored the entire exchange as he drove home his point. "The Third Reich urgently needs these specialists. And we have them here in Austria."

Austria had specialists. Austria had resources. Yes, Kitty thought, resources for war, for Hitler's vision of world domination. Edgar glanced at her, cleared his throat and refolded his napkin as Dorothea directed the soup to be served.

"It is our assessment," Edgar said, "that Hitler will either pressure our chancellor into a peaceful takeover, perhaps make him resign, or the German Wehrmacht will invade."

"Jesus help you," Kitty scoffed. She ignored her mother-in-law's frown and Margit's surprised snigger.

Kitty was busy recalling one of Captain Wallace's reports.

Germany's advances are not to be ignored. Germany's hunger will not be satiated. We urge the current administra-

tion of the United States of America and her allies to prepare
for the worst.

Kitty reflected—not for the first time since she'd moved to
Vienna—on Edgar's warnings back in Tokyo, less than a year
ago. Dominoes. This one was about to fall. She looked at the
table around her, stopping at Edgar, whose expression seemed
to say, "Just eat and get through this. Save your opinions for
home."

Kitty held her tongue and ate, but every swallow around the
lump of fear in her throat was painful.

The sound of rumbling, like thunder. Jubilant cries that reached
all the way up to the top-floor penthouse. Edgar was already
awake and striding across the room, pulling open dresser drawers. Kitty sprang from the bed and went to the window, looking
up into the sky.

"Edgar, it's airplanes." She turned to him, wide-eyed.

"Patrols, maybe." He joined her and peered between the
blinds.

Kitty opened the window and looked down onto the street
below. A group of people waving flags—scarlet, black and white
—were heading somewhere.

"Good God," she groaned. "It's happened, hasn't it?"

"Get dressed," Edgar ordered. "We're going to the
center. I want to get to the office and I'm not leaving you
here."

The phone rang out in the foyer. Kitty could hear it cut off
suddenly, and pictured Jerzy answering it. Edgar was buttoning
up his shirt and tucking it into his trousers as he left the
bedroom, still barefoot. She hurried to her closet and pushed
the dresses around, then laughed nervously, on the verge of
hysteria.

"What does one wear when one's adopted country is being invaded?"

Edgar was just hanging up when she came out wearing a plain black dress and did a double take. All of her accessories were black: her jewelry, her shoes. The black pillbox hat and veil were the finishing touch of her funeral attire.

In the next moment, Edgar had his socks and shoes on, and Kitty gulped down a cup of coffee. Jerzy was hovering in the background. She turned to him, rested a hand on his forearm.

"I am afraid," she said measuredly, surprised at how cool she felt. "At least, I believe I am. Are you all right?"

Jerzy's eyebrow curved. One single curt nod was all he allowed himself before Edgar called into the room.

"Are you ready?"

On Rennweg, they flung themselves onto a moving street-car, the conductor scowling at them and wagging a finger. Edgar apologized and pushed Kitty deeper inside. People were chatting excitedly. Military trucks zipped past on the road parallel to them. At one crossing, Kitty saw a tank.

This was real. It was happening. Her heart kick-started a surge of panic. From behind, Edgar put an arm around her.

"I don't know what I should be feeling. What should I do?" she whispered. "I am so scared."

"Not nearly as much as I am."

This did not reassure her one bit. And still she let him lead her, and she followed when he jumped off near the opera house. He went towards Heldenplatz but there was no sign of activity. Shop windows, usually opened at this time of day, were shuttered.

Suddenly, a siren sounded in the distance, growing louder and faster. A car flashed by with two white S-lines crudely painted on the side. It disappeared down the road, heading straight for Vienna's center. Edgar followed after it. Moments later, Kitty spotted the crowds of people. Among them, a group of men with swastika armbands on their brown shirts.

"That's SA. *Sturmabteilung*," Edgar said ominously. "They're like patrols, to supposedly keep the peace."

"Keep the peace?" Kitty's voice was high-pitched. She knew about them from reports out of Berlin. "A bunch of thugs are keeping the peace? Where are the police?"

No police. No firemen. But a lot of men in their hats and coats, with swastika armbands wrapped around their upper arms. They were forming rows of six, as if getting ready to march in a parade. And then Kitty realized that was exactly what was happening. The crowds were getting deeper as they lined the pavements and street. An entire truck was loading up with young children, waving flags and bunches of flowers. She choked on the acrid smell of smoke, of burning rubber.

"Edgar?" Kitty cried and grasped her husband by the back of his coat. The spectacle was terrifying. A civilian army of Nazis had been lying in wait and was now here in full force. "There are so many of them!"

Her husband turned his head, his eyes ice-blue. "It's the people's will. It's hard to fight against the people's will. That's why they're here now. This is what Austria wants."

"And you?" she cried after him. "Is this what you want? Because if it isn't, stop it. Stop it, Edgar!"

But her husband was tugging her through the thickening crowds. For a moment she thought he was going to join that very parade. But he veered off just as a group of jubilant young people pushed straight into them. Kitty's hand wrenched away from Edgar's. He swung back for her but she pulled away, staring at him as the crowd filled the space between them. In the distance, an explosion, directly behind Edgar.

A scream lodged in her throat and he pushed towards her.

"Kitty! Stay with me," he shouted.

A man jumped between them, raised his hand in a salute in front of her—"One country, one blood!"—before moving on.

"Without a shot fired," a woman exclaimed as she passed Kitty by.

"Come and see," someone shouted. But not to her.

Kitty stood still in the stream of people, gaping. She heard her husband. She heard them all. But she did not want to go and look. She did not want to watch.

The crowds were organized, forming a way for the paramilitary, for the Wehrmacht, for the new civic leaders, six rows deep. Suddenly a cheer turned into a roar. An entourage of black Mercedes crept forward on Kitty's right. *S-1*. Men, women and children raised their hands, like preachers giving a rigid blessing.

She had to flee. She had to run.

Kitty spun around, looking for an escape. On her side of the street, just a few steps away, an empty alley. Another tank rumbled and jolted into the square. Another blast, followed by the sounds of a brass marching band. The cheers competed with the beat of the drums.

"Kitty!" Edgar was at her side.

"I want to go home," she screamed. "Home! Take me home!"

He led her into the alleyway. They followed the maze of narrow passages. When they came to a dead end, Kitty beat the wall with open palms and swung to Edgar, wild-eyed.

"What now?" she sobbed.

He stepped up to her, and she wailed against his chest, then looked to him for guidance.

But he was looking elsewhere. He was looking up.

"I don't know," he said. "But we're all right, you and me. We're together. We're all right."

MARCH 1938

The Monday after the annexation, Kitty returned to the consulate.

The mood was not subdued as she had expected. There was nothing normal about the atmosphere at all. Some of the staff were overexcited. Others—like Kitty—were shell-shocked. But there was nothing between the two extremes.

The embassy doors usually opened at nine but Cooper had called everyone in at eight o'clock to discuss the influx of requests they would get for visas and passports. Kitty came through the side entrance and headed upstairs but paused at the sound of rattling coming from the foyer. She looked down, surprised to see a row of guards standing just behind the door, and a sea of faces in front of the embassy gates. She hurried upstairs.

Cooper stood in the center of the pool room, apparently waiting for her. Some of the secretaries were seated on the leather couch as if in a police line-up. Millie was standing near the windows on the far side of the room and gave Kitty a knowing look when she came in. Kitty muttered her apologies and undid her scarf.

"There are going to be thousands of people asking for help," Cooper opened.

As Cooper reported what Kitty had already witnessed and heard about, she locked eyes with Millie. Had she heard from Judith? From Khan and Big Charlie? What about Oskar and Artur? When Kitty's calls to Judith had gone unanswered, and she and Edgar were in the muck of their own debates, he had flat out refused to let her go to Alsergrund and check on the gang. They argued about what to do next. Kitty had suggested they go to America, he practically demanded that they sit and wait. His sudden patriarchal attitude and impatience with her left her reeling, wondering what had happened to the man she had fallen in love with.

Cooper cleared his throat. "For most of the people lined up outside, there is little or nothing that we can do. You will be tired, overworked and irritable, but I still ask you to treat each of the visa applicants with courtesy. When you can't do anything for them, when nothing else is available, give them your time and sympathy so that here—at least in this consulate—they will be respected human beings and not hunted animals."

He then looked at Kitty. "I'll need you to assist whoever needs assistance."

"Yes, sir."

"Beginning with keeping that mob out there in line."

Kitty unfastened her coat and hung it on one of the pegs. She hurried downstairs to the foyer and went into one of the front offices to peer out the windows. There was indeed a sizable crowd and when she stood up on tiptoe she swore the line went all the way around the corner. Men mostly, but plenty of women and children. Some older people as well. A crowd of anxious faces.

"*Wahnsinn*," she breathed, because it truly was insanity. "This is going to be a busy day."

Cooper appeared behind her. "I don't think we can wait.

There are SA troops out on the streets and reports that they are attacking Jews at each of the consulates. Let's get these people in here."

Kitty nodded and rejoined him at the entrance. He motioned the guards to open the floodgates.

For five American dollars, visa applicants hired other Viennese Jews as placeholders to reserve their spot in the long line. The walls of the consulate vibrated with the ringing of telephones. But the work could not distract Kitty from the heightened awareness that something dangerous was unfolding. There were the principles she held true as an American. Her adopted country, and the man she loved, had been taken over by a brutal regime. And the two things were pulling her in opposite directions.

Throughout the day, Kitty or Millie tried reaching someone at Alsergrund. But neither woman had success. So Kitty searched the masses that had swept into the halls of their building for Judith or another familiar face, but with no luck.

Cooper followed the normal process of obtaining a visa. An interview with a consular official was required of each applicant before one could be issued. Each individual foreign service officer could accept or reject any of the applications placed before him. But Cooper made the final decisions.

Uncertainties among the staff increased when word came through that the British and French diplomats were being called home. Given that Austria was no longer a sovereign country, Cooper telegraphed the Department of State and questioned the consulate's status in Vienna. Were diplomatic functions still needed? Two days later, the assistant secretary, George Messersmith, wrote back to say that D.C. had yet to determine Vienna's position. Kitty knew of George Messersmith from when both he and Nils had worked in Berlin. From what her brother had told her, Kitty had very mixed feelings about the man. Holding the cable, she read his response. He was giving them permission to continue functioning in their capacity. For now, the Vienna office would keep its doors open.

That night, at ten o'clock, after the last disappointed visa candidates were shown out and told to return in the morning, Cooper pulled the remaining staff together into the foyer.

"We need to do better. We've got to get organized. The functions which each of us must perform in this consulate now are in many respects more important than anything we've done before. All the officers here in Vienna have a very real opportunity for public service. I know we can depend on you all."

Earlier in the day, he had told Kitty to cancel all social events. He was going to roll up his sleeves and help process applicants. Every time Kitty came in that week, Cooper was there. His detailed reports did not stop. His communications increased and still he was working side by side with the other officers and administrators.

Kitty continued streaming information through their communication lines, keeping the Department of State appraised of the situation. He gave her more responsibility. More authorization. And she tackled it all with gusto. It kept her from despairing.

When Cooper got word that D.C. had decided to transform Vienna from a legation to a consulate general, his first request was for an increase in staff.

One afternoon, Millie waved Kitty to her before whispering, "Khan left me a message downstairs. He's being pretty secretive but it sounds like he and Big Charlie took control and got Oskar and Judith somewhere safe. When things calm down, they'll let us know what's next."

Kitty breathed a loud sigh of relief. "We can relax. At least for a minute."

She held out Messersmith's cable to Millie. The Assistant

Secretary of State had responded to Cooper's request for more staff. It was brief and indirect.

The Visa Section should not dominate consular work.

Millie looked up from it and wrinkled her nose, then directed her gaze towards the hallway. Kitty also turned to the heartbreaking scene. People were lined up on benches, children played with toys on the floor, and old people, hands folded in their laps, squirmed on the hard seats, their expressions in various stages of resignation or suffering.

"I want to respond to Messersmith myself," Kitty muttered. *If visa work should not dominate, what the hell else should we be doing exactly?*

Since the Anschluss, Kitty hardly slept. Besides the twelve- to fourteen-hour workdays, the images of anguish, her concerns about the gang and Judith kept her wound up.

In the meantime, Edgar had, to all intents and purposes, disappeared. He was sleeping at his office, and when he came home he was too exhausted to talk. Their meals—when they shared one—were submerged in unspoken thoughts. That parade, those city streets, the spectacle of terror had bruised them and their relationship, and she could not reach Edgar over a growing chasm, even when what she really wanted to do was grab his hand and pull him to her side of the gap.

"You don't understand," they accused one another, lashing out their frustrations.

The only information Kitty could get out of him was that his department was being reorganized. His colleagues were being replaced one by one. And she knew he meant they were being replaced by young men who were more sympathetic to the new Nazi regime.

"And you?" she asked once. After all, was he not personally involved with the once mysterious S-I?

He'd looked up at her without raising his head from the plate of food, as if he'd heard her silent reprimand. "Don't rock the boat, Kitty."

Their boat? Or the big cruiser, called Austria, sailing towards dark waters? A small part of her took pity on him. She felt the squeeze around him the same way she felt the squeeze around the men, women and children who filtered through the corridors of the American consulate, hoping, praying and begging for a way out, even if only on a tourist visa.

But there were not enough visas to give out.

Tirelessly, Cooper coached and counseled each of the staff, including Leland Morris and Harry Carlson, his two senior foreign service officers, on the particulars of U.S. immigration laws. One morning, the FSOs sat at the conference table, the secretarial pool along the wall, as Cooper held a meeting.

"Our job is to accurately implement policy," he said. "But we also need to respond humanely to the various level of immigration crisis. The American embassy in Berlin is including us in the total figure of visa quotas. This is the good news. Whereas we could only issue some fourteen hundred visas annually, we've been authorized to double that."

Kitty frowned. Nobody had to be a mathematical genius to understand that the growing need would never be served by that paltry number.

"Nobody gets a visa without an affidavit," Leland Morris chimed in. "They shouldn't even be in here if they don't have an affidavit. They need to submit those letters from American sponsors. And the other thing is, anyone sixteen years or above has to be able to read, or they will automatically be disqualified. Nobody who is at risk of becoming a public charge will be approved."

Kitty raised her hand at the back of the table. Cooper saw

her but he did not react. She raised her hand higher. He still did not give her permission to speak. She waved her hand then. He raised his eyebrows and turned away. Finally, she stamped her foot and sprang from her seat.

Cooper blinked at her. "What is it, Mrs. Ragatz?"

"Are there any plans from D.C. to change the immigration policy? I mean, it's the same as it was fifteen years ago. We're focusing only on the Jews right now but there will certainly be more political dissidents, priests, students and..."

She was thinking of Artur. Of Oskar.

"And?" Cooper asked, his irritation palpable.

"And others that the Nazis deem undesirable."

"Thank you very much for that, Mrs. Ragatz," Cooper said. "We are quite aware. And no, I know nothing about any changes. Perhaps you could call Senator Larsson and ask what his committee is actually up to?"

Stunned, Kitty sat back down.

Later, Cooper sidled by her. She had never seen him so angry. "*And others*, Mrs. Ragatz? Like husbands who have said nothing against the new regime?"

"Is that a crime?" Blood surged into her ears.

Cooper cocked his head, raised that eyebrow again. "Not yet, Mrs. Ragatz."

13

MARCH/APRIL 1938

A city without a soul. That was what her father had said on the phone. She had called to talk to him, as Cooper had suggested, though she knew Cooper had said it in spite.

"Every street looks like ours," Kitty told her dad. "I walk past the Polish, the Czech, even the Russian consulates, and there are lines of people hoping to get out. Then those Brown Shirts come by with their clubs and beat them off or humiliate them."

"Christ, Kitty." Her dad rarely swore. He was affected.

"Listen, a lot of the Jews who are now in Vienna fled Germany when the Nazis first took over. They know what to expect, but right now...?" How could she describe it?

Her father waited.

"Judith said few believed it would happen here. But it did, Dad. Nobody realized how short of a fuse there was..."

The Senator had agreed with her. "It sounds like the Nazis were just waiting for the right moment. Be careful, Kit."

She was not the one who had to be careful. Judith, Oskar, and Artur had to be. She still hadn't seen hide nor hair of anyone from the gang. And neither had Millie since Khan had come by, but Kitty often wondered how they were faring.

Even so, she took her father's warning to heart in the days that followed. She divided her time between helping visa applicants and Cooper's diplomatic briefs. He was constantly on the telephone. The words *regime, crisis, war* and *control* were injected into nearly every paragraph in his reports. One other word began infecting her documents as well: *anti-Semitism.*

To which, apparently, the American administration was not immune, because by the end of the third week, Mary Rosen stood before Kitty's desk, with one defensive eyebrow arched as usual.

"Goodbye," Mary said flatly.

"Are you gone for the day?" Kitty looked at the clock. It was only nine thirty in the morning.

"I've been let go."

"Let go?" Kitty looked around. As usual, there was a flurry of activity. The FSOs were losing their patience, were haggard and overworked. The girls in the room were also getting snappish.

Kitty waved toward the hallway, bursting at the seams with candidates and applicants. "You're one of the best in the pool. And we need people."

Mary hugged the nearly empty box of personal items tighter to her chest then stuck out her hand. "Apparently, I am no longer needed... not here. Goodbye, Kitty. And good luck."

That evening, alone in a pool of light from her lamp, Kitty ate a sandwich at her desk, a stack of files still to be sorted for Cooper by the next day. She overheard two of the foreign service agents talking in the hallway.

"No more kikes on the staff, thank God."

"Really?"

"Yeah. Under the pretense that it's dangerous, but Roosevelt's administration wants all the Jews gone."

"I'm not so sure," the other man said. "I think they're just shuffling personnel out of here for show. They want to pretend they're being respectful to the Germans. I think they're reassigning Gardener, for example, somewhere else."

The first man laughed drily. "Nowhere in Europe is going to be safe for the likes of them soon."

Her appetite ruined, Kitty dropped her uneaten sandwich into the wastebasket.

Much to Kitty's surprise, Edgar brought home a bicycle for her. Her husband was prone to blowing hot, then cold, these days but the bicycle—which might have otherwise made them laugh and send them on a silly ride through the parks—was procured for an ominous reason.

"I don't want you to ride the streetcars anymore," Edgar explained. "Too many SA patrols."

She had not had to say anything about her apprehension, and could not. Like many of the details she had begun keeping from Edgar, she did not tell him that two American tourists—a man and a woman—had pushed their way into Cooper's office. The woman had been pale and shaking. The man had held a bloodied handkerchief to his nose. They were from Ohio, and he had been beaten by a stormtrooper for not raising his hand in salute.

Cooper had taken down their information, then escorted them downstairs. He did not return until after he had gone to the Austrian authorities and railed at them. At least according to his reports, they had assured Cooper they would tell their "men" that tourists were exempt from having to salute.

Shortly after what all of the world was calling the Anschluss, the new regime assigned a new name to Austria. Kitty now lived in Ostmark. Just as most of them had predicted, Arthur Seyss-Inquart—S-I—was their new chancellor.

That night, Kitty watched Edgar eating in silence.

"Do you know him?"

He frowned. "Who doesn't know him?"

"I mean, personally, Edgar. Do you know Arthur Seyss-Inquart personally? Like you know the man who's just been made the new Gestapo head? Or the—"

In a flash, Edgar slammed a hand on the table. "I have no idea what you are accusing me of, Kitty, but right now you and I have jobs to do. You, in your corner of the world. Me, in mine. It would be best if we did not discuss these things or, I promise you, we will sleep as enemies."

Shocked, angry tears rose. "Is this what we have come to? Really, Edgar?"

"If you want to save this marriage, Kitty, then maybe you should consider quitting your job."

She stormed out, locked herself in the bedroom and paced the room, hyperventilating. She did not understand how he could be transforming like this right before her very eyes. All the joy—all the light he'd brought with him—had been sucked out of their lives in a matter of days.

With one arm, she swiped the dressers. Lamps and photos crashed to the ground. Glass lay in shards. The vase of fresh-cut flowers toppled over last.

Edgar slept in his study that night. She awoke to the mess, dressed in the clothes she had worn the day before, managed to brush her teeth and headed back to the office without cleaning up the bedroom or meeting her husband. She apologized meekly to Jerzy, wishing it was her husband who would be left with cleaning up. Poor Jerzy had not deserved it.

Still livid, Kitty grimly confronted the piles of communications from the policymakers and diplomats. Cables. Telegrams. Letters from Washington: George Messersmith. Secretary Cordell Hull. Ambassador Raymond Geist at the embassy in Berlin. All of their names rang of conflict. *Messer*. Knife. *Geist* in German translated into ghost. Even Cooper's proper last name, Wiley. She was playing with these thoughts when another cable arrived from Berlin. Again, a refusal to allocate more staff and more funds. And another flat-out no to raising the visa quota.

Feeling defeated, Kitty was about to leave for lunch when Cooper shouted for her to come in. Like almost everyone in the office, he shouted now. Kitty hurried and stood in the doorway. Cordell Hull, Secretary of State, was on the phone. Cooper waved for her to take notes.

"Just a moment," Cooper said. "I have Senator Larsson's daughter here." It was as if he could not call her by her married name any longer.

Cooper looked at Kitty. She signaled she was ready. "Go ahead," he said to the speaker.

"John, I wish to express to you and to your collaborators my appreciation of your efforts to keep us fully informed of recent developments in Austria," Hull said. *Ostmark*, Kitty corrected in her notes. "You are commended for the thoroughness, promptness and general excellence of the reports submitted."

"Thank you very much." Cooper said. "Cordell, I've been reporting to you about the ever-increasing list of arrests. There have been reports of suicides and other tragedies among the Jews, and also quite a number of the workers. Most notably those who were—"

"Communists," Hull interrupted.

"Socialists, if I may be so bold as to correct. And the Nazis are conducting house searches, plundering and confiscating property..."

"Yes," Hull said, "just like they did in Berlin."

Cooper did not respond and Kitty paused. He locked eyes with her. His were tired.

"The tragedy here is greater than Berlin," he addressed the speaker. "Berlin was gradual; here it came from one day to the next. And like a hammer. Our consuls should, for the present at least, be well staffed in order to cope with visa, passport and welfare cases en masse. We're in a state of siege, and this will go on, I guarantee, for a protracted period."

Hull blustered down the line: "George Messersmith was supposed to handle all this."

Cooper closed his eyes. "His answer was no, but—"

"Then I'll have to talk to him. But it's no good going over anyone's head on this."

"No, sir," Cooper agreed.

"We'll get back to you."

Cooper said goodbye and kept his hand on the telephone. "Did you get all that?" he asked her.

Kitty nodded, turned to the door. It was all futile. Bureaucracy was just futile.

When she was back at her desk, she struck the notes with her pen, making sharp jabs. All the girls were busy. Millie was listening intently to Leland Morris. Two other assistants were pounding away at the keys. But Mary Rosen's desk was still empty. They needed more staff. Immediately.

The clock read one. She hadn't had lunch. For the umpteenth time, Kitty thought of Judith and snatched up the phone, expecting it to ring on at her studio as always. She lurched out of her seat when Judith picked up the phone.

"It's me," Kitty said. "I'm worried about you. Where have you been?"

"You. I thought you'd be... We can't talk on the—"

"Put on your coat. I'm coming over."

"Before all this, Austria's nationalists were only rubber-soled anti-Semites," Judith said as she locked her studio door. "But overnight, they became rabid, overt government-sanctioned anti-Semites."

Her relief was so great that Kitty could not stop grinning at her friend despite her ominous assessment. She clasped the little woman's hand as they walked to the cafe across the road and took a quiet booth. Judith assured Kitty that everyone was safe. She confirmed that Khan's mother's bookshop had survived the looting.

"Apparently the SA don't read books," Judith quipped. Then her face went slack again. "But Charlie's sports club was shut down."

"Where are Oskar and Artur?" Kitty whispered.

"Oskar closed the nightclub and retreated to Artur's mother's in Lower Austria for a while."

Kitty held Macke in her lap, enjoying the comfort of the little white dog. "In just three weeks, we've had over twenty-five thousand visa applicants come to us personally. We have managed under one thousand interviews. Do you know what it was like before that?"

Judith shook her head.

"Three hundred callers a month. Thirty immigration visas and thirty visitors' visas issued per month." Kitty sighed. "Cooper is walking a thin line. Politically and with his humanitarian efforts. That's why he's making me write down all the commendations he gets."

"It's a hopeless situation," Judith muttered.

"The Department of State refused to authorize any more staff. They haven't authorized a budget for more salaries, but the personnel that were suspected of being Jewish? Miss Rosen. Mr. Gardener. Miss Horowitz. They've been sent away, just like that."

Realizing she was unloading on already heavy shoulders, Kitty reached for Judith's arm. "I'm worried about you and Oskar. The whole gang. Let me try and help you get out."

Judith began to protest and Kitty squeezed her arm.

"You can't convince me that you are not in danger," she said. "You can't hide out forever. I want to help. Let me."

Judith leaned back. "What do I need to do?"

"Do you know anyone in America who would write an affidavit?"

"Of course."

"Get it, Judith. Get them to send it. And then put your application in. You can always decide against it. But put it in."

"All right, Kitty."

"And from now on," she insisted, "we meet once a week. For coffee. Just like this."

Judith smiled, those big brown eyes shining behind her glasses. "I've missed you. The whole gang has missed you."

Kitty nodded. "I'll make sure to tell Millie you said hello. We'll go out somewhere safe. I hear Achmed Beh is keeping Nazi guests to a minimum, making sure the seats are filled with regulars."

It was time for her to go. She paid the bill, hugged Judith, and patted Macke on the head. On the way back to the office, Kitty picked up a paper and read the first page. A referendum to make the Anschluss official was scheduled in just a couple of weeks.

As she pedaled back to work, she watched the people on the streets. The initial euphoria had been replaced by fear. People were on guard. Their glances were furtive, and they spoke in whispers. The Austrians had not expected the violence, the quick arrests and utter barbarism that many of the citizens now felt justified to take part in. Maybe, just maybe, enough people were disgusted and determined to vote against the annexation.

Only Edgar would know what was written in the hearts and minds of the Viennese.

Eager to see him, she switched direction and headed for his building, but slammed on the brakes when she turned into his street. There it was. The swastika flag, hoisted on the flagpole before the department. Kitty stared at it then looked for Edgar's window.

She willed him to come to the window. She would not go into that building on her own. She willed him to come to the window and see her. And just then she realized what was causing the rift between them.

Even if he sensed her there—the way he had so many other times in other situations—his shame would prevent him from seeking her out.

14

APRIL 1938

Kitty felt the need to report and write down everything she was experiencing and witnessing.

She wrote letters to the family in Minnesota and, for the first time in a long time, to Nils in Tokyo. After the hysterics in the post-annexation celebrations in Vienna's center, the city had grown eerily quiet. Drivers honked less. Streetcars were nearly empty. Taxis, once heavily competing for a fare, were rarely to be found. In broad daylight, Vienna felt empty.

As she bicycled through the city, she noticed that those who were out walked with a funny step, allowing club-carrying SA patrols to pass by, fresh-faced bullies who were much too young to understand the consequences they would later carry.

The Gestapo had set up headquarters at the Hotel Metropole. People were arrested on a daily basis either by them, the SS or the municipal police for the slightest transgression—most of those actions nobody had dreamed would ever be punishable by law.

She had to slow down as a swarm of boys and girls dashed out of a school building. The boys wore brown uniforms and pioneer scarves around their necks. The girls were in white

blouses and black skirts. Their smiles were bright, their cama-
raderie and laughter nearly infectious. But Kitty knew what
they'd learned inside that building. The kinds of songs they had
sung. That the men and women who were responsible for
shaping their minds now measured the sizes of their heads and
compared the color of the children's hair to a chart. *Pure blood.
Nationhood! Loyalty to your Fatherland.* Only for the right kind
of people.

As arranged, Kitty met with Judith the following two weeks.
On the Thursday before the referendum, they met in a park
and bought small paper cups of coffee from a stand. Judith
found a bench in a secluded spot and the two women sat
silently for the longest time.

"I feel like I am going crazy," Judith finally said. "Like I am
the only one who is not with them, you understand? Although I
know that can't be true."

"You aren't the only one," Kitty reassured her.

Judith peered at her over her glasses. "Then why isn't
anyone resisting this?"

"It will happen," Kitty said. "This can't last forever."

Judith threw her a look, scoffed and turned away, but said
nothing.

The coffee tasted awful and Kitty considered tossing it.
"Are you meeting the gang tonight? Maybe we should all just go
out for drinks. We could go to Achmed Beh's?"

Judith shook her head. "We're not going to any of those
places any more. There are fresh faces there." She raised an
eyebrow and looked at Kitty knowingly. "Eager, arrogant blue-
eyed Aryan soldiers. The Black bands are all gone or they've
gone underground. Which is where we all are, now."

Kitty's heart sank and she felt a pang in her chest. Losing
Judith or Oskar, or Khan—any of them—would be one of the
worst things imaginable. They were some of the few genuine

people she knew in Vienna. Even Edgar was becoming a stranger to her.

As the weeks passed, Kitty was no longer certain whether she would ever stop feeling off-kilter. Like tectonic plates after an earthquake, everything had shifted, even her marriage. Despite having profusely apologized to one another one evening, followed by passionate lovemaking, Edgar seemed to purposefully take part in every business trip there was thereafter. When he came home, he was sullen and bleak. When she reached for him at night, sometimes his body froze beneath her fingers, his back rigid. Other times, he held her tight instead of making love, as if he were struggling to keep afloat. Her nightmares were dark.

Each time she went to work, she watched for predator faces. In front of all the administrative buildings in the city center, guards wore thick red armbands with black swastikas. They were delighted by their power and greeted each passerby with a challenging, "Heil Hitler," as if daring the other not to salute.

At the consulate, the types of candidates that were seeking a visa changed, too. Whereas most of the initial applicants had been educated and professional Jews, who had almost immediately lost their jobs after the Anschluss, now the applicants were coming from the working class.

She hated giving bad news. An engineer stood before her one day. He unfolded his affidavit and placed it before her, right side up, as if to make sure she got the full effect.

"That took a great effort," he said with a thick Austrian accent. "A long wait. A lot of effort."

Kitty's heart sank. "We can't do anything with that. We need proof of the data on that form. A certified copy of your income tax return. A notarized letter from your employer, confirming your salary. A statement from your bank, confirming your deposit value."

She finally looked him in the eyes. "Get it all complete, and then I can start a file for you."

Gravely, he folded the affidavit, put it into his pocket and gave her a sad smile. "It took a lot of effort."

"Just a little more," she said.

Dejected, she went to grab a cup of coffee, wondering if her day was going to get any better. Then Messersmith sent a cable. She read it quickly before bringing it in to Cooper. Her boss was to cut the remaining staff in half. Kitty handed him the message and a stream of cuss words followed. The room outside his office went still. Morris and Carson stepped out and listened, their applicants inside the office anxiously peering at Kitty for answers.

Cooper then strode out a moment later and leaned on Kitty's desk. He addressed the whole room. "Get your wives, your friends, your friends' wives in here. I don't care what their nationality is, but get them in here to work. I'll hire them myself."

He withdrew a wallet and dropped Reichsmarks onto Kitty's desk, then patted his pockets and tossed some American bills and coins on top of the German bills. "Now get to it. Call everyone you know. I'll pay myself."

By the following week, there were desks in the foyer, and a whole troop of semi-volunteers. Kitty forgave Cooper for his earlier insults and rudeness. Her admiration for the man increased tenfold. It was an admiration she could not feel for her husband though, and that not only stung, it was driving a wedge between them.

Once, when Sam was preparing for his first anatomy exam, Kitty was helping him, and he told her about the amygdala.

"It's like an alarm in the brain. It sends us into a fight, causes us to take flight or feign death. So, either an animal or human will confront the danger, or they'll run. And then there are those who just surrender."

"My amygdala always sends me into fight mode," Kitty had claimed.

Sam had studied her, his grin thoughtful. "Sometimes it might do you good to play dead."

On the Friday before the referendum, the city was lying in wait. Or playing dead. Even the planes had stopped patrolling the skies. Everything in Kitty wanted to fight what was happening to Vienna. Edgar was in flight mode, once again avoiding her at all costs it seemed. But then he came home that night with a smile on his face.

"There's hope yet, darling," he said. "I've been talking to our friends."

"Our friends?" Kitty murmured. His sudden mood swing put her on alert.

But Edgar was pulling off his tie, and shrugged out of his coat. She willed him to look her in the eye. When he did, his face turned soft with tenderness.

"Come here," he beckoned. "I've missed you. Please."

Kitty felt a pang of guilt. They had bruised one another with words and deeds, and she had not backed down. Instead, she had hit back just as hard as he. She desperately wanted for them to find their way back to each other.

"It's been a terrible time," she murmured and caressed a brown curl from his forehead. "I feel as if I've aged years."

He caught her hand, kissed her palm, then led her into the sitting room, before pouring a drink. He offered her one, but she declined.

Kitty perched on the armchair. "What's the happy news?"

"The referendum. There is still hope. Our chancellor might yet be able to turn the tides."

But Edgar was wrong.

On Sunday, the day of the plebiscite, the SA troops and

Nazi henchmen accosted citizens on the streets. Kitty heard them from the window, watched them on the street below. Two patrols pulled the janitor straight out of one of the shops across the road and marched him towards the polling station.

"You can vote," she heard one of the troopers cajole. "You have a right to leave work."

They returned for the owner of the little flower shop across the street.

Kitty wanted to go out. Look for the gang. For Edgar. She dared not. Later, she heard pounding on her neighbors' doors below. She went into the foyer, listened at the elevator shaft. Voices. One set commanding action, the other pleading for understanding. Had they voted yet? Where was their pin? The only acceptable one was the one that said *Ja*, indicating the person had voted for the annexation.

On tenterhooks, and with the results due soon, Kitty was chewing her fingernails to the quick. The results would not be in their favor. Couldn't be after what she had witnessed all day long. It grew dark out. She turned on the radio and sank into the armchair.

The situation was a nightmare. The Nazis were here. And there was no going back. Exactly 99.71 percent of the country ratified the Reich's annexation.

The phone rang. She thought it might be Edgar. It was Sam calling to confirm.

"No," Kitty said. "Not ninety-nine. Ninety-nine point seven one."

There was a pause before her brother half-heartedly quipped, "Wowsers, Kit. So, voter turnout was over one hundred percent."

Kitty could not even laugh. The Senator on the other line, uttered only single words.

Unusually, her mother only listened for a long time before simply saying, "Kitty."

"Yes, Maman."

"Are you all right?"

"I don't know." Tears burned at the back of her eyes.

"How is Edgar?" Claudette asked.

Moved by her mother's inquiry, Kitty had to choke back a sob before she could answer. "I don't know. I don't know where he is. He left to vote this morning and hasn't come back." She dreaded all the reasons why he might not yet be home.

Her dad took the phone next. "You want me to get you two out? I can get you out."

Kitty shook her head and just then, she heard the elevator coming up. She abruptly ended the call, leaped from the window seat and rushed into the foyer. Edgar appeared and slowly pulled off his hat.

"Where were you? I was so worried..."

He paused in his undressing and she knew that he saw right through her. She loved him, she missed him. She'd been afraid for him. He was safe. She did not want to fight, she only wanted her husband back in her arms. And there it was. Edgar's devotion and sheer love written all over his face. And one more thing: heart-wrenching remorse.

He reached into his coat pocket and lay something on the console next to the phone. It made a tinny sound. Red. White. Red. *Ja!*

She took a step to him. She could strike him, she could make love to him. She had no idea how she could still react.

He slowly hung his hat, his eyes on her, and suddenly he was there, taking her into his arms. She held her breath, tears welling up.

"Darling," he murmured. He stroked her hair, kissed her forehead. "Kitty. I'm so sorry. This has been so awful. I've been so insensitive to you. I'm here. I'm here. We are bigger than this and we can stay above it."

"But you didn't." She glanced at that pin, gasped into his

lapels, hung on to them, again not knowing whether to thrash him or to pull him inside of her. Finally, she pulled away enough so that she could drill into his soul.

"You voted yes," she said. "Because they made you. Tell me that they threatened to beat you. To beat me? To deport your American wife. Anything."

"Kitty, what—?"

"Or are you...? Are you with *them*?"

For a sheer second, something clouded those blue-green eyes. She recognized that it was the instinct to protect himself. But in the next moment, they were clear, somber. Deferential.

"Had I known that was what was bothering you all these weeks..." he said. "No, I should have asked. I should have been more considerate."

"I want to know," Kitty interrupted. "Are you with them? It's a simple yes or no answer."

Edgar winced. "Nothing is simple about this, Kitty. Nothing."

"Edgar!"

"There is no yes or no."

"Damn you!" She shoved him away from her. "You're dead! You're playing dead! Wake up! Fight! Flee! I don't care, but don't you dare just lay down and play dead!"

Edgar stalked away from her but not before she recognized the torture in his eyes. She had hurt him. Mortally impaled him, perhaps. Was it fair of her to kick someone who was already down? Like she'd seen those Brown Shirts do to an old man on the sidewalk?

At the bar, Edgar poured two generous tumblers of whiskey, added ice to hers. It was going to be worse than she'd thought. The glass tinkled as he handed it to her. She raised her glass— eyes still locked on his—and drank.

He sat down on the sofa. She took the chaise longue across

from him, folded her legs beneath her. She shivered although the room was warm.

"All right," she said. "Tell me."

"What is there to tell? I'm a coward. You're right. I submitted." He took a deep swallow.

That couldn't be all. She felt sick.

"I told you I'd be apologizing to you a thousand times, until you believed how sincere I am."

"About what?" Kitty said slowly. "That you're a sincere *Nazi*?"

She hadn't noticed that she was shaking her head, as if she was having a seizure. It could not be true. But then she realized she had to believe it. It had been right in front of her all this time. The wedding. His father. His mother. The things they said. Even Margit. But most especially, the people at their wedding. The caliber of the people at her wedding. They were likely the ones leading this race to the finish line.

"Not a sincere Nazi," she said suddenly. "A secret one. Is this your great day of glory? You were lying to me when you said you were helping Chancellor Schuschnigg to keep Germany out."

"I did not lie to you, Kitty," Edgar said. "I never lied to you." And his voice was so different. He was warning her.

She burst out laughing, the terror rising. "Who *are* you? I don't know you!"

He stood up.

She did too.

He took a step to her. "You know me, Kitty. You do."

She backed away, gaping at him. "Nils warned me. He warned me. Does my brother know what you are?" She doubled over with the realization. "Of course he does. What was it that you and Nils fought about, Edgar? In Tokyo? What was that all about?"

Edgar said nothing.

"Seyss-Inquart," she accused. "Is he one of your friends? Did you help him when he raised his rebellion back in thirty-four?"

Edgar raised his palms. "Kitty, it's not what you think..."

"Not what I think?" she shouted. "What should I think, Edgar? Who's telling the truth here?"

He suddenly spun to the couch, sank onto it, head in his hands. When he looked up at her, tears were rolling down his face. He jabbed a finger towards the window. "In Tokyo, Nils told me that one of the Department of State officials had sent a cable that quite literally..." He was indignant. "Everyone in Roosevelt's administration ignored. You put good people out here, who wrote good reports, and they got completely ignored."

"What, Edgar? What did we ignore?"

"The fact that the Nazi party was growing in Austria. Hidden underground. Everyone believed after the NSDAP was banned that membership dropped to about twenty percent again. It was growing, Kitty. All this time, it was growing."

He slammed his glass on the table. "Nils and I were fighting about you."

"Why?"

"Because he didn't want us to fall in love. He didn't want you here, in Vienna. But I promised..." Edgar looked pleadingly at her. "We have to survive this, Kitty. We have to. I promised we would. You and I both saw it coming. You knew it in Tokyo. You knew it. That's why I was so confident that we could make a good team."

"We're not a team! I'm not a Nazi!"

"And neither am I!"

Kitty yanked her hands through her hair. They stared at one another, Edgar's chest rose and fell.

He rubbed his head. "I'm not, I promise you. But my father..." He threw his arms into the air. "He definitely is. And has been. It's one of the reasons I went to France, and then to

England. To get away from him, to just be..." He drew in a shaky breath. "And no, I don't want this for Austria."

"Ostmark," Kitty bit. "It's *verdammtes Ostmark* now. You have people like your father to thank and..." She strode out to the telephone console, grabbed the pin and threw it at him. It was too damned small to give her any satisfaction.

He looked forlornly at it. "I'm no hero, Kitty. I'm not the kind of hero that Hollywood is so good at creating. I don't make noise, I don't go out into the streets and scream at the injustice of it all, and shoot up the bad guys. I don't rock the boat—"

"You love that expression," Kitty muttered.

Edgar flushed, pressed the heels of his hands to his eyes. When he released them, the rims were red. "You Americans worship your heroes. But heroes here? They get murdered. They get sent to detention camps. Prison. Or just disappear. We read about them after the fact."

Kitty felt sick to her stomach. *Captain Wallace reports... Captain Wallace acknowledges that Agent X never appeared. Captain Wallace warns that all assets are in danger. Agent Y seized by Gestapo.*

"If we comply..." Kitty gritted her teeth. "We're nothing but cowards. We've got blood on our hands. We know what is wrong. Edgar, we know what is wrong and we know what is right. I still believe that much about you."

Head hanging between his shoulders, Edgar lifted his whiskey glass and took a long drink. "I'm just a man," he whispered. "I'm just someone who is trying to do his best... by his wife. By the woman he loves."

Kitty went to the couch. She slowly got down on her knees. They were silent for a very long time.

"Edgar, no marriage can survive secrecy. Or lying. This mistrust is going to kill us."

Her husband slid down onto the floor next to her. He reached for her. She cradled his head in her lap.

"Can you forgive me?" The emotion was thick in his throat. "I'm going to be the best man possible in this *scheiß Situation*. I'm going to try."

She stroked his hair, and when he looked up at her, she saw sincere pain and remorse but the damage had been done.

"I don't know," she whispered. "Forgive? Maybe. But forget?"

She had sat quiet for far too long. She should have met Edgar head-on earlier. Sam was wrong. Sometimes playing dead, lying in wait until the danger passed, was not the best ploy. She and Edgar were going to have to fight for what they had.

15

MAY 1938

The Nazi pogroms escalated when it was announced that the *Blutschützgesetz*—the laws protecting German blood—were to take effect in Ostmark.

The revolt against the Jews broke wide open. Kitty now understood that the secret NSDAP members had simply been cloaked under various political party names and the protection that old-family aristocracy afforded. These secreted Nazis were now rising to the top as those they brutalized fled into hiding in a cruel twist of fate.

Wrestling with her own conscience was exhausting. Edgar justified his work by saying the only way he would possibly help put Austria on the right course was to do it from the inside. But Kitty would have to tell Cooper; she would have to ask whether her position at the general consulate was not a conflict of interest. She was afraid to. Cooper had been delegating more responsibility to her, proven that he trusted her. Had anything really changed, she asked herself.

She kept putting off telling her boss, while realizing that, if she did not talk to him then she was more like Edgar than she cared to admit.

One Friday, Kitty was listening to Herr Markowitz, the owner of a small electronic parts store. The authorities had seized first his business, then his home. For his troubles, they broke his leg and smashed his left ear. He was a humble man, and Kitty wanted desperately to help him. Herr Markowitz was in his sixties with salted gray hair and sad eyes. She was helping him down the stairs of the consulate when one of the guards called to her and met her halfway.

"There's a Judith Liebherr insisting on seeing you," he said. "I told her she has to wait in line with the others."

Kitty's heart leaped into her throat. "No. She should come to the office. Let her through, please. And could you help Herr Markowitz to the door? His wife is waiting outside."

The guard did as she asked and Judith appeared, looking anxious.

They embraced, but Judith was stiff.

"What's happened?"

"I came to bring you Oskar's affidavit," Judith said. "But he won't leave without Artur. And Artur refuses to think about it. His mother is elderly and he will not abandon her."

Kitty put an arm around her friend. "We'll figure something out. I'll file Oskar's affidavit with your documents and then you can be processed together when your interview comes up. Maybe Artur will have changed his mind by then."

But Judith was trembling now. "There's something else. Those SA hoodlums broke into my studio and ransacked it."

"*Verdammte Scheiße*," Kitty cried. "Are you all right?"

"Besides my broken heart? There's graffiti everywhere. They ruined my space. Tore up hundreds and hundreds of Reichsmarks worth of fabric. My drawings. I don't feel safe going back..."

"No, of course not. Where's Macke?" Kitty feared for the dog. Out on the streets, the Brown Shirts were kicking and beating humans, but they shot the dogs.

"With Bella," Judith said.

Kitty looked up the stairwell. "Come on, let's get this taken care of."

When they walked in, Millie had a receiver pressed to her ear, but she smiled and waved at Judith then at Kitty and pointed to Cooper's door.

"They're in there," she whispered loudly. "Morris and Cooper, Geist and Kendrick."

"Thomas Kendrick?"

"Something big is going on."

Kitty sighed and led Judith to the leather couch and asked her to wait. Millie hung up and came over, and Kitty told her about Judith's situation. Pulling Judith into her arms, Millie soothed in that East Coast accent before looking up angrily at Kitty.

"We could file a report," she said.

But Judith scoffed furiously. "With whom? It's a lawless country now."

Kitty bit her lip to check her own building fury. She then handed Millie Oskar's letter from America.

"Find Judith's file, would you? Add this to it. It's Oskar's."

Millie looked at it then at Kitty.

"I know," Kitty said quietly. "We're not playing favorites. We're just putting son and mother together, that's all."

Millie stood up and headed for the overstuffed filing cabinets.

Suddenly Cooper called Kitty from his doorway. He looked rattled. "Can you get in here?"

Kitty grabbed her steno pad and a couple of pencils. As Millie had said, the U.S. ambassador from Berlin, Raymond Geist, was inside and she shook his hand.

Seated near the window was Thomas Kendrick. He towered over her as he grasped her hand next. After greeting the rest of the men, she took her position at the other side of Cooper's desk.

"Go ahead, George," Cooper said to the speaker and Messersmith's voice came through.

"As I was saying, the president won't go to Evian, France, unless the Brits are there. Look, the public's sentiment about the Jews is like this. We've got a troubled economy, there's a general attitude against immigration, and the public complains about there being too many Jews already. Changing immigration policies right now would be self-destructive."

"Let me get this straight," Kitty interrupted Messersmith. She spoke fast, still furious about the attack on Judith. "You're all thinking about your careers at the cost of men, women and children being brutalized at the hands of Nazis? Is that what I'm supposed to write in this protocol?"

Everyone in the room turned their heads and stared at her. There was static on the line.

"Who was that?" Messersmith suddenly snapped.

Cooper landed on her with a hard look. "Arne Larsson's daughter."

Messersmith cleared his throat, said something ungentlemanly but Kitty was reading Cooper's angry words as he mouthed, "One more time," and pointed at the door.

Across from her, Kendrick was watching her with interest. He leaned closer to Cooper's desk—to the phone—his eye still on her. "She's not wrong... The way I see it, the British have the same hang-ups. But what Mrs. Ragatz has to understand is that everyone is awfully tired of war. Chamberlain is holding out—"

"Wrongfully so," Kitty muttered. "Look at the Sudetenland."

Cooper clapped his hands together once and bowed dangerously towards her, as if he were shooing away a cat. Kitty gestured that she was buttoning her lips.

Kendrick had a half smile. "Both of our countries are

dealing with restrictionist policies that are making us into the world's most skilled experts in misery."

Grateful for his gesture, Kitty copied down everything, underlining *the world's most skilled experts in misery.*

Cooper pushed himself away from the desk and circled it, directing his voice to the phone but looking at Leland Morris. "Leland has had to use the LPC clause quite a bit recently." LPCs were those candidates who were likely to become a personal charge of the state. "But George, we're not overfilling the quota. Not at all. We are simply *filling* it."

Kitty suddenly understood what this conversation was about. When Messersmith ran the American embassy in Berlin, the officers only approved about ten percent of the allotted number of visas. Cooper had told her that. Now Cooper was getting flack for meeting the quota one hundred percent. Each month.

"George, Berlin is recommending that we relax the restrictions around the LPC cases," Raymond Geist now said. "And we need our allies to take this situation very seriously. They must be convinced that increasing their immigration quotas is the right way to go. Or these people will be stranded in a theater of violence."

Kitty was about to open her mouth again, tell them about Judith, but Cooper shot her a warning look before addressing the whole group.

"Perhaps it is advisable at this point to ask ourselves what the real objective of the present immigration laws of our country are," Cooper said. "Is it to preserve our liberal attitude on immigration and at the same time adequately protect the interests of our country and people? Or is it not to prevent what I can only see as potential genocide."

"I think that's going over the top," Morris argued. Kitty glared at her pad as he continued. "The object is not, as some interpret it, to maintain the United States as an asylum or refuge for the dissatisfied and oppressed in other parts of the world. The laws' objective is not, as some interpret it, to keep out certain classes of persons on account of their race, religion or political ideas."

Grinding her teeth, Kitty paused in her writing and glared at him. He frowned at her.

Back in D.C., Messersmith raised his voice over the phone. "Leland is correct. The objects of our immigration laws and practice are set forth in the immigration statutes, John."

Cooper looked chastened as the assistant secretary of state continued. "It is not the job of any foreign service officer—you included—to read your own ideas into the law or to impose those ideas into actual visa practice. And until our leaders can sit down at one table—in Evian, for example, as has been suggested—then nothing changes. The United States is not an asylum. A visa is a privilege, not a right."

Cooper, deflated, glanced at the group, then at Kendrick, who held up his hands in surrender. He looked dolefully at Morris. "Understood, sir."

"Is there anything else?" Messersmith asked.

"I put in a request for a reimbursement for the staff's salaries that I've had to hire," Cooper dared. He pulled out a cigarette and lit it.

"John," Messersmith warned, "we've been through this before. You cannot possibly expect me to reward you for going against the department's orders."

Cooper propped his glasses on top of his head, and rubbed his eyes. "Yes, sir. I understand."

"Mr. Kendrick?" Messersmith called. "Our only hope now is that the leaders of the free world decide to change their policies together. Can we count on you to get Chamberlain to Switzerland?"

The Brit leaned forward. "I promise I will do all I can."

"Good. And good day, gentlemen. Oh, and John?"

"Yes, sir?"

"Your transfer in July has nothing to do with this."

Kitty looked up in alarm. Cooper was being transferred? Morris exchanged a look with Cooper and she knew. Morris would be replacing him.

"Of course not, sir." Cooper pushed the button on the speaker box and sighed.

"Well, you heard it here, folks." Cooper put his hands on his hips. "The Department of State incurred such expenses while entertaining the Queen and King of England in the U.S., there are no funds available for the salaries of our personnel."

Nobody cracked a smile. Raymond Geist scratched his head and looked at Cooper.

"Are you going to tell them? Or do I have to?"

Kitty looked at her boss, anticipating the details of the bad news. His expression turned sour.

"Tell us what?" Morris asked. "That you're being assigned to Latvia?"

Geist rested his folded arms on his belly. "The reason I'm in Vienna is to deal with the increase of attacks on American citizens, and John here was nearly one of them yesterday."

"What happened?" Kitty asked.

Cooper stubbed out his cigarette, exhaling noisily. "We were on the Prater Golf Course, and two stormtroopers accosted us. They wanted to know whether I was a Jew. I told them I was the chargé d'affaires at the U.S. General Consulate."

Geist forged ahead, "The patrol said that wasn't his question. Was John a Jew, was what he wanted to know."

Kendrick shook his head and muttered something.

Morris looked from Geist to Cooper. "What did you say?"

"He didn't," Geist said. "This guy's superior didn't even try to stop that little sh—" He glanced at Kitty. "Moron. It was as if he was testing his goon out or something. Of course Cooper isn't a Jew, but the kid wanted proof. Then one of the golfers—" He turned to Kendrick. "You know him."

The Brit raised an eyebrow. "Our favorite Gerry from the Abwehr?"

"That's the one," Geist confirmed. "He comes marching across the green and asks what's going on, accuses them of bad theater. He yells at the two Nazi numbskulls and assures them that Cooper wouldn't be playing golf if he were a Jew."

Morris chuckled and Kitty glared at him. It was not a joke. She'd had enough.

"Judith Liebherr is out there." She pointed to the door. "The Nazis ransacked her office. Tore up her sketches. Ruined her fabrics and her dresses."

Morris looked at her with such contempt it made Kitty freeze for a second. He waved at Cooper as if to ask him to shut her up, but Cooper ignored him.

She was relieved when he asked, "Who is Judith Liebherr?"

"A fashion designer. She designed my wedding dress. She's a friend. To me, and to Millie."

"And?" Morris asked, irritated.

"She's scared. Her application is one of thousands that are ready to go. All she needs is—"

"She waits in line like everyone else," Morris snapped.

"We're still trying to process interviews and time is running out," Kitty argued.

Morris pointed a finger at her. "If you were my secretary, I'd fire you right now. You are way out of line, young lady."

"Leland, come on," Geist said. "She's got a right to have her say, too. We're all on the same side."

Morris scowled but retreated.

Cooper sighed and sat down behind his desk. "Kitty is right. We have to get our countries to change something."

Kendrick uncrossed his legs and started to get up. "Right. I'll get on it. I'll do my best to convince Chamberlain to go to

Evian." He turned to Kitty. "It's good to see you, Mrs. Ragatz. Please pass along my greetings to your husband."

Kendrick looked back at the men in the room. "Let's hope our leaders do the right thing in Switzerland."

Concerned about Judith, Kitty strode over to the couch.

"How are you doing?"

Judith's hand fluttered to her throat. "I'll be... I don't know."

"Give me a minute, OK?"

"And?" Kitty asked Millie quietly. "Did you find Judith's file?"

Millie looked pale. "I did. But her affidavit isn't in there."

"What do you mean it's not in there? I made the file myself." Kitty grabbed the manila folder from Millie's hand and opened it, flipping through the clipped documents. "Come on. Come on..."

But the affidavit was not in the folder.

She glanced at Judith on the couch, then the folder. "This can't be," she muttered. "Look, the box is ticked. It arrived two weeks ago."

"Do you think it got filed elsewhere?" Millie suggested.

Kitty groaned at the row of cabinets and drawers. If it had fallen out, or got ripped out, and put elsewhere, it could be anywhere in those thousands and thousands of files.

She handed Millie the folder back. "Find it. Please."

She crossed the room to tell Judith the bad news and glanced over at Cooper, who was heading to her desk with what looked like more work. He looked as if he was about to call her back.

She should go and talk to him, she thought, but it didn't matter anymore if she told Cooper about Edgar or her potential conflict of interest. Morris would have her demoted or fired as soon as he took the helm. In the meantime, she was going to do what Cooper had set out to do and treat the victims with some human decency.

Kitty pointed to Judith.

"One hour," he called.

She smiled, relieved. "Right," Kitty said to Judith, "let's go for a walk. Take me to the gang."

16

MAY 1938

Kitty followed Judith through Floridsdorf, an industrial district in the northernmost part of Vienna. After Judith and she had walked for quite some time, her friend stopped at a long building with cans, wires and old rusted metal tables stacked neatly in the yard.

"Where are we?" Kitty whispered. The situation seemed to warrant silence and stealth.

"This was one of Big Charlie's places of work. He knew the owner pretty well before it shut down."

"One from his fan club?" Kitty asked, referring to the gang's inside joke that nearly the entire city used to be the wrestler's fan club.

Judith smiled sadly before producing a key ring. "It's a prime spot because there's a direct connection to the sewage tunnels."

"You mean the water system below the city?"

"That's right." Judith shut the door behind them and led Kitty through what had to have once been a production hall but was now empty. Only the marks left on the floor indicated that machinery had once been here. Painted stripes designated safety zones and walking zones. The industrial lamps above were turned off. The air was still.

They reached another heavy door at the back of the hall. There was an *Achtung!* sticker on it with a lightning bolt. Lights flicked and buzzed on when Judith flipped a switch. Stairs led into a cellar and Kitty followed her friend down another long corridor. Pipes clanged above their heads. It was cooler down here and dank. Another set of stairs. Another level deeper.

"When you said underground," Kitty muttered, "I didn't think you meant... literally."

Judith chose another key from the bundle she was carrying, unlocked a third heavy door and Kitty was blasted by stale cigarette smoke. Two lamps glowed above a motionless conveyor belt. Bottles of liquor, glasses, shakers and beer taps were on top. Was this a bar? There were tables and chairs arranged around a small platform with a microphone on it and a curtain behind it.

Kitty looked around, astonished. "Oskar moved Der Keller here?"

"I most certainly did," a voice said from behind that stage curtain.

Turning towards it, Kitty was already opening her arms to Judith's son. His dark hair was a little longer than the last time she had seen him; his eyes—big and warm like Judith's—squinted with pleasure as he took Kitty into his arms.

Oskar was one of her favorite people in the gang. There was something almost ethereal about him; it made him strong and fragile all at once. She kissed both his cheeks and squeezed him tighter.

"You needed that," she whispered in his ear. "And I can give you that."

Oskar's contemplative smile spread slowly across his face. He swept his arms over the room, encompassing what was left of his once very successful establishment. It was a sad gesture.

"The Gestapo stormed into Der Keller a few weeks ago," Oskar said. "They arrested and interrogated me. Threw the rest of my people and patrons out onto the street. Artur ran, bless him. He was able to escape. But they shut us down."

Just then Artur sidled out from behind a beaded curtain to the left of the stage followed by Hannes and Max, the two little street kids who brought him cigarettes. With one stuck in the corner of his mouth, Artur was dressed as Agnes in a long-sleeved blue gown sans the makeup and the Marlene Dietrich wig. Kitty had never seen him without either. He was half bald with short gray-brown hair around the crown.

Artur led the boys to the heavy door, holding a small cloth sack in his hand, and dropped a single coin into Max's hand.

"Is that all?" the boy complained.

Hands on his hips, the half-clad drag queen lifted the scanty sack as if it were obvious why.

Hannes stuck out his bottom lip, his big hazel eyes wide and his nose running. Artur fished out a handkerchief from the sleeve of his gown, and wiped it as well as a black streak from the boy's cheek.

He then turned back to Max. "Next time, I expect you two to go further than just around the corner if you want more money."

"Or go and sell your stolen coal to the Brown Shirts out on the streets," Oskar called. "See how far that gets you."

Dejected, the boys turned to go.

Oskar looked after them in exasperation. "Are they lazy or what?"

Artur chuckled. "They're kids."

"You imported the little street urchins," Kitty said after hugging him.

Oskar smirked. "Artur won't cut them loose. He thinks they're his."

"Where are Khan and Big Charlie?" Artur asked.

"They're at my studio, helping to clean up," Judith said, and then had to share the news about how the Nazi thugs had destroyed her studio.

Artur banged the table with a fist, then rubbed his face and lit another cigarette. Oskar sank into a seat at the nearest table, pulling his mother down next to him.

"What now?" Judith begged.

Kitty took her hand and grabbed Artur's to her left. "I'm going to help you all get out of Vienna. All of you. In six to eight weeks, you can get your visas. I've just put Oskar's affidavit on file. All we need to do is find Judith's. It's only been misplaced, but Millie is looking for it."

Oskar frowned. "Misplaced?"

"We'll get it settled," Judith assured him, and completed the circle by grasping his arm.

They sat like that for a while, the entire table holding on to one another, and Kitty looked at Artur pointedly.

"And you," she said. "I just need an affidavit, Artur."

He shook his head. "My mother is ill. I'm not leaving her alone."

Oskar let go of Judith and put an arm around his lover's shoulder. "Where he goes, I go."

"Judith, say something," Kitty urged.

Artur reached across the table for her. "We're Jews, and we're homosexual, darling. There are no hooks for our kinds of hats." He looked at Oskar. "There is no other place for us to go."

"That's not true," Kitty said, and he gave her a look as if he pitied her. "What about Paris? Oskar?"

Oskar shook his head sadly. "It's Frau Horváth, Artur's mother, who's important here. America is a pipe dream. Even England is impossible. The more time that passes, the tighter the Nazis are going to control who goes in and who goes out. My name is already in the Gestapo files. This club is all we've got left."

Judith slumped back into her chair. "Then if you stay, I stay."

"No, Mother. You're going to New York. Just until it's safe to come back," Oskar said. "And we're going to do like Big Charlie and Khan said. We're going to fight back."

"How do you mean?" Kitty asked.

Artur and Oskar shared another look before Artur answered, "Sabotage. Getting organized and recruiting help. We want to print leaflets, pamphlets, the like."

Judith smiled sadly at Kitty. "I asked for it, didn't I? I'm the one who wanted to know why nobody was resisting. Now, here they are, talking about resisting."

Kitty felt a rush of adrenaline. "Is there a way I can help?"

Oskar's eyes flashed brightly. Judith looked surprised. Artur sat back and folded his arms, one eyebrow raised and one side of his mouth in a smirk.

"If you're offering, we're taking it," Oskar said.

Kitty bit her lip. "Should I talk to Millie? We can trust her with our lives."

Oskar nodded slowly then leaped from his seat and came over, putting his arms around her neck and kissing the top of her head. "I love you, Kitty. You might be our little stray cat, but you throw the shadow of a lioness."

On her way back to the office, Kitty regretted speaking so quickly. Cooper was leaving. Her position was precarious as it was. And if she worked to help the gang, it would be one more thing she was doing behind Edgar's back. She already kept a lot from her husband as it was. Their relationship, their friendship, their intimacy was suffering because of it.

Since the wedding, she had shared very little with him about the gang. Save for Millie, he never asked about them. She believed he had forgotten that Judith and Khan even existed.

And wasn't that what the Nazis wanted to do as well? Get rid of exactly these kinds of people? The Big Charlies and Khans, the Oskars and Arturs of Ostmark?

With renewed courage, she decided she would just have to determine what her role would be. Not only at the consulate, but in helping to resist the regime. She invited Millie out for a drink after work and they headed to the tavern across the street where Kitty told her all about Cooper's meeting.

"Cooper made the mistake of putting his political position first," Millie said.

"What do you mean?" Kitty asked.

"He did everything not to appear overly sympathetic or benevolent. Or he'd never come up for the prime position he's getting."

Kitty disagreed. "He never feared criticism for doing the right thing by the people."

Millie shrugged. "I thought he was very stringent about implementing the immigration policies."

Now she knew how she might test Millie's openness to a fledgling resistance effort. "Cooper knows how to bend the rules without breaking them. If it were up to me, I'd be breaking them one after the other, as far as they go. You know what I mean?"

Millie tilted her head. "If Morris couldn't do it, Messersmith and Geist would rein you right back in."

"I'd like to see them try," Kitty said.

"Me, too," Millie laughed. She sipped her wine.

"I think Cooper's way is better." Kitty looked curiously at her. "What about you? Would you bend the rules?"

Millie placed her glass back on the table and studied Kitty. "You were with Judith today. And the gang?"

Kitty nodded.

"Uh-huh," Millie said. "Anything I should know?"

Kitty leaned forward and Millie mirrored her. "It's only an idea."

"Do tell," Millie whispered. "My lips are sealed."

Kitty's mind was reeling all that night and the next morning. She had nearly forgotten about Cooper and was surprised to see him standing at her desk.

He waved her to his office. "Got some time for me?"

She shut the door behind them, and Cooper rested his glasses on top of his head after sitting down. His finger briefly tapped a file on his desk then he lit a cigarette and peered at her. Her heart soared. Had he found Judith's affidavit? Was that her file?

"So," Cooper exhaled. "What are we going to do with you?"

Kitty swallowed. It was not her fault the files were such a mess. Not hers alone, anyway.

"Yesterday didn't go very well with Morris, did it?" he asked.

She wilted. This wasn't about Judith, it was about the call with D.C. "No, sir. It did not."

Cooper smirked. "You've got..." He seemed to catch himself, and smiled slyly at the file. "You've got what it takes, Kitty."

"Sir?"

He pushed the folder forward just a little. It was her personnel file. "I'm not going to beat around the bush. You're not cut out to be Leland Morris's assistant. He doesn't want you, you understand?"

Kitty nodded.

"So, what I've done is put a recommendation in for a new department. You're familiar with Captain Wallace?"

"Of course, sir."

"Anyway, the British are trying to make a concerted effort with the U.S. to share intelligence. I put your name in for heading a new secretarial pool with a group of our agents. You'll be setting up a new office downstairs to analyze intelligence. You can even choose the girls you want to help. You'll be responsible for preparing messages, recovering and intercepting messages from couriers, and getting information to those who need to know. How does that sound?"

"Incredible, sir," Kitty muttered.

She had to tell him about Edgar, though. Her husband was now a diplomat and legal adviser to the reorganized German Foreign Office in Vienna. Edgar was involved in policy. He had his finger in every pie. Surely the Consulate would question whether she should be working in such an important position with such a husband.

"I can't promise you anything," Cooper said, mistaking her debate with herself for shock. "You have my highest recommendation, though."

Kitty breathed more easily. She had a little time. She could still turn the job down. But if she did, she would be out of a job, period. Morris would never keep her on. And espionage was even better than the foreign service office. If she could ever accept it. If she was even offered the position.

"Thank you," Kitty said. "Thank you very much for your trust in me."

Cooper eyed her for a moment. "It's the best I can do."

"I understand."

Cooper came around and placed a friendly hand on her shoulder. "You keep your head down a bit more. OK? Stir the pot, but don't do it when others are looking."

She should tell him. If he found out about Edgar through a different source, he'd be disappointed. "May I tell you something?"

Cooper stepped back behind his desk. "I know you're disappointed in me—"

"No, sir. I'm not."

"Yes, you are. But I hope one day you will understand." He

turned in his seat and retrieved something from the console behind his desk. He dropped it in front of her. It was the latest issue of *The American Foreign Service Journal.*

"I just read that your brother, Nils, has been assigned to London."

Kitty nodded. "He's moving up in the world."

Cooper eyed her. "As will you, Kitty, I have no doubt. Just don't mess things up for yourself. OK?"

Feeling guilty, all she could do was nod.

Three weeks later, Cooper was gone. The tide of violence against the Jews continued to rise. Those who were looking to escape flooded the embassy—and then one day disappeared altogether. Morris got rid of Cooper's volunteers and part-time staff and began changing the processing system.

Meanwhile, in Millie's and Kitty's searches for Judith's affidavit, nothing came up. And when the results of the conference in Switzerland appeared in the papers, Kitty was angry that not one country had offered to raise their immigration quotas or make new policies.

Her fury grew when the Nazis published the results in the *Volkszeitung,* jeering about the fact that the world was not interested in intervening for the Jews in Austria and Germany.

When a couple of weeks later, Morris called her into his office and said that Agent Benjamin Roberts was prepared to make Kitty the new head of his analysis pool, she took the job without blinking.

She knew it was her only chance to protect the gang.

17

AUGUST 1938

The diplomatic pouch arrived on Kitty's desk on a hot August day. Her supervisor, Agent Roberts, handed it to her unsealed.

"You'll need to make two carbon copies. One goes to Mr. Morris upstairs."

Kitty nodded and withdrew the report. It was from British intelligence. Captain Wallace was back with more news.

Asset Pim claims Adolf Eichmann will be made head of Ostmark's *Zentralstelle für jüdische Auswanderung* (Central Office for Jewish Immigration) with headquarters in Vienna. As in Germany, expect all Jews to be processed through this department. Pim says all current documentation could be rejected and Jews forced to renew their application process. Expect confiscation of Jewish property and further barricades for obtaining visas from friendly countries. Pim also has knowledge that Eichmann is moving to Vienna within days. Location is same building as Fireman's residence. Notify Fireman.

Kitty looked up from the message. "Fireman" was Leland

Morris. Kitty knew enough about Eichmann that the idea of him living right next door to the U.S. general consul was more than a little uncomfortable.

She looked at the message again—*Pim has certain knowledge that Eichmann moving to Vienna within days*—and turned to Millie. It had cost Kitty nearly all of her energy, but she had extracted her from the pool by finding a superb secretary that Morris could not say no to.

"Who is this new spy, Pim?"

Millie tapped the eraser side of her pencil against her teeth before waving it. "Wait, Pim's come up a few times. We got that list not too long ago, remember? Pim's either a German or an Austrian informant, I can't remember which. But Captain Wallace seems to trust him implicitly."

Kitty was impressed. Signs were cropping up that there were plenty of nationals finding ways to resist the Nazi regime. "Then I say Herr Pim shares hero-of-the-week status together with Captain Wallace."

Adolf Eichmann would be a big fish to fry for them. He was not an unknown personality. Anticipating that Germany would give him the task of overseeing the expulsion of Austria's Jews, Kitty had already started a file on him. She made a copy of the message, went to the cabinet and found it, reviewing her notes.

Otto Adolf Eichmann, a German-Austrian, poor at school. Joined the Nazi party in 1927 and became a member of the SS in 1932, then the SD a year later. Tasked with handling all Jewish affairs and their emigration from Germany.

Kitty inserted the brief. Now Eichmann was on his way to Vienna.

She wondered whether Captain Kendrick had already received word, though it was quite likely. To the British expat, Eichmann would present another obstacle to helping relocate

Jews. She would ask Roberts whether she should send a copy to him as well.

In the meantime, the changes Morris implemented at the American consulate had created a more massive bottleneck. Fifteen thousand Viennese had submitted their applications in the last month alone, so Morris had decided to file all new registrations according to the application day instead of creating a file for each applicant.

Severely understaffed again, the FSOs were still processing all the pre-July registrations which meant they would not be able to deal with the new cases for at least two years. Worse yet, although Judith's interview was up, neither Kitty nor Millie had found her affidavit. Judith immediately sent word to her contacts in New York, requesting they send a new one—another delay that taxed Kitty's low reserve of nerves.

She closed Eichmann's file, took the second carbon copy of the message and winked at Millie.

"Going to go see my favorite guy," she said.

Millie pulled a face. "You want me to do it?"

Kitty shook her head. "I've got this."

The trouble with espionage, she was learning, was that for every report of intel they received, there was intel passed along in the opposite direction. The Gestapo, known for its intimidation but not for its savviness in collecting intelligence, did not stop trying to get closer to their fringes.

She and Millie were doing something similar. They had agreed with the gang that no top secret information would be shared. But something like this, about Eichmann setting up an immigration office in Vienna, she not only would share, but felt obliged to do so.

Kitty had been cautious since joining the intel analysis department. Edgar knew nothing about her new job. He thought she was still working for the FSOs upstairs. But he had noticed changes in her and remarked on them.

"You look like the cat who's swallowed the canary," he'd said one day, startling her. Another time he said she was glowing, then blurted, "Are you perhaps pregnant?"

She wasn't. And she did not want to be. Not if she could help it, and not here, in Vienna. She was feeling the ramifications of keeping secrets from him. Gone were the days where they completed each other's sentences, shared their thoughts, or even read to each other. Inevitably, one or the other would touch on a sore subject, and Kitty was frustrated by the ramifications. It was as if Edgar was hoping for another regime change so they could repair their marriage. She feared they would reach a point of no return. Then what?

It was easier to be swept away by the business of gathering intelligence on the Nazis, and the intrigues of espionage. More than once, she'd asked herself whether Khan, or Big Charlie, or even Judith would be capable of clandestine work. Could someone like Captain Wallace help the gang perhaps? Or someone like this new asset, Pim?

Upstairs, she relayed the message about Eichmann to Morris.

He read it, folded it and stuck it into a drawer in his desk. "You can tell Wallace to consider it done. No need to have Eichmann watched. I'll keep my eye on him."

"Very well, sir."

And Eichmann most certainly will have his eye on you, Kitty thought.

18

AUGUST 1938

In August, when all the businesses in Austria slowed down for the summer, Edgar and Kitty were practically forced to spend time in close quarters. She suggested a change of scenery. His most creative option was to take a week off at the Vienna Woods cottage.

"Just in case I have to go back to the office."

That suited Kitty just fine. She did not want to be far away from the gang, or from the intelligence department either. It surprised her how happy she was to potter about in the new vegetable patch her in-laws had given in to, and to put the last touches on the new landscape at the front of the house. In the former grain storage, she'd found a couple of usable tables and chairs she quickly refurbished and placed beneath the chestnut tree.

After overcoming a few awkward silences, Edgar and she were discovering that, away from the immediate confrontations on the streets and the papers, they still very much enjoyed one another's company and began choreographing a careful dance around their issues.

On one such morning, as they lingered over breakfast, Jerzy

appeared, bringing that week's newspapers. Kitty wrinkled her nose at the sight of the *Volkszeitung*. It was filled with Nazi propaganda under the guise of investigative journalism. Virtually every page was covered in photos detailing the Reich's road to becoming the absolute superpower. Irritably, she was about to hand it over to Edgar when a photo caught her attention. That profile, that figure, that jutting upper lip. Captain Thomas Kendrick.

Shocked, she unfolded the paper and gaped at the headline.

"What is it?" Edgar put down his egg spoon and leaned in.

"The Gestapo arrested Kendrick," Kitty said with disbelief. She turned the paper so he could see.

Her husband rose and read over her shoulder. She looked up at him in shock. There was something rippling over Edgar's face. Surprise? Disgust? She couldn't really tell. She turned back to the article as Edgar held the edges and they read together. Astonished, Kitty clamped a hand over her mouth.

Arrested on charges of espionage in Freilassing, Bavaria, the British officer was transferred by the security services to the Gestapo headquarters at the Hotel Metropole in Vienna. Captain Thomas Kendrick is a well-known British expat, who allegedly operated under the name of "Captain Wallace". At the behest of the German authorities and after delicate negotiations with the British, Kendrick will be expelled from Ostmark. The SD and the SS have confirmed that Herr Kendrick's complete espionage ring has been uncovered and further arrests will be made.

Kitty had to shake herself from the cold chills racing over her back and arms. All those assets! And relatively new ones, like Pim. But she had to make a cover story.

"You... know him," she said, the fear plain as day in her

voice. She hoped he would read it as shock. "He was at our wedding... Edgar..."

Mumbling that he knew, Edgar took the paper from her and dropped into his seat. "I had dealings with him over the department." He lowered it and looked at her. "I first met him at Oxford when I was there. That's how I know him. But this is... rather shocking."

She desperately wanted to call the office, but how could she without giving away the fact that she knew about Captain Wallace? Then she remembered that Nils was in London. Surely he would know something.

Edgar folded the paper and placed it on the table. "The poor fool. You never really know a person, do you?"

Kitty looked away from him, distraught. The birds were singing much too brightly in the chestnut tree and a warm breeze lifted the edges of the front page.

"If you don't mind," she announced. "I think I will call my brother. Maybe Nils knows something about it."

Edgar frowned. "Right. Do that."

But Nils was tight-lipped on the phone. "Kitty, I only know what the media is reporting."

"Surely that can't be true. Is he going to be OK?" She wanted to ask whether Nils knew anything about how internal agents might be handled. Whether the charges would mean imprisonment. Death, perhaps. Again, she was thinking of the other assets, like Pim.

"You'll just have to wait and see." Nils sighed. "How's Edgar?"

"He's fine," Kitty said dismissively. "He was shocked but not nearly as much..." She couldn't say *as much as me*. She couldn't tell anyone or let on that she was involved in relaying intel reports. She'd signed a secrecy act.

"He's fine," she repeated, feeling ridiculous.

"Good. Tell Edgar to call me sometime."

Anxious, Kitty rang the Larsson mansion in St. Paul next, hoping to speak to her father, but a sleepy Sam told her he was on a fishing trip.

Then her mother came on the line. "*Chérie*, how are you?"

"Fine, Maman. I'm sorry I woke you all."

"But how are you, *really*?"

Kitty frowned and looked at the receiver in her hand before answering. "I'm OK, Maman."

"What do you need to be more than just OK?"

Jolted, tears sprang into Kitty's eyes. She pressed a hand beneath her ribs and collected herself. How was she to explain the events, the emotions, the positive turmoil that had impacted her life since the Anschluss?

"I think a glass of Burgundy is on the menu tonight," she tried. "That will certainly help matters."

To her surprise, Claudette laughed softly. "A good Burgundy does always help. Kitty, I know it's none of my business. It can't be. It is not my marriage. And I know you called to talk to your father, but it's me who is here now. I can only tell you this: there are always ups and downs. This is Edgar's and your test now. There are outside forces working against you, *ma fille. Le diable en personne.* The devil could break you. Or he could make you stronger. Hold on to your husband, Kitty. Weather this storm, darling. *Je t'adore.* I miss you, *chérie.* You are my favorite daughter, you know."

"I'm your only daughter, Maman," Kitty whispered, but the joke fell flat. She swiped a tear away and said what she really meant. "I love you."

For the rest of the weekend, she exerted herself to pretend things were normal, that a British expat's fate had little impact on her. But, as she passed by a mirror in the hallway one afternoon and looked at her reflection, she hardly recognized herself. Who was she becoming?

Her earlier belief that she and Edgar could feel and understand everything about one another, pick up on the slightest cues, and be of nearly one mind—all that had come to an end on the very day of the Anschluss. And now, with all her secrets building up, the idea terrified her. And it wasn't just her secrets.

It was the lying that bothered Kitty the most. The lies from the Department of State. The lies from the Nazis. The lies her husband told her to protect his work and them. The lies she had to tell to keep her secrets. As she stared at her reflection, she realized she had been dredged in all those lies. And even more were to come.

Something urged her to prevent it. She frowned at her reflection. Did she love Edgar enough to salvage what she could? There was only one way to find out.

On Sunday, she suggested they pack a picnic, saddle the roans, and ride out to one of the lakes. Edgar readily agreed and they rode hard, Kitty relishing the exhilaration and shedding her anger and her anxiety. Thrilled by the ride, and driven to a primitive lust, she made love to her husband in the long grass. It was loud, and they were desperately passionate. Afterwards, he tried to linger with her in his arms, the heat radiating around them, the buzz of the insects, the scents of late summer carried on the slight breeze from the lake. He caressed her bare arm with lazy, soft strokes, his eyes half-closed. But the gesture was too intimate. Too foreign.

Frustrated, she pulled away, knowing he sensed her rejection. "I need to go for a swim."

Naked, she walked to the bank of the lake and jumped in, the cool water sliding over her. She kicked further and harder, clearing her head. When she came up, Edgar was already in the water, his anticipation apparent. She floated on her back.

"You're distracted," he said.

"It's just something Claudette said," she lied.

"We're not to talk about it?"

She shook her head. He came closer. She fought the urge to

dive away again. He pulled her to him and they touched foreheads.

"This is changing us, Kitty."

"Is?" she asked more mockingly than she wanted to. "It already *has*. I know that you're fighting your demons, Edgar. But so am I. Maybe I should try to understand you better. Do more to understand you better, I mean." She pulled back, brushed her hand over his wet curls, rubbed her fingers over the rough two-day beard, but her lust for him had been satiated. She saw him for who he was again. And he noticed it, too.

He searched her face. "You're so much..."

"What?"

"More sure of yourself." His eyes narrowed in contemplation. "Like a woman on a mission."

He can still read my mind.

She kicked away, afraid that she had already revealed too much.

When they returned to the cottage and led the horses back into the stable, Kitty remembered the emptied half of the barn. On their way out, she paused and pointed to the door.

"What was that for, do you think?"

Edgar shrugged. "Cows, maybe?"

"There's a trapdoor. Feel like exploring?"

Edgar looked reluctant but she grabbed the flashlight hanging on the wall.

"Come on. I'm curious."

He finally followed, grumbling, "It's just a trapdoor. No big deal."

They entered the empty barn and she looked for the iron ring she'd uncovered with her boot last time. But she couldn't find it. Edgar stepped to the left, and brushed back a thick layer of straw.

"Here it is."

He lifted the ring and Kitty frowned. Had she moved that straw back when she'd last been here? She couldn't remember.

Edgar heaved the door open and Kitty illuminated the stairs down to a dirt floor.

"What's this for, Edgar?"

He shrugged. "Came with the property."

"Like Jerzy," Kitty said.

He laughed in one breath. "Like Jerzy." He pointed to the dimly lit stairs. "You're going down there?"

There were cobwebs hanging across the staircase. The cool air was musty and old.

"Yes. Why not?"

Edgar looked at her as if she was crazy. "Too spooky."

"Ha!" She left him above, and shivered at the touch and tug of cobwebs, the dark corners and dank smell. There were some old crates, and a barrel, some odds and ends, but no skeletons. Just a hiding place for secrets, she thought.

She rejoined Edgar. Back in the late afternoon sunshine, they passed the low building with all the stored bric-a-brac, and she peeked in, an idea germinating; she willed it to stay below the surface.

"*Isch nur Klumpert*," Edgar said over her shoulder.

"One man's garbage is another man's treasure."

Edgar pulled her to him and kissed the nape of her neck. "Curiosity killed the Kitty. What's with you today?"

She gently shook him off, distracted. An underground space. A resistance group. A place to hide. Something like Oskar's club in the subterranean bunker.

"You practically grew up on this place," she teased lightly, fishing for hints as to whether she was onto something, "and you don't even know what's in all these buildings."

"Grew up," Edgar scoffed. "My parents bought the place ten years ago. I was already long out of the house by then. As a matter of fact, missy," he pulled her to him. "I was at Oxford."

"Right you are, guv'nor," Kitty said. She leaned into him until they reached the house, pretending that her heart was in it.

It wasn't until Monday morning that Kitty thought of Kendrick again. When Edgar announced at breakfast he wanted to go into the next village to run some errands, she said she would stay at the cottage to do some reading. Since their lakeside session, he was full of hope, as if he believed all was forgiven and forgotten.

As soon as he was gone, Kitty picked up the phone and called the consulate. Millie answered.

"The department is on red alert," her friend said. "The British are keeping their lips zipped. Apparently, Kendrick is being escorted out of the country today. And until he's safe, nobody's talking."

"Have we heard anything about the other agents? Especially that new one, Pim? Millie, he's a local. He or any other nationals will be up on charges of treason."

But Millie knew nothing more. Kitty fretted over it the rest of the week.

The world positively refused to be closed out. In another attempt to prove to Kitty that they were on the mend, Edgar insisted they go fishing. Jerzy arrived on the bank of the river later with an important message.

"Don't shoot the messenger," Kitty mumbled. The butler always seemed to carry the most awful news.

Edgar folded the note and gave Kitty a look that warned her he was about to disappoint. "I really need to take care of something."

She did not even pretend to object.

Edgar kissed her cheek. "I'll be back by Saturday morning. Promise."

That afternoon, Kitty called the office again and caught Millie just in time.

"Nothing on Kendrick," Millie reported. "But something else has happened."

"Go on."

"Judith called me today. She has the new affidavit from New York—"

"Thank God," Kitty breathed.

"But..." Millie's voice broke.

A photo of Josef and Dorothea Ragatz hung on the wall and Kitty stared at their stern faces as she squeezed the receiver.

"All Jews now have to go through Eichmann's Central Office. Not to us. Judith went there and... Kitty, she has to change her name," Millie finished angrily.

"She what?" Kitty glared at the images of her in-laws accusingly.

"If she doesn't change her name to a Hebrew equivalent, then she has to add a middle name. Israel for the men, Sara for the women." Millie was gritting her teeth. "She can be called Judis or Judith Sara. She chose the latter. And she had to drop her husband's *Austrian* last name! She is now Judith Sara Goldberg. All of her future business transactions have to be made in that name. And..."

Kitty balanced the phone at her ear and wrenched Josef and Dorothea from the wall, slamming them down on their faces. "And what?"

"Her affidavit has to contain her new name."

"Jesus—" Kitty bit her lip. Firmly, she said, "You tell her... Tell her..."

What? What should Millie tell her?

Kitty looked out the window. Edgar had taken the car back to the city. She couldn't even catch the last train if she wanted to.

"I'm back on Sunday night. I'll come straight over. We'll figure this out. And until then, she does nothing. Tell her that,

OK? She does *nothing*. No, to hell with that, I'll call her myself."

"Kitty." Millie was firm. "Everything is changing very quickly. You can't do anything from the Woods. You can't do anything for her right now. None of these processes—not the Nazis', not ours—even consider the human being behind the paper."

Kitty took in a deep breath and held it. That was it! They needed to tell these people's stories. What had her father once said? If you put a face on a policy, if you capture the constituents' emotions, more often than not, you could at least get people to listen.

"Here's what we're going to do. We start by changing things from the inside. You and I are not going to hand out leaflets and pamphlets on the streets of Vienna. I need your help."

Millie laughed abruptly. "OK... You know you can count on me."

After hanging up, Kitty leaned against the console and rubbed her face. She heard movement and looked up to see Jerzy standing in the doorway, looking embarrassed.

"You startled me," she said.

"Please forgive me, madame. I only wanted to ask what you would like for supper. The woman who cooks has an emergency, and—"

"Sorry, of course. She should go. Would you just grab something from the larder?" Kitty looked at him a little more closely. "And the wine from Burgundy. Thank you."

Dusk had settled in the backyard, the setting sun poking shafts of light through the branches of the chestnut tree. Cricket and early evening bird song surrounded her. Kitty lit some candles on the table. Jerzy brought the food and the wine and she waited until he began pouring.

Kitty asked, "What do you think is going to happen? To us? To Europe?"

Jerzy did not speak for a long time and she thought he hadn't heard her, but then, he slowly said, "Hitler will try to invade Poland."

"But France and England wouldn't allow it."

He stepped back, wiped the bottle's neck, then dropped his hand self-consciously next to his side. "What have the Allies done for the Jews so far?"

"Nothing," Kitty agreed.

"We are just Poles," he continued in that same measured tone. "Sandwiched between the Soviet Union and the Third Reich. They will cut us up like a cake and gorge on us while France and England will be relieved that it is not them. And if the Poles do not fight..."

For the first time since Kitty had met him, Jerzy was not only talkative but articulate. And for the first time, Kitty saw what made him so hard to reach. He had carefully hidden his real reason for remaining distant.

"You would go back and fight," Kitty asked. "Wouldn't you?"

His eyes held hers, and did not let go. She had to drop her head to escape his intensity.

Yes. Yes, he would.

PART THREE

OCTOBER 1938–FEBRUARY 1939

19

The streets of Vienna were shiny with rain. A cold wind gusted as Kitty cycled to the consulate. With the new construction and massive expansions the regime had undertaken in Vienna, it was difficult to navigate the disruptions to the public transportation system. Many Viennese had given up and were using their bicycles instead.

At the consulate, she greeted the guard, "I look like a wet cat." She shook herself off near the entryway. The woolen hat she'd just managed to find deep in her wardrobe had protected her head, but her blond curls were dripping with rain.

In the ladies' room, Kitty dried herself and her leather satchel off and was just about to head downstairs when she saw Leland Morris on the first landing. There was no time like the present.

"Mr. Morris," Kitty called. Clutching the satchel at her side, she dashed after him.

The consulate chief turned to her, his interest at the sight of her only mildly piqued. "What can I do for you, Mrs. Ragatz? I have to get to a meeting."

Kitty kept up with him. "Sir, I believe you know that I have a personal investment with some people in the city. People who are trying to get out."

"Vaguely, Mrs. Ragatz."

"You might remember Judith Liebherr? She's now Judith Goldberg."

"Congratulations to her."

"There is nothing to congratulate." Kitty gritted her teeth. "Sir."

Morris stopped in his tracks and turned slowly around. He was ready to dismiss her entirely.

She rushed on, "We lost her affidavit this past summer."

"She wasn't the only one." Morris sounded bored. "Lots of them were misplaced with that miserable filing system we had. Tell her to get another one."

"I did, sir. She has. It has just now arrived from New York. Her third one since April. She and her adult son were supposed to receive their visas this past summer but because of Eichmann's circus..." Kitty sighed with exasperation at Morris' waning attention. "Sir, her name is Judith Goldberg now because of Eichmann's policies, not because she willingly gave up her late husband's family name. We're begging for your help, sir."

Morris pointed down the stairs. "Along with the tens of thousands of others who have a similar story? Who now have to wait even longer to get out because they need to get a stupid *J* stamped onto their passports by the Nazis?"

Kitty nodded hopefully. "Exactly, sir. Our candidates are harassed over and over again about who they are, what they're planning on leaving behind. I've got it all right here, sir." She patted the satchel and slipped the strap over her head.

When she was abreast with him again, he tossed her an annoyed glance. "I'm going to be late, Mrs. Ragatz. What do you want from me?"

"I wrote a report for the Department of State."

Again, a sharp look from him. "You're not qualified to write reports."

He was wrong about that. She'd learned from Cooper, one of the best writers in the whole Department of State as far as Kitty was concerned. Morris's reports were terrible, and Kitty knew it because the U.S. and Berlin were constantly surprised when they received diplomatic and political news via American intel and not from the chargé d'affaires.

Without slowing down, Kitty followed Morris into the pool's office and stopped only when he was at his office door. With a flash, she realized she was not going to win him over by pointing out his weaknesses.

"You're right, sir. It's not my job to write reports, and that's why I'm asking you to just look at it. To consider it. I don't care if you even put your name on it."

He whipped around. "Me? Put my name on *your* report? Who the hell do you think you are, Mrs. Ragatz?"

She swallowed. "I meant, if you find it worthy of sharing with the Department of State." She prickled at that. It was a damned good report. "Listen—"

Morris scoffed and glared at his secretary, the third one in as many months. "When Secretary Hull calls, I don't want anyone disturbing me."

"Sir," Kitty said firmly.

His profile to her, Morris rolled his eyes.

"It was our fault we lost her affidavit. Judith has to give up her paintings, her apartment, her studio, everything to the Nazis. The roof over her head. And how is she to do that, if she cannot even book passage to America?"

"Mrs. Ragatz, I'm not so certain you truly appreciate our situation. We can't do more than we already are."

"I have a proposal. All I'm asking, sir, is that you read my report. And if it's not something you feel the Department of State should see or take action on, then please, toss it."

Morris's face rippled, his mouth twisted. He darted a sideways glance at his secretary. Poor girl. She had big shoes to fill. Millie was the only one who could really deal with Leland Morris. Kitty should have sent her up with the report.

She reached into the satchel and withdrew the fat envelope. She'd been working on it for nearly five weeks, thanks to Khan's and Charlie's help in procuring stories.

"What in God's name is that?" Morris pointed.

"Our applicants' personal stories could very well make a difference."

"A difference to what, Mrs. Ragatz?"

"Putting a human face on the tragedy unfolding here, Mr. Morris. A difference between life and death, quite frankly, sir." Kitty patted the top of the envelope. "Our report is in there, but so are letters to the Department of State from our Jewish candidates, who are stuck between the red tape in our embassy and the hurdles that Eichmann moves every day. I'm including them as exhibits to my report."

"You're not writing a legal case! Exhibits!" Morris exclaimed. Heads looked up. Flabbergasted, he yanked open his office door.

"I'm begging you," Kitty pleaded. "Just read them. Please."

To her relief, Morris snatched the packet from Kitty and fanned her with it as if to shoo her away. "I'm not promising anything. Now get back downstairs, Mrs. Ragatz."

"Thank you, sir."

He shut the door in Kitty's face.

His secretary winced. "Iceberg," she whispered.

Kitty smiled tightly. "Then let's hope those letters from the Jews work like salt and start melting him."

"I did it," Kitty announced when she returned.

Millie came around from her desk. "And? How did our Mr. Morris take it?"

"Not well..."

Millie arched an eyebrow. "You've really put yourself in the line of fire this time."

"You agreed we should do it!" Kitty reminded her. "I guess we'll see."

Millie smiled slyly and produced a cable from a dark brown folder stamped *confidential*.

"What's this?"

"Pim's back on the wire," Millie burst out.

Kitty stared at her. "Really? What did he say?"

"Why is it always a he?" Millie complained. "Maybe it's a she?"

Muttering appreciatively, Kitty read the cable then stared at her friend. "He wants to directly report to our offices. He needs a contact directly to our own assets."

She could hear Ben Roberts, their boss, speaking behind the door of his office. She leaned on Millie's desk. "What about me? What if I was Pim's direct contact?"

Her friend's eyes widened. "I did just say, why couldn't it be a she, didn't I?"

Kitty nodded. "It doesn't hurt to ask, right? I know Vienna. I can get around, deliver messages, retrieve information."

"Your husband also works for the regime."

"Don't be such a dud, Millie."

"I'd think this through before you go to Roberts with this. Just get your arguments all straight."

Kitty nodded. Her friend was right. This would require a good strategy.

A few days later, and just before Kitty was supposed to meet with Roberts, Leland Morris called her up to his office. She was not prepared for what she saw. Harry Carson, and the other FSOs, were in the room with him.

She checked to see whether the phone line was lit up. It was not. This was going to be an internal issue. She groaned inwardly, realizing her mistake before she even sat down. She had told all in her report. How the Jewish applicants had to wait an average of four to six months for their American visa. In the meantime, the regime expected those same persecuted people to meet all official requirements including the spoliation of their possessions. Then the Nazis gave the Jews only weeks to leave Austria, or be arrested. With their homes already in possession of the regime, the Viennese trying to get out of the country had to find a place of purgatory. They waited in countries like Switzerland, France or the Netherlands for the American documents, and that was at times financially impossible for a family.

Kitty had pointed out these failures in her report, and illustrated how a lot of it had to do with their internal processes in Vienna. Now, Morris was going to publicly chastise her. Carson and the other men may as well have all stood up and just thrown rocks the moment she entered the room.

Her muscles tensed at the sight of the papers on Morris's desk. Kitty recognized Judith's handwritten note attached to her new affidavit. Morris caught her looking at it, and held it up in the air for the others to see. The page contained nine illustrated women in a circle, in various dresses and in forms of repose. Two of them were dressed in ballgowns, the woman at seven o'clock wore harem-styled trousers and a top that exposed her belly through a sheer fabric. Her hair was tied up high over her head like a genie, and she wore large sunglasses. Another was in a pleated skirt, much like the one Judith had worn to Kitty's wedding, but the top was a chunky sweater, and she was holding a champagne glass. Yet another was dressed in a military-style skirt and jacket with a sharp cap on her head. In the middle, Judith's handwritten request that her documents be expedited as she would like to book passage to America, and continue working again in New York.

Morris held the page of illustrations as if a mouse by its tail. "We all had to admit that this is very good. Really good. I'm forwarding these freak letters on to Messersmith."

Kitty gaped at him and understood. He was going to forward the packet to Messersmith so that they could share a good laugh. Her blood boiled.

"This is not a joke. Frau Goldberg is deadly serious. The reason she drew this is because she wants you to see her as a real person. The Nazis have banned all clothing and fashion created or sold by Jews. All of it. She doesn't have a job. She doesn't have her studio. She has no rights. All she has is us."

"Yes, well, we'll get one of the vice consuls to look into it. In the meantime, we have several other drawings and clever missives that are begging for attention. But, Mrs. Ragatz, we have called you in here for a different reason."

Kitty looked from him to the others, but could not read their poker faces, except for Carson's. He looked embarrassed. Uncertain, she returned her attention to Morris.

He opened his hands. "I read your report, as did the others here in this room."

"Those were meant for your eyes, Mr. Morris. Yours and the Department of State, should you have chosen to share it with them."

"But you brought up very important points, I must admit. My colleagues and I are here to assure you that we understand the extreme pressure the Nazis are using to force out the Jewish population, but we all came together to apologize to you, for falling so short of your expectations."

"I didn't mean to offend—"

"By all means. It was right of you to point out our short-comings."

"But—"

"Mrs. Ragatz, we hope that you will pass along our apologies to your"—he lifted the pile of papers—"colleagues and friends. Isn't that correct, gentlemen?"

Each of them nodded.

"You have made it clear to us that we have an administrative challenge. And I am dealing with it via administrative measures. The efficiency of the visa employees has increased by suppressing the indiscriminate information they have been giving out at all hours of the day. Such pernicious practice gave rise to misunderstandings, incorrect information, and even showed favoritism. You, Mrs. Ragatz, are one such example with these"—he jutted his chin at the packet of letters—"stories. What should happen if we allowed our emotions to rule our every decision? I'll tell you. Chaos. Which is why I put every safeguard in place, to prevent the possibility of tampering with records. Suffice it to say, there is not a lot of evidence that any dishonest act has occurred inside the office. There is much evidence, however, to indicate that administrative confusion has caused errors which are of a nature to give rise in the mind of the uninitiated public"—he glared at her—"the belief that favoritism and corruption has existed. But we have not lost someone's affidavit since that time. Not one. I hope that I have made myself clear to your satisfaction."

Kitty slumped in her seat, began picking at a fingernail, caught herself and dropped her hand. She sat up again. "I'm going to assume that you will not be sending my report to Secretary Hull?"

Morris bared his teeth and, like a minister, raised his hands upwards. His congregation of foreign service officers rose. Nobody looked at her as they filed out of the office. When the door closed behind them, Morris fixed his glare on her.

"I don't care whose daughter you are. You overstepped your bounds, young lady, and for the last time. I have spoken with

Roberts, who is also uncertain what to do with you, Mrs. Ragatz. As for Miss Hoffmann, I regret that her complicity with you in this matter will force my hand to either offer her old job with the pool or reassign her as well."

Kitty hung her head.

"In the meantime, I will keep the letters from your friends and colleagues, I will make certain that Mrs. Goldberg's affidavit is filed properly and she will be put back into the queue without exception."

"Thank you," Kitty said. "That is most—"

"But you, Mrs. Ragatz. You are another matter altogether. Since our most valuable intel assets have been arrested or quieted, there is not much work for you in that department. It is also clear that with the intensifying activities of violence exhibited by this Nazi regime, your husband's position with the German Foreign Office creates a grave conflict of interest. I have recommended that Roberts put you on temporary leave for an indefinite period of time."

Kitty's chest squeezed tight and she had to take short breaths. This day had been long in coming, ever since John Cooper Wiley had announced his transfer. She knew it could not have lasted, and she had gone out on a limb, made Morris really sit up and take notice, but for all the wrong reasons. She'd failed miserably. She'd failed Judith. The gang. And most of all, she'd failed herself.

"I want to offer my sincerest apologies," she pleaded. "My intentions were not to—"

"No, of course you did not *intend* to, Mrs. Ragatz." Morris steepled his hands beneath his chin, his gaze direct. "But I understand your passion for the role you have and how you might have been misled to feel obliged to take us on. You have proven again and again that your bleeding heart extends beyond these consulate's capabilities. Our job is to serve Americans first. The Jews—and all other visa applicants—come second. The worst of it is, you seem to hold little regard for those of us who are working under excruciating circumstances."

"No, sir," Kitty protested. "You're wrong there. I care very much—"

"I'm curious about whether you care enough."

"Enough about what?" she cried angrily.

"About those excruciating circumstances we are in." Morris's head bobbed slightly, as if he were taking her in from head to toe. "Our most important intelligence assets were those working from inside the regime. Without them... Well, after Wallace... it's kind of a vacuum of intel, now. Have you ever considered that the information your husband is privy to might be... valuable to our work here?"

Kitty's eyes widened. "You want me to spy on my husband?"

The ends of Morris's lips twitched upwards. "You would have valuable access to the details of his work. You could write one of your reports then. You could—"

Clenching her fists, Kitty rose and squared herself against him. "Sir, now it is you who is overstepping his bounds. May I please have a piece of paper and a writing utensil?"

He peered at her for a couple of seconds before taking the top sheet from his stationery pile. He pushed it over to her and held out a pen. Heart pounding in her ears, Kitty bent over his desk and wrote hurriedly.

Morris cast a glance at it and raised his eyebrows. "I didn't think you would give up so easily."

Tears stung the back of her eyes. To hell with giving up. She was just getting started. In a low voice, she said, "You have no idea."

He lifted the sheet and, with exaggerated care, placed her letter of resignation into a desk drawer. "I will keep this, Mrs.

Ragatz, but I'd like you to take a few weeks and consider my proposal. I know how much your work means to you. Take a vacation. We'll talk. And then we'll see whether I must accept your hasty retreat."

Kitty braced herself on the edge of his desk. "It's going to be a real pleasure to prove you wrong."

20

NOVEMBER 1938

Kitty's desperation flared against a backdrop of a sickly orange glow. Vienna was ablaze.

It was the middle of the night. She and Edgar witnessed the spectacle from the rooftop of their apartment building as soot-brown clouds crawled upwards and across the pulsing horizon. In the distance, occasional sirens scraped the air. Not nearly enough trucks and men, Kitty thought, for all the fires burning. The buildings had been aflame for hours.

Tinny cymbal-like rings interrupted the night. Like that fiery horizon, they too were coming from the north. Kitty believed it was from Alsergrund, Judith's neighborhood. Oskar's and Artur's district. Where Khan lived with his family. Where Big Charlie was. That's where the sound of destruction was coming from.

In comparison, Rennweg—the entire street—was dead still.

Kitty hugged herself in the thick bathrobe. It was cold but she was not shivering from the biting November temperature; she was shaking with dread. Edgar had his arms wrapped around her but there was a palpable distance of inches between them; that space between their bodies felt like miles. Heart-

broken for a hundred more reasons, Kitty pulled away and went
to the railing.

The violence began with the news a few days before about
an assassination attempt on Ernst Röhm. The radio announced
that Hitler's third secretary died from his wounds later that
same day. The Führer's henchmen happened to all be in
Munich, celebrating the Beer Hall Putsch when Goebbels took
the microphone and screamed about the ungrateful Jewish
immigrants. How dare they attack one of theirs like this?

Kitty had turned to Edgar, aghast. "He is giving civilians the
license to destroy all Jewish property... all Jewish businesses."

"They'd never do that." But Edgar had gone pale. "Surely,
they never would."

They did. Goebbels' words lit the fires that burned in
Vienna now.

She faced her husband. His features were barely distin-
guishable in the darkness, but she felt his eyes on her. "I can't go
on like this."

There was a vacuum between them, and Edgar was trying
to close it by moving toward her.

"It's the Jews now," she said, deflecting his attempt to reach
her. "Tomorrow, it could be me."

"Kitty."

"It could be you." Tears rolled freely as she jabbed an
accusing finger into his breastbone. "Tomorrow, it could even be
you, Edgar."

The next day, the paper's headline called the pogrom
Kristallnacht. The English papers translated it into the tragi-
cally poetic *Night of the Broken Glass*. The Nazis called it
something more official: *Judenaktion*. Jewish Action.

Their phone was not working. Kitty wanted to call home, to
let her family know she was well and not to worry. Edgar

offered to accompany her to his office and make the call from there.

Khan was lingering against the lamppost when Kitty and Edgar stepped out of their building. She was not surprised to see him and her relief was so great, she rushed to him, leaving Edgar behind.

"Where is Judith?"

"Bella's," Khan said. "With Macke and Big Charlie. She wants you to come."

"What about the others?" she asked. "We were just headed to Edgar's office to place some calls."

Khan glanced at her husband, who stood a few steps away now, and remained silent. Kitty understood. He did not want to speak in front of him.

Edgar's jawbone twitched, but he was resigned.

"Go to the office," she said to him. "I'm going to check on my friends. I'll meet you there."

"I don't want you to go alone, Kitty."

"I'm *not* alone."

Edgar closed his eyes briefly, offered Khan his hand like the afterthought that it was.

"How are you?" he asked Khan.

Khan narrowed his eyes. "This time? They defiled my mother's bookshop. Apparently all Russian literature is communist literature. Communist literature to these... ignoramuses... means Jewish literature."

"I'm so sorry." Edgar sounded sincere.

Kitty swiped a hair away from her face. "Are your parents all right?"

Khan's scowl grazed Edgar. "They have no idea what my parents had to do to flee the Soviets. We're Muslim, by the way."

They again. And he was accusing Edgar. He was not completely wrong to do so, but it was still wrong. Kitty knew her husband's heart was broken and heavy, even if for possibly different reasons.

Edgar put a hand on her shoulder now. "I'll wait for you at the office."

When her husband was out of earshot, Khan asked where Millie was.

"She left for Berlin on Saturday, to her new post there."

He took in a shuddering breath. "I am glad to hear it." Then, "Judith asked me to find Oskar and Artur."

"Do you know where they are?"

"I'm going to have to guess at the club. They weren't at Artur's mother's. We tried calling but there was no answer. It's the only other place I can think of."

Kitty took out her key and retrieved her bicycle from the storage room. Khan pedaled and she clung to his waist, perched behind him on the cargo rack. From the first district, he followed the Danube River, then pulled up along the road and wheeled the bike to a hiding place near the bank.

"Follow me," he said, and led Kitty to the mouth of a tunnel.

"Where are we?"

"The water and sewage system of Vienna," Khan said. "This will get us to Floridsdorf and Oskar's club without being detected by Brown Shirts, police or Gestapo. They're crawling everywhere."

He produced a flashlight and lit the entrance. The smell of sewage hit Kitty like a gut punch and she took shallow breaths between pinching her nose. The sound of water grew louder when they climbed downwards.

"Stay with me," Khan warned. "The rats are not to be messed with."

She realized that he held a small pistol.

Shivering and swearing, she jumped each time at the squeaks and peeps. Something scuttled past her feet and she clutched Khan so hard he nearly lost his balance. Eventually, they reached a point where they could walk more comfortably, even stand straight, but she did not stop cursing beneath her breath. Her shoes were the least sensible pair she could have for these tunnels, and she was freezing through her thin coat during the arduous trek.

It took nearly half an hour before Khan stopped and flashed the light indirectly in her face. "Are you OK?"

She nodded, but her chattering teeth gave her lie away.

He inserted a large key into the steel door of the tunnel wall and pushed. They were in a quiet room, followed by a normal-looking door. He shut them in, completely muffling the sounds of water behind them. Khan leaned his ear up against the second door and immediately pulled back. He put a finger to his lips, his eyes wide before turning off the flashlight.

Kitty pressed against him, listening with him. She could hear a lot of voices behind the door. Someone was howling, or sobbing. Was that a child's voice? Then another man answered in an indifferent tone. There were muffled popping sounds, several of them, and Kitty immediately thought of flashbulbs.

Khan pulled away from the door and whispered into her ear. "If I open this now, they'll smell the sewage and, whoever is in there, will know that we've been using this route. I need you to go up to the road. Go and find out what's happening. Pretend you're just a passerby."

Kitty frowned. "Alone?"

"Yes, Kitty. Alone." Khan turned on the flashlight and illuminated the contours and features of his skin and face. His light gray eyes showed resignation. He reached for a strand of her hair and pointed the flashlight at it. He was right. Khan would draw too much attention to himself.

He led her back into the main tunnel, down a more quiet branch of it until a ladder appeared. Khan climbed up to the manhole, first. He removed the cover and motioned for her to hurry up past him.

Kitty looked out onto the deserted street. It was part of the industrial area. Nobody was about. She crawled out onto her hands and knees and quickly headed in the direction Khan indicated.

He'd been right. Something had happened. Three cars were parked at the manufactory, and police milled about. She stopped in her tracks when she saw two of them pushing and dragging Oskar towards one of the vehicles.

"Oskar!" she called, panicked. "Where are you taking him?"

The officer who was putting him into the car threw her a disgusted look. "You know this man?"

Oskar cried frantically, "Artur! They murdered Artur in cold blood."

"Yeah," the policeman snapped. "And we're about to find out how the pansy here was involved."

"*Sois prudent, petit lion,*" Oskar cried. "*Ils cherchent la moindre raison pour nous d'etruire!*" *Be careful, Little Lion. They're looking for any reason to destroy us.*

Kitty clamped a hand over her mouth when the door slammed shut.

The policeman shoved her out of the way, gave her another look over, and grumbled something in dialect that she could not make out before climbing in behind the steering wheel.

When the engine started up, Kitty was spurred into action. "He didn't do it! He couldn't have! Oskar? Who did this?"

Oskar jerked his head towards the other side of the road. Kitty scanned the area but all she saw was a cloth sack on the ground. Then she recognized it. The sack that Max and Hannes used to collect coal. Her insides withered.

Two detectives tried to prevent her from going inside the building, but Kitty pushed past them and ran to the far door with the *Achtung!* sticker on it. She hurled herself down the two flights of stairs. The door to the once secret club was propped open. The first thing she saw was Hannes crying quietly at the nearest table. Max was across from him, his arms wrapped tight around himself and his teeth chattering. Beyond, where the stage was, a group of men blocked the view. One was putting a camera away and she caught a whiff of sulfur.

When he stepped aside, Kitty moved toward the stage. She saw a dim pool of light. The fabric of a ruby red sequin gown. The blond wig at the far corner of the stage. Artur's hand dangled off the side.

Kitty took one more step and she was standing over him. Artur's eyes and mouth were wide open, empty. A dark hole. A pool of blood beneath his smashed open head.

Kitty dropped to her knees as someone tried to grab her. They wrangled her back onto her feet. As she passed the boys, she called to them. Max returned a defiant stare. Hannes burst into fresh tears.

The detective sat her at another table. He asked her questions. Two other men appeared. Gestapo, this time. They also wanted to know why she knew the place. What she had to do with *these people*. What her name was. Then they said, "Frau Doktor Ragatz, we now have a file on you."

They shoved and pushed her back upstairs. And they warned her to stay away.

21

NOVEMBER 1938

The grief. The anger. The sheer futility of Artur's death. It was exhausting.

For a wad of Reichsmark and his little brother's freedom, Max had led the Brown Shirts to Agnes. That was what Oskar told the gang as they sat in Bella's living room. After Artur's lover had been processed at the police station, his only saving grace—his ticket to mercy—was a close contact within the police department. A lieutenant who did not want Oskar to spill his secrets. But he'd warned Oskar that even that favor would quickly run out.

Khan went to the window, and drew the drapes closed. Big Charlie's frame nearly encompassed the entire dining table where he sat. Kitty hugged her legs against herself on one end of the peach-colored sofa. Judith was in the opposite corner, Macke curled up next to her in his sugar-donut position. Her hand rested on the armchair where Oskar sat silently weeping.

He suddenly fell back and flung an arm over his forehead as if stabbed with pain anew. Stray tears appeared from beneath his elbow and rolled down his cheeks. He had a bruise beneath his left eye. A cut lip.

"This is the second time they've tried to press charges against me. The third time, it will be straight to Dachau." He sat up again, angry now. "How dare they accuse me of Artur's murder!"

Macke lifted his head and whined. Kitty clutched a damp handkerchief in her fist and reached across the sofa to touch her friend's leg. Judith looked at her, the lenses of her glasses smeared with tears.

"I've got double the trouble against me," Oskar continued. "Like Artur said, I am a Jew and I'm a homosexual. It's only a matter of time before they just lock me away for those reasons alone."

They, Kitty thought. The unnamed. The specters of the regime, moving like a swarm that landed, devoured and destroyed everything in its path.

Bella came in from the kitchen with a tray of tea and porcelain cups, but Big Charlie grumbled that he needed a shot of something stronger. She wrapped her cardigan around herself and went to a hutch behind the table and withdrew a bottle of clear liquid. Six shot glasses followed. Kitty rose, and helped her serve. A moment later, they all raised their glasses.

"To Artur. To Agnes," Kitty said.

Everyone repeated it, and Bella was the first to empty her shot.

After tossing her own down, Kitty realized that the clock on Bella's mantelpiece read past five. She peeked behind the drawn curtains and saw that it was dark outside, and snowing. She had not even tried to reach Edgar.

Khan folded his arms over his chest, his normally smooth face slack with distress.

"What are you and your family going to do about the bookshop?" she asked softly.

Khan shook his head. "What should we do? We keep going."

Judith rose and tenderly caressed Oskar's face. "Those monsters," she said quietly. "They're getting rid of us in the most horrible ways possible."

Macke whined from the couch and jumped down, balancing his front paws delicately on Judith's knee. Kitty went and picked him up, turned her head away to avoid those eager licks, and rested her chin on top of his head.

One strap of his suspenders sagging over his shoulder, Big Charlie was pouring another round of schnapps for everyone.

"That's enough," he growled. He was not talking about the liquor. "I've had enough. We're going to organize ourselves and fight these bastards."

He handed out glasses to everyone and Kitty clinked hers with his.

Big Charlie wiped a hand over his mouth. "Bella has agreed to let Judith and Oskar stay here for now."

"What about you and Khan?" she asked.

He turned his huge hands toward himself. "I'm too difficult to hide. A bit too well-known. Vienna, is, after all a small city. And—"

"The whole of it is your fan club," Kitty interjected.

He nodded. "So, I'm going to leave here tonight and you will only hear about me through Khan from this point on." He put a heavy hand on her shoulder. "You need to get Judith and Oskar out of the country. Yesterday."

"I'm supposed to meet with Morris on Friday but I'm on thin ice, Big Charlie. I can't ask for any favors."

"I don't need Morris, that *Depp*. I need equipment. If I get equipment, I can take care of the rest."

"What equipment?"

Big Charlie jerked his head towards the windows and shared a meaningful look with Khan.

"He knows a guy," Big Charlie said.

Kitty raised an eyebrow. "Khan knows a guy?"

Big Charlie nodded. "He's really good at... let's just say, he's really good at producing hard-to-get documents. And he's got the equipment we need. Stamps, templates, passport booklets. Dyes, and the right paper. Except that he's in Berlin and he wants payment up front."

Kitty looked from one friend to the other and realized they were already privy. All of them. "Are you serious? You are talking about forging documents to help people get out of the country."

Breaking the rules. Taking the situation into their own hands. Going up against the regime. Kitty thought of Kendrick. He'd risked his life as Captain Wallace and had supplied American and British agencies with important information. In the end, many of his assets had been arrested, but not all if she were to believe the confidences Nils had shared with her. But those that had been caught were facing a Nazi execution.

Now the gang was considering taking charge and possibly changing the course of many lives, at the risk of their own.

Bella drifted over. "We're not the only ones, Kitty. Many people are resisting. As a matter of fact, we could get the assistance we need quite reliably. We need to distribute leaflets, flyers... keep up people's spirits. Recruit others who will have the courage to sabotage the regime."

Big Charlie pointed to himself again. "I can't get to Berlin. And Khan? No offense, my friend, but your eyelids won't measure up to Aryan standards."

"You don't think so?" Khan blinked rapidly at Kitty.

They never stopped with the jokes.

"So, we'll need you to carry the payment over the border," Big Charlie said.

"Me?" Kitty took a step back.

"Doesn't your husband regularly travel to Berlin?" Bella asked.

Kitty knew the gang was not suggesting that Edgar carry the

money. They were suggesting she join Edgar to Berlin and carry the money. Which would mean making up with Edgar in a way that her request to join him would feel genuine.

"We'd get everything we need," Big Charlie said. "And open up a route for... let's just say a lot of effective equipment. Not just printing presses, stamps and documents."

"Weapons," Kitty guessed. "Explosives. For real damage."

"Wireless radios," Bella added.

Head spinning, Kitty went to one of the dining room chairs and sat down. On the table, the untouched tea in Japanese porcelain cups. She stroked the delicate handle of the one nearest to her. Cherry blossoms. Women in kimonos. Picnickers beneath the flowers. She shook her head. If she did this, did she have any good reason not to accept Morris's offer to spy on her husband? Her marriage would fracture for good and her decision, to do this or that, would be the final blow.

She looked up at Big Charlie, pleading with him in silence.

Measuredly he said, "We are not the only ones who need help. There are thousands in Vienna—"

Judith tore herself away from Oskar and stood behind Kitty's chair. She wrapped her arms around Kitty. "I know they are asking you to do something very risky. Give her some time, boys. In the meantime, I'm wondering if you could do something for me. Alsergrund is too dangerous for me to return to. Khan said they started cordoning sections off and herding the residents into new districts, but I need some things from my apartment."

Kitty clasped her friend's hand and twisted to face her. "I'll go, but only if you promise that you will leave immediately."

Judith released her and glanced at Oskar. He'd covered his face with both hands. "I'll go if he goes."

Big Charlie cleared his throat and scratched his head. "I'll send Khan with you, Kitty. And you do everything he tells you."

Kitty stood up. "Edgar is going to Berlin in three weeks."

Oskar suddenly revealed his battered face, and he sat up. She saw a flash of hope.

"I just need to get my head around it," she begged. "I'll go to Judith's first. Tell me what you need."

At the first sign of trouble, Khan and Kitty got off the bicycle and hid it behind a tavern. Where once Viennese workers drank their Gösser beers in the afternoons, now the establishment stood empty and destroyed.

Dreck Sau!—dirty pig!—was splashed red across the front wall.

Alsergrund looked like a war zone. Smoke invaded Kitty's lungs. She had to pick her way through shattered glass. Nearly every window was smashed. Doors hung from their hinges. Paint blackened out the Hebrew inscription on the doorbells and signs of shops. Earlier, the regime had ordered those inscriptions, whether the local Jews spoke or read Hebrew or not. If they had the letter *J* in their pass, they had to have Hebrew inscriptions on their properties. Then there was the graffiti. Hateful, violent slogans about rats, vermin, and pests. Demands for purifying the nation's blood.

Khan suddenly pulled her into a doorway and peeked around the corner. He flattened himself against the threshold. "*Sturmabteilung.*"

Brown Shirts. Voices and footsteps followed but they were heading away from them.

Kitty locked eyes with Khan. "I'll go," she said.

He grabbed her arm. "There's an alley three hundred meters east of Judith's building. Blue door. Make sure nobody sees you. That's where I'll be."

By the time Kitty arrived at the apartment building, her jaw was so tight it hurt. She took the stairwell. The atmosphere was eerie. There were entrances left carelessly open, and she caught sight of people's things strewn about. A pair of dark brown men's shoes were lying in the middle of the corridor.

Judith's apartment door was miraculously locked. Kitty inserted the key. When she stepped in, she was shocked by the disarray in the apartment. She had always felt at home here, among the Jugendstil lamps, the exotic potted plants, the peaceful, layered shades of green and white décor, the art and sculptures, and the bookcases filled with art books. But the scattered personal items, the tossed clothing: these were the remnants of a woman on the run.

Kitty moved to Judith's bedroom and stopped at a large, gilded mirror. Tucked into the upper part of the frame was a photo. Judith, Khan, Sarah and Millie with Kitty in the background in her wedding gown, her arms opened to encompass them all in. She didn't remember having posed for that photo. Worse still, she couldn't remember feeling that happy.

In the closet, she found a few practical things for Judith to wear. Sweaters, trousers, a pair of short boots, a coat, underthings. Bella had given her a knapsack, but warned Kitty not to take too many things, not to stuff it full or she would draw attention.

She went to the toilet and plucked the toothbrush from its cup, a brush, and a second pair of sunglasses resting near the basin. She left the jewelry as Judith had instructed. If anyone stopped Kitty, they could accuse her of looting what was now considered Nazi property. Next, Macke's thick leather leash and a collar with the rhinestone stud. She turned it over, examined the even stitching on the leather. Between the layers, Judith had told her, she'd hidden American hundred-dollar bills.

In the living room, on a tilted drawing table, Kitty found one of Judith's sketchbooks. She jammed it into the rucksack as well as a handful of colored pencils. Her friend had not requested them, but she would need to divert her energies into something she loved.

As she was about to leave, Kitty heard voices in the corridor. She held her breath. Steps sounded downwards in the stairwell, sharp commands, another voice protesting. The slamming of the entrance door.

Her blood cold, Kitty peeked through the peephole. Nothing more. Just silence. She stepped out, locked the door behind her, and cursed under her breath at her shaking hand. She slung the rucksack over her shoulder before hurrying down the stairs. Through the glass of the front entrance, she saw two SA patrols passing by, jostling an old man with a white pointed beard between them, faces pulled into jeers. She waited. She pushed the doors open, went in the opposite direction. It was not where she was supposed to go. Kitty had to somehow find a way back to Khan, but those men were heading in the same direction she needed to go in.

At the next corner, she turned left. The street was empty, but there was a sweater strewn on the ground. A brick-red smear, head-high, on a wall sent a chill through her. Kitty hurried. And as she neared the end of the road, she heard first the gunshot, then the screams.

Heart pounding, she hid in the threshold of a building. A German Wehrmacht *Lastwagen* passed by on the adjacent street. She stopped in front of a shuttered store and waited before going around the corner. Down the road, where she intended to go, several patrols milled about. From the trucks that had just passed by, Wehrmacht soldiers were shouting at people to get out. The road was cordoned off. There were guards standing at barricades, checking a woman's papers.

"*Sind Sie deppert?*" Thick Viennese dialect. Just like Edgar's, but she now found it vile.

As if at the mercy of a marionette's string, Kitty's back

pulled taut. She turned slowly around. It was one of the SA troops that had passed by the entrance of Judith's building earlier. He must have followed her.

"*Was machen Sie da?*" He opened a palm, wiggled his fingers. "*Papiere.*"

Kitty, her heart in her throat, her blood thick as tar, automatically tugged at the straps of the rucksack.

"*Was ist da drinnen?*" What is inside here?

Then she remembered she didn't have to speak German. "Sorry, I don't understand," she said in English.

Uncertainty flitted over his face. She waited until he was right before her. His dark gray eyes were glassy, and he flashed her a tight-lipped smile. He was about her age.

"What are you? British?" he asked in English.

"American."

"What's in the bag?"

"Some things of mine."

"What are you doing here?"

"I'm just passing through."

"You come to loot the properties?" he sneered. "Take souvenirs of Vienna?"

Kitty shook her head. He gestured for the rucksack. She slowly handed it over.

"Why is there a leash in here? I don't see any dog. And these? These sketches. Are they yours? A toothbrush. Who are you taking these to?"

"They're mine. They're my things."

He did not believe her. He eyed her as if he were considering her for dinner. "Documents."

From her coat pocket, Kitty withdrew her papers, her face on fire. She noticed the interest the interaction was drawing from the guards at the barricade.

"Do you know it is illegal to help the Jews?" the little runt said as he reviewed her documents. "It says here you are married and a permanent resident here."

This got her. She switched into her best Viennese dialect.

"Do you idiots know that my husband is the legal adviser and a diplomat with the German Foreign Office? You can ask your supervisor over there to give Dr. Edgar Ragatz a call. I'm on my way to his office now, but I got sidetracked when I saw all this waste here. I can only imagine how delighted SA-Lieutenant Goering is going to be about the uselessness of all this property now. Property, do I need to remind you, that the Reich hoped to confiscate. For you Germans? But surely they'll forgive little runts like you for having your day of sophomoric fun. Be my guest, arrest me, take me in, the Aryan wife of an Aryan diplomat who is witnessing the destruction of the Reich's property."

She had him. His eyes were wide, his cheeks splotched red. His contempt was palpable but so was his lack of confidence now.

"And yes, these are my things." She snatched the rucksack away from him, then her papers. "I'm going to walk away now, you *Depp*, and if you want to shoot me, do so. I'm sure there are enough people high up in the offices who can't wait for a little *Schlappschwanz* like you to hang from your tiny balls as a lesson for others like you."

She shoved past him and strode back the way she came.

"*Halt!*" he called. She expected to feel the bullet. But halfway down the block, still nothing happened.

Heart racing, black pins before her eyes, Kitty reached the end of the block, turned the corner and raced in the correct direction. Bäumlegasse. She nearly screeched when Khan stepped out of the shadows.

"Are you OK?" he asked. "I got worried back there."

Kitty nodded, not trusting her voice yet. With a shaking hand, she passed the rucksack with Judith's belongings to him.

"Tell Big Charlie I'm doing it." Her lungs hurting, she struggled to take in a full breath. "I'll carry the cash to Berlin. I'll find a way to convince Edgar to take me with him."

Khan clasped her upper arms. "Thank you, Kitty. Oskar was right when he said you are a lioness."

22

NOVEMBER 1938

Kitty biked to Edgar's office, relieved to see that the light was still shining in his window. Inside the Foreign Office building, she went to the woman at the front desk.

"Would you be so kind as to call Dr. Ragatz, please? Let him know his wife is here?"

"Certainly, Frau Doktor."

The woman directed her to Edgar's office after hanging up. Four men in Nazi officer uniforms passed by and Kitty lowered her head, her blood chilled.

"Lots of traffic today," the woman muttered.

Jittery, Kitty went upstairs and Edgar met her on the threshold. She was stunned to see her sister-in-law standing near the window. Margit's cheeks were splotched pink as if she'd been crying. She looked to be in pain but acknowledged Kitty with a wan smile.

"I didn't expect to see you here," Kitty said. "It's been a long time. I hope you are well."

Edgar looked flustered. "Margit has just—"

"Just? Forget it, Edgar," Margit snapped. She snatched up her handbag on the chair across from his desk. "What do you know about it? You have one another. Perfectly suitable couple. Who cares about what I want?"

"What's that supposed to mean?" Kitty scoffed.

But Margit shoved past her brother.

"Listen to me," he hissed to her.

"Not here," Margit snapped.

Brother and sister glared at one another before Margit snapped, "Forget that I ever said a thing. Sorry, Kitty. Goodbye."

"Goodbye?" Kitty stepped aside as Margit dodged into the hallway. The door closed softly behind her with a click.

With an exasperated sigh, Edgar moved to his desk before asking whether Kitty was all right. "You disappeared. I've been worried about you."

"If you had seen what I have," she said acidly, "you should be terrified."

He closed his eyes. "Drink?"

She nodded.

Behind his desk was a wall-to-wall bookshelf and a credenza next to the window. He went to it, opened a cabinet and retrieved glasses and cognac.

Kitty went to the black leather seats across from his desk and picked up a silver photo frame from the corner of the table.

It was one of their wedding portraits. She looked up at her husband, pouring drinks from a decanter. He still cared about her, she knew that. It was she who could not forgive him but she had to at least try. If she was going to get to Berlin, she had to convince him that she could. An idea was stirring in her about Oskar as well, but it would mean she would need her husband. And it would be a test.

He handed her a glass of cognac. Edgar was examining her. His concern was sincere and it touched her.

She put the photo back down. "I didn't know you had this in your office."

"You don't look all right at all. You're shaking."

"I was accosted in Alsergrund. They wanted papers. I had to use your name to threaten them."

A shadow passed over his face. "Brown Shirts? Did they hurt you?"

"No. Like you said, I'm just shaken. Alsergrund is blown to hell, Edgar."

"Damn it, Kitty. What were you doing there anyway? You can't change anything by going down there. Are you *trying* to draw attention to yourself?"

She bristled. "Not at all."

He threw his hands up, and put the desk between them again. "Do you understand that you are playing with fire?"

"*I'm* playing with fire?" she protested. "I'm not the one working inside the regime."

"Keep your voice down."

He was right, but her fury had reached boiling point. "Those were my friends there last night. My friends, who are terrified."

"Your friends?" Edgar shot back. "Really? Those stray puppies of yours, Kitty?"

"I can't just go out on the street and not see what is happening, Edgar."

"Then stop looking," he shouted.

"Are you kidding me?" she cried. "Those same people who were out there looting last night, Edgar. Burning down places. Terrorizing Vienna's citizens! They'll be at the next cocktail party by Saturday and they'll be taking Communion this coming Sunday."

"Sit down," Edgar demanded.

"To hell with you!"

"Kitty! Sit down!"

Defiant, she perched on the arm of the chair to his left. He yanked his seat back and dropped into it, rubbed his face with both hands and then over his hair until his curls stood up at the base. He stared at her.

"I called your family. I didn't want them to worry. Your father insists you come home until things calm down."

"Home?" She couldn't return to America, though every cell in her body yearned for it. *Run. Flee.* But she was a fighter. Icily, she said, "I thought this was my home, Edgar."

Her husband's expression crumpled. "You have no idea how terrified I am for you. For us."

She watched him for a moment. She could beg him now to stop. To leave the German Foreign Office. To stop doing what he was doing. To come to America with her. But the gang was depending on her to get to Berlin. She had to make peace with this man.

Stretching a hand across the desk, she leaned forward. "I know you are scared. I'm not giving up on us. I'm not. But you're right. I don't feel safe. Especially when you travel all the time. I don't feel safe out on those streets."

Edgar grasped her hand and kissed it. She caressed his fingers with her other hand.

"What happened out there?" he asked softly.

It hit her then. All the events of the day. The violence. The fear. The despair. Artur's body. The blood. She had to fight the tears. "Artur was murdered by stormtroopers."

"Jesus," Edgar breathed. "Good God, Kitty. I'm so sorry."

"They're not my strays, Edgar," she choked. "They're my *friends*. They're real people."

He was next to her then, lifting her up. She was in his arms, engulfed by him. She let herself be carried, surprised by how much she needed it. Uncertain, because she did.

"Go ahead, Kitty. Take a moment."

"I don't need a moment," she cried. Forcing herself to push away from him, she held him at arm's length. "I need your help,

Edgar. I need your damned help. I need you on my side right now."

She saw his apprehension. He was pulling away because of it.

"Oskar was arrested and he thinks he might be arrested again," she said, clutching him. "The authorities let him go, but they beat him. And he's convinced they'll hang the murder on him."

"Why Oskar?"

"Artur was... his lover."

"We can't choose who we love," he muttered. He turned away from her and reached for his glass. "I don't mean you, or us. I mean, I do, but not in a bad way... *Scheiße*, I'm making a mess of this." He faced her again, apologetic.

She took his hands in hers. "I know what you mean."

"No. You don't. Margit asked for my help, too..."

Kitty had nearly forgotten. "What about her?"

"She's in love. With the wrong kind of man, apparently. Someone my parents will not approve of."

"She came here to tell you that?"

"It's about the cottage at the Vienna Woods. I'm thinking about taking it over."

Kitty could care less about the house in the Vienna Woods. "So?"

"She was hoping she could have it. Since, you know, I got Uncle Andreas' penthouse. She wants to have her own place. But I reminded her that you and I have invested the most time into it. Your gardens, your vegetables. Anyway..."

Margit and her problems were so small in comparison, and so typical for a woman of her status, it was cliché. Kitty remembered how they had surprised Edgar's sister at the cottage once. Edgar had informed his parents that he and Kitty would spend the weekend there. When they arrived, they were both irritated to find Margit was staying in the guesthouse, first of all, and secondly that she was up there without having told anyone. Now it made sense. Margit had a secret lover.

"Poor, poor Margit," Kitty said sarcastically. "I can't believe this takes precedence right now. My friend was murdered, Edgar. *Murdered!*"

"All right," her husband said. "We'll save Margit's problem for another day. Give me Oskar's full name. You know I can't help him personally, Kitty. It could get me fired. And that would be the least of it. But I might know someone who would be willing to represent him."

He reached into the middle drawer and withdrew a pad of paper.

"Tell me everything you know," he said.

Kitty went to his side of the desk, hugging herself. She could not stop shaking as she told him what she'd seen at the manufactory. "We have the right to know the truth, don't we?"

Edgar nodded, and kissed her hand again. "You know that I love you above everything. I really do. I would do anything for you."

He would not do *everything*, though, and it hurt so much she had to look away. She dared not challenge his decisions now. Right now, she was asking him to use his pull for her purposes.

"I'll get this to Oskar," she said and took the information from him.

"Kitty? I'm going to Berlin in three weeks."

She still knew her husband well enough. It was almost too easy. Her expression remained anticipatory.

"Why don't you come with me?" he said. "Millie's there, right? You could visit her. Spend a few days touring around. We can make it an early anniversary gift to ourselves."

Afraid that he, too, could read her mind as easily, Kitty leaned in and nodded against his forehead so that he could not see the satisfaction in her eyes.

23

DECEMBER 1938

Three weeks later, and up until the moment Kitty arrived at the train station in Vienna, she was still not sure whether she would —whether she could—go through with carrying the money for Khan and Big Charlie. She stood on the platform now, a box of Sacher chocolates in her hand.

It's not a problem if you don't go through with it, Khan had assured her. *But you need to know by the time you pick up the box.*

OK. I'll know before I go into the chocolate shop.

If you do this, go in, touch your hat and—

My hat? What if I'm not wearing a hat.

Wear a hat, Kitty.

Of course I'll wear a hat. Sorry.

Go to the woman wearing a white and red blouse. Tell her you are looking for Hershey's chocolates.

Hershey's? Where can you get American—

Stop interrupting. Millie is an American, right? You want Hershey's.

Right. Hershey's. OK. I understand.

The woman will tell you she doesn't carry Hershey's. You

have to say that it's a pity because you're feeling quite nostalgic. That's her code. The woman will offer you a box of Sacher chocolates. Pay for them. Take the box. The money will be in the box.

The money was Judith's, those American bills literally unleashed. Oskar had also gathered funds from trusted friends of Der Keller. Kitty did not know the sum. She had not seen the money. She assumed it was beneath the tray somehow. Stuck to the bottom of those chocolates. She could not know because she would have to unwrap the box to find out.

Our contacts in Berlin will collect the money.

How?

From the train station, you'll go through the main entrance onto Invalidenstrasse. About fifty meters from the exit doors, there is a ladies room on the right. Go in there. Set the box on the counter. You will forget the box of chocolates.

Wait in the middle stall. If it's occupied, wait until it's free. Someone will slip a business card for Dr. Bodemann on it. That's your signal that you can leave the restroom. Don't stop to do anything. Just leave and forget the box of chocolates.

That was it. It seemed so simple.

"You ready, darling?" Edgar startled Kitty out of her reverie. The huge clock above the train schedule read five past one.

She clutched the box of Sacher pralines. It looked completely normal. Pink box. Gold lettering. A pink fabric ribbon tied on top.

"These are for Millie," she said.

Edgar nodded, and ushered her to their platform. The conductor whistled and called for everyone to board if they wanted to get to Berlin.

24

DECEMBER 1938

The train rocked past the lakes south of Berlin. Across from Kitty, Edgar awoke from dozing, caught her gaze and smiled with a little embarrassment. He ran a hand over his curly brown hair and shook himself awake.

"Was I snoring?"

She placed the latest edition of *The American Foreign Service Journal* down. "Not at all. You don't snore."

He eyed the Sacher box next to her and reached across the aisle but Kitty placed a flat palm over it, careful not to crush the pink ribbon.

"You didn't feel tempted to just take one?" he teased.

She tried to match his relaxed manner despite her heart flipping over in her chest.

"I told you, these are for Millie."

Edgar arched an eyebrow. "*Es war nur ein Schmäh.* I was only teasing, Kitty. The way you're protecting that box, you'd think you were carrying a bomb."

Kitty held her breath for a second. "Not a funny joke to be making these days," she muttered.

"Why didn't you just buy some when we arrived in Berlin? It's only a box of chocolates."

"But it isn't." She pointed to the label, the double meaning not at all lost on her. "Sacher is a specialty of Vienna, not Berlin. I happen to know that Millie loves Sacher."

Whether that was true was of no consequence. Though the pink and gold box certainly marked a special brand of Austrian chocolates, it was only Kitty's cover. But the way those pralines weighed on her, they may as well have been explosives.

When she spotted a policeman coming through the carriage, Kitty did a double take. Subtly, she placed her journal over the box and smiled casually as the man yanked the handle of their compartment door. He half-heartedly examined the identity papers Edgar held out for him and glanced down at Kitty's journal before nodding and leaving them.

Edgar eyed her hand beneath her ribs. "It was just a routine control."

Kitty realized she had stopped breathing. "Of course. It's just... After Artur..."

The train suddenly rocked and swayed again as it navigated a curve. The houses and buildings were growing denser. They were coming into Germany's capital. She glanced down at the journal and the box beneath it, her heart kicking up into her throat.

Had the saleswoman at the shop been trustworthy? What if she was Gestapo? What if Kitty was being followed right here on this train? The conductor had eyed the journal in a suspicious manner. What if she had the wrong box?

"Are you having second thoughts?" Edgar asked.

She masked her surprise. "About?"

"The chocolates."

Kitty smiled sweetly at her husband and tucked the box further away from him. "Out of sight, out of mind."

She hoped so anyway.

. . .

The train screeched to a halt in Berlin's main station and Kitty yanked open the sticky varnished door, the Sacher box pressed up against her. With the sudden heat of anticipation, she ached for a breath of fresh, cold air, but the stink of stale cigarette smoke was all she got.

Edgar helped her down from the train and they walked along the platform, looking for the correct exit. Kitty spotted the sign for Invalidenstrasse, her heart hammering now, a thin sheen of sweat building on her forehead. In the corridor before the exit, she found the toilet Khan had directed her to watch for. Edgar was hurrying towards the double doors that led to the street when she halted.

"I just need..." she called after him.

He turned around, his brow furrowed. "But the hotel is only a few minutes away by taxi."

"It can't wait."

Kitty went in, her legs like jelly. On the narrow ledge under the mirror, she balanced the pink and gold box and washed her hands beneath a thin stream of water. She had to crouch to examine herself in the cheap mirror, her image wavy and liquid. She wore a red pillbox hat and a red cashmere winter scarf around the collar of her tan wool coat. Her curls were pinned back from her face, her blue eyes were wide with anticipation. After hesitating a moment, she stepped into one of the stalls. She closed the door and waited. She did not have to use the toilet, but she felt as if she would throw up.

At the sound of the door opening, she froze. High heels clicked on the tiled floor and came to a halt at the row of sinks. Water running. Kitty bent down and peered beneath the space between the stall door and the floor. A long brown fur coat. Black high heels. Thin ankles. The squeak of the tap and the water stopped. The woman was wiping her hands. Then she moved towards Kitty and stepped into the toilet next to hers.

There was a tense, still moment. Kitty held her breath. The woman's heels scratched the tile and a card appeared on the floor of Kitty's stall. Kitty stared at it, but did not pick it up. *Dr. Eugene Bodemann, Institute for Law* in Berlin with an address and telephone number.

Kitty quickly unlocked the stall door, did not even stop to pretend to wash her hands. She hurried out and panic seized her when a man in a black leather coat shoved through the entrance of the train station. She froze. But he walked right past her. When she spotted her husband in the street outside, bending into the window of a cab. Kitty clutched her valise, gathered her wits, and strode out.

Edgar opened the rear door for her. "Everything all right?"

Still shaken, she nodded and crawled into the cab.

Edgar looked in. "You forgot the chocolates."

She looked at her valise. She could say she had packed them—

"I'll go fetch them," he called.

"Edgar, wait!" She tried to grab him but Edgar was faster, already at the door of the train station again. "Don't bother!"

Kitty dashed out of the cab, ready to tackle him if she had to. She stopped just inside the corridor. Edgar was holding open the door to the ladies' room for a woman wearing sunglasses, a broad black hat, and a brown fur coat. She stepped aside, looking down her nose at Edgar. Kitty was about to call to him that she would go in and get the chocolates but how could she when this woman had likely taken them already? But where was the Sacher box? The woman had only a handbag and it was too small for it.

The stranger turned her head slightly towards Kitty, then clicked away towards the station platforms.

Edgar stepped back out. In his hands, the pink and gold

box. The bow and everything appeared untouched. He handed it to her with a smile and half a bow.

"After protecting them from me for hours, you can't possibly forget them here."

Stiffly, Kitty took the box. Nothing had changed about it. It was as heavy as when she had purchased it.

Edgar held the door open to her, encouraging her with another pleasant smile. The cab driver was impatient but Kitty was not listening to him. She got back into the vehicle and put the box on her lap. It burned a hole through it by the time they reached their hotel. It weighed a ton as she carried it onto the elevator. It was ticking—she swore it—when they got into the room.

Only when she heard Edgar showering did she feel it was safe enough to check. She undid the bow, looked at the creases critically, and opened the box. Twenty-four pralines lined up in four solid rows. She lifted the paper tray. Nothing there. She traced a finger along the edges, then the bottom, and found nothing. She put it all back together and concentrated on getting the bow tied up the same way as it was before.

Scrutinizing her work, she realized something: it could be a different box altogether, couldn't it?

"Never again," Kitty breathed, and fell backwards onto the bed.

The December air was crisp and cold beneath a cloudless winter blue sky. Millie had suggested a popular cafe near Unter den Linden where the Berliner pastries and coffee were cheap but excellent. It would be easy to find, she'd joked, by the powdered sugar around people's mouths. But after arriving in the city, Kitty was not in the mood for any jokes whatsoever.

From her hotel, she crossed a garden, lightly coated in snow-fall, and stopped to watch three children playing a game of soccer with a rather worn leather ball. She saw a teenage girl with short-cropped dark curls who looked as if she had just received the best news in the world by her excited and secretive smile. But when Kitty reached the main road, she halted in her tracks, horrified by the sight along Berlin's famous broad avenue. She had seen black-and-white photos of the city in the *Volkszeitung*, but it was a whole different sensation to see it in real life and in color.

A row of red flags and swastikas created a veritable parade of the Third Reich's presence. An entourage of black limousines sped by. Across the road, Nazi officers in brown and black uniforms, and long black leather coats, strode purposefully by the row of swastika-bedecked pedestals. What was most perverse were the colored Christmas lights and wreaths that had been added for holiday flair.

With the cumbersome Sacher chocolates for Millie in her hand, Kitty reorientated herself and found the cafe, the windows steamed over. She was relieved to see her friend and hugged her before taking a seat across from her. The cafe was bustling with Germans and tourists alike. In the corner opposite their table, a man in a heavy wool coat sat reading the paper and sipping a cup of coffee. Still unsure whether she wasn't being followed, she shifted in her seat. Kitty was on high alert.

"I took the liberty of ordering Berliner and coffee the way you like it," Millie said.

"With whipped cream?" Kitty asked half-heartedly. "And these Berliner? They look just like American donuts."

"Sweet yeast dough, fried, with apricot jam inside. Absolutely healthy and good for you." Millie grinned and patted the box of chocolates. "Thanks for these but you didn't have to bring them all this way."

Kitty scoffed. "You have no idea."

Millie smiled uncertainly. "Is everything all right?"

"Nothing is all right."

"I can see that. Your letter broke my heart. Poor Artur. Poor Oskar. How is the rest of the gang holding up? How is Vienna? Edgar?"

"Those are all very complex questions with very complicated stories. For that we need to go for a walk." She looked meaningfully at Millie, then let her eyes skirt around the cafe and back to the man who was giving her goosebumps.

Millie nodded. "I'll pack these up to take with us."

"Do me a favor?" Edgar would have chased her down the road had she forgotten the Sacher again, but she couldn't wait to get rid of them. "Can you just leave the chocolates?"

Millie looked at her quizzically but did as Kitty requested.

Outside, they walked in silence as Millie led Kitty along the canals. Soon enough, they were alone and Kitty stopped at a landing, gazing at the cityscape. She hugged herself and shivered.

"Where do you want me to start?"

Millie winced. "*Kristallnacht.*"

Kitty told her everything leading up to the discussion of creating a resistance movement in Bella's living room. That was where she stopped. She had been sworn to secrecy, and that meant even Millie could not know, but Kitty had an idea that she'd been turning over and over in her mind. She studied her friend, who was still emotional by Kitty's descriptions about Artur and Oskar, about Judith's apartment and the Brown Shirts who had accosted Kitty in Alsergrund.

"This spectacle..." she whispered and jutted her chin at the swastika-covered avenue beyond. "It's ten times louder—screaming, really—than in Vienna."

Millie looked knowingly at her and bent forward before lowering her own voice. "I know how you feel. I asked to be reassigned. I want to go back to the States. I can't take this anymore. It's... menacing. We're going to look back at this time and ask ourselves why our countries didn't do more..."

Kitty narrowed her eyes and opened her purse to remove *The American Foreign Service Journal.* She opened it to the article she wanted Millie to see.

"Can the American Foreign Service be improved? Written by FSO," Millie read. She looked up at Kitty. "Is this you?"

"No. But it should have been. Keep it. Read the articles in there. They'll ring familiar."

"Are you going to go back to the consulate?" Millie asked.

What Morris had asked Kitty to do—to inform on her husband's associates, on the Nazis, but quite possibly putting Edgar into harm's way if she didn't do it right—was a huge risk. And she'd just experienced how nerve-racking it would be. But the gang was counting on her.

"I'd like to work for Ben Roberts again," Kitty said, glancing down at the canal. "But only because the alternative is being at home all the time. I don't even know if I can play the good diplomat's wife, especially with a diplomat who is..."

Millie squeezed her shoulder. "How are you two holding up?"

Kitty laughed softly, biting back the bitterness. "I don't know. I don't know if we really are holding up. It's all a facade. Or becoming one. To be honest, it's tragic. Edgar and I... we were... I thought we were the real thing, you know?"

Her friend squeezed her shoulder again and clicked her tongue. "Calling it a tragedy, that is the truth. You two were something to envy."

Were. Kitty lowered her head, surprised by the rising tears.

Millie tucked the journal into her purse. "All the American consulates and embassies received a memo from Leland Morris last week."

"About what?" She was glad for the change in subject, but wary.

"Form Thirteen. Listen to this. *Morris* created a new system whereby all applicants can stop coming to the consulate..."

Kitty couldn't believe it. "Like we had suggested in our report? The report he's angry about?"

Millie smirked. "He's handing out forms and requesting that the Jews return them with a self-addressed envelope. And *Morris* is taking credit for it being his idea. It works so well, that Messersmith asked him to write all about it to the other embassies and stations."

"That's just genius," Kitty said sarcastically. "Good on you, Leland Morris."

Millie turned to face her and leaned against the railing. "Kitty, you do have what it takes and you are in a position of power whether you recognize it or not. Politics is just a bunch of moving parts—like a puzzle box—and you need to keep examining those little sliding panels on that box to find the right door. Look at Irena Wiley. She's a diplomat's wife. Not once has that woman underestimated her role or felt less powerful because she is 'only' Cooper's wife. Edgar is in love with you," Millie said. "Really. I might seem silly sometimes—"

"No," Kitty said. "I know exactly how talented and smart you are."

Millie smiled. "He's really in love with you, Kitty. I've seen it. And you're underestimating how very much he is conflicted. But you can change that."

"How?" Kitty scoffed. "Without being forced to live against my values?"

"You know what Irena once said? 'John thinks of himself as the head. But I am the neck. And it is the neck which directs the head.' She knows where he should turn; where he should focus. Be the neck, Kitty."

Millie opened the bag from the cafe and withdrew one of the sugary dough balls. "Berliner?"

Kitty took it, bit into it and watched Millie enjoying hers. She decided that Millie was not only right but that there was no choice other than to ask for help. She would risk exposing the gang's intentions, but she knew she could not go back to the embassy. Kitty's work in helping the Jews and those hunted by the Nazis would have to veer off in a new direction. A path she had already embarked upon just by coming to Berlin.

"I need your help," Kitty said. "Before you get transferred out of Europe."

Millie brushed her hands and put her mittens back on. "What do you need?"

"I need you to get a message directly to Pim."

The surprise in her friend's expression flickered between concern and interest. "I can't promise anything. I mean, I'm not even working in intelligence any longer, but..." Millie pursed her lips, then put a hand on Kitty's forearm. "I know someone who does, though. Leave it with me. What do you need me to relay?"

Kitty looked out on the frozen canal. A large Neo-classical building was right across the water, a Nazi flag waving in the winter breeze, a Christmas tree bearing a huge star stood in the middle of the plaza. She studied Millie for a moment. Her gut said she could trust her, that the gang could trust her.

"It's a matter of life and death. Listen carefully..."

Three days later, Kitty stepped out of the cab and looked up at the Berlin train station before turning and taking her valise from the taxi driver.

"Thank you."

Edgar put an arm around her shoulder and led her to the doors, then held them open for her. Kitty walked into the corridor that led to their departure platform, her eyes grazing the ladies' room as they walked by.

"Just give me a minute," Edgar suddenly said, and headed into a gift shop. He waved her away. "I'll meet you at the platform, darling. Go on."

Kitty frowned and watched him go inside. After speaking with Millie, she'd needed another day to get rid of the feeling that she was on pins and needles. As he'd promised, Edgar had kept his meetings and business in Berlin short. Millie's words about Edgar's devotion to Kitty had affected her greatly. She did not want to go back out into that city of black and red, and instead announced they would celebrate their upcoming anniversary early. She created a romantic nest in their hotel room for their last two days.

Edgar had been perplexed only for a moment before taking full advantage of the situation. They had ordered room service, talked, and made love, played music and danced. Kitty had even read to him from her latest novel.

Not even her secrets ruined those moments for her. She was becoming a separate entity from Edgar, and there was something thrilling about it that spurred a new passion. It added a new layer of excitement to their lovemaking for her.

A man's voice announced that the train to Vienna had arrived. She checked the clock. She hoped Edgar would not be too long. She checked for their platform and waited at the top of it. Soon, she spotted her husband's stride. She could recognize him miles away with that confident, easy gait. When he appeared from behind a crowd of passengers seeking out their trains, Kitty frowned. He had something in his hand. It was flat and silver with a sheer white ribbon on top. He reached her, holding it out to her already, beaming at her with that dimpled grin. A box of pralines.

She stared at it as he bent to kiss her cheek. "An early anniversary gift. For both of us," he explained. "So that I don't have to ask your permission next time I want a piece of chocolate."

25

JANUARY 1939

Pacing in front of the consulate, Kitty peered up and down the streets. Where were they?

Judith had finally gotten her emigration papers from Eichmann's office. She had fourteen days to get out of the country. Though the police cleared Oskar of Artur's murder—and they had Edgar to thank for that, even if indirectly—Judith was angry that her son had not been granted his exit papers yet. Either way, Oskar guaranteed Kitty that he would be here this morning and obtain his mother's visa or, at the very least, find a country where Judith could safely wait for it.

Now, Judith and Oskar were twenty minutes late. She looked up at the building and saw Leland Morris standing in the window. He cocked his head and tapped his wrist. She nodded and marched to the corner and back. There was no sign of her friends.

More concerned now, Kitty wondered what the hold-up might be. Were they in trouble? Khan had informed her the money she'd carried to Berlin had arrived and that the gang would take delivery of the equipment in bits and pieces. He was squirreling the parts away throughout the tunnels beneath

Vienna, she guessed. She didn't know, because Big Charlie had told them that information was to be shared on a need-to-know basis only.

"For protection," he'd said.

A tapping on the window above startled her. Morris waved for her to come upstairs. Kitty flung her arms out and sighed. Whether she liked it or not, she would have to face him. Upstairs, he was waiting for her and closed the door after her.

"Where is your friend?" He returned to his desk.

Kitty shook her head.

He sighed and folded his hands as if in prayer. "I was wrong about you."

"How do you mean?"

"You're not just an entitled troublemaker hiding behind her father's name, are you?"

Kitty frowned. "I don't know how I ever gave you that impression, Mr. Morris. I did my job with the utmost sincerity and professionalism."

Morris scratched his nose. "Agent Roberts and I had a long talk. He said we lost a valuable asset in you, but—"

Kitty held up a hand to stop him. "I don't think I need to hear this right now. I don't need your apologies. I don't even need for you to admit that you took my idea and made it your own with Form Thirteen. I know you're short-staffed, Mr. Morris. But..." She reached into her coat pocket and withdrew her own letter. She put it on the desk.

Morris did not move to open it.

"This letter of resignation should replace the one I wrote by hand. It is official. I will not be returning to work for you. Or for Agent Roberts. Though I hold nothing against him," she finished pointedly.

Morris finally took the envelope, opened it, read it and replaced it. "I accept your decision, Mrs. Ragatz. Would you now go find your friend, please? She can leave as soon as today, if she so wishes."

Kitty brightened only a little, still worried about where Judith might be. "I will go do that. Thank you, sir."

Too little, too late, she thought as she jogged back down the stairs and out the doors. And chastised herself for thinking it.

Kitty took the tram to the second district. The Cafe Rembrandt, just around the corner from Bella's apartment, made her stop in her tracks. She and Judith had occasionally met there before the Anschluss but now she was shocked by the sight. A white Star of David was painted across every window and someone had daubed *Jud* just between the menu boards on the ground before the entrance. The cafe looked otherwise completely abandoned.

With dread weighing her, she reached Bella's apartment block, but when she took the stairs and knocked, nobody answered. Not even Macke barked behind the door. Bella had hardly budged out of her apartment since Judith and Oskar had taken up residence with her, and all three had grown pasty from lack of fresh air and exercise.

Back downstairs, Kitty was relieved when Bella appeared from around the corner. She hurried to meet her halfway.

"Where are Judith and Oskar?"

Bella looked surprised. "I thought they were with you? She and Oskar wanted to go to Alsergrund."

"But why?" Frustrated, Kitty rubbed her face.

"She said she wanted to grab some things, some photos of Oskar or something, to see whether there was anything she could still salvage in case she had to leave right away."

A young man on a bicycle pedaled up the street, wearing a swastika armband and brown uniform. His look of suspicion pierced Kitty with fear, but he passed by.

"I'm going to Alsergrund." Kitty said. She gripped Bella's

elbow and led her to her apartment building and saw her safely inside, and promised to get word to her.

Alsergrund had changed once more. The Jewish shops were now proper German shops. *Metzger, Hüte,* a shop for soaps and perfumes. *Jews not welcome* hung on the windows and doors. Billets reminded Kitty to follow Führer and country into greatness.

The base of Judith's apartment building was covered in graffiti that had been scrubbed off over and over, only to be desecrated again and again. As soon as she walked into the building, she knew the reality that Judith had had to encounter: there were new families living in these apartments. German families.

On Judith's floor, however, her place was open and some of her things were still inside. Before Kitty could go in, the apartment door opposite opened and a large woman with a shiny, red face stepped out, her light brown hair sticking out from beneath a dingy headscarf. She eyed Kitty critically, head to toe, and folded her arms.

"Are you here to collect the items?" she demanded. She had a wholly different accent to the Viennese.

"Pardon?" Kitty asked. "What items?"

"My sister should be moving into that apartment soon and they still haven't cleared it out. Aren't you with the German *Mädeln?* The inventory is done, we just need you to clean out all that crap."

Kitty stared at her. No, she was not a member of the Hitler Youth movement, but it could be useful if the stranger thought so. "Yes, of course. The inventory."

The woman shrugged and shifted in the doorway. Behind her a baby screamed, and she seemed oblivious to it. "The government is right to seize those thieves' properties. That Jew lady and her son came back trying to claim everything as theirs. Good thing the authorities already confiscated paintings and valuables. Dragged that Jew lady out by her stupid, short hair."

"When?" Kitty asked, feigning disgust.

"This morning. And some young man with her. Now go on. My sister is coming this weekend. Go!"

Heart in her stomach, Kitty stepped into the apartment. The paintings were gone. The drawing table was gone. All of the fineries—the Jugendstil lamps, all the fixtures, the art, the vases, the record player, the sofas—they were all gone. Only a few things were left, like books, and linens and household items that one normally reconsidered taking with them if they moved. All of Judith's plants were dead.

Kitty hurried through the rooms and stopped at a scurrying sound coming from the bedroom, followed by a growl and a muffled yap.

"Macke?"

In the bedroom, photos were scattered across the parquet floor among clothing and underthings. Judith's glasses lay halfway beneath the bed.

Now the dog whined. Kitty dropped onto all fours, knowing she would find Macke under the bed. He was shaking.

"Hey, buddy," Kitty's voice shook as well. "Come on out, little guy."

Macke whined again, wiggling and licking his nose. She picked up Judith's glasses and placed them on the mattress, then scooted beneath the bed, taking his bird-bone body into her hands and gently pulled him out. He immediately began licking her face, but still shivered. She held him for a while until his shudders settled down, then she rose, picked up Judith's glasses, and left the apartment.

The Gestapo headquarters were fifteen minutes away on foot and across the Donau. She would figure out what to say by the time she reached them.

.   .   .

Hotel Metropole was a Ringstrasse building in the center of Old Town, right on the curve of Morzinplatz. A building that had once welcomed dignitaries and tourists, and now housed the Reich's secret police. Kitty went inside.

"Good morning." She leaned on the front desk, which was more like a telephone booth.

A middle-aged guard in wire-rimmed glasses was sitting very low inside. For a second, Kitty mused that the Nazis must be very paranoid if they felt the need to protect their receptionist behind bulletproof glass. The guard looked up with mild irritation from a stack of index cards. There was a small typewriter to his right. He eyed Macke in her arms with unmasked irritation and the dog growled low in return.

The guard flicked his attention to her. "How can I help you?"

"I'm looking for some friends of mine."

"Did you check with the police?"

She hadn't even thought of it. "Neighbors reported they had been taken away by plainclothes policemen. That would be you, right? The Gestapo?"

Dramatically, he opened a large black book with several columns and a long list of perfect Germanic script. "Names?"

"Judith Liebherr..." Kitty took in a breath, anger bubbling in her throat. "Judith Sara Goldberg, I mean. And Oskar Israel Goldberg."

Even from his bent head, she saw the deep frown, the way he pretended to actually look for their names on half of the filled page before he closed it, his expression set.

"I have no people with those names here."

"Are you certain?" Kitty asked. She had half expected it but now she felt unsure. Perhaps she had truly misread the situation, maybe she really needed to go to the police.

Kitty stepped away from the booth and glanced around. After setting Macke on the ground, he got right to sniffing along the wooden base. She was standing in a large marble foyer, and could hear doors down either corridor to her right and left as they opened and shut with soft sucking sounds. She looked back at the guard. There was a wooden ledge behind him and a single crutch propped up against it. His or someone else's who was trapped in here for questioning?

"OK," Kitty said, patting the wooden counter. She then reached into her coat pocket and withdrew Judith's glasses. "I think you're wrong, though. I think they are here. Judith Goldberg is going to need these. She can't see without them, and if you want her to sign anything, she's going to need to be able to read, right?" She shoved the glasses through the gap in the window.

The guard peered over to his left before he reached for them. "You need to get that dog out of here."

"Make sure Frau Lieb—" Kitty glared at him. "I mean Frau Goldberg gets those glasses."

He placed them on the ledge behind him and stared defiantly back. Just then, two men appeared to her left and one exclaimed surprise. Kitty looked down. Macke—leg lifted against the base of the pedestal—was relieving himself.

The guard, peering over the glass, demanded that she clean it up. Kitty snatched up Macke and bolted for the door. Only when she had put some distance between herself and the Hotel Metropole did she stop to kiss the top of his head.

"You are a wonderfully bad little boy. I'm going to get your mama out of there."

She would try again later. But she had to inform the gang about Judith and Oskar. She was absolutely certain—from the moment the guard had taken the glasses—that Judith was inside with the Gestapo.

. . .

The next day, Kitty was back in the den of lions, but this time without the dog. She could see that someone had scrubbed the pedestal of Macke's marking.

"Any information about Frau Goldberg?" Kitty asked the same guard.

He glanced up, recognition flashing across his face, but did not answer. Judith's glasses, however, were still sitting on top of that ledge. She felt an all-too-familiar rage bubbling up.

"They still have rights," she hissed. "You still have to offer her due process."

When his only acknowledgment was a look of apathy, Kitty pointed to the bench next to the booth. "I'll be sitting right here until someone comes and tells me whether my friends are here, and if they are, on what charges and how they can be released."

He stared at her as she backed away. She soon heard his voice behind the glass, low and angry, then the slam of the telephone in the cradle. A door opened far down the corridor to her right and she heard two sets of footsteps.

A beefy-faced officer with large, rough hands, and a second one, with a high forehead and thin blond hair, headed straight for her.

"Good day." Kitty braced herself and rose.

Wordlessly, they stepped on either side of her and dragged her to the front entrance, down the short flight of stone-worn steps and used her body to fling open the door. Kitty tumbled onto her knees on the sidewalk. Her left one burned with pain. The muscle men turned around, slammed the doors behind her, and Kitty got up on all fours. She stared after them. Passersby ignored her completely, but their silent judgments fell thick and fast on her.

That evening, at Bella's apartment, as Kitty nursed the scratches and scrapes on her legs, Khan warned her not to go back to the headquarters, and not to return to Bella's apartment.

"You've raised their hackles, Kitty. They might have had you followed."

"I am going to be there every day until someone tells me something," Kitty told them both. But she agreed that returning to Bella's could be dangerous.

Khan told her how to leave a message for him. They agreed that, if she wanted to contact the gang, she would move the big, terra cotta flowerpot from the left corner of the Juliet balcony facing Rennweg to the right of the balcony.

"But how should I get a message to you?" Kitty asked. "The Gestapo will certainly be watching."

"The flower shop across the road," Khan said.

Kitty expressed surprise, remembering how the SA troops had harassed the owner into voting in the referendum.

"I've been wondering when we'd get to this point. Listen, the flower shop owner puts out a card rack with postcards every day." Khan looked at both her and Bella. "Kitty, you buy some postcards. Take them home. If you need to leave us a message, you're going to write it on one of them and put it at the very back of the stack of cards with the Vienna opera house on it. When Bella sees the pot has been moved, she'll go retrieve it."

Khan then bent over a pad of paper and created a basic code for her that would appear absolutely normal to anyone reading the back of her card, even if they wondered why somebody's card was stuck in the card rack.

"If we need to contact you," Khan said, "Bella will call you, and she will eventually share a recipe with you. You should go to the card rack and check it. Same place, same way. I'll keep working on a code so that we can communicate more specifically."

Kitty shook her head in wonder, kissed his cheek and hugged them both goodbye.

"For now," she added. "It's only goodbye for now."

·   ·   ·

On the third day, she returned to the Gestapo headquarters again. This time, the police must have been waiting for her because no sooner had she stepped inside than a wholly different man in a gray suit and blond brush cut blocked the way to the guard.

"Step this way, Frau Doktor," he said.

Kitty's blood went cold. They knew who she was.

He beckoned her upstairs and she followed him to a well-appointed office near the end of the corridor. The herringbone wooden floors creaked and popped as he took his spot behind his desk. The window looked out onto the banks of the Danube, the sky winter-washed in shades of blue and gray.

"I understand that you are looking for a friend," he said. "I'm Franz Josef Huber, the chief of state police. I can tell you that your friends are here."

Kitty quietly gasped. "On what grounds?"

He shifted, examining her. "We know who you are, Frau Doktor Ragatz. The fact that you are here, inquiring about a Jewish woman and a Jewish homosexual, piques our interest. What we are not certain about is whether you understand the impact this is having on Dr. Ragatz."

Kitty's heart seized. "This has nothing to do with Edgar."

"No. But your insistence in harassing our personnel will get back to him, and that, my dear Frau Doktor, would put him in quite a precarious situation. Having a wife with a reputation for being a... how can I put this delicately? A Jew lover. It fosters complicated implications." He steepled his hands. "Frau Doktor, if I may be so bold as to advise you. It does not pay to associate with the wrong kind of people."

"Wrong kind of people. Indeed." Kitty bent slowly forward, enunciating each word. "Where is she? Where's Judith, and where's her son?"

Huber cocked an eyebrow and took in a deep breath. He looked to his right and picked up two files. "Oskar Israel Goldberg is on his way to Dachau. He was caught in the arms of another man last night and, as you know, that is against the law."

"That can't be true," Kitty protested.

"You are so certain. I'd be curious," the chief said smoothly.

She couldn't give away that Oskar had been staying with Bella all this time. She couldn't put Bella into these men's sights.

"Dachau?" Kitty said. "Without a trial?"

He tipped his head. "He shall get his due process."

"What about his mother? Judith has an American visa, ready to go. She could be on the next train to catch a boat. Let her go, and I will personally escort her out of the country."

He looked amused. "I don't think so. You see, Frau Goldberg seems to know where we can find someone else we're keen to speak to."

Kitty froze.

Slowly, Huber opened a file and placed two photos in front of her. Big Charlie was the first one. The second one was from Judith's mirror, the one from her wedding where she posed with the girls and Khan was circled in red.

Kitty had to blink away the black pins.

"It is clear that you know Alikhan. What about Karl Grossmann? He goes by Big Charlie. Our customs guards seized a shipment of printing equipment and blank passports sent over the border from Germany. The two men we arrested finally gave us Karl Grossmann's name. We know that Alikhan and he are working together." He replaced the photos, closed the files and folded his hands on top of them. "Therefore, Frau Doktor, we will bring you Frau Goldberg if you tell us where we can find Big Charlie and Alikhan. Call it a trade."

Kitty willed herself to look him in the eye. "I don't know Big Charlie. And I don't know where Khan is. He was simply one of the many guests at my wedding."

"That's unfortunate, Frau Doktor. And not just for you. You see, we are trying to figure out what you could possibly have to do with these people, but perhaps there is something we should know about your husband?"

Kitty said nothing. She knew anything she would say now would be twisted sheerly for Gestapo purposes. She could barely control her breathing. Her limbs were numb.

Huber's look bored into her. "Your husband is a very influential man, as is his father. Very well connected, and sometimes —like you, Frau Doktor—not always with the right kind of people. It would be a shame if Dr. Ragatz and you were found to be connected to traitors within the Reich."

The chief pushed himself away from the desk and came around, Kitty turning her head to keep him in sight. She nearly fainted when he went to the door, opened it and extended an arm to her.

"You are free to go, Frau Doktor. Take some time and think long and hard about what your next move is going to be."

Kitty stood. She did not want to go anywhere near him but she had to. To get out of here, she had to.

He escorted her all the way to the entrance, and her eyes skirted over the front booth. She could only see the top of the guard's head, the typewriter pinging, one letter at a time.

Huber held the door open to the street. By the time Kitty was in the fresh air, her legs were rubbery and weak. Around the corner, she ducked beneath a small bridge and leaned against one side, gasping for breath.

Oskar was headed to Dachau. But Huber had said nothing about transporting Judith anywhere. Which meant she was still in that building. What Kitty needed to do now was to find a way to warn Khan and Big Charlie that the Gestapo was searching for them. She pounded the cement base with her fists and sobbed. She had "stirred the pot," "rocked the boat," tried to be the hero. How many times had she been warned? The

Gestapo was squeezing in on her. And now on Edgar because of her.

With a start, she thought of the embassy. Morris would be wondering what had happened to her. Maybe that was it. As an American, she could find safety there. And what? Call her dad, who would make sure she left—and leave the gang behind? Spill everything to Morris—who made a joke of everything?

No. She was on her own now. She had chosen this. She would notify Khan as they had arranged, and she would make sure he and Big Charlie were at least safe.

The walk back to Rennweg steeled her for her next steps. Kitty stopped at the flower shop and chose three different cards. The Rathaus. The gardens at Palais Liechtenstein where she and Edgar had celebrated their wedding. A steamboat on the Danube.

"These would be nice for family and friends," she explained aloud to anyone who might overhear her. She paid for them and returned to her apartment.

Quickly checking the rooms, to her relief she found that Jerzy was not there. Kitty went straight to Edgar's study, retrieved the code Khan had written and straightened out the sheet. She scribbled the warning that Khan had given her if she suspected that the police or Gestapo were closing in. She did not suspect, however. She knew.

Absolutely certain that the weather is getting colder.

They had to take action. She had to help them find a hiding place. She looked up then as if she'd just been hit on the head.

On the wall, Edgar's uncle's hunting scenes and dead animals had been replaced with photos and collages of her and Edgar, most of them from their honeymoon in the Alps. Coming around the desk, she studied the photo of Edgar and her at the cottage, sitting on the horses in the stable yard just before riding off.

Behind those horses, there was the empty barn. The cellar. And the storage house. And acres and acres of woods. There were places to hide on the cottage property.

Kitty hurried back to the desk and tapped the pen against it. How could she make herself clear? She checked Khan's list. There it was: *meet me* with the code *Perhaps you will join us.* Khan would have to get a message to her to let her know how. She would direct them to the Vienna Woods cottage, wait for them there, and help them get situated. Her mind was racing with all the details and possibilities of being discovered, and the security measures she would have to build in.

She hid Khan's code in her credenza, taping it to the top of a drawer, then grabbed the postcard and the two others she'd purchased and headed to the elevator. She pushed the button, thinking her plan through.

As soon as she safely placed her postcard into the card rack, she would exchange the other two postcards, thereby giving her a reason for being at the shop again in case Huber had put his goons on her. Then she would move the flowerpot on the Juliet balcony and wait for Bella to call her.

As subtly as she could, she checked for anyone that looked suspicious, found nothing, and hurried across the road. She stood at the card rack, slipped her postcard in, and removed two random cards. The flower shop owner looked quizzically at her as she asked him to exchange her earlier purchase.

She was just about to cross the road again when she saw Jerzy entering the building. Two men came up the walk just then, and Kitty froze.

The two Gestapo muscle men. They stopped Jerzy before he entered the building. Kitty ducked back into the shop and looked out the window, uncaring if she looked strange. The smaller man with the high forehead handed Jerzy a cardboard box, pointed upwards—to her apartment—and then turned and left. The big meaty one looked around, then the two of them crossed the road opposite and went through the park. Kitty was holding her hand beneath her ribs, and released a slow breath.

The flower shop owner was watching her. "Madame?"

Kitty shook her head, looked to the left, but did not see the men in the park. She ran across the street and into the building, hearing the elevator click and whirr as it made its way back down. When it arrived, she got in, inserted the key for their suite, and heart hammering, watched the floors pass by.

Jerzy was still in the front foyer, and his face showed alarm at the sight of her.

"Good afternoon, Frau Doktor. Are you all right? This just came for you. Two Gestapo..."

Trembling, she took the big box from him. It was tied shut with a string and was surprisingly light with the contents inside loosely packed.

"Did they say what was in it?" She held it against her.

"I'm afraid I don't know," Jerzy said. "But let me help you with that."

Goosebumps rose across Kitty's arms as Jerzy pulled the string and opened the box. Kitty looked inside. The first thing she saw were Judith's glasses atop Judith's handbag, then her appointment diary, and a pen. A typed note on an index card was near the bottom. Kitty fished it out.

> We regret to inform you that Frau Judith Sara Goldberg was found dead in her holding cell. The cause of death is heart attack.

There was more, but Kitty dropped the box, the contents spilling across the black-and-white tiled floor.

26

FEBRUARY 1939

It was her fault. Judith's death was her fault. Oskar, in Dachau, was her fault. And it was the fault of the Department of State. And it was the fault of the Nazis. And the Gestapo. It was Edgar's fault. But mostly, it was her fault.

She had tried to fix everything and she had done it all wrong. She had rocked that boat, and caused everyone to fall into deep water. Judith's money had paid for nothing but traitors. With no time to arrange anything, Big Charlie and Khan disappeared into the complicated network of tunnels beneath the city. They were on the run and those tunnels were now regularly patrolled by secret and military police. She had no idea whether they were safe.

The day after Judith's box had arrived, Edgar had returned from Rome and the Gestapo showed up minutes later and took Edgar in for questioning. Kitty had not even had a chance to prepare him for it. He returned that night, at first silent, then he exploded.

For days, he vacillated between anger and pity for her, but their words wounded one another to the point where Kitty was left numb.

"I don't know what you were thinking," he shouted. "Do you? You have no idea how much danger you have put yourself in. Forget about me. I'll be fine."

Kitty's fear and anger constricted. "That's right, you'll be fine, because you have your father to run to."

"When in God's name have I done that? When, Kitty? Just name one time—"

"But that's it! You don't run. You don't flinch. You just get down to it, business as usual. You promised me you would do everything to try and change the direction."

"Sure, Kitty. And now? Every move I make, they'll be watching me."

"You can't give up."

He strode over to her, fast and mean. She had never felt so small around him. "You are the one who sent them for me, Kitty. I told you once, I told you a hundred times, but you don't know when to stop. You have their attention, all right. Congratulations! Now what?"

She grabbed for him, truly sorry for the ordeal she had put him through. Needing his arms around her because her heart was splintered into a million pieces. Judith and Artur were dead. Dead. And Oskar was out of their reach in Germany, in a detention camp. But as Edgar paced back and forth in the sitting room—even sidestepped her when she tried to reach for him—she realized he was slipping away from her for good.

"Can you forgive me?" Kitty pleaded. "Please, forgive me. You always ask for my forgiveness."

"I can't," he snapped.

"Why not?" she bit back. "What's changed, Edgar?"

He spun on his heel, eyes wide and wild. He swept his arm violently across the room. "*Die verdammte Welt*, Kitty! The whole fucking world! And they have cornered you. They will try to corner me. And when they do..."

Kitty folded her arms. "Then it's a damned good thing the world is round."

"Kitty?" Edgar was watching her from his side of the breakfast table. It was days after their most bitter fight.

She pushed away her plate of scrambled eggs and *Semmel*. She'd picked at the bun but had left the eggs untouched. "Hmmm?"

"I've got some news. I met with my father."

She did not look up. "About what?"

"The cottage. I told you a while back. My parents haven't been using it all that much, and I offered to take it over. I've made an agreement with Margit that she can use the guest-house, as long as she tells us in advance."

Kitty shook her head, not understanding.

"Margit wanted the property, remember?"

"The lover," Kitty said flatly.

"I thought it might be a good place where you can... Now that you're not working, I mean. Maybe you'd just like a place to get away to. The gardens? The horses? Where you might clear your head."

"Clear my head?" she asked tersely. "Or hide me away?"

Edgar cleared his throat. "Or maybe you will reconsider going to Minnesota for a visit? I think it would do you good."

Hiding her away, then.

She looked back down at the plate. More than anything, Kitty longed to say yes. Of course she wanted to return home. She longed for the comforts of order and peace, of feeling safe inside the dark, old oak interiors of the Larsson mansion. Of sprawling across Sam's bed as he lay on the floor with his pillow under his head, and talking about God and the world until all hours of the night. She yearned to drink a cup of coffee beneath the red maple in the garden with her father, and get his perspectives. She even yearned to see her mother, because Kitty needed to hear how Claudette had been right and she had been wrong.

Yet, going home and sticking her head in the sand was not going to change anything. Two of her friends had been murdered. Another was trapped in a concentration camp. And Big Charlie and Khan were in hiding until the Gestapo had better things to do.

And then she gasped. If Edgar took over the cottage, she could finally secure it for Big Charlie and Khan. Careful to contain her growing excitement, Kitty cleared her throat. *Be the neck.* He had to believe this was his idea.

"You're right. I'm not myself. How could I be? I'm grieving. There is no medicine for that."

Edgar nodded as if he'd expected that to be her answer. "That's why I'm thinking you might be able to recover a little. At the cottage. It will be ours. You can plant that vegetable garden like you'd always wanted. Finish the landscaping. I know it's still early for the season, but there's plenty you could get started on. Besides..." A shadow rippled across his face.

"What?"

He took a deep breath, then released it slowly, crumbling an eggshell beneath the tip of his butterknife. At the sound of the door to the butler pantry, Edgar's look flicked past her. Kitty glanced over her shoulder. Jerzy was coming in with a stack of platters to put away.

"What is it, Edgar?"

Her husband's jaw tensed. "Germany marched into Czechoslovakia early this morning. Without a fight."

Porcelain shattered on the floor and Kitty leapt out of her chair. Jerzy was bent over a broken blue-and-white *Augarten* platter. She rushed over to him, but he waved her away, two of the largest pieces already cradled in one palm.

"Excuse me," Jerzy said. "Please. Forgive me."

She put a hand on his forearm. "Let me help."

The creases in his brow grew deeper. When he raised his head, she saw anger in those bright, blue eyes.

"Poland will be next," he whispered so low she thought she was imagining it. She bent closer as Jerzy said, "But they must fight. Someone must stand up to them."

Suddenly, Edgar was on the ground with them, the hearth brush and dustpan in hand. Jerzy reached for them but Edgar did not let go.

As Edgar swept up the floor on his knees, Kitty rocked back on her heels.

In late March, in between the cottage and returning to the city, Kitty was repotting the red geraniums on the Juliet balcony when the phone rang. She pushed the loose earth down, stood up, and brushed her hands before heading into the hallway.

"*Grüß Gott. Frau Doktor Ragatz am Apparat,*" she answered.

"Kitty, it's Millie."

"Millie, my goodness." Kitty nearly burst into tears. All she had done was send Millie more heart-wrenching news. "It's so good to hear your voice."

"I had to call you. I'm finally going to D.C. I'll be working for the Department of State."

"That's incredible, Millie." This time the longing to return to the States hit Kitty square between the eyes.

"And, Kitty..."

"Yes."

"We have reason to celebrate."

"We do?"

"He said yes."

Kitty frowned then gripped the phone. In the small mirror opposite, she saw her reflection. Her blond hair had grown long enough that she now tied it back. She had been feeling older and weary in the two months since Judith's death, but now her blue eyes shone and her heart beat faster.

"That took long enough," she said quietly. "Wait. *He* said yes."

"Yeah, *he*. And *he* sent me a box of chocolates. I'm going to pop the champagne tonight."

Khan might have been clever at inventing code on the spot, but so was Kitty, because back in Berlin, she had fashioned the message to let her know when and whether Millie was successful in reaching Pim. According to that code now, not only had her friend been able to reach Pim, but the asset was a he, not a she. The chocolates meant he would be in contact with Kitty directly.

She heard Millie hesitate on the other line. "What about...?"

"The family is fine," Kitty hurried, knowing Millie would understand she meant the remaining members of the gang. She had managed to safely get Big Charlie and Khan to the Vienna Woods but with phone taps everywhere, she could not be explicit.

"Everyone's fine," she assured.

Millie sighed. "I'm glad to hear it."

"Congratulations, again," Kitty said. "When do you leave for D.C.?"

"In a couple of weeks," Millie said. "I'll be stopping at the embassy in London first."

"Millie... Tell Nils that I'm all right. He needn't worry."

Millie was silent on the other end for a moment. "I can do that."

"And I hope your date goes well," Kitty added, just in case someone really was listening in.

Millie thanked her. "Funny how you always meet people twice, right?"

Kitty nodded, grateful that Pim had come back to her, full circle. Perhaps now she and the gang could really make a difference and avenge Judith's and Artur's murders. Even get Oskar out of Dachau. She felt a renewed surge of power. She had a team.

PART FOUR

JUNE–NOVEMBER 1939

27

JUNE 1939

The gray sky contrasted with the rolling, bright green hills. As a Minnesota girl, Kitty knew that color of sky meant a serious thunderstorm was brewing. What she was not certain about as Khan jammed the gear of the *Lastwagen* into place and climbed the next slope, was whether she had perhaps jumped the gun.

It *felt* safe, but what if it wasn't? They were taking the winding, mountain roads towards a small iron and steel town between Graz and Vienna. The truck Khan was now driving had suddenly appeared at the Vienna Woods cottage one day. The keys were stuck in the ignition. Big Charlie and Khan had searched the entire vehicle for a clue as to why it was there. They found it, glued to the bottom of the seat, in a brown envelope. *Marketplace, Mürzzuschlag. Saturday morning. Keep the change. Very generous. Thank you. Truck courtesy of the orphanage.*

They were in the throes of resistance work. After weeks of interpreting secret messages from Pim, which he posted on page three of the *Volkszeitung* via advertisements for everything from typewriters to insurance, Kitty not only knew how to extract from his code, but how to decipher his cryptic instructions, his first ones being to clean her slate. To do nothing for weeks, and give no reason for the Gestapo to keep trailing her.

But his messages kept coming and not just through the newspaper, but through various clandestine channels. Eventually, Kitty pieced together information about an insurgent group that she finally correctly interpreted as being called the O5. She had no idea who they were, how they had come together, but Pim had pointed out that she could see their handwriting—literally—on the wall.

Amidst the splattered graffiti in Vienna, on building foundations, on signposts, in the corners of flyers, and billet boards, she stumbled on the simple O5 symbol in chalk. Sometimes in yellow. Sometimes in green. Sometimes in white. But that resistance group was there, and the more she looked, the more she found them. They led the gang to supply depots—a copy machine, paper, ink and other materials, so that they could write and produce leaflets and flyers. She had clandestine meetings with a new network of couriers responsible for taking her communication back to Pim, who, in turn, instructed them to keep recruiting and adding members to their cell. But the most brilliant was her cover, which, in April, he told her to begin building up.

A nearby parish priest was involved with an orphanage in Upper Austria. Kitty recruited him and delivered her vegetables to help supply their kitchens, and also with resistance propaganda, falsified documents, passports, and other materials needed to help get people out of Germany hidden in the truck and the crates.

In the meantime, Khan recruited his sister, mother and father, making the bookstore the place where they could distribute their missives and messages to the city couriers. Bella then pulled in a niece who'd studied at the University of Vienna, and established a small network made up of expats and students who offered safe houses not just for resistance members but for people who needed to hide from the Gestapo and any enemies that could or had renounced them.

Big Charlie vetted the best candidates from his fan club, and recruited them to assist their efforts. Despite he and Khan having to remain hidden in the Vienna Woods, they were all working, and making an impact.

She and Khan were wearing the standard farmer's blue overalls, her hair done up in a loose chignon beneath a scarf. They were going to a farmer's market. Pim's cryptic instructions meant that they were to wait until someone approached and made contact with them there.

The gang's main goal was to establish an escape route for the Jews in Vienna. But to coordinate their own efforts better, she needed to get the equipment for forgeries. After begging Pim for better communication, and in person with his O5 group, he'd resisted until now. Now they were invited to meet up with some of the engineers and members of the O5 in the Semmering Mountains.

She was anxious, wondering whether he'd be there in person. Kitty had begun to envision what Pim might look like. Mysterious. Young. An intellectual, in wire-framed glasses. And she could not wait to shake his hand, tell him how much she admired him, how very glad she was that he had escaped the Gestapo when Kendrick had been arrested.

"I bet they're socialists," Khan said.

Kitty knew how he felt about communists, but said nothing. From what she had learned, the O5 was a mixed bag of political and religious leanings, banned together to purge Austria of the Nazis.

"Why do you think they're called the O5? What does it stand for?" Kitty asked Khan.

He shrugged.

It didn't matter. They were part of it, and it had given Kitty that renewed purpose under the guise that she was volunteering. Edgar had appeared relieved that she had a project, and had bought the story about the orphanage and the vegetables.

"Your sister-in-law was back this last weekend," Khan said.

"Did you finally catch sight of Margit's lover?"

Khan shook his head. "Just a little from his frame. A boxy guy. Cap on his head. Definitely not her class, though."

"Much trouble?" Kitty asked.

"*Nee*, Big Charlie and I are very good at taking turns and keeping watch from the hill. Signals and all."

It gave Kitty sweet pleasure to be using Josef and Dorothea Ragatz's country home from which to run their resistance. The cellar beneath the barn was now well lived in, and rigged with a number of creature comforts.

When the coast was clear, the men slept in the old grain house among the bric-a-brac on folded-out cots, which they dragged up from the cellar. They had a key to the guesthouse, and used the toilets and showers. Two miles away, in case someone came to stay at the property, Khan and Big Charlie fashioned a hideaway in the woods. They had fresh water nearby, some provisions, and a camouflaged lean-to that they could quickly set up and dismantle.

But Margit was a thorn in their sides. Whereas the neighboring farmer and his wife looked in on the grounds like clockwork, Margit's appearances were still sporadic and sudden, making it very inconvenient for the men. Especially with the addition of Margit's lover.

"Well, it's been going on for some time," Kitty said. "I'm reluctantly giving her the benefit of the doubt and saying it's true love. Poor Margit. And poor you. I tried to get Edgar to put an end to her visits, but..."

"We're getting used to it," Khan said. "And as soon as she and that guy are gone? Big Charlie really loves that indoor shower."

Kitty laughed a little.

He squinted at her. "You heard from Oskar?"

She sat back and faced the road. "I got a letter. A lot of it was redacted, but he did get one of my parcels. He says the labor is hard but his attorney might be able to make some headway."

"Your husband's friend?"

Kitty huffed. "More like an acquaintance. God forbid Edgar get his hands dirty." Especially now that the Gestapo had questioned him. Her conscience still stung from that.

They were entering the valley, a large slate-gray river flowing quickly by.

Kitty looked down at the map. "Take the next right."

The marketplace was between the church and the city hall in a narrow plaza. Khan and Kitty set out their crates, built up the booth, and set up their *Vienna Woods Produce* sign. She was on edge as customers came by and picked up heads of lettuce, and rifled through the large white radishes. Some purchased them and some remarked on Kitty's accent.

"*Nicht ganz wienerisch,*" one woman in a green wool blazer criticized. *Not exactly Viennese.* She peered at Kitty and Khan in turn. Someone then called behind the woman, and she turned around, greeted a man in a suit and coat, and then turned back to pick up her sack, casting Khan one more suspicious look.

"I'm as original Viennese," Khan replied in dialect, "as you are Hungarian... Frau Varga."

The woman huffed and turned away, and Khan rolled his eyes at Kitty. But Kitty was busy watching two policemen striding across the square. They each had a billy club swaying at their hips. She cast a nervous glance at the city hall where posters of the Führer hung on the walls.

That was when a man in a Tyrolean-styled hat, a feather stuck in the band, approached. He was wearing a pair of Lederhosen and only a vest though the early mountain air was still remarkably chilly. He ordered five kilos of cherries, three heads of lettuce and a dozen white radishes, then handed a Reichsmark to Kitty.

"Thank you," she said, and opened the box of cash.

"Keep the change," the man said.

Kitty looked up. The man was gazing steadily at her. She studied the bill in her hand. In the corner, in pencil, O_5. Her pulse quickened. Was *this* Pim?

"Very generous," she said, remembering the exact words on that note Big Charlie had found in the truck. "Thank you."

Unsmiling, the man gave each of them a brisk nod and turned away.

Kitty caught Khan's attention and jerked her chin to the cashbox. She turned the bill over and found an address. Eight o'clock was written lightly in pencil beneath. She removed the pencil she had stuck into their clipboard, crouched behind the stand, and erased it.

They found a sturdy block house at the address the man had given them, but Khan and Kitty made their way to a shed at the back of the garden. Two men stepped out of the dusky shadows. Her pulse settled a little when she recognized the Tyrolean hat and feather. She and Khan were patted down.

"I'm Habicht, and this is Simon," the man said afterwards. "Not our real names, but our call names."

No Pim. Kitty had been naïve to think he would be here in person. But it was time to ask some questions and get some answers. The men ushered Kitty and Khan into the shed, and then opened a cellar door from the floor. Below, the space was much more comfortable than what Big Charlie and Khan had available to them at the Vienna Woods. A lamp burned on a makeshift table propped on two sawhorses. There were two stools, and a chair. Habicht indicated Kitty and Khan should take the stools. Simon stood across from them. In the light, his features were revealed. He was youngish and had short brown hair, wore a Dutch cap and also a pair of *Lederhosen*. There was a large scar running from his knee to a withered calf.

Habicht took off his cap, revealing white hair beneath. She realized that the men shared the same sharp nose and clear gray eyes. They had to be father and son.

Kitty settled back. "I'm really glad that you took the time to meet with us. I know the risks this presents."

"We fought Pim on this from the start," Simon said as if warning them. "We're not used to... foreigners." His eyes slid over both of them. "But Pim made a strong case."

"If we're going to work together," Habicht said, "we can only communicate with one person from your group. Nobody else will have contact with us."

Kitty began lifting her hand but then put it down. He was looking at Khan. Khan was street smart. Khan knew all the hiding places in Vienna.

"And that means Pim will only have contact with that person," Habicht finished.

"But," Kitty protested. "He trusts me. Pim came to me—"

"When you called," Simon said and spread his legs wide apart. "He explicitly does not—"

Habicht held up his hand and turned sharply to Simon, then looked back at Khan and Kitty. "So. Who is it going to be?"

Khan glanced at her and pursed his lips, then looked at Habicht. "She deserves to be the one."

The older man scowled. "This isn't a popularity contest. This is serious business. The fewer contacts, the less likely any of you will have the chance to give the rest of us away. It's for your protection, you *Depp*. But you two should choose who that will be."

Simon scoffed, and Habicht's hand came back up.

Kitty raised her own hands in surrender. "Khan should be the one."

"Good. That's settled. You can go."

"I want to send a message to Pim," she hurried. "We have a real mission. We need to help the Jews leave the country as soon as possible."

Khan rose suddenly and stepped between Simon and Kitty. "Just give her the assurances that we need. She's worked so hard to get this far. She's put herself, and her husband at risk. Just let her know whether it's been worth her while."

Kitty shot him a grateful look.

Father and son also seemed to come to a conclusion.

"We understand you want to forge documents," Habicht said.

Kitty looked up hopefully. "Yes. We have someone who—"

Habicht held up a hand, his brows knitted in anger. "We don't want to know anything. But Pim told me you are to get what you need. Everything." He looked at Khan. "Now, it's you I talk to and nobody else."

Kitty climbed the steps to the top again. Simon remained silent at her side as she reached the outdoors. It was raining, the storm finally broken. She moved beneath the narrow eaves.

"You're doing the right thing," Simon said in the dark. Clouds of air rose between them. She was unable to make out his features.

"How so?"

Simon's silhouette nodded in the dark. "He didn't want it to be you. But he wanted to let you and your friend choose."

"Pim didn't want me? But..." *Why?* Had she done something wrong? Had she offended him?

Somehow she knew that, even if he could tell her, Simon would not answer any of her questions about Pim.

"I just have one question that has nothing to do with Pim, or your work here."

Simon shifted next to her in the dark.

"Why O5? What does it mean?"

"Oesterreich," Simon said.

"Pardon?"

"We're not Ostmark. We're Oesterreich."

Whatever that meant. But Kitty dropped it because Khan suddenly appeared in the doorway. With some relief, she climbed into the truck next to him and faced him.

He put the vehicle into gear. "I've got what we need. We're going to talk about a new system. Where do you want me to take you?"

Miserable, and feeling quite excluded, she mulled it over for a moment. With Edgar on a short business trip in the Sudetenland, she could stay with Big Charlie and Khan at the cottage. It might be the last time they would be able to speak freely with one another, and she wanted to be there, to be part of the plan.

"I'll stay at the cottage tonight."

"All right." He was quiet for a moment. "Does Edgar ever ask why you spend so much time up there?"

She blew softly and looked out the window at the dark landscape. "I think he's probably relieved when we don't have to confront one another."

Khan grunted. "Are you relieved?"

Kitty was glad it was dark, so that he could not see that she had to blink back sudden tears. Quietly she said, "I'm very sad that this is the state we have reached."

"You never really know who you are until your back is up against the wall. But he helped Oskar."

She frowned and shifted to face him. "I didn't think you liked Edgar."

"*Nee*, Kitty. I don't dislike anybody. The Nazis, yeah, I dislike them, and that's mildly put. But your husband? You know our saying. He's got a lot of 'shadows to jump over', but he stepped up when it mattered. The way I see it, he's trying to protect himself so he can protect you."

Kitty stared at Khan for a moment, then turned to the window wondering whether she could reconcile herself with his perspective. It was not easy.

But Pim made everything else easier. A month later, Kitty was able to safely courier twenty-two newly forged passes, exit visas, transit visas and identity papers to the network. It was working, and she was thrilled, but the urgency to help more and faster grew. Edgar returned from Berlin with the news that Italy and Germany had established a new military and political alliance.

When he told her that, she lowered herself onto the sofa, feeling numb. Jerzy still predicted Poland would be next. But what were Italy's goals?

"Is this what you were doing in Rome when Judith died? Preparing for this?"

Edgar's face remained stony. "What I'm trying to tell you is that we need to brace ourselves. Hitler is hell-bent on war."

"You're certainly right about that. Judith was murdered at Gestapo headquarters, so even if it's my own personal war, Edgar, there will be one."

His face paled. "What do you mean?"

She retreated. She'd said too much already. "Never mind."

"No. I want to know what you meant." He stood with his hands on his hips.

"Look, Oskar is still in Dachau, God knows under what conditions. And you're out there helping to build up Hitler's power. You want to fight?" Her voice was a decibel higher. "Then why won't you fight for us? For our marriage?"

Edgar dropped his hands to his sides, his face slack. He slowly shook his head, his eyes watery blue. "Kitty, *mein Liebling*. This has to stop. Your accusations... They have to stop."

She gasped, the tears flowing freely. "Is that your idea of being a diplomat? That's how you're going to negotiate with me? I have to *stop*? You know what, Edgar, I used to admire you because you were a leader. But you have done nothing in all this time."

Edgar shut his eyes, swaying before her. Then he took her by the chin and tenderly caressed her cheek with his thumb. "Sometimes, a leader is someone who recognizes that others can do better than he and steps aside when that's needed. I thought you knew that."

She pulled away. "What is that supposed to mean? Who did you step aside for?"

He winced, those dimples creased. He dropped his head and retreated to his study then, the door closing softly behind him. Kitty stared after him. An hour later, unable to stand the silence and inactivity, she left him a note that she would be at the Vienna Cottage.

If Edgar had given up, then he had no idea how that was going to drive her to do more. From now on, she thought, they were on completely separate pathways.

28

SEPTEMBER 1939

The priest reached for the basket in Kitty's hands and smiled, but his attention was on the road beyond the village church-yard. She looked over her shoulder.

"It's safe," she assured. "I wasn't followed."

"Bless you, Kitty. I'll get these into the right hands."

She left the basket with him and climbed onto her bicycle. The passports, transit visas and other forgeries for thirteen people were in the priest's hands now.

That made three hundred and twelve people between May and August. All the forged identity papers that Big Charlie and Khan produced with painstaking attention to detail were helping the persecuted of Vienna and beyond. The one thing Kitty wished for was to hug them each and wish them peace and strength. In the name of Judith Liebherr. In the name of Artur Horváth.

She pedaled on to the next village, her legs tired from the long road, and thought—not for the first time—of Pim. She wondered how she could miss someone she'd never met, but it was the thrill she missed. The secret communication between

them. Though she looked each day, there were no more advertisements on page three of the *Volkszeitung* for her.

In the meantime, Khan had cracked the mystery behind the
meaning of O5. After she told him about Simon's answer, he
brightened.

"'O', for Oesterreich," he declared, "and five for the fifth
letter in the alphabet: 'e'!"

At first she had doubted him, but Big Charlie had laughed
loudly, convinced that Khan was right.

Khan then went so far as to tell her that the instructions he
received now were not coming from Pim at all, but through a
different O5 resistance member. Her job was simply to follow
orders, to do as she was told, and she did. Her life was on the
line. The Nazi regime was cracking down on resistance
members ever more.

Reports trickled in that the SS and Gestapo raided entire
districts, incarcerated their victims and delayed their trials.
When Kitty was growing up, the Senator had a wisecrack about
such methods, referring to the American Westerns he loved,
and called it a situation of "shoot first, ask questions later."
Except that the Nazis were no joke. If she was to believe the
news that came from other couriers and underground publica-
tions, Hotel Metropole was the site of misery, torture, and
death. Nobody would be able to convince Kitty that Judith's
death had been anything but murder at the Gestapo's hands.

Vienna was not alone in the efforts to tighten security. In
Upper Austria and in Styria, secret police infiltrated two
groups. In Tyrol, an entire clandestine network had been rooted
out and its members executed.

Black propaganda meant jail time, sabotage was cause for
death. Every step was a risk. Every attempt to prevent Nazi
activities was a game of cat-and-mouse, life-or-death. And every
precaution was necessary to gain the upper hand.

To Kitty's relief, Margit had stopped coming to the guesthouse. For weeks, Khan and Big Charlie hadn't seen her, and Kitty supposed the love affair with the mystery man was over. At the next opportunity, Kitty invited her sister-in-law out to lunch, but Margit said she was not feeling well and asked that they do it some other time. That clinched it for Kitty. She was certain that Margit was suffering from a broken heart.

Then on the first of September, Kitty was rummaging in the kitchen larder, looking for canning jars, when she heard the unmistakable sound of radio static over the wire. It was coming from the butler pantry. She paused, then pressed an ear up to the wall. There was music, and a man, speaking in urgent Polish, crackled through. All Kitty understood was, "Long live Poland!" Then the national anthem, and static again—it had to be Jerzy in there, with an illegal wire. She was about to leave the pantry, when she heard an English broadcast.

"... the German air force and German army unexpectedly invaded Polish territory without a declaration of hostilities..."

There was a low cry, then a crash from inside, the sound of broken glass. Kitty rushed out, and found Jerzy propped up against the vitrine, shards of a wine glass scattered against the far wall.

His face was contorted and he looked wretched. "My wife and daughter. They live just south of Warsaw. She is..."

Kitty stared at him.

"She is... Jewish. My wife is Jewish."

Kitty clamped a hand over her mouth. Without thinking, she asked, "And you?"

He closed his eyes and shook his head then reached into the collar of his tunic and withdrew a golden crucifix on a thin chain.

"I should never have left them. I should have..." His hand closed over the crucifix.

"What are you going to do?"

Jerzy straightened, and brushed his face with one hand. "I don't know."

"But you do, don't you?"

Edgar was calling for them from the dining room. Kitty studied the Polish man for a moment. She patted his shoulder on her way to the door.

"We're in here," she called but met Edgar in the hall.

"Is Jerzy in there?"

She glared at him. "He needs to be alone right now. Are they broadcasting on the local radio?"

Edgar nodded and she marched into the study where their radio was already tuned into the Reich's broadcasting system.

The announcer's voice was reaching an excited and feverish pitch when she turned up the volume.

"Early this morning, the German Wehrmacht was forced to defend itself against shots fired by Poland."

"It's propaganda," Kitty grumbled. "Lies, lies, and more lies."

She spun away from the radio, but Edgar leaned over it, one arm crooked against the wall, his forehead on top. One strap of his suspenders hung loose at his side.

A live broadcast of Hitler's special session with the Reichstag followed. "This night, for the first time, Polish regular soldiers fired on our territory. Since 5:45 a.m., we have been returning the fire and from now on bombs will be met by bombs."

Reports described the Blitzkrieg, which consisted of air bombardments and raids on Poland's infrastructure followed by a massive land invasion plowing its way through large swathes of the country. Infantry, the announcers reported, was already picking off any remaining resistance.

"Those bastards," Kitty repeated over and over.

. . .

Two days later, Britain, France, Australia and New Zealand declared war on Germany. Canada followed. But the United States declared its neutrality.

Kitty called the Senator when she heard. "Congress has to do something."

"They don't want it, Kit, they just don't. All they see is the danger of allowing subversive persons into the country."

Kitty sighed heavily. She saw Jerzy passing between rooms. What could she do? Should she give him a fake visa for his wife? Could Big Charlie make one for them? How? It had to be in Polish. She shook her head.

"Kit? Are you still there?" Her father's tone indicated a lecture was coming.

"Yeah."

"You should come home. Don't you want to be where you are safe?"

"The only thing I want is to stop suffering from the sensation of futility and utter frustration."

The Senator sighed heavily. "I take it that's a no. Then may I suggest you don't try to save the world, Kit? Just do what you can for those you can."

He had no idea. None.

The following day, the Soviet Union invaded Poland. Vienna was half a day by train from Warsaw, the war was that close. But Jerzy's wife and daughter were already unreachable.

Days later, Kitty arrived at the Vienna Woods cottage by wheeling her bicycle onto the eleven o'clock train from Vienna and riding to the property. The branches of the chestnut tree behind the cottage swung on the September breeze. The roses growing alongside the house's wall bore huge heads in red, coral, pink and yellow. The window boxes were bursting with red and white geraniums.

She went to the barn and was startled to find Khan in the doorway, face to the sun.

"*Servus*," he said lazily, squinting at her. "We worked all night. And I've figured out a better hiding place so we can transport more at one time."

Big Charlie came out of the adjacent door, wiping his ink-stained hands on a dirty rag. Whereas he'd been huge and fearsome just a year ago, Kitty saw that the underground life—literally, underground—was not good for his health. He'd shrunk, and looked flabby. Khan's normally smooth face revealed signs of stress and lack of sleep, too. He had lines at the corners of his eyes and dark rings. He looked as if he were walking in his sleep right now. His hands were stained with ink.

"Bring her the crates," Big Charlie said.

Khan reluctantly pushed himself away from the threshold, stumbling to the hayloft.

"Is he drunk?" Kitty asked.

Big Charlie tilted his head. "Maybe?"

She raised an eyebrow, bent down below him to catch his eye. "Did you two raid the—"

"We're not thieves, Kitty." Big Charlie chuckled, but then looked worriedly where Khan had gone. "It's the chemicals. We had to adjust the dyes for these new passes. They got to his head, is all. We got all the photos processed, all the documents are set."

Kitty smiled. "I know you're not thieves. But there's a bottle of schnapps in the house you definitely deserve. I'll fetch it for you."

Khan appeared again, lugging the vegetable crates.

"See these?" he asked.

Kitty ran a hand over the exterior. Everything about them looked normal. But Khan removed heads of lettuce from one. There was a solid bottom. Not unusual. But he pressed the side of the crate and the bottom popped up a little bit. He tugged the thin piece of plywood up and there they were: the passports and identity cards. Along the bottom of another crate Khan revealed, all lined up in a row, were freshly printed ration cards.

"Holy smokes. This is really neat." She grinned at both men.

"Not all of them contain documents. Only the greens. The lettuces, the broccoli, the cucumbers. OK? Potatoes, carrots, and tomatoes have none. It's the easiest way we thought you could identify which were which."

"This is brilliant," Kitty declared and laughed.

She picked up a few of the identity cards and rifled them in her hand. Men, women, children, of all ages, would get these passes to freedom, to food, and even to jobs. She tried a crate of cucumbers for herself, pushed the tiny release on the side, and pulled the bottom open. This crate contained their hardest task to date: the newly adjusted passports to fit the regime's recent changes. She opened the first one. The thin spine crackled satisfactorily, but Kitty nearly dropped it into the dirt.

She stared at the photo. Closed the book and checked the front. It was a German passport, all right.

"Something wrong?" Big Charlie asked.

"Hey," Khan drawled. "You don't like the work we did?"

Kitty shook her head, and opened it to the photo again, and pointed to it. "This is our butler." She checked whether the two men understood the implication. "Edgar's and my butler."

Except Jerzy wasn't Jerzy any longer. He was Heinrich Gustav Dopplar, born 1901. An engineer from Vienna.

"Why is your butler..." Khan stumbled over and peered at the passport. "Wait. I made an exit visa for him."

"To where?"

"Just out of the Reich. Nothing fancy. No destination."

Kitty clutched her throat. "This is not good. Not good at all."

Big Charlie scratched his head and shuffled some of the crates.

"Who am I delivering these crates to?" she asked.

"The church," Khan said. "You're going to take the truck and leave it with the priest there."

"This could be a trap." Big Charlie was echoing her own suspicions.

"I'm not sure. I'm..." She scanned the farmyard. "People are not always as they appear to be, and Jerzy..."

She did not know how else to express it. On the day she received the box of Judith's effects, Jerzy caught her when she'd fainted. That moment had built a fragile bond between them; one that continued to build with each new step towards war. It was thin, but it was there.

"I'm going to find out what this is all about," she finally said. "But you and Khan should go to the hideaway."

She carefully put the passport back into the crate, fitted the bottom and helped Khan load them onto the truck. Last, she put in her bicycle.

"Get some rest, you two, but stay away from here for the time being," she said.

Big Charlie put his heavy hands on her shoulders. "Be careful, Kitty. It might be just as it appears. A trap."

Filled with dread, she climbed into the cab and started the ignition. The village was just over half an hour away, plenty of time for Kitty to mull the situation over. She kept checking her rearview mirror to see if anyone was following her. Save for a farmer or two and a postman, there was nobody.

She found the priest at the rectory and brought him to the back of the truck.

"We might have a problem," she said. "I recognized one of the people in the passports. Non-Jew."

The priest's eyes widened. "What do you want me to do?"

"When is the pickup of these crates scheduled?"

"Tonight. They're taking the truck tonight. But I'm supposed to ask for one man's passport to hand over directly."

Kitty grasped his arm. "Whose?"

"Heinrich Gustav Dopplar."

She bit her lip. "Who told you this?"

He narrowed his eyes. "I'm not allowed to say."

"Damn it," Kitty muttered. She kicked the dirt next to the truck. "I'm afraid we've been betrayed. Let me take care of this."

"How?"

"I'll meet them when they arrive." He was beginning to protest but Kitty grabbed him by the forearm. "I'm still an American citizen and the daughter of a senator. If I get arrested, I have a better chance of getting out alive than you. Understood?"

When he agreed, Kitty went to the truck, opened the cab door, and retrieved Khan's pistol strapped to the bottom of the driver's seat.

It was nearly dark when an automobile appeared at the top of the hill just above the church. It reached the crest and the headlights suddenly turned off. Kitty watched as it silently coasted down into the churchyard.

Two men got out. In the dark, she could only make out their silhouettes; one shorter and more square, the other, lean and tall, wearing a Fedora hat. She waited at the door of the rectory until they knocked. Two raps. Pause. Three more.

Blood thundering in her ears, the pistol cocked, Kitty opened the door. As she had guessed, Jerzy was the square-built man. He took a step back as she aimed the gun at him.

"What is the meaning of this?" she demanded.

The man in the Fedora was not someone she recognized. He was in his forties, lines on his face, and thin lips. He put a protective arm before Jerzy, and he reached for the pocket of his coat.

She swung the pistol on him, her finger on the trigger. "Give me your weapon."

Reluctantly, the man handed her his gun. "Who are you? Where's Father Michael?"

"Get inside," she waved her weapon, keeping it pointed at the men, and spoke in English. "I'm a good shot, so no funny business."

The stranger frowned, but Jerzy pursed his lips and nodded.

"It's all right," he said to the other man, then to her in English, "We're all friends here. I just need the passport, Frau Doktor. And there's someone I still need to say goodbye to. She's waiting at the guesthouse."

Kitty watched from afar as Jerzy rapped on the door of the guesthouse. The door flew open, and Margit stepped outside.

"You made it," Kitty overheard from her hiding place. "I was so worried about you!"

Jerzy took Margit into his arms, and Kitty could tell by the way their clothes bunched up that he was hugging her tightly. She heard Margit sob, then Jerzy was tenderly kissing her face. He put an arm around her waist and led her into the house.

The next time Kitty saw the two of them, they were in the window of the sitting room. Jerzy suddenly strode over, pulled the curtains shut and stopped only for a second to look out. Kitty dropped the binoculars, crept out of the bush, and returned to the truck. She would have to drive it back, then cycle back to the property. But by the time she returned, it was nearing light. She did not want to be alone in the barn. Instead, she headed out into the woods to find Khan and Big Charlie, and let them know that—for perhaps the first time ever—maybe there was a reason to believe in coincidence.

With the curfew in place in the city, Kitty did not return to Vienna until nearly seven the next morning. She showed her documents at three checkpoints, security growing ever tighter since the war.

The apartment was dim in the morning light when she closed the elevator gate. For a moment, she thought it was completely abandoned, that Edgar had already returned to the office. She jumped when she found him in the sitting room, sprawled in the armchair, an empty whiskey bottle on the table, the glass next to it half full. His shirt was undone. His eyes were open.

"Jerzy's gone," he said.

"I—" She couldn't know about it. "You startled me. What do you mean, Jerzy's gone?"

"There was a report that the Polish commanders were executed by the Wehrmacht."

"Report on our wire?" she asked.

"From the BBC. Jerzy had a wire for the BBC."

"Good God," Kitty said. "In our home?" It was illegal.

"In our home." Edgar waved the nearly empty glass again. "The SS is now hunting down anyone left of the Polish Army. And Jerzy is heading there. To some sort of home front army."

Kitty sank onto the sofa across from him.

"Margit will be devastated," Edgar said. He cocked an eyebrow at her. "He told me about them. She was in love with him. But he would never leave his wife. Now he's going back to see if he can save his family."

"Margit and Jerzy," Kitty said. She had sensed how tortured the butler had been about Edgar's sister. "Who would have thought?"

He cast her a sideways glance. "I thought you were..." His breath hitched. "I thought you were gone, too. Or... that something happened."

She looked down at her lap. She should have called. But after getting the story from Jerzy, she'd offered to take him back to the cottage. To say goodbye. He had been shocked to find that Kitty was behind the forged passports but then he had taken her hands, and held them in his.

"I could have guessed," he'd said, and swore to keep her secret. "Thank you. For your courage, I thank you."

Edgar pushed himself up. "I never asked Margit who the man was. I never showed her any interest."

"Me either," Kitty said softly. "You'd told me there was someone, but I never asked her if I could be of any comfort."

"He was afraid of me," Edgar said. "He thought I would turn him in."

"Did you fight?" she asked.

Edgar shook his head. "I let him go. Here I am. Still here. I know you consider me to be the most repulsive being on this planet. And I can't blame you. I can't prove to you that I am not."

She studied her husband. He was suffering and badly. Scooting to the edge of the sofa, she reached for his arm. "That's not true. I don't believe you to be the worst person on the planet. You let him go, didn't you?"

"The road to hell is paved with good intentions." Edgar winced. "Jerzy did not do right by my sister. And I can't judge him, can I? I don't do right by you."

"I don't know what to do next," she said. "How I can keep..."

He gasped softly. "Ah. Yes. How can you keep living here? With me. Well. Your father called. Seems the Department of State is urging all Americans to leave now. He wants you to come home, Kitty. I can't say I disagree with him."

"I'm not going anywhere."

"So you'll stay here and suffer on."

She leaned against her husband and wrapped her arms around his neck. Holding him like this was what he needed and she could give him that. For this moment, at least, she could give him that much.

29

OCTOBER 1939

Approximately three weeks after discovering Jerzy's and Margit's affair, Kitty received a mysterious package. It was empty save for a postcard of Hotel Metropole. With some trepidation, she flipped it over. In English, in printed letters scrawled across the back, she read:

SiX o'clock. lOvE, Pim

Her heart leaped at the sight of his name. The "O" and "E" was O5, the alternative sign for the Vienna resistance. After nearly six months of her clandestine life, O5 jumped at her immediately, from the chalk marks around the city, to its appearances in messages, notes, on placards, and deliveries.

If one was looking for the call letters, one could find them. But the "X" in the six? Why was it also capitalized? And where at six o'clock? There was no obvious address where one would normally be written on a postcard. Kitty turned it over and examined the photo. Was he asking her to meet at the Gestapo headquarters?

Judith. Oskar. They'd been tortured in that house of horrors, as had so many others since.

She ran a finger over the card, and stopped at a point where the surface was slightly more raised. She held the postcard up to the light. The "X" was to the left of the hotel in the picture, just the corner foundation of a building. She knew that there was a tavern there. She had walked by it on her way home those three times she'd gone asking for Judith. Kitty looked at her watch. It was four fifteen now.

"All right, Pim," she whispered. "It's a date."

Zum Wohl was a typical Viennese establishment. Dark oak tables layered with sticky varnish, hardwood stools with green suede upholstery. Corner booths hidden in the shadows of dimmed lamps. Facing the entryway, Kitty took a table in such a booth. Through the glass front, she could see the first three floors of the hotel that served as the Gestapo headquarters. Her pulse fluttered.

She was one of three patrons. Two men, who barely looked up from their newspapers, were seated at one of the smaller round tables in the center of the dining room. One of them, leg crossed over his knee, was absorbed in a paper attached to a newspaper stick. There was no flicker of interest, no sign of recognition, no nod of acknowledgment that she was even there.

"What can I bring you?" the waiter asked.

"*Ein Verlängerter*," Kitty said. She was already jittery but coffee was better than alcohol. "Unless you have whipped cream?"

He cocked an eyebrow at her and she waved her hand.

"Never mind. I never asked."

Kitty watched the door again, every person passing by was a reason for her skin to prick in anticipation. A man suddenly appeared in the window, then pushed his way in. Pim? He was wearing a long, gray wool coat and a hat. He went straight to the bar and greeted the waiter, who was preparing Kitty's coffee. No glance in her direction, not even a look around as to who else might be inside.

Kitty watched the man as subtly as she could and perked up when he slid the waiter something across the bar. The waiter looked at it, nodded, and the man pressed his hat down and left. The waiter took whatever was on the bar and slipped it beneath the counter. He then carried the tray over to her table, placed a glass of water down, then her coffee, the spoon rattling against the white saucer.

"Anything else?"

She waited, anticipating that the waiter would hand her whatever that man had slipped to him. Kitty shook her head. "This is fine. Thank you."

"You're an American?" he asked.

Her heart fell. "Yes."

"I can tell by the accident."

"Accident?"

He flushed. "*Dialekt.*"

"I see."

"We are at war. There is no milk to be had. But I do have this."

He reached into his pocket and Kitty sat forward. The message? But the waiter placed a small toffee wrapped in gold foil onto the table.

"It's all I have to sweeten the coffee," he said.

It was definitely not what the man had slipped the waiter over the bar but when he left, she unwrapped it, discreetly examined the foil, and was disappointed to find nothing.

"Would you like the paper?"

Kitty nearly snapped her neck at the familiar voice. She choked. Oskar! He was the man from the small round table in the middle who'd been reading the paper.

He was gaunt, and gray-faced. From beneath his hat, the hair on the sides of his head was shorn close. His big brown eyes flashed at her, surrounded by dark rings. He was offering her the newspaper stick with the latest edition of the *Volkszeitung*. His wrist and hand were thin, the veins popping out, the hand of a much older man, maybe twenty years added to Oskar's thirty-five.

"Greetings from Pim," Oskar murmured. "He wanted you to see that I am alive. But this will be the last time we'll see one another, my dearest lioness. At least until things are over."

Kitty opened her mouth to speak, still trying to find her voice, but he brushed a finger over his lips.

"It's an interesting issue." Oskar lay the stick across the table for her. She reached for it, touched his hand, confirming for herself this was not a dream.

"*Vielen Dank*," Kitty finally managed, her throat closed tight with emotion.

Oskar's eyes creased at the edges but not quite into a smile. He touched his hat and, with a slight limp, strode out the door.

She wanted to go after him. She wanted to tackle him and take him into her arms. She wanted to know how he had managed to get out of Dachau. She wanted to grieve over Judith with him, to tell him that because of the gang, she was sure that what she was doing with the resistance was the only right thing for her now.

But he was gone. The moment he stepped out the door, he vanished, as if his presence had been a mirage. *Pim sends his regards.* Startled, she stared at the door. Pim had done this? Had he gotten Oskar out of Dachau? She was looking for answers but the only clue she had was the newspaper in front of her.

Kitty stroked the varnished wood of the newspaper stick, turned it to her and glanced at the front page. She had to pretend to read because her eyes were swimming and she had to blink back the tears. Oskar was alive! She turned the page, her head still trying to process what she had seen.

At first glance, at the bottom right-hand corner on page three, she found the familiar square of advertisement. This time for a natural herbal tonic with the story that explained why this particular brand was the best for one's ailments. Kitty's pulse kicked into high speed. Herbal tonics were messages for sabotage operations.

Her mind clicked through the three paragraphs of text, picking through the coded message that was now so obvious to her, she wondered how it was not obvious to anyone who actually took the time to read these advertisements. Like the Gestapo.

1. *Cherries delivered in season.*
2. *Two days. Filtration.*
3. *B-hybrid plants. HQ, 1108*

Her legs and arms numb, Kitty looked up at the front entrance and beyond, at the Hotel Metropole across the street. *HQ.* The Gestapo headquarters. The intended target? November 8th, written in American with the month first. The intended day. Cherries were explosives. B-hybrid meant the explosives would be distributed over several couriers to get them into the hands of the right people. And in two days, she should take delivery of the explosives at Khan's family bookstore. That was the filtration.

Something made her eye flick back to page two to the spread of photos. At the end of the captions of two of them, written in black ink, *O5* jumped at her. She studied the images. Hitler was on parade again, standing in the front of an open car, his hand raised in that Caesar salute. But next to it, a photo of workers carrying beams and building materials into a building. Beneath, the caption read,

Munich prepares to welcome our Führer! Preparations for the 16th anniversary of the Beer Hall Putsch, November 8th.

November 8th. The same date as her instructions in the advertisement. She sensed that her activities in Vienna were not scheduled by coincidence. This was going to be a very large clandestine operation.

Her blood racing, Kitty rifled through her purse, found a black pen, cupped her hand over the photo caption, leaning as if to push her cup away, and scratched out the O_5. She closed the newspaper, stood up and took it to where the other issues hung on sticks near the front entrance.

The gang would not believe her when she told them she'd not only seen Oskar, but that he'd delivered their next assignment. She had touched him. It was him.

And Pim had somehow rescued him from certain death.

30

NOVEMBER 1939

"Two sidearms, one Luger, and enough explosives to create the damage needed. All hidden among my underthings." Kitty winked at Khan and Big Charlie before carefully opening the well-worn suitcase before them.

Inside were women's clothing and toiletries, which she pushed aside from the edges of the case. Both men leaned in with anticipation.

"The first thing the police do is check for secret compartments," she said. "Perhaps tear the lining in hopes of finding something. But thanks to Khan's inspiration, not this sweetheart."

She closed the case and pressed the catches on the side of the locks extra hard. She heard the softest whisper. Carefully, Kitty loosened the top outer shell and Khan chuckled behind her. When Kitty revealed the weapons, the explosives and an envelope strapped into place, Big Charlie made a satisfied noise.

"German engineering does it again," he said, bouncing his head in appreciation. "Probably a Jew."

Khan laughed softly. "Or a frustrated Soviet-bred engineer?"

They grinned at one another and Kitty clapped them both on the arms.

"I'm glad you're impressed," Kitty said. "It's Pim's gift to us. But I don't think anything could top the gift of Oskar."

Big Charlie sniffed. "I hope he'll be all right."

"I trust Pim with my life," Kitty declared. "With our lives."

"*Tja*," Big Charlie muttered. "It never hurts to be too careful. Trust nobody."

He was right, of course but, Pim had guided them through half a year of sabotage, forging documents, taught them the precious art of security, and got them networked with goodness knew how many other resistance groups so that they could work as one. Which was exactly Big Charlie's problem. He felt that, the more people involved, the greater the threat for discovery. But for Kitty, Pim was a beacon of hope.

She removed the envelope from the bottom of the hiding place. "Our instructions and a floor plan of the Hotel Metropole. I'm to pass this on but first, I have to take a train to Geneva. I've booked passage to London. And the cover story is perfect. Edgar has suggested several times that I go visit my family, and just get away. But I didn't want to leave you two behind. So, it's only a short trip to London. That's all. I'll visit my brother, Nils, and return."

Big Charlie rubbed her shoulder gently. "You don't have to worry about us, Kitty."

"Sounds easy enough," Khan said, still examining the case. "But, Kitty, each new operation is just a step closer to being caught."

She leaned against him fondly. "I had a friend in Paris. An actress. She used to say that if you don't get stage fright, that's when you know you're going to disappoint the critics." She stretched out her hands to them. Her nails were chewed down. "Believe me, I'm nervous. So, we'll be fine."

· · ·

In the middle of the night, the day she was to leave, Kitty awoke to the sound of Edgar's irritated voice. It was coming from his study. He suddenly switched to a tone he used when he was trying to get someone to calm down.

She tiptoed into the hallway. His door was ajar, light streaming onto the tiled floor. Quietly, she stepped in. There was a pot of tea next to his files, a sure sign that he'd been working. He was facing the window, the phone at his ear.

"No, Mother. I didn't know. I don't understand why you're making such a fuss. *Um Himmels willen*, of marrying age? What is this? The nineteenth century?"

Kitty leaned against the threshold and he glanced over, making an apologetic face.

"*Entschuldigung, Mutter*. I didn't mean to be disrespectful." He sighed. "Margit is an adult. She can... Yes, of course it disturbs me that she did not stick to our agreement. No. You don't need to do that. I'll take care of it. Promise."

He placed the receiver into the holder none too gently then turned to the windows and rubbed his hair. She saw him take in a deep breath.

"Why is she calling so late?"

Edgar gave her a lopsided smile but it did not erase his anger. "She's engineering a disaster."

"Your sister doesn't deserve it."

But that only served to increase his agitation.

She brushed a hand over the high-backed chair in front of his desk before sitting down. She would be leaving him later that day, and finally seeing Nils for the first time in two years, but only if she pulled off her mission.

The anticipation of it made her wrap her robe tightly around her. She looked down at her lap. Nearly a year ago, she and Edgar had stood on the roof of their apartment, she in this very same robe, as Kristallnacht shattered the veneer of the city.

Edgar was still pacing behind his desk when he suddenly

stopped, as if realizing she was still there. He pointed to the pot. "Tea?"

"No, thanks. It's probably what's keeping you up."

He blew out his cheeks, rubbed his face again. "If that was all. When does your train leave?"

"Twelve."

"That's a humane time. I'd take you to the station myself but... I have to leave very early this morning."

Business again. He looked forlornly at her, and she wondered, not for the first time, whether everything was becoming too much for them.

She cocked her head and drummed her fingers on the table. "Are you going to miss me?"

Edgar looked crestfallen, glanced at the phone, then closed the file in front of him. "More than you will know."

"What's wrong?"

"Nothing I can't fix. I just... Something came up." His jaw twitched. "When you reach Geneva, you're going to feel a lot safer than you do here."

"Ha! I imagine you're right. It will be strange."

"With all that has happened to us..." Her husband reached across the desk and beckoned for her hand. She gave it to him and he stroked her fingers thoughtfully. "Did you imagine that when we married, we'd have a family? That I'd come home from work and you'd tell me about the children? That we'd be busy entertaining and posturing for Vienna's society and aristocrats?"

Kitty pulled lightly away. "We never talked like that. Not seriously, anyway."

Edgar laughed sadly. "We didn't, did we?"

He needed to escape. Suddenly, everything in her wanted to tell him what she was really up to; to get him involved, to make him her partner. Maybe, just maybe, she could recruit him. He was failing and miserable. He'd once said they were a team. But in two years of marriage, had they ever really been?

As if calculating the hours, Edgar was looking at the clock on the wall behind her—the wall with the photo collage of their adventures in the Alps, at the cottage, in the early days of their courtship.

"You better get to bed," he suddenly said. "You have a long day tomorrow."

He was so serious that Kitty laughed. "You know, I am used to traveling. Even if the two of us haven't gone anywhere in almost a year." She struck a pose, showing her profile and splaying her finger from her chin to down between her breasts. "I'm still young and strong."

When she faced him, he had that sad look again. "You're the most beautiful, fascinating woman I have ever known, Kitty Larsson."

Her brow knitted at the way he used her maiden name.

He pushed his chair back, then was at her side. She craned for a kiss, but he pecked her cheek. "Good night, darling."

To her great surprise, she was disappointed. She rose to find that he was already holding the door open for her.

"Won't you come to bed?" She would settle for just holding his hand in her sleep.

But Edgar caressed her cheek to soften the rejection. "Not tonight. I must prepare for the morning."

As the door closed softly behind her, she wondered how many nights the two of them had left.

She spotted her identical suitcase the moment she headed for the coffee bar adjacent to the Hauptbahnhof. Trains clacked away behind the station, the tram rang its bell, but she was focused on that one piece of luggage. She stepped up to the bar, every sense on high alert, and placed her suitcase on the floor next to the stranger's. A woman with an elegant blue coat and a matching pillbox hat was right next to Kitty. She also had wavy blond hair, but was a tad older, Kitty guessed. The stranger lifted her coffee cup, drained it, and then quietly excused herself as she bent down to take the handle of Kitty's case.

Kitty ordered a coffee, stirred it with a spoon, and took a sip. She dropped some coins onto the counter, took another sip, and glanced around. Her heart froze at the sight of the red-faced Gestapo man and his smaller sidekick. The men who had tossed her onto the street outside of Hotel Metropole. They were standing just outside the bar. They were waiting for her.

The woman who'd been next to her was nowhere to be seen. There were three ways this was going to work out. Either those men were here by coincidence, which Kitty—she reminded herself—did not really believe in, or they were here for something else. Worse yet, the woman was a rat and had led Kitty here for capture.

Kitty was laying her bet on the latter.

31

NOVEMBER 1939

Kitty was in one of the better-appointed rooms in the Metropole. She stared at the wooden panel, six-feet high. The wall above it revealed a water stain beneath the deep hunter green paint. A gleaming oak table and a matching bench with carved oak leaves stood in the corner of the room. Opposite, a fire crackled and popped in a large beige tiled oven.

The whole situation felt medieval to Kitty. She should be on her way to Nils right now. Instead, she was being held captive by the Gestapo.

The door opened. Kitty took a step back and waited. SS-Obersturmbahnführer Franz Josef Huber appeared. He was cool, and immaculate in his perfectly tailored jacket, jodhpurs and gleaming black boots. She detested the accoutrements. The black triangle patch on his right arm, the fighting eagle on the collar, the billed hat that he now took off.

He held up a hand as if to convince her that he came in peace, then spoke in heavily German-accented English as he crossed the room to her. "Now, Frau Doktor, before you begin making protests about how you are an American and you have *rights*, I would like you to sit down and simply relax."

Relax?

"I am the daughter of a United States senator." Her neck went hot at the sound of her own voice. It was shaking but she pressed on. "America has so far declared neutrality and requires your cooperation to stay as such."

"As we are well aware," Huber said amiably.

"I was on my way to Geneva when your goons collected me. I demand to know why I'm here."

"There is a situation." Huber took a chair to her left and folded his hands on the table. He studied her as she reluctantly took a seat opposite. "What do you know about the activities at your husband's holiday home in the Vienna Woods?"

Kitty stiffened. It felt like an eternity but she managed to manipulate what she hoped was a puzzled expression.

"The vegetables I deliver for the orphanage?"

Huber's left eye twitched. "Your vegetables. Yes. Such as you store in the root cellar."

Kitty sat back. "I'm afraid I don't understand your line of questioning. Why am I here to talk about my vegetables? What state interest could you possibly have in it?"

"Your mother-in-law, Frau Ragatz, also thought your business was very innocent. Until she went up there looking for clues about her daughter's secret hideaway, and made certain discoveries."

Now Kitty's fear involuntarily flashed like a lightning strike. Edgar's telephone call. Margit's clandestine love affair. Dorothea Ragatz's inability to let anything go that she was not controlling herself. What had that witch of a woman discovered?

Kitty tried to set an expression that made her look and feel indignant and innocent. But the effort of not letting on, of being numb, was revealing itself in the light sheen of sweat building on her brow. She brushed back her hair in a motion of annoyance.

"So my mother-in-law was digging around my husband's property? And what did she find? She can't leave her daughter in peace. Margit came to the guesthouse to get away from that woman."

"As I've been given to understand," Huber said. "It seems that the family tension goes all around, with both children. She claims she still has rights to the property. But what we're interested in, Frau Doktor, is the cellar where you stored your vegetables."

Her chest hurt. This was not about the suitcase. Not about the explosives. It was about Dorothea discovering Big Charlie and Khan at the cottage. Were they here? Had they been arrested?

"What about it?"

Huber's smile was patient. "I'll show you in a moment. In the meantime—"

A knock at the door and a young policeman stepped in, brought an envelope to the chief and with the click of his heel, and a salute, he left. Kitty watched Huber open the envelope with great anticipation, but her mind was unwinding the reel of possibilities at a hundred miles an hour. If she was here about the cottage, that meant that the operation to detonate the Gestapo's headquarters was still on. It was the first time she realized the resistance group was prepared to put innocent lives on the line. If Big Charlie and Khan were incarcerated here... If she...

Huber withdrew several photographs and she was forced to return her attention to him. He flipped through them, then fanned them out on the table.

They were images of the stable yard, the barn, dirt tracks from what Kitty could only guess was the truck, the truck, and then the inside of the well-lit cellar. Kitty had to keep from gasping in wonder. The equipment that Khan and Big Charlie had was missing. Save for a stack of *Vienna Woods Produce* crates, and scuff-marks on the floor—revealing clearly that the cellar had been well lived-in—there was nothing. Except for the next photo that Huber pulled from the bottom of the stack. This one was of a large bottle of black ink, half full, and the remnants of the paper Khan and Big Charlie had used to produce ration cards.

Where were Khan and Big Charlie? Where was the machinery? Or was Huber not showing her everything on purpose? Had they and everything else been seized and he was leading her on to confess?

Huber's tone was mocking. "I see that you are quite shocked."

Say nothing. Not a word. Kitty pretended to study the photos.

"Your husband doesn't know where the truck came from."

Edgar was here, too? Also being questioned? Kitty was having difficulty catching her breath.

"The orphanage lends it to me. I use it to deliver my vegetables and the goods from around the area."

"And the ration cards?"

She was about to say she knew nothing about them but then she peered down at the photo with the ink and paper. "Is that what those are?"

Huber slammed a palm on the table and Kitty jumped back. His smirk was one-sided and he clicked his tongue. "Yes. That is what those are."

"If you're suggesting what I think you might be suggesting, I'd like a lawyer," Kitty said. "And I'd like to call the consulate general."

Huber narrowed his eyes. "For what? We haven't charged you with anything."

Another knock on the door. Huber stood this time and went to it himself. Kitty watched his expression go cold.

"Is she in here?"

Kitty half-stood as Josef Ragatz, in full SS regalia, strode in. She had never seen him like this, had never actually witnessed the man at his work. But he was dressed to the nines for this show. Agent Roberts had drilled her in recognizing paramilitary and Wehrmacht ranks by their insignia. Her father-in-law was Standartenführer, which meant he was very high up in the echelons. But the promotion had to be new. And Edgar had kept it from her.

She sank back down onto the bench. Josef kept his head bowed as he strode to the table, folded his hands and pierced her with a glare.

"My entire family is here for questioning, and this is your doing."

"Mine?" Kitty said. "I wasn't the one with a secret lover at the cottage."

She felt bad for that, for diverting his attention to Margit. Knowing her sister-in-law, she'd probably told them everything about Jerzy by this point. And that meant Kitty was in even bigger danger. One more connection to her and Edgar would only make things worse. But maybe she was getting the girl all wrong. Margit had led her secret life for a long time, without Dorothea finding anything out. Until now. Why now?

"Perhaps you can tell me," Josef said, "what you know about this man my daughter was in love with."

So maybe they did not know about Jerzy. "You could hardly say Margit and I had a close relationship. Why don't you ask her?"

Huber leaned against the door, watching her intently.

Josef bared his teeth. "I did."

Kitty waited, the silence pressing on her. Her heart thudded so hard, she was certain he could hear it. *Do not speak. Do not volunteer any information.*

It was Josef who broke it. "Margit discovered that several hundred Polish officers were supposedly executed."

He watched her reaction. She gave none.

"She went into hysterics. In the middle of our dinner party. I can only assume that the man she thought she was in love with was Polish."

Kitty sat slowly back, but the thought that Jerzy might have been among those murdered made her feel sick to her stomach. "I'm still waiting," she said measuredly, "to learn how I am involved in this."

Josef looked pleased, as if he'd been waiting for her to open this door. "Dorothea wanted to know what our daughter was hiding. She went up to the property only to discover clues that someone else had been using the cottage's facilities. She called the police. The police discovered the cellar. They called the Gestapo. And now we are all being questioned. *I* am being questioned."

"Indeed," Kitty said. Her father-in-law was being questioned about possibly being a traitor. Or harboring one. Or two. She arched an eyebrow. "I want that phone call now."

"You think you're still in America."

Kitty eyed his uniform. "Far from it, Standartenführer Ragatz. Far from it. But I am still an American citizen. And I know my rights."

Josef Ragatz smacked his lips and turned to Huber, who was standing at the door.

Huber shrugged. "She was heading for Geneva when we found her."

"Luggage?" Josef barked.

"Clean."

Found her. Not arrested her. Which means they might have followed her to the train station. But not seen the suitcase exchange? This gave Kitty some hope. With a show of annoyance, she rose. "Where is Edgar?"

Herr Ragatz stood up, marched over to her and snatched her hands. Yes, her hands looked awful. Maybe there was a little dirt beneath one of her short nails. But now she knew what he was looking for. Ink stains. The way there had been on Big Charlie's hands. Or Khan's. She had little doubt their fingerprints would be found and, if the Gestapo had not yet arrested them but later discovered their identities, they would connect Kitty to the two of them immediately. Huber already had a file on her.

She yanked her hands out of Josef's. She had to get out and soon. "Before you touch me again," she said defiantly. "That phone call? And I want to see my husband."

Leland Morris might have been an administrator, but he was quick to bring down the law. He claimed Kitty's diplomatic immunity and reminded the Gestapo that the last thing they wanted was to cause a diplomatic crisis. But it had been twelve hours since she'd been brought in for questioning. It was the middle of the night of November 8th.

Kitty was still not certain whether the O5 operation was a go. She had no idea when any explosives were supposed to go off, or where, or how many, or who the targets were. Or whether Khan and Big Charlie were indeed in the building, and Huber was just trying to corner her.

Her heart sluggish, her skin prickling at every sudden noise, when Leland Morris and Edgar walked in, her first instinct was to scream that they all had to get out of the building. But she had to know whether Khan and Big Charlie were there.

The first thing she noted was Edgar's stony expression. He strode over to her and grasped her arms, his eyes filled with dark shadows. "*Um Himmels willen*, Kitty? What have you been up to?"

"Nothing!" Kitty cried. She shifted to Morris. "Really! Why isn't anyone asking Margit? I have no idea who else was using the property. Didn't the Gestapo find anyone?"

Morris took her hand, businesslike and controlled, and led her to the table. Edgar did not follow, but began pacing.

"Are they pressing charges?" she asked.

"No," Morris said. "They don't have any evidence that you were involved. Where were you headed when the Gestapo brought you in?"

"Geneva," Edgar said. "Nils is supposed to meet her."

Morris eyed her. "Your brother?"

Kitty nodded.

"Can you make sure she gets out? She needs to leave Vienna," Edgar growled angrily. "I can't have my wife suspected of acts of treason."

Kitty looked at him wildly. "You can't, can you? God forbid you get a black mark on your record!"

Edgar glared back at her with contempt, as if he were listening to a child having a tantrum.

"Maybe Doctor Ragatz is right," Morris said. "We should get you out of here until—"

"Don't you *dare* tell me only until it's safe." She got up and paced to the door, opened it and faced a startled guard. Edgar shut the door behind her.

She whirled back to him. "We need to get out of here. You're right about that, Edgar. We need to all get out of here, *now*."

"We're working on that," Edgar snapped.

"No. Now." She swung to Morris. "*Right* now."

Morris pushed away from the wall and sighed. "All right. I'll go put some pressure on Huber."

As soon as Morris was gone, Edgar snatched Kitty against him and pressed his mouth close to her ear. His grip was strong, his tone was terrifying. "It's over. You're going to get in that car with Morris and you are getting on a train to Geneva. And then you will wait until I contact you and tell you what to do."

Kitty twisted her head away, her skin searing under his

touch. She had never seen him like this. He was dark and dangerous, and she realized that she'd always known he could be like this.

"I'm sorry," she said acidly. "I'll go but I wouldn't lay your bets that I'm at your beck and call. That's not one you're going to win."

Edgar gripped her wrist hard. "One more word, Kitty, and you are going to ruin everything... for me."

"For *you*?" she cried.

Morris and Huber walked in soon after, Huber looking resigned. He motioned them out the door.

"You're free to go, Frau Doktor."

Edgar nodded at him. "I apologize for this."

Huber pointed a finger at him. "Your family has been cleared. But the cottage is off limits. We will do everything we have to in order to locate the traitors."

Kitty felt hysteria bubbling up in her throat. She wanted to laugh with relief. Khan and Big Charlie had gotten away, for now.

"Of course," Edgar said. "You can expect our full cooperation."

"Oh, yes," Kitty said acidly. "You can expect our full cooperation indeed. Dr. Ragatz is very good at reminding me of the expected etiquette in Vienna."

Huber blinked. "Thank you for your time, Frau Doktor. We apologize for the fright."

"Fright?" she bit back. "Inconvenience is more like it. I'm supposed to be on a train to Geneva."

Edgar grasped her by the elbow and led her stonily downstairs into the foyer, Morris on the other side of him.

At Morris's car, she wrested herself away and shook her husband off. "Don't touch me. Don't you ever, ever touch me again," she hissed as Morris went to the other side of the vehicle.

"You are no longer my husband. You never were. I have no idea *who* you are."

She yanked the door open and slammed herself into the seat next to Morris. Edgar leaned in.

"Kitty?"

But she did not acknowledge that she heard him and yanked the door shut.

She shot Morris a pleading look. "Can we go, please?"

The car pulled away from the curb, and she did not look back.

When she got to the main train station and had to show her passport at the checkpoint, her legs felt like jelly, and her heart was heavy. Khan. Big Charlie. They were gone to her.

Glancing down the platform before boarding, she half expected to see Edgar coming after her—and suddenly had the feeling that she would never see him again.

Her husband was lost to her as well. It was all over.

32

NOVEMBER 1939

In western Austria, as the train pulled into the last stop before the Swiss border, Kitty stared out the window and the people waiting on the platform. As guards boarded to check their documents, she was filled with terror once more. What if here, right now, they had been given instructions to find her? What if the Hotel Metropole had been attacked? What if Big Charlie and Khan had been arrested and given her name? All it would take would be one phone call to the Feldkirch train station. But the older man who checked her papers looked at her once, then handed them back to her.

Still shaky, Kitty replaced them into her handbag and looked out the window. She was startled at the sight of a rail schedule right before her. In white chalk, scrawled in the upper right-hand corner of the steel post, was O5. This was not for her, of that she was certain.

The train whistle blew and they pulled away from the platform, and she kept those call letters in sight for as long as possible. A sense of lightness filled her as they passed dark forests and open fields. So many places to hide. So much country to cover. There might be tens of thousands of police and security officials working for the Nazi regime—her husband included—but as she looked out at the landscape, she knew that there would be more resistance building up. She felt it in her bones.

Then a thought entered her mind. If the Gestapo did not find any equipment, save for that half bottle of ink and those paper discards—which was just sloppy—then how had Big Charlie and Khan emptied the cellar before the Gestapo got there? And how had they known that they were coming? That Dorothea was coming? Had they? Then she thought of something. With the big operation planned to bomb the Metropole, Pim had likely instructed Khan and Big Charlie to clear everything out, just in case.

Satisfied with that answer, she fell asleep.

Edgar had predicted the relief she would feel when she reached neutral Geneva and he was not wrong, though she was unpleasantly surprised at how many uniformed Nazis were roaming about, and apparently guiding a complicit Swiss immigration department. She watched with some horror as one of the Swiss guards stamped a red *J* into a woman's passport. The same *J* used by the Third Reich.

At the sound of Nils calling her name, Kitty turned and ran up the platform. She dropped her case on the floor and sprang into her brother's arms. He held her tight.

"Edgar rang to tell me what was happening."

Nils was murmuring things to her, but Kitty pressed into his great overcoat, two years' worth of pent-up emotions pouring out of her. She felt as if she had just left a battle, as if she had been shelled and bombed by one awful event after another. Judith. Oskar. Losing Khan and Big Charlie now.

And Edgar. The loss of a man she thought she'd known, and thought she would spend the rest of her life with.

Angry again, she wiped away the tears. "Get me out of here. Just get me to England."

Nils put an arm around her shoulder and picked up her case, then led her to the exit. "I've got a car waiting."

Kitty slipped into the back of the waiting vehicle, and clung to Nils's arm. He tapped on the glass between the front and back seats and the driver pulled away from the curb and stopped at the first intersection. Kitty watched as two German Nazi officials crossed the road in front of them. One stopped, peered through the windshield, and she froze. But the German went on, and Nils put a hand on her knee.

"You all right?"

Only when the driver continued did she nod.

Nils leaned in close to her and whispered into her ear. "Pim sends his well-wishes."

Snapping her head around, Kitty stared at her brother. "Are you—?"

But Nils put a finger to his lips, his eyes flicking towards the driver. "No, I'm not. But not another word until we're in the plane."

Kitty was on tenterhooks all the way to the tarmac. She boarded the airplane, and lowered herself into her seat. Nils sat opposite her, still mum. Only when the airplane had reached altitude did he lean forward.

"You'll be debriefed in London."

"Debriefed? By whom? Christ, Nils, what is going on here? How are you involved?"

Nils looked regretful. He took her hand and kissed it. "You'll find out everything in good time, Kit. All in good time."

But she was much too traumatized. She wanted answers. Now. "Who is he? You're not him, so who is he?"

Nils pressed his index finger to her lips and repeated, "All in good time, Kit."

She clamped her mouth shut, wondering whether all this

time how her Viking brother had been involved, and if she could not trust him, then whom could she trust?

Landing in London gave Kitty the sense of safety she'd ached for without even realizing how much she'd needed it. Another car was waiting for them, but Nils remained tight-lipped. He was good at that, and she copied him. This time, as they motored north of London, she slept.

The sound of gravel beneath the tires jolted her awake. It was dusk and they were pulling up outside a large red-brick country estate. Kitty's mouth dropped open as she peered at the figure at the top of the terrace. Captain Thomas Kendrick—Captain Wallace—removed his hands from his pockets and jogged down the steps to her side of the car.

She leaned forward as he opened her door and smiled down at her.

"Welcome onto British soil, Frau Doktor Ragatz. Jolly good to see you looking so well."

33

NOVEMBER 1939

Kitty and Kendrick were alone in the cozy sitting room. A fire crackled in the hearth. Kitty pressed herself against the corner of a walnut and pale blue satin sofa. She had demolished the sandwiches and cake already, realizing that she had not eaten in nearly two days. Next to her teacup was a glass of warm cognac.

The secret service officer crossed his leg in the armchair opposite and stirred his tea before placing it on the side table next to him. After convincing her that British SIS was well aware of the O5's activities, and was aware of the plan to bomb Hotel Metropole, Kitty revealed to Kendrick the whole story about her arrest at Vienna's central train station, and the situations that had led to it.

"You were extremely lucky to get out of there when you did," Kendrick said.

"What about the Gestapo headquarters? Did they..."

Kendrick winced. "The mission failed."

Her heart fell, certain that she had had a hand in botching it, but Kendrick seemed to sense her disappointment.

"It's not your fault," he said. "A mole infiltrated the group that was responsible for planting the explosives. Their leader was arrested but he was not the only one. The rest scattered. Including your two friends."

"Khan and Big Charlie?"

"There are no records of their arrests. In fact, there is still a manhunt out for them."

Kitty sighed in relief, but was terrified of what should happen if they were found. And that Huber would most certainly connect her to them.

"Edgar might be in trouble," she said. "The Gestapo might use my husband to get to me if they find my two friends."

Kendrick's eyebrows rose slightly. "Indeed."

She stared at him. "Are you Pim?" she asked softly.

Kendrick looked towards the fire. "He's on his way. But meeting him..." He crossed his other leg. "Hotel Metropole was a botch-up, but there was also something else."

"What?"

"An attempt on Adolf Hitler's life this evening. We're waiting for the details."

In Munich. The photo of the builders in Munich, for the anniversary celebrations. Kitty opened her mouth, her eyes widened. "Were we a decoy? Were O5 operatives put in danger to be used as a distraction?"

Kendrick folded his hands and leaned back, his foot bouncing. "Now, that is an interesting theory, Frau Doktor."

He picked up his tea and sipped, his eyes never leaving hers.

She was not quite a guest. She was not really a prisoner. She was also not even an insider. Kitty had the distinct feeling that she was something of all three and also very much in limbo. And her fate seemed to hinge on Pim.

With all that she had gone through, with all that was working in her head, Kitty was surprised that she slept through the night so soundly. When she awoke, it felt as if she'd slept for days. Hail was falling like gravel against her window and the landscape beyond the circular drive was misty and gray.

A dress that was not hers, but came with the luggage she'd taken from the cafe in Vienna, lay on top. It would fit just fine. There was a knock on her door just as she'd finished changing and Nils stepped in, a stack of newspapers in hand.

"Sleep well?"

She nodded and he handed her the papers. The one on top was that morning's issue of the *Voelkischer Beobachter*, the Nazi party's official newspaper. She read the front-page article, turning her back on Nils. At almost half past nine the night before, a bomb went off at the Bürgerbräukeller in Munich, where the Beer Hall Putsch assembly had taken place. The report detailed that Hitler had left the building just moments before, and admittedly much earlier than intended. The Führer —the paper stressed—was unharmed. But, among other bystanders, some higher-ranking officials had been injured.

"It says here the assassination attempt is the work of British secret agents," Kitty said, lifting it for her brother to see. "They're even implicating Prime Minister Neville Chamberlain."

"This is their way of stirring up hatred for the British," Nils said.

"So, if the Brits didn't do it, who did?"

"A man was arrested in Constance. A German carpenter. He was trying to flee into Switzerland. Kendrick is keeping tabs on that. I think the regime knows it's an anti-Nazi military conspiracy. They just won't admit to it because they want the British to be the enemy."

Kitty hugged herself. "Which can only mean one thing: Germany is setting its sights on England?"

Nils blinked. It was his way of saying yes. He strode to the table in the corner and tapped an index finger on it, mulling something over. "I'm just going to go ahead and say it, Kit. There have been more arrests in Vienna. Members of O5."

She lay the papers on the end of her bed. "Do we know who?"

Nils shook his head. "Only the leader of B-Group. He was in charge of—"

"Planting the explosives," Kitty said. "Kendrick mentioned a mole, said he'd told secret police the entire plan."

Nils rubbed a hand over his head. "If you had been there when they'd found out, Kitty? If they had connected you to the members in the Vienna Woods... You would not have gotten out if it weren't for Pim—"

"Edgar," Kitty said at the same time. She locked eyes with her brother and went to him. "Edgar got me out of there."

"Pim, Kitty. Pim got you out of there."

"Who is...?"

Nils nodded slowly. Outside the window, the sound of a vehicle coming to a halt on the gravel. He tore his gaze away and pulled back the curtain. "He's here."

Holding her breath, Kitty went to the window just as a driver opened the back door of a black sedan. A man's leg appeared before the driver blocked the view with an umbrella. The passenger stood and Kitty saw the stride to the front door. She could recognize that gait anywhere, damn the umbrella, the hat, the heavy foreign overcoat.

This was her husband walking up the stoop to the estate house. Edgar was in London. And he was Pim.

34

NOVEMBER 1939

"Kit? Do you want me to come with you?"

"Where?" She spun to Nils, her brother's complicity putting up her guard.

"Downstairs. Or do you want me to bring him up here?"

She shook her head and turned to the window. The driver was getting back into the car. Heavy mist clung to the treetops of the forest across the way. "I'm not ready."

"Take the time you need, Kit. I know it's a lot to digest."

She scoffed.

"Can I do anything?"

Her head was spinning. She couldn't think. She couldn't see straight. "Please. Just leave me alone."

She heard the door click shut. Staring out onto that gray landscape, she was propelled back in time. The very first warning flags she had seen. Nils and Edgar suddenly falling out, then their little meeting at her wedding reception with Kendrick. Edgar's many trips and nights away. The countless drink parties, events, and gatherings. Edgar always—but not quite—friendly with nearly everyone, encouraging her through their game of gossip to reveal everything she had learned about the people she'd met and spoken with.

It was difficult to breathe. She paced the carpet, clutching her sides. On occasion, another memory would make her stop and she groaned. Tears rolled down her face and she was shaking, tormented as she focused on her own miserable failure of never seeing Edgar for who he really was, hearing him but never listening to what he'd really been saying to her every time he'd defended himself.

Everything she had assessed, assumed, anticipated about her husband, it was all now in question. She had misread so many clues and cues. Had she? Or was all of this a lie? Was she a pawn in some awful game? Was Kendrick playing her for the fool? Edgar? Even Nils!

Kitty had no idea how long she had been at it, trying to remember—agonizing over every single minute lost—when she heard movement in the hallway. Outside her door, low voices. She suddenly remembered Tokyo, when Edgar had come to her hotel room door and told her he loved her. Staring at the doorknob, willing it to move, but wishing he'd go away, she clutched her throat.

Then the soft rap. "Kitty? May I come in?"

"All right," she whispered, her anger hot.

She strode over, gripped the knob, and flung it open to her husband's steady gaze. He was ready for it. She was not. Both Kendrick and Nils were with him, but at the sight of Kitty, Nils murmured to the big Brit and they excused themselves.

She backpedaled to the window, staring at Edgar as he stepped in. He was wearing one of his suits. His blue-green eyes were heavy with remorse and concern. He was freshly shaven, and he'd trimmed his hair. He looked normal but she had never known this man. Not ever. Not really.

Edgar came slowly towards her, as if she were a dangerous animal.

She was. "Don't. Stay over there."

He halted in his tracks, in the middle of the room, and eyed the two armchairs next to a round walnut table.

"Where are my friends?" she demanded.

Edgar looked chastened. "Oskar is in safe hands. He is in France. Bella got on the train to Paris yesterday. I saw to that."

I saw to that. How much had he seen to in all this time?

"Big Charlie?" she pressed. "Khan?"

"They have simply vanished. Maybe to Prague? Maybe to the south? But those two have always been pretty resourceful..."

"You warned them?" Kitty choked. "They knew you—"

"No, Kitty. None of you did." Edgar opened his hands. "Not until that morning. It was such a close call. My mother rang, remember? She threatened to go to the cottage and snoop around because she was sure Margit's lover was there. I had to get Khan and Big Charlie out in a hurry. And we missed the ink. The paper."

"All this time you've been orchestrating me. All this time, you've been deceiving me," she sobbed, her initial relief for her friends shifting to anger again. "I should have known you knew everything when you bought those damned chocolates."

Edgar cocked his head. "The chocolates? You mean... in Berlin? What about them?"

"Don't you dare pretend with me right now."

Edgar shook his head. "I'm not pretending, Kitty. My sole reason for taking this risk—of meeting you here—is because I can finally tell all. And it looks like you and I both have catching up to do. May I?" He indicated the armchair.

In answer, she stepped away, towards the bed. She bumped the lamp on the nightstand table, snatched a pillow and hugged it to her as she perched on the edge of the mattress.

He loosened his tie, unbuttoned his suit coat, and sat down, one leg crossed over his knee. "You first?" Edgar suggested.

Kitty scoffed. "I don't think so."

"Are you really that surprised, Kitty?" he asked gently. "I mean, now that you know?"

She nodded. Then shook her head. How could she be? Now confronted by the truth, it all made sense. All of it. But that did not dilute her anger, her sense of betrayal and sheer confusion. "You did your job well," she said bitterly.

He closed his eyes. "I had no choice. You are smart enough to realize that."

Kitty buried her face into the pillow and took three deep breaths, her mind still reeling. She looked back up at him. "That's what you always said. You didn't have a choice. But you had many, didn't you? You had so many."

He nodded slowly. "Many. And I was always torn, Kitty. Torn between deceiving you and protecting my position. It was not fun. There was no fun in it at all. I have always loved you, but..."

"You drove me to do the things I did." Kitty was defiant. "I started to loathe you."

"And if despising me is what led you to discover your courage and resilience, then I am happy to take some credit for that. Hate is all right, Kitty. If it was apathy you felt, then I would know all is lost between us."

"You dare to still have hope?" She tossed the pillow off to the side and jumped up, pacing in front of the bed.

Edgar leaned on the table, his head in his hand, watching her. "Do you know how often I thought that you were onto *me*?"

She swung to him, surprised.

"The first time was before our wedding when you took me to Achmed Beh. With Sam? You mentioned that I looked so uncomfortable. Remember that? Achmed Beh was the place I met with so many of my assets. Where I received messages. I was so worried that you were testing me. That Nils might have accidentally given that clever brain of yours a clue."

Kitty stared at him. "Did you know the gang already?"

He shook his head. "None of it, until you were in contact with Pim. And what you all did... God, Kitty. Such courage. Your determination. I don't know the extent of what you did before all that, and I don't dare to ask. It's not why I am here."

"Then why are you here?" she asked, her suspicion rising again.

He took in a deep breath. "I cannot tell you how often I wanted to be in this very situation with you, but I almost needed you to believe that I was the passive, reluctant idiot working for the regime. It broke my heart each time you... It's why I asked that someone else be my direct contact. I was too close to giving myself away to you."

Kitty moaned softly and swiped a fresh tear away. "Dear God."

Gently, Edgar said, "I felt how much you admired Pim. I realized that, if you'd had the chance, you would have escaped me to be with someone whom you..."

"You just sent me away. In Vienna, you just sent me away with Morris, and I swore I would never be able to forgive you for that. With hardly a goodbye. With... I don't know. There was such revulsion between us. It was my fault, of course, that the Gestapo... We'd gotten too comfortable at the cottage..." She realized she was rambling, her thoughts, the stream of events, jumbled in her head.

"I'm not going to lie." Edgar pushed himself up. "You were becoming a liability to my work. It started the day you got yourself a Gestapo file. And then when I received word that you were looking to be in touch with Pim directly, I don't know... Maybe I just didn't want to keep this secret from you any longer. That's why I decided to go ahead and contact you. Kendrick was wholly against it at first. Nils was outraged. But I convinced them. I had an idea that it was not your first attempt at clandestine work. Then Nils found out you'd been working with intelligence analysis. And I thought, well, if you'd been that discreet for so long, then one thing was certain—you had the ability and you had the guts."

"Ha," Kitty said softly.

He came to her, gently took her arms.

This close, she could not look him in the eye. "Now what? You, here, in England, Edgar. The Gestapo will suspect something."

He nodded, his eyes betraying fear. "You're absolutely right. It's dangerous for me to be here, on this estate. There are spies, double agents, everywhere. But I have taken every precaution. It took a lot of convincing, but my plan was to meet you here before the Hotel Metropole operation. But as fate would have it..." He opened his arms. "Now, I'm here as part of a diplomatic mission to help clear up the assassination attempt on the Führer. I convinced my superiors to let me come, on good faith that I would also help clear up your role in the cottage affair. Which is why you will be heading to the United States. And we will not see one another for quite some time."

"Why?" Again the panic. "Where will you be?"

He gave her that look he did when he was about to disappoint. An expression she'd gotten to know very well. "You know I can't tell you that."

"And what should I do in all that time?"

"Kendrick and his team will be debriefing you. I have suggested they start profiles on all the people we know. Everything you have ever heard about, heard of, heard directly or picked up in your work with the consulate, at all the events and functions. With me. With Cooper. Nils wants to have you debriefed at the U.S. embassy as well. And..."

"And?"

"Kitty, you could request an audience in Washington. You know the stories first-hand. Nils has wrangled a meeting with the Department of State, and you will tell them how very

serious the Nazi party is about annihilating the Jewish population, and murdering dissidents. If nobody does anything soon,
Hitler will be knocking on their doors himself, because his ulti-
mate goal is world domination. And if I am right about where
things are heading, he will do so with Japan in tow."

Kitty walked slowly past him and back to the window. The
view was unchanged but so much had shifted for her. She
looked over her shoulder. Her husband was waiting. "And what
about us?"

"That depends very much on you." He stood next to her.
"There is nothing I want more than your forgiveness. Kitty, the
last thing I want is to lose you. I love you above everything. If
you tell me, I will quit now. I will come to America with you.
And that will be that."

She slowly faced him, fresh tears falling. "I can't ask you to
do that," she whispered. "How could I ask you to do that when
all I've done is accuse you of doing nothing... and all this time
you were... doing everything."

Tentatively, he reached a hand for her cheek. Just as carefully, she leaned into it.

"What can I do for you?" he asked. "To help you reconcile
yourself with me, Edgar, your husband and Pim, the man you
thought was better than me?"

"How can I reconcile myself with you when I don't even
know who I am right now?" she whispered.

"From the day I met you, I knew that you were a woman of
conscience and extreme courage. I cannot tell you how beautiful it was to watch you discovering that about yourself."

Kitty took in a deep breath. "You're not the person I thought
I'd fallen in love with. Not at all."

Edgar let her go, crushed. He went to the bed, and sat down
as if his legs could no longer carry him.

Kitty shook her head slowly. "You're not the same person..."

She crossed the gap between them, her voice firm. Strong. "You are... you are so, so much more. So much more."

He looked down at her as she dropped to her knees beside him. She reached up and caressed his face, his half-grin, his dimples, that hope pooling in his eyes pulled at her heart so hard, she choked back a sob.

"You said I wasn't very boring," Edgar said.

"No, you are not very boring." She smiled back. "And you said it would take you years to peel back all the layers of me. I had no idea that I would have the opportunity to do the same. I stopped paying attention. And, Edgar, I am so, so sorry for that. I stopped trying to understand you."

She wrapped her arms around his neck and held him, her body molding against his. "God, I've missed you."

"I need to tell you something," he whispered into her ear.

"I love you."

It was some time later when Nils and Kendrick lost patience and knocked on the door.

"What now?" Kitty asked, pulling away from Edgar's embrace. They were lying next to one another on top of the bed, where they had held one another for a good part of the day.

"Are you two still in there?" Nils asked through the door. "Edgar? Has she murdered you?"

Kitty pressed her face into Edgar's forearm as he sat up and swung his legs over the bed. Grinning, he nudged her and she also rose.

"Call the police," Kitty called back.

"That's it," Nils boomed, and entered the room.

Kendrick followed, stepping in cautiously, relief flooding his face. "You two seem at least amiable."

Nils spread his legs apart, put his hands on his hips. "And?"

"We didn't get that far," Edgar said. "I think you two should do the honors."

"What?" Kitty asked, dreading any further surprises. "Do the honors of what?"

Nils brushed a hand over his head. Only now did she notice that his hair was thinner. "You and I are going to D.C. I've got you a meeting with Wild Bill Donovan and the Department of State. The Senator will be there, too."

Kitty scoffed. Donovan was a good friend of the family. She had once famously beaten him at cards when she was sixteen or seventeen. In fact, she had cleaned house on all of her father's guests that night, but Donovan had lost the most money. He was a brilliant diplomat, a bit risqué, which earned him his nickname, and a man she greatly respected.

"Why does he want to see me?"

"The president has put America on war footing. Donovan confessed that Roosevelt expressed interest in him doing a little snooping around in Europe as an emissary," Nils said. He shrugged. "It might be a good opportunity for you to share your story. A good opportunity for your, you know... career. Unless you want to try applying to the Foreign Service Office again."

Kitty scoffed. "I don't think they're going to have me, Nils." She looked at Edgar, whose expression was unreadable. "But what about us?"

"If the Americans don't snatch you up as an asset," Kendrick said, taking a step forward. "I've got someone who would be interested in talking to you on our side of the Atlantic."

Edgar grasped Kitty's hand. "I know her personally. And I think the two of you would get on really well. That is, if you would be interested in moving to London and working for the British."

Kitty held his gaze. She had just found her husband again. "And you?"

"I need to set some things into motion. There's a long way to go. We've only gotten started. And if you want to be a part of it, we'll be a part of it together."

"Sincerely?"

"If you only knew how sincere I am." He pressed his lips to her hand. "We make a good team, darling."

She gazed at her husband. Judith and Artur were dead. The rest were scattered to the wind and they could still use her help. Hers and Edgar's. If the resistance in Austria could use anything, it was the help of all the Allies.

She faced Kendrick and Nils.

Nils nodded once. "You're good out in the field, Kit."

"I can't imagine what would happen if we properly trained you," Kendrick added. "But if you go to the Americans, maybe you can help us to coordinate efforts with those who would like to intervene in Europe's war."

Kitty let Edgar draw her to him. He put his arm around her waist and she gazed up into those steady blue-green eyes. He kissed her forehead, the feel of him so sound, so familiar again, that she again ached for all their lost time. She held tight to her husband and faced her brother.

"When do we start? Because there is still a lot to do."

A LETTER FROM CHRYSTYNA

Dear reader,

Thank you for reading *The American Wife*. If you enjoyed it, please consider recommending it to other readers and leaving a review. If you'd like to keep up to date with all my latest releases, just sign up at the following link. Your email address will never be shared and you can unsubscribe at any time.

www.bookouture.com/chrystyna-lucyk-berger

For background information on this series, follow my monthly historical and cultural background blog on www.inktreks.com or sign up to receive it at www.inktreks.com/#newsletter

I hope to meet you on Kitty's and Edgar's next journey,
Chrystyna Lucyk-Berger

www.inktreks.com

facebook.com/inktreks

twitter.com/ckalyna

instagram.com/ckalyna

goodreads.com/ckalyna

bookbub.com/authors/ChrystynaLucykBerger

AUTHOR'S NOTE

I owe many thanks to those who documented their experiences. Many inspirations came from my research at the DÖW (Dokumentationsarchiv des österreicheschen Widerstandes/Archives of the Austrian Resistance) in Vienna, from scholars and witnesses such as Oliver R. Rathkob, Dietrich W. Botstiber, and most especially Melissa Jane Taylor whose work on John Cooper Wiley and Leland Morris was positively key to shaping Kitty's story. Many thanks go to all the helping hands: Roderick Martin in Vienna, Sam Nohra in Washington, D.C., Theresa König in western Austria, Lesya Lucyk in Minneapolis, the team at Bookouture and especially Jess Whitlum-Cooper, my editor in London. Your invaluable assistance, your research, and your insights made writing this novel a wholly enriching and enjoyable experience.

All key historical figures are fictionally portrayed in this novel.

Kitty Larsson and Edgar Ragatz are products of my imagination and composites of many different figures. The inspirational women behind Kitty Larsson include Amy Elizabeth Thorpe, Muriel Gardiner, Virginia Hall, and Maria von

Maltzan, as well as a number of other brave women who made it their duty to resist the Nazi regime, sometimes at the cost of their own lives. Edgar Ragatz's background, as well as Pim's, were heavily inspired by several German and Austrian dissidents who stood up to the Nazi regime. His character and his family background were inspired by many key figures of the time.

The events that took place within the Department of State and at the American consulate in Vienna, under John Cooper Wiley's leadership and Leland Morris's, are based on factual letters and reports, but their character portrayals here are purely fiction. The interior layout of the consulate, and the formation of a new intelligence analysis department within the consulate were completely fabricated. However, it was not unheard of for American and British diplomats to share important intelligence, especially to support interventionists' efforts.

Form Thirteen did come to fruition in Vienna on Morris's watch, but was not an idea—to my knowledge—that had been stolen from someone else.

My most exciting find when researching resistance in Austria was how many people did organize themselves to stand up to the Nazis. The O5 was a Viennese-based network founded by some of the most powerful, intellectual and elite Austrians. Because the documentation on O5's activities are scant, I pulled together various anecdotes from clandestine activities that happened within the Reich and applied my fictional license to the details.

Furthermore, Thomas Kendrick did exist, and did work as "Captain Wallace", and was extradited by the Gestapo. Back in England, he went on to head British MI6 during the Second World War and helped develop many important spy operations.

Lastly, all of the members of this novel's "gang" were also based on composites. Agnes'/Artur's murder was inspired by the murder of a real drag queen after two little boys led SA stormtroopers to the club. Judith's illustrations of nine dresses submitted to the consulate was inspired by fashion designer Louise Kuschnitzky, who illustrated a written plea to American authorities as she waited in limbo for her visa. There are reports of such missives being referred to within the Department of State as "freak letters" and passed around by senior members for their amusement... That is a story which I could never have made up.